CAUGHT IN THE LIGHT

Robert Goddard

CORGI BOOKS

CAUGHT IN THE LIGHT
A CORGI BOOK : 0 552 14597 1

Originally published in Great Britain by Bantam Press,
a division of Transworld Publishers Ltd

PRINTING HISTORY
Bantam Press edition published 1998
Corgi edition published 1998

Set in 10/12pt Plantin by
Phoenix Typesetting, Ilkley, West Yorkshire.

Corgi Books are published by Transworld Publishers Ltd,
61–63 Uxbridge Road, London W5 5SA,
in Australia by Transworld Publishers (Australia) Pty Ltd,
15–25 Helles Avenue, Moorebank, NSW 2170
and in New Zealand by Transworld Publishers (NZ) Ltd,
3 William Pickering Drive, Albany, Auckland.

Reproduced, printed and bound in Great Britain by
Cox & Wyman Ltd, Reading, Berks.

Robert Goddard was born in Hampshire, where he and his wife now live. He read History at Cambridge and worked as an educational administrator in Devon before becoming a full-time novelist. His previous novels, which are all published by Corgi Books, are *Past Caring*, *In Pale Battalions*, *Painting the Darkness*, *Into the Blue* (winner of the first W.H.Smith 'Thumping Good Read' Award), *Take No Farewell*, *Hand in Glove*, *Closed Circle*, *Borrowed Time*, *Out of the Sun* and *Beyond Recall*.

Acclaim for *Caught in the Light*:

'Scintillating plotting . . . Goddard's ability to pull the wool repeatedly over the reader's eyes remains dazzling'
Sunday Times

'This is his best book yet, a sinuous structure of twists and traps leading to an unexpectedly sinister climax'
Daily Telegraph

'When it comes to duplicity and intrigue, Goddard is second to none. He is a master of manipulation . . . It is a hypnotic, unputdownable thriller'
Daily Mail

'A literally spellbinding foray into the real-life game of truth and consequences'
The Times

'Sheer gripping power'
The Times Metro

'A compelling, edge-of-the-seat tale . . . once again, it proves that Goddard really is the master of the modern mystery thriller'
Irish News

Also by Robert Goddard

and published by Corgi Books

PART ONE

COMPOSITION

Chapter One

I was in Vienna to take photographs. That was generally the reason I was anywhere then. Photographs were more than my livelihood. They were part of my life. The way light fell on a surface never failed to tug at my imagination. The way one picture, a single snapshot, could capture the essence of a time and place, a city, a war, a human being, was embedded in my consciousness. One day, one second, I might close the shutter on the perfect photograph. There was always the chance, so long as there was film in my camera. Finish one; load another; and keep looking, with eyes wide open. That was my code. Had been for a long time.

I'd come close once, in Kuwait at the end of the Gulf War, when some weird aptness in the knotted shape of a smoke plume from a burning oil well made my picture the one newspapers and magazines all over the world suddenly wanted. Brief glory from an even briefer moment. Just luck, really. But they say you make your own – the bad as well as the good.

I went freelance after the Gulf, which should have been a clever move and would probably have worked out that way, but for life beyond the lens taking a few wrong turnings. The mid-Nineties weren't quite the string of triumphs I'd foreseen when my defining image of the Gulf madness made it to the cover of *Time* magazine. That's why I was in Vienna, rather than in Bosnia or Zaïre or anywhere even faintly newsworthy. But, still, I was taking photographs. And I was being paid to do it. It didn't sound bad to me.

The assignment was actually a piece of happenstance. I'd done the London shots for a glossy coffee-table picture book: *Four Cities in Four Seasons – London, Paris, Rome, Vienna*, a European co-publishing venture that netted me a juicy commission to hang round moody eyefuls of my home city in spring, summer, autumn and winter. I'd given my own particular slant to daffodils in Hyde Park, heat haze and traffic fumes in Piccadilly, rain-sodden leaves in Berkeley Square and a snow-patched roofscape in WC1. I'd also reconciled myself to the best and truest of what I'd delivered being tossed aside. It was, after all, only a picture book. It wasn't meant to challenge anyone's preconceptions or make them see instead of look. And I wasn't Bill Brandt. Any more than my French opposite number was Henri Cartier-Bresson.

It was just after an obliging cold snap over Christmas and New Year that I handed in my London-in-winter batch and got the message that Rudi Schüssner had walked out on the job in Vienna for reasons nobody seemed to think I needed to know about. Rather than call in someone new, they offered me the substitute's role. The Austrian publishers had liked what they'd seen of my stuff, apparently. Besides, I was free, whereas the French and Italian photographers weren't. And I was glad to go. Things at home weren't great. They were a long way from that. A week snapping snowy Vienna didn't have to be dressed up as a compliment to my artistry for me to go like a shot. Anyway, *The Third Man* had always been one of my favourite films.

They put me up at the Europa, on Neuer Markt, halfway between Stephansdom and the Staatsoper, right in the heart of the old city. I'd last been to Vienna for a long weekend with Faith before we were married: a midsummer tourist scramble round just about every palace and museum in the joint. It had been hot, hectic and none too memorable. I hadn't even taken many photographs. On my own, in a cold hard January, it was going to be different, though. I knew that the moment I climbed off the shuttle bus from the airport and let my eyes and brain absorb the pinky-grey dome of light over the snow-sugared roofs of the city. I was going to enjoy myself here. I was going to take some great pictures.

The first day I didn't even try. I rode the trams round the Ringstrasse, getting on and off as I pleased to sample the moods of the place. The weather was set, frozen like the vast baroque remnants of the redundant empire that had laid the city out. I hadn't seen what Schüssner had done with spring, summer and autumn. I hadn't wanted to. This was going to be my Vienna, not his. And it was going to give itself to me. I just had to let it come. A photograph is a moment. But you have to wait for the moment to arrive. So I bided my time and looked and looked until I could see clearly. And then I was ready.

Next morning, I was out at dawn. Snow flurries overnight meant Stephansplatz would be virginally white as well as virtually deserted. I hadn't figured out how to cope with the cathedral in one shot. Its spire stretched like a giraffe's neck into the silver-grey sky, but at ground

9

level it was elephantine, squatting massively in the centre of the city. Probably there was no way to do it. I'd have to settle for something partial. In that weather, at that time, it could still be magical.

But, then, there's always been something magical about photography. It certainly seemed that way to the Victorian pioneers, before the chemistry of it was properly understood. Pictures develop and strengthen and hold by an agency of their own. You can stand, as Fox Talbot did, in a darkened room and watch a blank sheet of paper become a photograph. And even when you know why it happens you don't lose the sense of its mystery. That stays with you for ever.

Perhaps that's why what happened at Stephansplatz that morning failed in some strange way to surprise me. I'd brought the Hasselblad, but I didn't take a tripod, though technically I should have. I'd always shied clear of accessories, arguing that all you needed to do the job were a good pair of eyes and a decent camera. Plus spontaneity, of course, which you don't get fiddling with tripod legs. I just prowled round the square, looking for the right angle, for some way to give scale as well as atmosphere to the scene. I backed off to the north side, where there was some shelter from the wind, and took a decent shot of the snow slashing across the dark flank of the cathedral. But Schüssner could have managed that. I was looking for something more distinctive, something that would carry my own grace note.

I didn't find it. It found me. With my eye to the camera, I tracked across to the blurred reflection of the cathedral's west front in the glass façade of the Haas-Haus, then slowly down and back until the curve of Kärtnerstrasse was an empty white arena beyond the black prow of medieval buttressing, with a shop sign

10

gleaming like a golden snowflake in the distance. Then, just as I steadied the camera, a figure stepped into view round the southern side of the cathedral, red coat buttoned up against the chill, and I had a piece of composition you'd die for. I pressed the shutter release and thanked my stars.

The figure was a woman, dressed in boots, overcoat, gloves, scarf and fur-trimmed hat. I'd have expected her to hurry across the square, head bowed. Instead, she stopped, turned and looked at me as I lowered the camera, then walked towards me. She was frowning, I saw as she approached. She almost seemed to be angry, her dark eyes seeking and challenging my gaze. My first impression was of a pale high-cheeked face framed by the soft black brim of the hat, of eyes that could see as far as they needed to – and quite possibly through whatever stood in their way.

'Did you just take my photograph?' she said. The voice was English, unaccented, surprisingly deep.

'You were in the photograph I took,' I replied. 'It's not quite the same thing.'

'It is to me.'

'Is there a problem?'

'I don't like having my picture taken.' Her nose was broad and flat, almost as if it had once been broken. Somehow that made her more striking still. That and the aggression in her eyes which camera-shyness didn't seem to me to go anywhere near explaining. 'Especially not by somebody I don't know.'

'That must be difficult for you. I expect you get a lot of requests.'

'Funny,' she said, looking me up and down. 'I thought I'd be safe in Vienna from smart-arse Londoners.'

'In January, at dawn.' I glanced round the square and nodded. 'It was a good bet.'

There was a moment's silence, when the only sound was the wind mewling round the cathedral and flapping the camera-strap against the collar of my coat. She should have walked away then, or I should. But neither of us moved. Incongruity turned towards fascination, and I realized I was no longer sure how this would end.

'It'll be a great picture,' I said neutrally.

'What makes you think so?'

'I'm a professional. Trust me.'

'Do I have a choice?'

'About the picture? Not really. About breakfast? Well, that's a different matter. You can have it with your husband back at your hotel. Or with me at the Café Griensteidl. It's on Michaelerplatz. Maybe you know it.'

'Better than you know me, that's for certain.'

'You said you didn't like having your picture taken by a stranger. This way I wouldn't be one, would I? Not any more.'

'What about your wife? Won't she be expecting you?'

'She's not with me this trip.'

'And my husband's not with me. That's how I can be sure of breakfasting alone.'

'Please yourself.'

'I will, thank you.' And with that she did move, round on her heel and smartly away across the square.

I watched her until she'd vanished down the street beside the Haas-Haus, and wondered as soon as she was out of sight why in hell's name I'd behaved as I had. Though she wouldn't know it, it was actually way out of character. For a moment I'd very much wanted not to let our encounter fizzle into nothing beyond a figure in red in the background of a photograph. I'd wanted that with an acuteness I couldn't fathom. It wasn't just disquieting, it was positively eerie. As if I hadn't any idea of what was really going on in my head.

I tried to shrug the sensation off as I made my way down Kärtnerstrasse to the Opera House and took some speculative shots of its snow-hazed bulk from various vantage points. But I was cold now and oddly dispirited. I carried on round to Heldenplatz and managed some perspective views of its wide-open arctic spaces. Then I gave up and retreated to the Griensteidl.

And there she was, waiting for me. She was at a table near the far end of the café, so tucked away that I didn't see her until I went to grab a newspaper from the rack and recognized her coat and hat on the nearby stand. Then I glanced round and saw her, watching me quite calmly from a distant table.

'You did know the place, then,' I said as I joined her.

'I know less than I pretend.' The anger was gone from her eyes, but their intensity was undimmed. Her hair was short, expertly cropped in some fashionable bob, and an engagement ring sparkled beside the wedding ring on her left hand as she trailed it round her coffee cup. 'Like you, I imagine.'

'Why do I get the feeling that you *are* like me – in lots of ways?'

'I don't know. But I do know what you mean.'

'I'm sorry if I . . . said anything stupid back there.'

'Why be sorry? If you'd been more polite maybe I wouldn't be here now.'

'I usually am, you know. Polite.'

'Promise me you won't be . . . with me.'

'All right. That's easy.'

'No, it isn't. Polite means dishonest. Impolite means honest. And honest isn't easy.'

13

The waiter came over and I ordered coffee and a croissant. The uncertainty was delicious now. Just what were we talking about?

'My name's Marian Esguard.'

'*Esguard?* That's unusual.'

'My husband's an unusual man.'

'He seems a negligent one to me.'

'You don't know him. And that's good. That's actually great. I can't remember when I last talked this much to somebody who didn't know him.'

'Shall we keep it that way, then?'

'Yes.' She smiled faintly for the first time. It warmed her eyes. There was a sudden sense of exuberance, of joy, on a short leash. 'Who are you?'

'Ian Jarrett.'

'A photographer.'

'Right. Here for the winter light.'

'And you're wondering what I'm here for.'

'No. Unless you want me to.'

'I told you to be impolite.'

'But just how impolite? That's the question.'

'A question for you to answer, not me.'

'You can at least tell me what brings you here.'

'I'm not sure. Boredom. Desperation. The need to get away. The need to think.'

My breakfast arrived. She watched me sip some coffee. Then she reached across the table, tore an end off my croissant and ate it, slowly and studiously.

'Hungry?'

'I think I must be.'

'Have it all.'

'You never can, in my experience.'

'Nor mine.'

'But there are always new experiences.'

14

'So there are.'

'Tell me, Ian, what's the worst thing you've ever done?'

'I killed somebody once.' Hearing myself say what I never normally volunteered was more of a shock to me than it seemed to be to her. 'Hit a pedestrian late one night about five years ago while I was driving home.'

'An accident?'

'Oh yes. And I was sober, too. But I still killed them.'

'Of course.' She nodded. 'It doesn't make any difference to them, does it? The fact that you didn't mean to do it.'

'You talk as if you know the feeling.'

'I do. When I was a child I goaded a schoolfriend into walking out onto a frozen canal. The ice broke. She fell through and drowned. An accident. But she stayed dead.'

'That must have been worse. At least I didn't know the pedestrian I hit.'

'I never told anyone I'd encouraged her to do it. Never a soul. Till now.'

'Why tell me?'

'Because . . .' She hesitated, searching my face, it seemed, for some kind of reassurance. 'Because I want us to do anything we want. And nothing we don't.'

'Are you sure?'

'Yes. I am.' She looked straight at me, unblinkingly direct. 'Are you?'

'Anything and nothing?'

'Exactly.'

'Whatever that means?'

'Whatever.'

That was the last moment when I could have laughed it off and put up some kind of social smokescreen. But then the moment passed. And all I did was nod slowly in agreement and return the frankness of her gaze.

'Staying in Vienna long?'

'Long enough.'

She smiled, more broadly than before. 'That makes two of us, then.'

'I thought I might go out to Schönbrunn this morning. Take some pictures of the palace and the park. Why don't you come with me?'

'I shouldn't. For all kinds of reasons.'

'But you will?'

'Oh, I expect so, don't you?'

'I'm not sure I know what to expect.'

'Neither am I.' She drained her cup and replaced it in the saucer with exaggerated care. 'Isn't that why we're going?'

I don't know why I thought of Schönbrunn. I hadn't really been intending to go there that morning. But it was bound to be quiet so far from the centre on a freezing-cold weekday. We both needed time, before the next step caught up with us.

And it *was* quiet. The palace floated silently in its snow-covered park like some vast yellow ghost, so remote from the dusty, tourist-choked clamour I remembered that my visit with Faith could almost have lain in the future rather than in the past.

'They say Franz Josef preferred it here to the Hofburg,' I said as we walked out slowly behind the palace through the snow-blanked gardens towards the Neptune Fountain and the colonnade of the Gloriette on the hilltop beyond. 'He kept his mistress in a villa near by.'

'You obviously know Vienna better than I do,' said Marian. 'Who's Franz Josef?'

'You must have heard of him. The famous Austrian Emperor. The old fellow with the walrus moustache and the chestful of medals.'

'You've lost me. But I'm no historian.'

'Neither am I.'

'No. You're a photographer. So shouldn't you be taking photographs?'

'Later. Just at the moment I don't seem able to concentrate.'

'Why not?'

'Why do you think?'

'You need to be alone. Is that it?'

'Maybe I need to be. But I don't want to be.'

'Sorry if I'm distracting you from your work.'

'You're not sorry.'

We stopped there, beneath Neptune and his frozen fountain, and turned to look at each other. Until that moment, we hadn't so much as touched. 'What's happening?' Marian murmured.

'Something that's never happened to me before.'

'Nor me.'

We were breathless now, expectant yet apprehensive. Then we were kissing: her lips against mine, her tongue, her nose and cheek, the butterfly flicker of her eyelashes, the warmth of her breath, the leather of her glove cool against my neck.

She broke away and stared at me, as if terrified, then headed along the path that led round the fountain and up to the glade of fir trees beyond, glancing back to see me following, moving faster, almost running.

I caught up as she entered the screen of trees behind the nearest of Neptune's Tritons. We kissed again. Snowflakes shaken from the branches around us dampened her face as she arched back across the parapet, yielding or still resisting, there was no way to be sure. But there was no way to stop, either.

'Let's go back to my hotel,' Marian whispered. 'Now.'

'Where are you staying?'

'The Imperial.'

'The best, so they tell me.'

'Come and find out.'

'Talk to me about something,' she said, staring into my eyes as the taxi sped us back through the city. 'Anything.'

'I can't think of anything.'

'Tell me about your work.'

'I just take pictures.'

'Is there one photographer you particularly admire?'

'None living.'

'Dead, then?'

'Roger Fenton, maybe.'

'Why?'

'He was the very first war photographer. In the Crimea. He had to work it all out from first principles, but he still managed to come close to something like art. And his landscapes . . . But you don't want to hear this.'

'I don't want to think, either. Keep talking. Was he successful, this Fenton?'

'Very.'

'Healthy, wealthy and wise?'

'Hard to say. He was the most famous photographer of his generation. But he gave it all up when he was still a relatively young man. Sold his equipment and negatives. Packed it in.'

'Why?'

'Nobody knows.'

'But you have a theory?'

'For what it's worth.'

18

'Go on.'

'I think he realized he'd done his best work. That it was only going to be downhill from there. So, he quit.'

'That must have taken a lot of courage.'

'Or despair.'

'Or temptation,' she countered.

'What was there to tempt him?'

'The unknown.' She twined her fingers in mine. 'The place you most want to go. For all the risks attached.'

Marian had a suite on the first floor of the hotel: an opulently furnished pair of rooms looking down onto the street through high, thick-curtained windows. The door closed solidly behind us and she turned a switch to lower the shutters, filtering and thinning the grey winter light. It was warm and silent. The imminence of passion – of heat and flesh and broken taboos – hung almost tangibly in the air.

'This must be expensive,' I said.

She shrugged. 'My husband's paying. He likes me to spend his money.'

'Won't we pay, too – in the end?'

'Maybe. But first . . .'

'Yes?'

'We can have what we'll pay for. And make sure it's worth the price.'

She took off her coat and gloves. We kissed slowly and lingeringly, knowing this time that we wouldn't stop. The madness of it was part of the pleasure. I didn't know her and she didn't know me. But nothing was going to be held back. Already, I sensed it was going to be better than it had ever been before, her desire fitting mine like the skintight leather she'd just peeled from her fingers.

And it came so close. As close to perfection as I could dream of it being. Morning drifted into afternoon as we surrendered to each other, at first with clumsy eagerness, then in subtle variations on a theme that always had the same savoured ending. So much released and discovered, about the mind as well as the body. What we were capable of. What we couldn't have admitted to any but the strangers we were even then ceasing to be. Each climax found and surpassed a new limit. By the end there were no inhibitions left. We'd been shocked into a drained and exhausted tenderness.

'You can't photograph that, can you, Ian?' she said as we lay on the bed, still warm from the heat of all we'd done. 'You can't capture it in any picture.'

'I wouldn't want to.'

'Then what *do* you want?'

'You've already found that out.'

'Tell me anyway.'

'I want you.'

'Well, you've got me now.'

'But I can't keep you.'

'That's lucky for you, isn't it? You can fuck me and forget me. Most men would envy you.'

'I'm not most men.'

'I noticed.'

'And I'm not very good at forgetting.'

'Well . . . you have to have some weakness, I suppose.'

I refused to laugh. 'What's yours?'

'Strangely enough . . .' She smiled. 'The same.'

It wasn't the first time I'd been unfaithful to my wife. It wasn't even the second. But, still, I'd never known or done anything like it before. The intensity of the experience was bewildering. Already the question wasn't

20

whether it would be repeated, but whether I could even bear the thought of it not being repeated.

I stayed at the Imperial that night, returning to the Europa only briefly to pick up a change of clothes. We dined in the hotel's grand luxe restaurant. Marian wore a black dress that looked as if it had been made for her by a top designer, but no jewellery and very little make-up. My mind's eye kept flashing back to just a few hours before. I tasted her rather than the wine and relished the recency of the memory.

'What are we going to do, Ian? I don't mean tonight. I mean . . .'

'Eventually.'

'Yes.'

'I don't know. You have a husband. I have a wife. And a daughter.'

'You didn't mention her before.'

'She's fourteen. It's not as if . . .'

'I have no children.'

'The truth is, Marian, we hardly know the first thing about each other.'

'But you've realized already, haven't you?'

'What?'

'That what we do know is all that matters.'

'I know I've never felt like this before. Never felt so much so soon.'

'Neither have I.'

'What is it?'

'It's a chance in a million.'

'Then we should make the most of it.'

'And to hell with the consequences?'

'Just now, consequences don't seem to matter.'

'Liberating, isn't it?'

'It could get to be a habit.'

21

'Yes. I know exactly what you mean. A habit you can't kick.'

'For the moment, I don't even want to try.'

We went back to her suite long before we'd eaten or drunk enough to slake our appetites. The chambermaid had pulled the mirror-panelled doors across between the two rooms. We watched our reflections in them as I unzipped her dress and slid the flimsy layers of silk from her body and pulled her down onto the thick-piled carpet, in the lamplight's glow. The sustained urgency of our lovemaking was alarming me now. Already, it was certain my life had changed. But what had it changed *to*? As Marian had unwittingly predicted, the temptation to find out was irresistible. But it was also frightening.

We fell into bed and a pit of slumber. I woke from it as if I'd only had my eyes closed for a few minutes, though it must by then have been the early hours of the morning. Marian was still asleep, but mumbling to herself, breathing heavily and tossing her head on the pillow, as if trying to throw off some stifling weight.

'I won't let you do this, Jos,' I heard her say. 'I won't let you.' A moment's silence, then, in a louder voice, 'You can't stop me. I'll show you what—' Suddenly she was awake. She jerked up in the bed, coughing and panting and throwing out her arms. 'Oh . . . Oh God . . .'

'Take it easy,' I said. 'You must have had a nightmare.'

'I'm OK.' She fell back against the pillow and began to breathe more easily. 'God, I'm sorry. I don't know . . . what happened.'

'You were talking in your sleep. Is Jos your husband?'

'I *named* him?'

'You did.'

'Just goes to show . . . you can't get away from some

people . . . as easily as you think. Yes, Jos is my husband. He'd be touched to know, I'm sure, that he was in my thoughts.'

'Are you afraid of him?'

'Why should I be?'

'It sounded as if . . .'

'He means nothing to me. Not a thing. And he knows that. There's no reason for me to be afraid of him.'

'But you were dreaming about him.'

'Some sort of automatic guilt mechanism, I expect.'

'It doesn't seem to have kicked in in my case.'

'It will. And when it does I probably won't see you for dust.'

'You're wrong.'

'Am I?' She'd reached out for me in the dark and was teasing me now, with her fingers as well as her words. 'Prove it.'

'I can't. Not yet. But I will.'

'All right. I'll give you the benefit of the doubt. Meanwhile, there's something you can do for my guilt problem.'

'What?'

'Take my mind off it.' She pulled me closer. 'Any way you like.'

Early next morning, while Marian was in the bath, I left the hotel and went across to the Café Schwarzenberg on the other side of the road for hot black coffee and a cold-dawn's-light appraisal of what had happened and what was going to happen. Her husband meant nothing to her, she'd said. But was that true? More to the point, did *she* mean nothing to *him*? I'd detected fear in her voice, for all her denials. And I was a threat to him now, whether he knew it or not. Just what was I getting myself into?

23

Then there was Faith. Our marriage had been running on empty ever since the accident had thrown my affair with Nicole in her face. I still suspected she'd only patched it together then for Amy's sake. But Amy was away at boarding school now. And that had largely been Faith's decision, one that could have been intended to pave the way for a separation. But at a time of her choosing, not mine, and certainly not to make things easier for me. If I tried to turn this into something more than a five-night stand, Faith and I were going to have to acknowledge that we no longer loved each other. And it wasn't going to be easy.

Nor was walking away from Marian at the end of my week in Vienna, though. We'd been together for just twenty-four hours, yet already I couldn't bear the thought of us being apart. A chance in a million, she'd called it. And she'd been right. It was also a chance I knew, soberly and surely, I wasn't going to let slip.

'I have to take some photographs today,' I said over breakfast back in her room. 'The publisher wants the job wrapped up next week.'

'Then you'd better jump to it.'

'Will you come with me?'

'I'd like to. But look what happened at Schönbrunn. Not a lot of pictures.'

'I'll have to go back there.'

'Why don't you hire a car? It would give us more time . . . for other things.'

'My budget won't run to it.'

'Mine will.'

'Actually, there's another problem.' This was how it was bound to be, I knew: the spilling and sharing of secrets, one by one. 'You remember the accident

24

I told you about? The woman I killed.'

'You never said it was a woman.'

'Didn't I? Well, it was. And I . . . I've not driven since.'

'You lost your licence?'

'No, no. It wasn't my fault. At least, not officially, although I've often wondered . . . I lost my nerve, if you want to know the truth. The thought of how easily it happened just wouldn't go away.'

'Does it upset you to talk about it?'

'Not any more. But, like I told you last night, I'm not very good at forgetting.'

'Some things you have to forget.' She reached out and touched my cheek with a gentleness that seemed to soothe some wound of her own as well as mine. 'Sounds like you need a driver. Can I apply for the job?'

'The pay's lousy, the hours are diabolical and the boss won't be able to keep his hands off you.'

'I'll take it, then.'

So I got to have my cake and eat it, too. Marian hired a smart Mercedes and took me out to the farthest suburbs and beyond, as well as round all the obvious, and some of the not so obvious, photogenic corners of the city. The weather held in finest winter mode and everything went too smoothly to be true. I took some pictures I reckoned I'd be proud of, and Marian and I . . . Well, what did we do? Fall in love? Develop an addiction to each other? Indulge a seductive compatibility of mind and body? I wouldn't know what to call it. But I know what it felt like: the real thing, experienced for the first and surely only time.

'You haven't tried to take my photograph again,' she goaded as we explored the snowy grave-lined avenues of the Zentralfriedhof, Vienna's vast central cemetery, halfway through the week that was already accelerating towards its end – and our crisis. 'Why's that?'

'You made your views pretty plain on the subject, as I recall.'

She pouted. 'But that was before we'd been properly introduced.'

'I'd like to take your picture, Marian. I'd like you to want me to.'

'You talk as if it really matters.'

'I'm a photographer. It's bound to matter.'

'Why?'

'Photographs – the best ones – capture the reality of things. And of people.'

'How long have we had them?'

'Photographs? Oh, a hundred and fifty years or so.'

'Who was the first person to have theirs taken?'

'I'm not sure. Fox Talbot's wife. Or one of his servants at Lacock. Then again, Daguerre might have—'

'Lacock *Abbey*, near Chippenham?'

'Yes. You know it?'

'I went there once. I . . . can't remember much about it.'

'William Fox Talbot invented photography at Lacock during the eighteen thirties. There's a museum at the house devoted to the subject.'

'It can't have made much of an impression on me, I'm afraid. Sorry.'

'Never mind.'

'But I'll make up for it.' She ran skittishly ahead and turned round, smiling back at me. 'Take my picture here.'

'Why the sudden conversion?'

'Because half the people in this cemetery must have died before photography was invented. But they were just as real as you and me. Maybe more so.'

'How could they be more so?' I raised the camera to my eye and stepped to one side, widening the angle to capture the long, pale perspective of bare trees and brooding gravestones beyond Marian, in her blood-red coat. She was grinning at me stubbornly. 'You're real enough for me.'

'It's just that I'm so happy I reckon there's a good chance I'm dreaming all this.'

'Well, you're not.' Her smile was the making of the photograph. It looked so genuine, and yet so glaringly inappropriate in that snow-draped avenue of the Viennese dead. 'And now we have the proof.' I took the picture in that instant and felt a ludicrous sense of triumph that she'd allowed me to do it. 'Thank you, Marian.'

'What for?'

'For letting me capture your reality.'

'Oh, you've done that all right.' She was still smiling, more broadly than ever. 'Didn't you know?'

On our last full day together in Vienna, we went out to the Donaupark. From the top of the Danube Tower, its railings bristling with frost, I got some crisp and effective shots of the UNO-City office blocks and an evocative view of Stephansdom's spire, as distant now as our meeting beneath it seemed. More distant, for sure, than our parting.

Over lunch in the tower's revolving restaurant, with Vienna slowly tracking round below us, we each waited for the other to say what had to be said. Eventually, I told myself as well as her, 'There's no way I can avoid leaving tomorrow.'

'I know.'

'I wish—'

'I know that, too.'

'When will you go?'

'I have a flight booked for Friday.'

'And then . . . we can meet?'

'There's a problem, Ian.'

'Your husband.'

'Jos wouldn't . . .' She gazed out through the window at the snow-bleached horizon, struggling to compose her thoughts and words. 'He lets me do much as I please. Like this trip, for instance. But . . . there are limits.'

'And I'm beyond them?'

She looked back at me. 'In England, you would be. He'd feel I was making a fool of him. As I suppose I would be. And that would make him very angry. Which wouldn't be a good idea. Not at all. Believe me, I know. From bitter experience.'

'Do you have to tell him?'

'Look at me, Ian. What do you see?'

'A beautiful woman.'

'If that's true, it's because of you. I wouldn't have to tell Jos I was having an affair. He'd know at a glance.'

'I'm not going to give you up.'

'I think you may have to. Unless . . .'

'What?'

'It's all or nothing, as I see it.'

'I'm ready for that.'

'Are you? What would your wife say? And your daughter?'

'Whatever they wanted to say. It wouldn't make any difference to me. I've made some mistakes in my life, but this wouldn't be one of them. Come away with me, Marian. We'll make a clean break of it. A fresh start. Together.'

'Can we really do that?'

'I don't think we can do anything else.'

'You're right, of course.' She reached across to clasp my hand. 'We can't. I've known that all along.'

'Then why didn't you say so?'

She smiled. 'Because I wanted to hear you say it first, I suppose.'

We went back to the Imperial and made love. The sex was searing and committed, like two drowning people clinging to each other. The experience had deepened every time, until now it took us to places I wouldn't have believed existed. She let me photograph her afterwards, lying naked on the bed, her lover's eyes playing with the camera lens. The pictures, too, were a proof of our sincerity. What they meant could never be denied.

'What time is your flight tomorrow?' she asked as we lay together in the encroaching twilight.

'One o'clock.'

'I'll drive you to the airport.'

'No. Let me say goodbye to you here. In the best kind of way. Let me have that memory to hold in my head.'

'When will you tell your wife?'

'Straight away.'

'You're sure?'

'Oh yes. I'm sure.'

'Me, too. Amazing, isn't it? I love you, Ian. Do you realize that?'

'I realize I love you.'

'I wish I could fly back with you.'

'Why don't you?'

'Because Jos is away on business until Friday. I can't tell him until then. And I'd rather wait here to do it than in his house.'

29

'Isn't it your house, too?'

'Not really. Esguards have lived there for generations. And I've never been one of them. Not where it counts, in the blood. It might have been different if I'd produced a son and heir, but . . .'

'You don't have to tell me why that never happened, Marian. Unless you want to.'

'I want to, but I'm not going to. The less we know about each other's marriages the better. By Friday night they'll be history.'

'Three days from now. It sounds a long time.'

'Just long enough' – she rolled onto her side and stretched out her hand to me – 'to put a real edge on your performance.'

'I think I can guarantee that.'

'You can phone me here in the meantime and tell me what to expect.'

'Where shall we meet?'

'You've got this irritating practical streak, you know.' She let go of me and sighed. 'It must be your photographer's mind. Exposure times. Light readings. Focal points. All that detail.'

'Well, talking of photography, you mentioned you'd been to Lacock. Could you get there on Friday night?'

'Lacock? Easily. Why?'

'There's a wonderful old inn in the village. The Sign of the Angel. You know the kind of place: oak beams; creaking floors; log fires; antique furniture; and nice cosy bedrooms.'

'Sounds great. Especially the cosy bedrooms.'

'I'll book the cosiest one they have.'

'You'll be able to show me round the Abbey. Explain all that stuff about Fox Talbot I seem to have missed.'

''Fraid not. The Abbey will be closed at this time of the year.'

'Never mind. There'll be other opportunities.'

'Lots, I hope.'

She kissed me lightly on the cheek and settled her head on my shoulder. 'As many as you want, Ian. Starting Friday.'

We went no further that evening than the Café Schwarzenberg, where we lingered over wine and coffee and our vaguely formed plans for the future. But the complexities of life in England seemed too many to grasp while we still had one Viennese night to savour. We'd resolved to meet at Lacock when a decisive break with our pasts had been made, and that seemed as much as we were capable of for the moment.

'Tell me how Fox Talbot came to invent photography,' said Marian, as we finished our last coffee. 'I'd better start boning up on this kind of thing now I'm going to be living with a walking authority on the subject.'

'I'm hardly that. And it's a long story.'

'Give me the potted version.'

'Are you serious?'

'Yes. I'd like to know.'

'Well, ever heard of a camera lucida?' Getting no answer, I went on. 'It was a drawing instrument popular with amateur artists in the first half of the last century. Basically an adaptation of the camera obscura. I don't suppose you've heard of that, either.'

She pouted. 'As a matter of fact I have. Besides, I know enough Latin to have got ahead of you. Camera lucida: light room. Camera obscura: dark room. Right?'

'I'm impressed. Anyway, it works like this. Paint one

31

wall of a darkened room white and drill a pinhole in the opposite wall. Given decent light, an inverted image of the scene outside the room will be cast onto the white wall. Put a lens in the pinhole and you can turn the image upright and focus it. Install a mirror in the room and you can reflect the image onto a sheet of paper and trace it. Shrink the room to a box and you have a portable drawing device. That's the camera obscura. It was in widespread use by the end of the seventeenth century.'

'You know it all, don't you?'

'You did ask.'

She smiled. 'Go on.'

'OK. The camera lucida on the other hand comprised a small prism mounted on a telescopic stem. You stood it on your drawing board, adjusted the angle and looked down into the prism at the reflection of the scene in front of you. Then you moved your eye just far enough towards the edge of the prism for the images of the scene and the sheet of paper below to merge, apparently *on* the paper. All you had to do was trace what you saw. It was invented by a man called Wollaston at the end of the eighteenth century.'

'But we're still a long way from photography.'

'Not really. It just took a few decades for someone to have the idea. Why not try to fix the images created by these devices as permanent pictures? William Fox Talbot, Wiltshire squire and amateur scientist, spent his honeymoon in the Italian Lake District in the autumn of 1833, trying unsuccessfully to rival his wife's drawing skills using a camera lucida. When he got home to Lacock, he started experimenting with ways of removing his dodgy draughtsmanship from the equation altogether. The light-sensitive properties of silver nitrate were well known to him. What he did was treat a sheet

32

of paper with a salt solution of the stuff before exposing it in a camera obscura. The result was a negative photographic image – light for dark, because light darkened the silver chloride. But if the paper was transparent, it could be re-exposed to create a positive image on another sheet below it – the key to photographic reproduction.'

'So that was it?'

'Essentially, yes. But it took him several years to get that far. And several more to find a really good fixing agent. Outdoor photography of people and objects didn't become a practical possibility until about 1840. And it was complicated by the simultaneous discoveries of the Frenchman, Louis Daguerre. He achieved the same results using copper plate rather than paper. But the daguerreotype, as it was called, couldn't be reproduced. That's where Fox Talbot had the edge.'

'You make it sound simple.'

'It was. Beautifully simple. But the best ideas always are. Someone else could have thought of it before Fox Talbot. Thomas Wedgwood, son of the potter, seems to have gone a long way towards achieving the same thing thirty years earlier, but he died before he could make much of it. Tragic, really. We'd give a lot now for thirty extra years of photographic history, I can tell you.'

'How do you come to know all this, Ian? I can't believe most photographers are caught up in the subject the way you are.'

'That's their affair. To me, the dawn of photography is just about the most magical period in history. Until then, everything – every tree, every building, every human face – was just an artist's impression. At some fundamental level, not quite real. But a photograph is different. A photograph is almost as good as being there.'

I caught her quizzical look. 'What's wrong?'

'Nothing. It's just . . . so weird. That I should meet you, of all people.'

'What's weird about it?'

'The sheer . . . improbability of it, I suppose. Almost as if . . . I knew I'd find you here.'

'I'm not sure I understand.'

'You're a photographer.'

'So?'

'Fascinated by the invention of photography.'

'What about it?'

She shook her head. 'It's just crazy, that's all.'

'Marian—'

'Shush.' She pressed her fingers against my lips. 'I can't tell you exactly what I mean. It's too complicated and too incredible. But I will, I promise. At Lacock. It'll make more sense there. It was an inspired choice of yours, really. Besides, whetting your curiosity like this means I can be sure you'll turn up.'

'You can be sure of that anyway. There's no need for guessing games.'

'This isn't a game.'

'What, then?'

'Wait and see.' She grinned. 'There are some things I don't give up as easily as my virtue.'

I thought at the time she was setting up some subtle joke at my expense about photography, though I couldn't for the life of me figure out what. It didn't really seem to matter. She'd promised to explain at Lacock and that was good enough. My impatience to see her again wasn't going to turn on one minor mystery.

In fact, I'd more or less forgotten about it when I left the hotel next morning with just enough time to book

34

out of the Europa and catch the shuttle bus to the airport. I didn't want to go when it came to the point, not just because I'd infinitely have preferred to stay with Marian, but also because there was a flak storm of condemnation from Faith to be ridden out before we'd meet again, all of it justified. I'd have no answer to as many accusations as she cared to throw at me. And then there was Amy. She'd have to be told, too. I was dreading that even more.

But it was all worth it. The certainty struck home as I stopped outside the Café Schwarzenberg and looked back at the hotel to see Marian watching me from the window of her room. We waved to each other across the slushy grey bustle of the Ringstrasse and I held her gaze for as long as it took a tram to caterpillar slowly between us. Then I turned reluctantly away and headed on. Towards all the many consequences of what we were doing. And a future I was willing to trade them for.

Chapter Two

They say time seems to pass more quickly as you grow older. They also say there's a good reason for that: the brain measures time by how much of it there is to remember, so each year is a smaller proportion than the one before of your life to date. It's a sour little trick to be the victim of, because it means pleasure, however intense, grows ever more fleeting. Sure enough, my five days with Marian in Vienna seemed like so many hours when I ran through them in my mind on the flight home. Not that it really mattered, because we were going to be apart for an even shorter period. And there's the flip side to the trick: pain obeys the same rule as pleasure.

Maybe that's why I charged at the problem of explaining myself to Faith and Amy like a horse rushing a fence. I wanted to be over it and away. I wanted to be two days in the future, and I opted for the easiest and quickest route. I was a photographer, after all. I knew about brevity. It came with the job. And speed was part of what had drawn Marian and me together, the bloom on the dark fruit we'd bitten and swallowed.

Besides, infatuation makes you selfish. It doesn't

leave room for much else, certainly not sensitivity or responsibility. It made me believe that what I wanted was all that counted, so long as Marian wanted it, too. And she did, just as urgently as me. I knew that. And so I knew it had to happen. Watching the tops of the clouds above London, spilling and pluming like the contours of an undiscovered landscape, I felt elated by the madness we'd set in motion. Everything before was drab and monochrome. I was about to see in colour for the first time.

I'd lived at the house in Barnes for the best part of ten years. When I stepped inside that afternoon, I realized with a kind of delayed shock that it had always been more Faith's home than mine, decorated, run, furnished and inhabited by her, merely used by me. I stood in the hallway, my bags at my feet, the traffic noise from Castelnau a background hum behind the tick of the clock and the buzz of the fridge and the click of the radiator. There'd been no danger of returning to a cold house. Faith's thermostatically controlled domesticity was lying in wait for me.

I turned and looked at the framed photograph of her and Amy hanging beside the barometer on the wall. It was one of my better efforts, capturing their unposed smiles, their snub-nosed twinkling-eyed resemblance and, just within the camera's grasp, their ease together, their certainty, their indissoluble kinship.

'You take pictures, Dad,' Amy once said to me. 'But there are hardly any of you. Why's that?' Because the photographer is never quite part of what he sees, Amy. Because the price of clear vision is the distance you need to focus in. I like to see, not be seen.

It didn't take me long to pack the little I needed. I'd

be back for the rest later, when the dust had settled and our plans were clearer. Faith would be reasonable, I knew. There'd be no scissored suits or burned books. She'd let me off lightly in the end. I phoned Tim Sadler when I'd finished packing and asked if he could put me up for a couple of nights. Tim qualified as just about my best and oldest friend. We'd met at university, where we'd both specialized in photography during our art degree course. He'd been doing most of my developing for several years at his small trade processing lab in Fulham. He was too fussy and set in his ways for my line of work, but his pernickety nature made him the ideal developer. It also made him fastidiously loyal to friends. Besides, he'd heard this tale before and knew better than to press for details.

'Does this mean what I think it means, Ian?'

'Sort of.'

'A cooling-off period?'

'A bit more than that.'

'Well, be my guest anyway. And give my love to Faith – if you have the chance.'

It was a nice idea, but hardly practical. I had only one message for Faith and it wasn't of love. I'd been on a form of marital parole since the affair with Nicole and I was about to break bail. Not for the first time, Tim was going to be harbouring a fugitive.

Faith came in at six, the clip of her office heels on the path warning me a few seconds before her key turned in the lock. The door was still closing as I walked out of the lounge and looked at her, groomed and smartly suited, briefcase in one hand, keys jangling in the other. Her weary expression turned towards suspicion as our eyes met. Already, at some intuitive level where our years

38

together, the good as well as the bad, merged in her memory, she knew.

'Not unpacked yet?' she asked, noticing the suitcase further down the hall.

'There's something I have to tell you, Faith.'

'What?' She dropped her briefcase and stared at me. 'What's happened?'

'I'm leaving.'

'You've only just got back.'

'I mean I'm leaving . . .' I looked away, gesturing helplessly. 'You. This house. Our marriage. It's over.'

'*Over?*'

'Finished. Done with. I can't—'

'Can't what?'

'Make it easy when it isn't. Be fair when I'm not being. We've had our problems before and ridden them out. But not this time. This is the end.'

'It's Nicole, isn't it?' She crashed the keys down on the telephone table and stepped closer. Her face was flushed, her breathing rapid. She was more shocked than angry. But soon the balance would change. '*Isn't it?*'

'No.'

'That bloody woman.'

'It isn't Nicole. It's someone . . . you don't know.'

'Who?'

'It doesn't matter who she is. What matters is that I love her.'

Faith tried to laugh, but her eyes were closer to tears. 'I doubt you do, Ian. I doubt you even know the meaning of the word.'

'Nothing you say will make any difference. I'm sorry, truly sorry, to tell you so . . . bluntly. But there really is no other way.'

39

'I forgave you Nicole. Have you forgotten that?'

'No. Of course not.'

'I could have made things a lot harder for you.'

'I know.'

'Not just then. Other times. I've given you far more than you've ever deserved.'

'I know. Faith, for God's sake—'

'What about Amy? Have you considered how she's going to react?'

'She's a level-headed girl. She'll understand.'

'Oh, she will, will she? Well, just in case she doesn't, perhaps you'd like to explain it to me. I mean, the way it works. Why it's so easy for you to walk out on fifteen years of *my* life as well as yours.'

'Who said it was easy?'

'It must be. Otherwise you wouldn't be doing it.'

'You know things haven't been right between us for a long time.'

'And this is how you put them right?'

'You're not listening, Faith. I've fallen in love with somebody else. It's as simple as that. If I stayed now, I'd be living a lie. And I'm not prepared to do that. I'm doing this for your sake as much as mine.'

'Bullshit. You're doing it because you want to.'

'All right. That's true, of course. It's what I want. But in time you may come to see that—'

'It's what I wanted all along without realizing it? Is that going to be your twisted justification for running off with whoever this bitch is?'

'I'm sorry.' I held up my hands to signal my abandonment of the argument. 'This is getting us nowhere. I have to be true to myself, Faith. I've made my choice. I'm leaving.'

'Go ahead then.' Her eyes were red and brimming

now. She blundered past me into the kitchen, catching my camera bag with her foot and slewing it across the floor. 'Do as you please.' She ran water from the tap onto her fingers and rinsed some of the tears away.

'You can contact me through Tim if there's anything—'

'There won't be.' Her voice was thick with emotion. I wanted to hug and comfort her, but my own words held me back.

'Obviously, as soon as I'm settled—'

'Get out, damn you!' She turned and glared at me. 'If you're so determined to be . . . true to yourself . . . and false to me . . . then you're right. There really is nothing else to say. Whatever you've got with this woman won't last, even if it is more than sex, which I doubt. Either way, when it's over, and that'll be sooner than you think, I won't be waiting for you. Walk out of this house now and remember, it's an exit only. There's no way back.'

'Faith—'

'What's stopping you? It's what you say you want. So go ahead.'

'All right, but I just—'

'Just nothing. Get out. That's all I'm asking you to do. Get the hell out.'

I gathered up my coat and bags and retreated to the door. Holding it open, I looked at her down the length of the hall, standing defensively in the kitchen, her arms folded, her face set and blank, her whole body trembling faintly. A favourite phrase of Tim's ran through my mind: *The things people do to each other.* God, it was true. I felt guilt and remorse at one remove. They should have enveloped me. But for the moment they couldn't touch me. I recognized them only as theoretical emotions. The real thing was what I felt for Marian. It made everything else seem not just worthwhile but irrelevant. Without another word I stepped out through the door and pulled it shut behind me.

Tim lived alone in a small terraced house in Parsons Green, well set in his contented ways, which revolved in neatly described circles round his cat, his classical music collection and his processing lab half a mile up the road. He viewed his friends' emotional crises with the pained bafflement of someone who'd never experienced anything even remotely similar, although I'd often wondered if he harboured a secret passion for Faith. They were alike in many ways. And that evening at his local, the White Horse, he told me, as he had on numerous occasions in the past, that I was mad to treat her so badly.

'You're probably right, Tim. But falling in love isn't much different from going mad. Just rather more fun.'

'I wouldn't know, would I?' he responded, slipping out a self-deprecating smile. 'I'll have to take your word for it. You're certainly not the same man I had a drink with a fortnight ago.'

'How do you mean?'

'You look about five years younger and you can't stop grinning, which doesn't make any sense considering you're in the process of turning your life upside down. So I suppose it has to be love.'

'I've never met anyone like her before.'

'Naturally not.'

'She's just . . . utterly extraordinary.'

'Of course.'

'And we're doing the right thing. I know we are.'

'Good.'

'I'm only sorry other people have to get hurt along the

way. I wish it could be avoided. But it can't. You do see that, don't you?'

'Are you asking me for my approval, Ian? I'm not sure I can give you that.'

'Let's say I'm not, then.'

'After all, this may be simpler than five years ago, but in the long run it could be a great deal more significant.'

'It's bound to be.'

'What about Amy, for instance?'

'I'll go up and see her tomorrow, before Faith has the chance to make it sound worse than it is.'

'She wouldn't do that.' Tim sounded disappointed at needing to contradict me. 'Besides, how could she? Let's be honest. There aren't a lot of extenuating circumstances, are there?'

I stared hard at him, then we both smiled. 'No, Tim. There aren't. Not one, since you mention it. Except that I can't seem to stop myself.'

'I reckoned not. It's why I haven't bothered trying to talk you out of it.'

'Perceptive, as usual.'

'Just a gift for observation. Too generalized to make me as good a photographer as you are. You've always had an obsessive streak, Ian. I wouldn't have thought it made you very good at mixing business with pleasure, though, like you must have been doing in Vienna.'

'I managed.'

'So you *did* bring back some pictures?'

'Yes.'

'Which you'll want me to print?'

'Of course.'

'Tomorrow?'

'I was hoping so. Then I could deliver them on Friday.'

43

'Before taking off with the woman of your dreams.'

I shrugged apologetically. 'Something like that.'

'This is going to cost you a few friendships, you know. A lot of people are going to take Faith's side. You do realize that, don't you?'

'Yes. But the friendships that really matter will endure.'

Tim sighed and drank some of his beer, then gave me a purse-lipped frown that amounted to a limited kind of blessing. 'I suppose they will. When all's said and done.'

I took the train to Bury St Edmunds next morning, then a taxi out to Amy's school. I'd phoned ahead and arranged to see her during a free period before lunch. This was the worst part of the whole enterprise. I knew she was going to be upset and I knew Faith would end up doing most of the consoling. But still I wanted to be the one to tell her. I wanted her to say she understood, even if she didn't. In short, I wanted it all.

But it was soon clear to me I wasn't going to get it. We walked out along the bank of the river that ran through the grounds, a chill, grey East Anglian mist turning the players on an adjoining hockey pitch to wraiths and the school building beyond them to a ghostly outline of the country house it had once been. Beside me, huddled in her uniform duffel coat and striped scarf, Amy looked too young and trusting to be burdened with what I had to tell her. But tell her I did, as gently as I knew how.

'Surely', she said disbelievingly, 'everything was all right at Christmas.'

'This has happened since Christmas, Amy. I've simply met somebody I realize I can't live without. It's

44

not easy. These things happen. People change. They grow apart.'

'Is that what you and Mum have done?'

'Sadly, yes. But it doesn't mean we love you any less. Either of us.'

'You just won't be together any more?'

'No. I'm afraid we won't.'

'Are you going to get divorced?'

'Eventually.'

'And then you'll marry this other person you've met?'

'I hope so. Her name's Marian. You'll like her.'

'No, I won't.'

'Come on, Amy. You've never met her. How can you say that?'

'I don't want to meet her.'

'You'll change your mind. This isn't the end of the world.'

'But it means nothing will ever be the same again. Quite a few of the other girls have divorced parents. And that's what they say. It alters everything. Spoils it. Makes it . . . complicated.'

'Life is. I wish it didn't have to be. But it is.'

'It didn't have to be with . . . Nicole.' Amy stopped. 'Did it?'

'Who told you about Nicole?' I said, taken aback to discover that my efforts to shield her from the truth five years before had evidently been in vain. 'Your mother?'

'Nobody told me, Dad. I just listened. I think I do that better than you.'

'Maybe you do.'

'But it's not going to be like it was then?'

'No, Amy. It isn't.'

'I'll just have to get used to the idea?'

'We all will. But remember. What the other girls have

45

told you isn't quite true. It doesn't alter *everything*. I'll still love you. You'll still be able to count on me when it matters.'

'Will I?'

'Oh yes.' I hugged her and sensed her struggling not to cry. 'As fathers go, you could do worse, believe it or not.'

'I believe it.' She pulled away and forced herself to smile. 'Honest I do.'

'Just not a lot worse, eh?' I aimed an elaborately slow punch that landed on her nose as softly as a butterfly. When she was younger, she used to squeeze her eyes shut and giggle as my fist approached. But she was older now. This time she kept her eyes open. And she never even came close to laughing.

A strained discussion with Amy's house tutor, late-running trains and a more than usually chaotic rush hour in London meant it was early evening before I got back to Parsons Green. To my surprise, Tim wasn't home yet. I let myself in with the spare key and seized the chance to telephone Marian. I was badly in need of her reassurance that the damage I was strewing round so blithely had a purpose as compelling for her as for me. But she was out, maybe walking off the same impatience I felt for our rendezvous at Lacock, maybe just having an early dinner. Guessing what I might do in her shoes, I rang the Schwarzenberg and persuaded them to page her. But she wasn't there either. I gave up and decided to try the Imperial again later.

Before I got the chance, Tim arrived, looking like a man with something to worry about. And pretty soon I had something to worry about as well.

'I developed your Viennese films.'

46

'How'd they come out?'

'They didn't.'

'What do you mean?'

'There's nothing on them. All six films are blank.'

'*Blank?*'

'The whole lot were exposed. It's as if you had the back of the camera open when you wound on. Every frame's a blackout. There's nothing there. Not a single picture to prove you even went to Vienna.'

'What have you done?' I shouted, shock unhinging my thought processes. 'Where are my photographs?'

'I don't know.'

'You . . . botched this somehow?'

'No, Ian. I just did my normal job. There must be something badly wrong with your camera.'

'There's nothing wrong with it. It's working perfectly.'

'The results suggest otherwise.'

'Tim, for God's sake tell me you're joking. Where are my bloody photographs?'

'They don't exist.'

'They *must* exist. I took them.'

'I believe you. The trouble is, you lost what you took. I don't know how or why.'

'Well, I certainly don't.'

'It's a mystery, then.'

'Just a minute.' I stepped closer. 'You didn't wreck this job for me, did you, Tim? As some sort of mark of your disapproval?'

'Of course I didn't. What do you take me for?'

'Sorry. I . . .' His hurt look was genuine. There was no doubt about it. 'I'm not thinking straight. I just . . . don't understand.'

'Neither do I.'

'*Exposed?* The whole lot?'

'Every single one.'

'This is insane.'

'But true.'

I struck out at thin air in frustration and began to walk up and down, thoughts whirling in my head. It couldn't be true, but apparently it was. I was scheduled to deliver my portfolio of Viennese photographs the very next day. But I had none to deliver. Except . . . 'There's one film left,' I announced, snapping my fingers. 'It's in the camera now. A few last shots of Vienna – nothing important.' That wasn't quite true, of course. It contained the pictures I'd taken of Marian at the Imperial, which naturally I hadn't wanted Tim to develop. 'But it'll prove the camera isn't at fault. I'll take the film to the lab, if that's all right by you, and develop it myself.'

'Now?'

'Why not? Is there a problem? I know my way round the place. I won't break anything.'

'I know you won't. But—'

'Then humour me. I'd like to do the job myself. It's not that I don't trust you.'

'Sounds like it.'

'I'm going to be in one hell of a jam if I've got nothing to show them tomorrow, Tim. Let me do this my way, will you?'

He shrugged. 'All right. But my bet is you'll just get another load of duds. It has to be the camera. Either that or . . .'

'What?'

'There *is* only one other possible explanation, Ian. And you don't need me to tell you what it is.'

*   *   *

Sabotage. That was the explanation Tim hadn't cared to name. Like he'd said, it was as if I'd opened the back of the camera when winding on the film. Only I hadn't, of course. But somebody else might have. It certainly looked as if they had, because the film I developed that night was the same as the ones Tim had developed earlier: black and ruined. Including the frames I hadn't even used. Which suggested they'd been wound on with the camera open, then wound back, in a deliberate and calculated act of destruction.

I must have sat in Tim's darkroom for an hour or more, trying to reason out a response to what had happened. The camera looked fine. It was old enough to make light seepage a remote possibility, but not on a scale to account for total exposure. The films had come from a regular source and I'd already used several from the same batch without any problems. There were the X-ray machines at the airports to consider, of course. They could have been wrongly adjusted. Still, it would have to have been a pretty gross error to produce such a devastating result. No, no. The overwhelming probability was that the films had been got at, before or after my arrival in Vienna. As to why, I hadn't the inkling of an idea. As to who, just about the only person who'd had an opportunity to do such a thing was the one person I had to believe, for the sake of my own sanity, couldn't be responsible.

I phoned the Imperial from the lab. It was late enough now to be confident of finding Marian in her room. And so she was.

'Are you all right, Ian? You sound . . . I don't know . . . odd.'

'There are some problems with the pictures I took of Vienna.'

49

'Serious problems?'

'You could say that. You don't remember seeing anyone . . . tampering with my camera, do you?'

'No. I'd have told you at the time if I had.'

'Yes. Of course you would.'

'Is this going to interfere with our plans?'

'What? No. No, why should it?'

'I can't wait to see you tomorrow. Christ, I literally ache to touch you again. You know that?'

'I feel the same.' It was true. Even the professional disaster I was staring in the face couldn't diminish my desire for her.

'How were things . . . with your wife?'

'Much as I expected.'

'But dealt with?'

'Oh yes.'

'Now it's my turn. Wish me luck.'

'You think you'll need it?'

'Not really. You've booked us into the place at Lacock?'

'Yes. The Sign of the Angel. I'll go down there tomorrow afternoon.'

'And I'll join you in the evening.'

'What time?'

'Hard to say. Nine o'clock at the latest, I suppose.'

'You'd better give me your home phone number. Just in case.'

'In case of what?'

'I don't know. Delays. Difficulties.'

'There won't be any, Ian. Trust me. I know what I'm doing. I love you, remember. Nothing's going to stop me. I'll see you at Lacock.'

'All right, but—'

'No buts. Just be sure you're waiting for me when I arrive. I'll expect a warm welcome.'

'You'll get it.'

'I'm going to hang up now. Otherwise, I won't know how to. Until tomorrow, my love . . . I'll be thinking of you all the time.'

She rang off. I put the telephone down and stared at the strips of useless film lying in front of me on the lab bench. Something was going on and part of me dearly wished not to know what it was. In twenty-four hours I'd see Marian again. Then, somehow, it would all be all right.

Friday was grey and cold and still, London a drab and grubby ghost of itself. I had to get out, had to start moving, not despite the hours at my disposal but because of them. I telephoned my agent and pleaded a family bereavement as justification for postponing delivery of the Viennese photographs until Monday morning. Then I asked yet another favour of Tim: take some pictures with a new film in my camera and develop them immediately to see whether they came out. That would rule in or out one possible explanation for what had happened. Pending the result, I preferred not to face the other possibilities. My thoughts were concentrated on surviving until I saw Marian again. I promised to phone Tim later, then set off. Only to find I'd left my departure just too late. A car I recognized very well was slowing to a halt at the kerbside just as I stepped onto the pavement. As it stopped, the driver lowered the window and looked out at me.

'Where are you going, Ian?' Faith asked. Her voice sounded calm enough, but her expression was tense, her jaw set in a clenched line.

'Does it matter?'

'Amy phoned last night.'

'Ah. Did she?'

'You should have warned me you meant to tell her straight away.'

'Maybe I would have done, if I'd got the chance.'

'Don't give me that. She's our daughter, Ian. You *should* have consulted me.'

'Well, neither of us were in a very consultative mood, were we?'

'I'm going up there this weekend to try to repair some of the damage you've done.'

'What can I say? She had to know, Faith.'

'You could say you're sorry. You could say you've taken leave of your senses. You could even say you want to put things right.'

'What would be the point? You said there was no way back.' A mad idea burst into my mind so abruptly then that I didn't realize at first just how mad it was. 'While I was in Suffolk yesterday, you didn't . . . drop by Tim's lab, did you?'

'Pardon?'

'Tim's processing lab. Did you, Faith?'

'Why the hell should I have gone there?'

'Some films of mine have been mysteriously ruined. You wouldn't happen to know anything about it, I suppose?'

'Are you out of your mind? You think—' She slowly shook her head, evidently dismayed that I should even hint at anything so absurd. 'God, Ian, I think you're falling apart, you know that? Maybe this Marian is the sort of woman who can drive men crazy. In your case that seems to mean paranoid. You ought to listen to yourself some time, you really ought. You'll be hearing from Malcolm. I'll leave you to find a solicitor of your own.' She let in the clutch with a roar and accelerated away down the road.

I watched her go. The stupidity of what I'd said hit home even before she'd turned out of sight onto the main road. It was illogical as well as unlikely, if not downright impossible, for Faith to have been responsible. She and Tim would have to have been conspiring against me. And if I started believing that . . . then I really might begin to fall apart.

Faith would certainly have found some evidence for her view in what I did next. I took the Tube out to Heathrow and lay in wait at Terminal One for the late morning and early afternoon flights from Vienna. I could easily have asked Marian which flight she was going to catch, of course, but I reckoned she'd have forbidden me to meet her off it. This way, I could explain that I'd surrendered to a sudden romantic impulse.

The only problem was that she didn't catch either of those I was on hand for. I waited by the barrier as first one then two Vienna flights emptied, and there was no sign of her. I began to worry, even though I knew she could have flown to Gatwick or arrived by an early flight while I was still in Parsons Green. Emptying a pocketful of coins into a payphone on the concourse, I rang the Imperial, who confirmed that Mrs Esguard had checked out. Gatwick, or some indirect route, had to be the answer.

But it wasn't an answer that gave me much peace of mind. I caught the next express coach to Reading and a train from there to Chippenham. It was as grey and cold in Wiltshire as it had been in London. And the taxi driver seemed to think I expected a metropolitan level of conversation.

'Everybody loves Lacock except me,' he announced as we left Chippenham. 'Not real, is it? Not genuine.

Bloody museum village. Slice of medieval Olde England. Strictly for the tourists. And the film crews, of course. You're lucky there isn't one swarming over the place today. Not in that game, are you? Only you look as if you might be.'

'Appearances can be deceptive.'

'You're right there, mate. Dead right. What do they say? The camera never lies? They must be joking. It was invented at Lacock, you know: the camera. Back in the last century. More's the pity, I say. We'd all be better off without photographs, if you want my opinion.'

He may have gone on to explain *why* we'd all be better off without them, but by then I wasn't listening. He had a point about Lacock, of course. I was well aware how idealized a vision of an English village the place represented. And therefore, in his terminology, how *unreal* it was.

But unreality was more or less my state of mind at the time. Nothing quite fitted, or seemed in tune. I booked into the Sign of the Angel like a man in a dream, spent just long enough in the low-ceilinged double-bedded room to dump my bags, then headed out into what remained of the afternoon.

It was strange to find myself breaking the habits of a professional lifetime by walking around without a camera. It was also a measure of how rapidly and completely I'd departed from normality. I followed a footpath I remembered north out of the village and over the fields to Reybridge, where I crossed the Avon and doubled back to the meadows on the opposite side of the river from Lacock Abbey. The building was exactly as it had been when Fox Talbot took his first photographs of it in the 1830s: a grey stone jumble of cloisters, turrets

54

and chimneys. Fox Talbot himself might have stood exactly where I was standing on a winter's afternoon 160 years earlier and pondered how to preserve the image of what he saw. And maybe that was the taxi driver's point. An image was all a photograph could ever be. Even if my pictures of Marian had survived, her absence would be just as real.

It was a fleeting reality, though, one due to give way in just a few hours to a renewal of all the pleasure and sense of purpose we'd discovered together in Vienna. As soon as I got back to the Sign of the Angel I phoned Tim.

'Your camera's fine, Ian. Perfect working order.'

'As I thought.'

'And that means . . . what exactly?'

'I'm not sure.'

'When will you be back for it?'

'I'm not sure about that either. I'll phone you over the weekend.'

'Faith called round to the lab at lunchtime.'

'What did she want?'

'A shoulder to cry on, I suppose. A mutual friend to agree with her that what you've done is inexcusable.'

'Which you did?'

'Well, I didn't *dis*agree. How could I? Actually, she seems to be almost as worried about you as she is angry. She asked me a strange question. Was I sure you'd really met another woman in Vienna or could you be making the whole thing up?'

'I haven't left her for a figment of my imagination, Tim.'

'That's what I told her. But I didn't get the impression she was convinced. I suppose in some ways insanity's easier to deal with than infidelity.'

'You reckon?'

'What I reckon, Ian, is that you're as sane as I am. But you're also mad to be doing this.'

'Thanks for the vote of confidence. It's much appreciated.'

Confidence was something I could have done with more of as the winter's dusk faded into evening. I walked round to the George for a couple of drinks, but by seven o'clock I was back in my room at the Sign of the Angel, waiting, waiting, waiting. Eight o'clock came. Then nine, Marian's self-imposed deadline. Still there was no sign of her. I grew more and more anxious, insecurity nibbling away at my reserves of logic. She wasn't so very late, when all was said and done. As soon as she arrived, the fretful hours I'd passed alone would vanish from my memory. I knew that. *Just as soon as she arrived.*

At nine thirty-two the telephone rang. I grabbed it in a panic. 'Marian?' I said, assuming it was her for the simple reason that nobody else knew I was there.

The line went dead as soon as I'd spoken. I put the telephone down, wondering if I'd somehow broken the connection by answering too quickly. A minute or so crept by. Then it rang again.

'Hello?'

'Ian?' It was her. My heart jumped.

'Marian, where are you?'

'I'm not coming.'

'What?'

'I'm sorry. I realize now . . . I can't.'

'What are you saying?'

'It's all a mistake. As bad for me as it is for you.'

'You don't mean that. Hold on—'

'You won't see me again. Or hear from me. That's the

56

only way to do this. I'm sorry about the photographs. I had to make sure, you see.'

'Sure of what? Where are you? What's going on? Are you in some kind of—?'

'Don't try to find me. You won't be able to. Goodbye, Ian.'

'Marian, for God's—'

Too late. Already, I was talking to myself.

PART TWO

EXPOSURE

Chapter Three

'What are you going to do?' Tim looked at me with a sympathetic frown that was somehow harder to bear than any amount of disapproval. 'This is a hell of a mess.' We were in the White Horse at Parsons Green early on Monday evening, the other side of a weekend I'd spent partly in Lacock and partly in my own kind of hell. I'd poured out the whole pitiful story to Tim because I needed to tell someone besides myself what I'd been through. 'In effect, you've walked out on your marriage for nothing.'

'That's one way of looking at it.'

'And you've managed to antagonize your agent as well as one of your best clients at the same time.'

'Correct.'

'Your professional reputation is going to look pretty sick after a fiasco like this.'

'Thanks for mentioning it.'

'Do you think you were deliberately set up?'

'I don't know what to think, Tim. But nobody gains by doing this to me. I prefer to believe – maybe I *have* to believe – that Marian was on the level in Vienna.'

'So why didn't she turn up at Lacock?'

'Loss of nerve. Or worse. Maybe her husband took steps to prevent her leaving him.'

'You have no idea where they live?'

'None.'

'And no way of finding out?'

'None I can think of. I phoned the Imperial and cajoled them into checking their records, but it turns out she somehow failed to register her address.'

'Suspicious in itself.'

'Yes. And she paid her bill in cash, so they've no way of tracing her.'

'And consequently neither have you.'

'None at all. Apart from just . . . looking.'

'Looking where?'

'Anywhere.'

'That sounds pretty hopeless.'

'I know.'

'Besides, she admitted sabotaging your films. Doesn't that prove she was planning to cut you adrift while you were still in Vienna?'

'I think she may just have been desperate.'

'On account of her husband.'

'Yes. There was something about the way she described him – or didn't. Something . . . fearful.'

'You're saying she might need rescuing?'

'Possibly, yes.'

'By you?'

'Who else?'

'On the other hand, she could be an accomplished actress who got a kick out of making a fool of you.'

'I don't think so.'

'I did say accomplished.'

'I still don't think so.' I drained my glass and looked at him. 'Same again?'

'I've only just started this one.'

'So you have. Back in a minute.'

I stood up and went to the bar for a refill. When I returned to the table, Tim's frown had deepened.

'What's wrong?'

'That won't help, you know.' He pointed at my glass.

'It'll help me sleep.'

'And then?'

'I'll start looking.'

'What about work?'

'If I get offered any, which after the Vienna cock-up is doubtful . . .' I shrugged. 'It'll just have to wait.'

'How long?'

'As long as it takes.'

'You're determined to go after her?'

'Yes.'

'Rather than try to patch things up with Faith and lose yourself in your work for a while?'

'Yes.'

'Why?'

'Because I have to know why she did it. And to do that I have to find her.'

'She told you not to try.'

'Yes. But I'm no good at following instructions. Ask my agent. I'm going to try all right. And, the way I feel at the moment, I can't imagine I'll stop. Until I learn the truth. Whatever it might be.'

Bold words for what was actually the only thing my self-respect would let me do. Marian needed me as much as I needed her. I was determined to cling to that belief because there was, quite simply, nothing else to cling to. And I wanted her, too, more than ever. The memories of our days and nights in Vienna were goads to the flesh as well as to the mind. I couldn't bear the loss of so much so soon without fighting to regain it. And the only way I could fight was to start looking for her and to go on looking just as long and as hard as I needed to.

It was a desperate course, no question. But the alternatives were worse. Faith had made it clear she wouldn't have me back. Besides, I couldn't have gone back even if she'd asked me to. I loved Marian, even more potently now I couldn't see her or speak to her or touch her. As for photography, the loss of my Viennese pictures had shocked me into a raw-nerved abstinence. I hadn't taken a single photograph since. I'd made a pact with myself. The next photograph I took would be of Marian.

My first recourse was to return to Vienna, hoping I might be able to pick up her trail there. A doorman at the Imperial remembered her well and seemed to think that when he'd hailed a taxi for her on the morning of her departure she'd said she wanted to go not to the airport, but to one of the railway stations: the Süd-Bahnhof. It was a destination that made no sense, since trains from there headed south, into Hungary and Italy. But then nothing else made sense, so why should that be an exception? I hung around the concourse at the Süd-Bahnhof pondering the point, then wandered out into the park of the Belvedere Palace, where I'd walked with Marian and taken one of the best of my lost pictures of snow-draped Vienna. The snow was gone now, succeeded by rain and slush and a dismal air of wasted chances.

I went everywhere we'd been, asking waiters and

passers-by and people at nearby tables in cafés if they remembered me and my glamorous companion of a couple of weeks before. A few thought they did, but none had any recollection of seeing Marian since. I took the 71 tram from outside the Schwarzenberg down through the suburbs to the Zentralfriedhof, and plodded round the avenues between the graves, wondering if she was waiting for me there, if I'd glimpse the red of her coat somewhere ahead of me through the trees. But I didn't. She wasn't there. Or anywhere else I tried. And the longer I remained the weaker grew the visual impression she'd left on the only places where I'd ever seen her.

I flew back to England and the onset of a relentlessly wet February. I moved my few belongings out of Tim's house – despite his assurances that I didn't have to – and rented a bedsit over a pizza parlour in Notting Hill Gate. It wasn't much of a place, but then it didn't need to be. I didn't intend to spend much of my time there. It was just a base for my search operation.

But where was the search to start? I reckoned I had two admittedly imprecise clues. Marian had said the house she lived in had been in her husband's family for generations. That sounded rural, if not manorial. And Esguard was a highly unusual name. It should be possible, given enough time and effort, to track it down. She'd also said there was no problem getting from there to Lacock. That implied a drive of an hour or so, maybe two at the most. I allowed seventy miles as a maximum distance and checked a map to see what lay within that radius of Lacock. Most of the southern half of England was the answer: Exeter in the west, Birmingham in the north, London in the east, Bournemouth in the south. Not much of a help, but it marginally narrowed the field.

I scoured the telephone directories covering areas

inside the circle and drew a blank. No Esguards. Then I went through those for the rest of the country with the same result. That left me back at the beginning and eager to try my luck on the ground. My reluctance to take photographs, whatever their origin, had an even stranger partner in the sudden loss of my horror of driving. Maybe it was just a matter of necessity. Faith was no longer available to ferry me around. And I wasn't going to get far on foot or public transport. Somehow everything – even the memory of that wet night on Barnet Hill when I'd taken a stranger's life in a moment of carelessness – had faded into insignificance compared with the task I'd set myself. Tim had said I had a streak of obsessiveness. But he was wrong. Extremism was nearer the mark. About photography. About Marian. About finding her.

I bought a second-hand car and gritted my way back to competence with a saturation dose at the wheel. The pattern of my search became a compulsion in its own right. I headed out of London along the radial routes, starting with the A23 down through Surrey and Sussex, working my way slowly west. Each route took several days to cover as I diverged either side, stopping at every town and village to ask the locals if they knew anyone living in the neighbourhood by the name of Esguard. I tried the pubs, post offices and estate agents as well. Nobody could help, but I went on asking, pushing to the back of my mind the fear that nobody would ever be able to. There was a kind of logic to it. If she'd lied to me, I'd never find her. But if she'd told me the truth . . .

February faded into March with nothing gained except a desperate kind of equilibrium in my life. As long as I was looking for Marian I didn't have to acknowledge the futility of what I was doing. My pursuit of her was also a flight from myself: from what my wife and daughter thought of me, from the sick joke I'd doubtless become among friends and colleagues and anyone who'd known me as a competent level-headed professional.

I wonder now if I'd ever have stopped, if eventually I'd simply have widened the circle as often as I needed to in order to sustain the search. To have given up would always have seemed worse than carrying on. There's no way to tell how and when it might have ended. Defeat, once admitted, would have been terminal, I'm sure of that. That's why it was bound to be so long coming. I was slowly zigzagging my way across England towards a dead end, but I never once let myself believe it. Wherever I went, I asked questions and studied faces: the same question with the same answer; the same face sought with the same result. I put identically worded advertisements in the personal columns of the national press every Saturday: 'MARIAN, PLEASE REMEMBER VIENNA AND RESPOND, IAN.' But nobody ever wrote to the box number. I hired private detectives to cover London, Birmingham, Bristol and Cardiff. But they turned up nothing. I became a ghost hunting a ghost, haunted by a past I couldn't forget and a future I couldn't give up.

The first stirrings of spring frightened me. I couldn't stop time passing, but as it did so Marian retreated deeper, day by day, into my memory. Even the season of our love was passing. Tim, the only friend I saw anything of, urged me whenever we met to break the spell she'd cast on me and face up to the realities of life. Faith had set the wheels of divorce in motion, as I knew from the letters her solicitor – formerly *our* solicitor – had sent to me. So far, I hadn't replied. But I'd have to sooner or later. And it wouldn't be long before Amy was home for Easter. Ignoring Faith was one thing, neglecting my daughter quite another. Tim pointed all this out to me as patiently as he could, throwing in occasional laments for the photographic career I was steadily demolishing. But none of it made any impression. I didn't expect anyone to understand what I was doing. I didn't really want them to. It was a private crusade, in which any compromise, however slight, was likely to prove fatal. Somewhere, somehow, sometime, I'd find Marian. And when I did . . .

The flat in Notting Hill, entered in clean spring sunshine. It was a Friday and I was back from a week-long foray in the West Country, weary and empty-handed and sick at heart from all the loneliness and pointlessness I could deny to Tim but not to myself. There was a letter lying in the narrow hallway, the address handwritten. One of the other tenants must have slipped it under the door. They often did when mail for me lay around the communal entrance for days on end. I picked it up and looked at the writing. I don't know why, but something told me it was Marian's. I'd never seen her write a single word, but the style was what I'd unconsciously expected hers to be. The postmark was London W11, as local as could be. I ripped the envelope open.

There was a postcard inside, but no message was written on it. The picture on the front was a fuzzy print of a country church. The caption read, 'St Andrew's, Tollard Rising, Dorset.' I sank slowly to my haunches and fell back against the wall behind me. Then I began to cry, tears of sheer overwhelming relief. It wasn't much. It was hardly anything at all. But it was a consequence, however cryptic, of the weeks of searching I'd sustained. It was some kind of message, albeit unwritten. It was almost an answer.

Tollard Rising was about thirty miles from Lacock. The irony was that I'd already been there and drawn a blank. It was among a string of villages I'd visited during a day's drive along the Fordingbridge–Shaftesbury road. Tollard Rising itself lay near the western end, where the Dorset–Wiltshire border meandered along the hilltops of Cranborne Chase. It occupied one of the more exposed locations, a huddle of old stone cottages round a small squat-towered church, boasting neither pub nor post office. Commercial life, such as it was, took place down the hill at Tollard Royal. I'd given the place short shrift at the time. Now the postcard had arrived, as if to rebuke me.

It had been a weekday before, and the village, as a consequence, eerily empty. There was more life to be detected on a sunny Saturday morning, but it was of no immediate help to me. A fellow washing his Range Rover echoed the comment I was used to hearing. 'Esguard? Don't know anyone of that name round here.' But someone had to know. Otherwise . . .

The church was damp and cold, despite the sunshine. The interior smelled of age and must and past times layered one upon another. Services were fortnightly, according to the porch notices. This was an obscure satellite parish, its affairs administered at arm's length by the vicar of Witchbourne Hinton ten miles away. The graveyard was the usual yew-fringed plot of old and new stones, more old than new, with lichen and decay well established: one weeping cherub, a few Celtic crosses and two or three large ledger-slabbed graves in the southern lee of the tower. Beyond lay farm fields and a sunlit descent into Blackmoor Vale. The only oddity that struck me was an ornate stone-arched gateway leading from the churchyard into what was now a sheep-cropped pasture. There was another, more modest rear entrance, still apparently in use, but this gate looked as if it had once served some significant purpose. The only building visible in that direction was a farm. The gate itself was sealed with a rusty chain and padlock.

I looked at the church. No obvious clues stared back at me. The postcard was surely one in its own right, though. It had brought me to this place. Why? What could a virtually redundant old church have to do with Marian? The man down the road hadn't recognized the name Esguard. It hadn't featured on the cleaning rota or the list of church wardens. But it *was* a rural location, as I'd suspected. And . . . Then it came to me. There were names all around me, on the gravestones. '*They were just as real as you and me,*' Marian had said of Vienna's foregathered dead at the Zentralfriedhof. '*Maybe more so.*'

I started a systematic search from grave to grave, scraping out the lettering on the older stones with a penknife, though even then some remained illegible. After half an hour with nothing to show for my efforts, I reached the grander ledger-stoned graves closest to the church.

They were also some of the oldest and most heavily weathered. It was as much as I could do to trace the inscriptions. But I persevered, progressing painstakingly from the first – Colonel something something Wheeler, Royal something, plus wife and son, all dead within a few years of each other in the 1820s – to the second, where I probed meticulously with the penknife at the faint lichen-blotched outline of a name until . . .

ESGUARD. It was there in front of me. JOSLYN

MARCHMONT ESGUARD. Marian had referred to her husband as Jos, surely short for Joslyn. And now I was looking at Joslyn Esguard's grave. There was no mention of a wife or children, only some kind of address – Gaunt's Chase, Tollard Rising – and a record of his death – 23 June 1838, aged 62.

I sat staring at that slab for a long long time. Was this the only Joslyn Esguard I could hope to find? Or was he an ancestor of the one I was actually looking for? I couldn't tell, but now at last I sensed I was on the track of an answer. I'd had to have the way pointed out to me, of course. I'd never have got this far on my own. Was Marian really my informant? If so, the postcard had to be a plea for help – the only kind of plea she could risk or contrive. The Esguards were an old family. She'd said so herself. Yes, that had to be it. She was married to this dead Dorset squire's great-great-great-great-grandson. And now I had an address. Gaunt's Chase. '*Esguards have lived there for generations.*'

But where was it? I asked at the post office down in Tollard Royal, but learned nothing. I tried the pub with the same result. Then I made for Witchbourne Hinton. Parish records didn't fade as fast as human memory. I found the vicar in his gardening clothes, tackling an overgrown hedge. He was a placid, comfortably built, rural cleric in late middle age, happy enough, it seemed, to take a break from his labours to satisfy my curiosity. And it was immediately obvious that *he* knew the name Esguard. For a very particular reason.

'You're the second person to enquire about the family this year. Are you acquainted with the lady who came last month?'

'I don't think so. Who was she?'

'I can't recall her name. A pleasant woman. Tall.

71

Dark-haired. In her forties, I imagine. There was something . . . professional . . . about her.'

'And she was asking about the Esguards of Gaunt's Chase?'

'Yes. But I couldn't help her any more than I can help you. I don't know the family or the house. As for the grave at Tollard Rising, well, as you've seen, it's more than a hundred and fifty years old. You'll understand that I devote most of my time to those of my parishioners who are still alive.' He grinned. 'Or, at any rate, rather more recently deceased.'

'Aren't there . . . records?'

'Of course. Those for Tollard Rising are held at the County Record Office in Dorchester. As I explained to the lady. That would include any certificate of marriage contracted in the parish by the late Mr Esguard, a possibility she seemed particularly interested in.'

'Marriage? Did she say why?'

'Not really. She described it as a question of historical research. Which is why I referred her to Mr Appleyard, our eminent local historian. Since she didn't come back to me, I can only assume he was able to satisfy her curiosity on the point.'

Derek Appleyard, retired schoolteacher and dedicated chronicler of the last thousand years of Cranborne Chase lived in a surprisingly modern bungalow at the corner of a wood halfway between Tollard Royal and Sixpenny Handley. His wife was preparing lunch when I arrived, but I only had to hint at an interest in his speciality for him to usher me into his study. His wife announced she'd eat without him and I had the impression she meant it.

The study was his research centre, crammed with

books, papers, folders, box files and computer disks, plus a framed map of Dorset *circa* 1600 on one wall, and a huge aerial photograph of what I assumed was his corner of the county on another. He was a spry, stooping old chap, who combined scholarly eccentricity with a cigarette habit that meant every surface in the room was finely covered with ash. One day, I imagined, the whole lot would go up in smoke, very possibly him with it.

'I confess myself puzzled, Mr Jarrett. First one Esguard researcher, then two. Odd, distinctly odd. What, pray, is it all about?'

'It's too complicated to explain.'

'Do you know that's exactly what Miss Sanger said. Are you sure you're not acquainted with her?'

'I'm not *absolutely* sure about much, Mr Appleyard, to be honest. But I don't think I am. Did she leave you with any way to contact her?'

'Yes. A telephone number. That's even odder, actually. She asked me to let her know if anyone else came by enquiring about the Esguards. But she led me to expect a woman, not a man.'

'Sorry to disappoint you. But I can save you the effort of contacting Miss Sanger. If you give me the number, I'll do it myself.'

'Good idea. She gave me a card. It'll be in here somewhere.' He began rooting through a desk drawer. 'Charming lady, I must say.'

'What did you tell her?'

'The little I know. There was a large house up on the downs near Tollard Rising called Gaunt's Chase. It dated from the late seventeenth century. Rather a pleasing William and Mary construction, to judge by surviving prints, though the exposed location can't have made it very comfortable. I can point out the exact site on the OS map. The Esguard family owned it, along with a substantial surrounding estate, including most of Tollard Rising. There's a gate from the churchyard that once led onto a carriage drive from the house.'

'I saw no drive.'

'No. And you wouldn't see the house, either, if you followed the route of it. The estate was broken up in the eighteen thirties, presumably to pay off creditors. The house itself burned down in 1838. I believe Joslyn Esguard died in the fire. The site was then cleared. I've looked for traces of it and, though there must be some, I've failed to discover them. Mind you, I can't claim to have mounted an exhaustive—'

'What about the Esguards today?'

'Same story. We have Joslyn Esguard's grave as you saw it. Plus memorial tablets inside the church to his father and grandfather, who I think are buried in the crypt. But with Joslyn's death the family seems to have come to an abrupt end. If there were any of them left, they must have moved out of the area. Understandable, perhaps, in view of the loss of the house and estate.'

'The vicar said Miss Sanger was particularly interested in finding out whether Joslyn Esguard was married.'

'Yes. Well, I suppose it would increase the chances of the line having continued if he was. But I couldn't help her. I know the name in connection with the house. The family's of no intrinsic significance. Not to me, anyway. But to you and Miss Sanger' – he shrugged – 'matters are obviously not so straightforward. But, then, what else should one expect of a lady in her line of work?' He held up her calling card. 'Psychotherapist and hypnotherapist, it says here. With a practice in Harley Street, no less.' Smiling, he handed me the card. 'What

74

do you think, Mr Jarrett? Was she here as an amateur genealogist? Or in a professional capacity?'

I drove as close to the site Appleyard showed me on the map as I could, then clambered over a gate into a field and struck out across it, with the wind in my hair and a distant vision in my mind of a seventeenth-century mansion dominating the empty bench of land where it sloped gently south-west, away from the escarpment of the downs, before descending in enfolded valleys towards Blackmoor Vale. I could see the clustered roofs of Tollard Rising and its church tower to the south, farm buildings and woodland below me straight ahead, and a vacant horizon above and to the north. Gaunt's Chase had stood there once. I had Appleyard's word for it. Maybe the track snaking up from the farm to some barns beyond the next field followed part of the route of the carriage drive. Maybe the trees in the dip where the barn nestled were a survivor of some prettified Georgian land-scaping. But nothing beyond maybes survived of the house. It hadn't merely been destroyed by fire. It had been erased.

Which rendered Marian's reference to her husband's ancestral home all the more tantalizing. There couldn't be another. This was the right place. The postcard proved that. But it was all gone, long ago. The Esguards had moved on, if they'd survived at all, leaving only their dead behind.

Yet there was more to it than that. There had to be. If only because I wasn't the only one looking for them. Daphne Sanger's interest, professional or otherwise, was clearly more than historical curiosity. She'd been sufficiently eager for news to add her home telephone number to the card she'd left with Appleyard. Which meant I didn't have to wait till Monday to find out what was driving her in the same direction as me.

'Hello.'

'Is that Daphne Sanger?'

'Yes. Who's calling?'

'My name's Jarrett, Miss Sanger. Ian Jarrett. We haven't met. But it seems we both know Marian Esguard.'

'How did you get this number?'

'From Derek Appleyard. You visited him last month.'

'Yes, but—'

'Do you know Marian, Miss Sanger?'

'Know her? What do you mean?'

'It's simple enough. I'm looking for Marian, and it seems you may be looking for her, too. Is that correct?'

'No. Of course not. If you know anything about Marian Esguard, Mr Jarrett, you'll know how ridiculous that suggestion is.'

'I met her in January. I think she may be in some sort of trouble. If there's anything—'

'You *met* her?'

'Yes. In Vienna, two months ago. How did you come to meet her, Miss Sanger? Is she a patient of yours? Or a friend?'

'This is ridiculous. I don't know what you're talking about.'

'You must. Why else were you in Tollard Rising last month?'

'I'm not sure that's any of your business.'

'You asked Appleyard to alert you if anyone came enquiring after the Esguards. Well, I came. And I'm prepared to tell you what brought me. In return for as much as you can tell me.'

'It's really not as—' She broke off, as if to think. Then she said, 'The woman you met in Vienna, Mr Jarrett. Could you describe her to me?'

'Marian? Well, if you insist.'

'I do.'

'All right. She's in her late twenties or early thirties. Medium height, slim build, short dark hair, pale complexion. She has a slightly flattened nose, large eyes, striking looks. Likes to wear red. Is that close enough?'

'Yes. Too close to be any kind of mistake.' She sounded mollified, but also puzzled. 'Very well, Mr Jarrett. I think we should meet.'

Jack Straw's Castle, Hampstead Heath, was Daphne Sanger's choice of rendezvous, not mine. It was predictably crammed with the younger Hampstead set at lunchtime on a Sunday, but maybe their noisy self-absorption was just the camouflage my companion required. She was waiting for me at a corner table when I arrived shortly after opening time, a neat, solemn-faced woman in her forties, dressed expensively but discreetly, with plainly cut ash-blond hair, gold-rimmed spectacles and startlingly long slender fingers, currently caressing a slim cigar.

'Sorry it isn't quieter,' she said. 'But crowds have their advantages.'

'Safety in numbers, you mean?'

'Safety *is* an issue, Mr Jarrett. Perhaps you've already realized that.'

'Marian's safety is uppermost in my mind.'

'Ah, yes. Marian. Of course. It's very strange to hear her called that.'

'Why?'

'Because it isn't her name. Not, at all events, the name she gave me.'

'But you recognized it well enough over the telephone.'

'Yes. Confusing, isn't it? If you'll forgive me for saying so, Mr Jarrett, you do look confused. And a little . . . how shall I say? . . . harassed.'

'I've had a rough time lately.'

'Personal or professional?'

'Both.'

'And what is your profession?'

'Photographer.'

I'd never have expected such an apparently self-possessed woman to register shock so transparently. Her jaw fell and her eyes widened. I thought for a moment she was going to drop her cigar in her gin and tonic. '*Photographer?*'

'Yes. What's so remarkable about that?'

'Don't you know?'

'No. Should I?'

'No,' she said after a moment's deliberation. 'I suppose, after all, you probably shouldn't. Tell me how you met . . . Marian.'

'Tell me her real name first.'

'Her real name? I have cause to doubt either of us knows that. Eris Moberly was the one she gave me. I took her on as a client last summer.'

'What kind of client?'

'I'm not sure I can disclose that. I'm a psychotherapist, Mr Jarrett. Just about the most confidential branch of medicine there is.'

'Why are you disclosing anything, then?'

'Because Eris Moberly is missing. Has been since early January.'

'You mean . . . since before I met her?'

'It seems so.'

'When you say "missing" . . .'

'I mean I can't find her. When she broke several appointments after Christmas I tried to contact her. She'd never given my secretary a telephone number, however, and her address . . . turns out not to exist. Louth Street, Mayfair. Sounds real enough, doesn't it? But a fiction nonetheless.'

'Are we sure we're talking about the same person? I've no reason to believe Marian deceived me about her identity.'

'Haven't you? What did she tell you about herself?'

'Not a great deal. We didn't have long enough to . . . become familiar with each other's pasts.'

'What did you have long enough for?'

'Look, we met in Vienna in January, by chance. There was . . . immediate attraction. We became . . . emotionally involved.'

'You became lovers?'

'If it's any of your business, yes.'

'I wish it weren't. Regrettably, I have to tell you that the woman you're "emotionally involved" with has a profound psychological problem. It wasn't a chance meeting. Let me ask you this. Did she know you were a photographer before introducing herself?'

'No. That is . . . Well, yes, in a sense. What of it?'

'It's why she chose you, Mr Jarrett. And why she used the name Marian Esguard.'

'What do you mean by that?'

'I'm not sure I'm at liberty to explain.'

'*Not at liberty?* I love this woman, Miss Sanger, and she loves me. We agreed to leave our spouses for each other when we came back from Vienna. And I went

79

through with it. I left my wife for her. Then . . . something went wrong.'

'She vanished?'

'Yes.'

'Leaving you with no clues to her whereabouts?'

'None. Except . . . her husband's name: Jos. And an
implication that they lived in some sort of ancestral
country residence.'

'Gaunt's Chase?'

'She never identified it. I was led to Tollard Rising by
a postcard of the church, sent to me anonymously. By
Marian, I think.'

'Do you have the envelope?'

'Yes.' I took it out of my pocket and showed it to her.

'I can't be sure. I've never seen her handwriting.'

'But I have.' Daphne Sanger nodded slowly in recognition. 'I'd say that was almost certainly written by Eris
Moberly.'

'You see. She wants me to find her, Miss Sanger. She
needs me to find her.'

'Possibly.' An afterthought seemed to occur to her.
'Jos is short for Joslyn, of course. Surely that satisfies you
Esguard is an assumed name.'

'I'm not sure it does.'

'Then let me tell you this. My enquiries haven't been
restricted to Tollard Rising. I've traced a marriage
certificate for Joslyn Esguard and a birth certificate for
his bride. Marian Juliana Freeman. She was born in
Chichester in 1787. She married Joslyn Esguard, a man
eleven years her senior, in 1809. The marriage seems to
have been childless, assuming they lived throughout it at
Tollard Rising; there's no record of a birth there. Nor is
there any record of the original Marian Esguard's death.
But I'm sure you can see what it all implies. Eris may

80

have sent you the postcard simply to show you where she obtained her alias. In other words, to put an end to your search.'

'Why such an elaborate charade?'

'Because elaboration upon reality is at the root of her psychological difficulties.'

'So you say. For reasons you're not free to share with me. Well, if you can't discuss your patient – sorry, client – with me, what about her husband?'

'I know nothing about him beyond his supposed name, Conrad Moberly, and Eris's description of him as wealthy and emotionally detached.'

'Could he be a descendant of Joslyn Esguard?'

'He could be. Theoretically. But if you're suggesting Eris is using the relationship between Marian and Joslyn, whatever kind of relationship it was, as some sort of convoluted code for her feelings about her husband . . .'

'What if I am?'

'Then I have to tell you you're wide of the mark.'

I took a deep breath, letting her see how frustrated I felt. 'Do you have any idea where Eris Moberly is now, Miss Sanger?'

'None.'

'Do you think she may be in danger?'

Daphne Sanger hesitated a long time before replying. 'It's possible. There are . . . worrying ramifications to her case.'

'I want to help her. Don't you?'

'Of course.'

'Then don't you think we should . . . pool our resources?'

She frowned. 'To do so would involve a gross breach of confidence on my part.'

I shrugged, trying to imply I might walk away from

the problem unless she gave me a good reason not to. 'Until you tell me more than you have so far, I don't see how we can make any progress. Do you?'

'No. I suppose not.'

'Then what do you suggest we do?'

She clunked the ice cubes round in her glass to make the tonic fizz, stared thoughtfully down into it for a moment, then looked up and said, 'I suggest we meet again in a day or two at my practice. I'll have made up my mind by then as to whether it would be appropriate, in all the circumstances, to explain to you what this is really all about.'

'And how will you make up your mind?'

'That's the bit you're not going to like, Mr Jarrett.' She shaped a cautious smile. 'I'm afraid you're going to have to win my trust. And I'm not a naturally trusting person.'

Daphne Sanger's method for assessing my trustworthiness was to call in a couple of references: a friend to verify my account of myself as far as he could, for which role Tim was tailor-made; and my wife to confirm I really had run out on her, which Faith naturally wasn't going to deny, especially when asked by a psychotherapist, the sort of person whose help she'd more or less told me I badly needed.

I warned Tim to expect a call from Miss Sanger and let him believe I was consulting her for the sake of my mental well-being. I left Faith to make what she liked of it, then sat back and waited for the results. My visit to Harley Street was fixed for Wednesday afternoon, which gave me two clear days to check Miss Sanger's credentials – they proved to be impeccable – and drive down to Tollard Rising again.

Nothing had changed at St Andrew's Church, or at the sloping swathe of farmland that had once been the deer park and landscaped vistas of Gaunt's Chase. For an idea of what the place had looked like I had to call at the local-studies library in Dorchester and leaf through various old county histories until I came across a reproduction of an oil painting by Canaletto, no less, of the house as it had appeared in 1753. A four-square, red-brick construction, faced in pale stone, with tall chimneys springing from a broad-hipped roof, it sat starkly in a strangely empty park, with only the rolling hills in the background to remind me that it was the same corner of Cranborne Chase where I'd seen nothing but fields and barns and fences. The county histories were principally interested in its architecture – 'restrained Dutch Palladian of the 1690s, possibly the work of William Talman' – and the circumstances surrounding Canaletto's commission to paint it – a flirtation with the role of patron of the arts by Nathaniel Esguard, grand-father of Joslyn. The Esguards' money was airily attributed to substantial holdings in the East India Company. Their eventual decline and fall – along with that of Gaunt's Chase – was undocumented, apart from the terse caption to Canaletto's depiction of the house. 'Destroyed by fire, 1838.' Canaletto's original was evidently in the hands of a private collector in Texas. Everything, it seemed, was either long ago or far away. And of no obvious concern to me. Except that Daphne Sanger's Eris Moberly and *my* Marian Esguard had decided that it should be.

'Take a seat, Mr Jarrett,' said Daphne Sanger as I entered her ground-floor consulting room in Harley Street. It was furnished and decorated in soothing shades of green, blending with the shadows of an over-cast late afternoon. 'It doesn't have to be the couch. I only have one because so many people expect me to.' Her self-assurance seemed magnified in this, her particular domain. It was warm and comfortable, yet oddly impersonal – odd because the lack of clutter, the lightness of her presence, somehow contrived to lower my defences. As no doubt it was meant to. 'May I call you Ian?'

'By all means.'

'And what will you call me?'

'What did Eris Moberly settle for?'

'Daphne.'

'Daphne it is, then. How did the positive vetting go?'

'Positively. Tim Sadler made all the right noises. And your wife . . . seemed pleased to hear you were coming to see me.'

'She thinks I'm mad. Or says she does.'

'From her point of view, your recent behaviour hardly looks . . . rational.'

'What about from *your* point of view, Daphne?'

'I have the advantage of knowing rather more of the background.'

'And am I to share that advantage?'

'Yes. I've decided to set my ethical reservations to one side.'

'I'm glad to hear it,' I said, exerting some effort not to look it. 'Where do we begin?'

'With any doubts you may have that Marian Esguard and Eris Moberly are in fact the same person. Listen to this.' She pressed the play button on a tape recorder stationed on the desk in front of her, and a voice that made me start with surprise floated into the room between us. '*My name is Eris Moberly.*' It could have been

84

Marian whispering to me in the darkness in Vienna. Daphne must have been able to read the startled recognition in my face even as she switched the machine off and looked across at me. 'Those doubts, if there were any, are now, I trust, dispelled?'

'Yes. It's Marian.'

'Or Eris. I suggest it will avoid confusion if we stick to the name she used here.'

'All right.'

'As to Marian Esguard, are you sure you've never heard of such a person in another connection – a historical connection, perhaps?'

'I never have.'

'Absolutely certain?'

'Completely.'

'Very well. As I told you, Eris Moberly became a client of mine last summer. She came to me because of my work as a hypnotherapist. She saw an obvious application of hypnotherapy to her singularly bewildering experiences, in particular the concept of regression to a previous incarnation.'

'You do that sort of thing, Daphne? Here in Harley Street? I thought reincarnation was the preserve of stage hypnotists.'

'I do *not* do that sort of thing. Eris consulted me specifically *because* of my scepticism about reincarnation.'

'I don't follow.'

'She wanted me to supply an alternative explanation for her symptoms.'

'And what were those symptoms exactly? Are you going to tell me she believed she was a reincarnation of the original Marian Esguard? You don't expect me to swallow that.'

'What I expect you to do is listen to this tape.' She ejected it from the machine and laid it on my side of the desk. 'I asked Eris to record an account of the events that had prompted her to consult me. This was the result. Go away and listen to it. Try to relate its contents to the state of mind of the woman you met in Vienna. Then come back here and tell me what you think we, as the only people party to her secret, ought to do about it.'

'Fair enough. I'll listen to it.' I stretched out my hand to pick up the tape, and held the pose, my fingers resting on it as I looked her in the eye. 'Are you sure you didn't regress her hypnotically? Are you sure this isn't some piece of parascientific dabbling that blew up in your face – and mine, too?'

'I never hypnotized her. Not even for the most conventional of purposes.'

'But she wanted you to?'

'Yes. As a kind of last resort.'

'So why didn't you?'

'Because it would have been too dangerous. Listen to the tape, Ian. Then you'll understand just *how* dangerous it would have been. And still might be.'

I listened to the tape lying on the narrow bed in my tawdry flat in Notting Hill Gate, wishing I could have had Marian lying beside me rather than Eris's voice rising and falling in my ear. I wanted her to come back to me. But it seemed she couldn't. Instead, I was condemned to follow, wherever her words took me. Into a life I hadn't known. Hers.

Chapter Four

My name is Eris Moberly. I'm thirty-two years old, married, with no children. That isn't a regret, by the way, either for me or my husband, as far as I know. I wouldn't describe our marriage as perfect. Conrad's too withdrawn for that. He isn't . . . emotionally demonstrative. On the other hand, he seems content with what we've got. So am I. What I'm saying is that this . . . problem . . . hasn't sprung from difficulties elsewhere in my life. I'm happy and healthy and, thanks to Conrad, wealthy. I've enjoyed the eight years we've been together. I don't want to say any more about it than that. It isn't relevant and Conrad wouldn't approve of me pouring out my secrets to a stranger anyway, so . . . let's keep him out of it.

The same goes for my family background. It's all standard, boring, upper-middle-class stuff. I wasn't abused as a child. I had a good education and a stable upbringing. My parents did their best for me. My father's a civil servant, retired now. My sisters are both married, with children. I suppose I don't see as much of any of them as I'd like. Conrad can be . . . difficult at times. Not that he'd stop me going on my own if I wanted to. Which I do. Just not as often as I should. You get . . . settled in routines, don't you? You think you'll do something some time soon, and then you find another year's flashed by and you still haven't done it.

What's happened to me recently has had that benefit, I suppose. Routine's a thing of the past. Ordinary life has changed. I'm not the person I used to be. I suppose I never will be again. I mean, even if you can make this stop, it won't go away completely, will it? She'll never leave me. I'm not sure I'd want her to. But even if I did . . .

You said you wanted . . . what did you call it? . . . A sequential account of how it started, so here goes. Conrad suggested we get out of London for Easter, which sounded great to me. We booked into a country house hotel near Bath for the long weekend and went down there on Thursday night. It all started as pleasantly and relaxingly as you could want. On Good Friday we visited Wells and Glastonbury. We spent Saturday in Bath. Then, on Easter Sunday afternoon, we drove out to Lacock. I'm sure you've heard of Lacock Abbey, where Fox Talbot invented photography. We toured the house and looked at the oriel window, the subject of his famous first photograph. Then we visited the photographic museum they've set up in the lodge at the entrance to the abbey. I suppose you could say that's where it began, except, of course, that it came into my mind as something I remembered very well, something I'd always known. It didn't seem weird or worrying. It was just . . . a piece of knowledge I'd carried about with me since . . . well, I couldn't have said when. A long time, for certain. It wouldn't have struck me as significant. It probably wouldn't have struck me at all, in fact, but for being at Lacock, where photography was invented. I'd never been there before, you see. I'd never consciously thought about it.

The museum has a section devoted to the history of photography. Not just Fox Talbot and the quaint old box cameras knocked up for him by the village carpenter, but displays and information about the other pioneer photographers and the inventors who paved the way for them. We were standing in front of an illustrated panel describing how close Thomas Wedgwood came to inventing photography about thirty years before Fox Talbot, when I turned to Conrad and said, without thinking there was anything the least remarkable in it, 'I wonder why they've overlooked Marian Esguard.'

'Who?' queried Conrad.

'Marian Esguard,' I repeated. 'It's only the lack of actual examples of her work that prevents her being acknowledged as Fox Talbot's forerunner.' Then I added, making a joke of it and feeling completely light-hearted, 'Male chauvinism in operation again, I suppose.'

Conrad was surprised as well as mystified. He'd never heard of Marian and, what's more, he'd never heard me say anything before that suggested I knew the first thing about photographic history. But, then, if you'd asked me, I'd have denied knowing anything about it myself. The name – and the remark – had come to me quite spontaneously.

It might have ended there, as a soon-to-be-forgotten throwaway remark. But Conrad never likes other people – especially me – knowing more than he does. He wouldn't let it drop, said I was making it up, though God knows why he thought I'd want to. In the end, we had some silly bet about it. I lost, and had to pay up. Conrad wouldn't let me off. I knew he wouldn't, of course, but I didn't expect to lose. I was utterly confident I knew what I was talking about. We went to the person serving at the counter and asked them. They knew nothing about it. We looked through a couple of reference books they had on display, which were comprehensive enough to include Marian. But they didn't mention her. Eventually Conrad insisted the curator be called. He tends to take things to extremes. And by then he sensed he was going to win, which he always enjoys. Anyway, the curator was away, not surprisingly on Easter Sunday, but somebody with a detailed knowledge of photographic history *was* unearthed. And he sided with Conrad. Nobody, apparently, had ever heard of Marian Esguard. He suggested I try the Royal Photographic Society's library in Bath, but he made it pretty clear he didn't think I'd find anything.

We had to go back to London on Monday and the library wouldn't be open till Tuesday, so I reckoned I'd have to drop the subject. It wasn't really very important, after all. Just a stupid misconception on my part. But it wouldn't go away. At first I thought it was pique at being proved wrong, but I knew it couldn't be. Conrad gave me too much practice at that. No, I was frustrated by the discrepancy between what I was sure I'd read or heard about Marian Esguard and the official record, from which she'd been mysteriously deleted. And I realized I wasn't going to be able to leave it there. I wanted to know why she'd been edited out of history.

The days are my own during the working week. Conrad's always very busy and I'm always very idle. He thinks I spend my time mooning around Bond Street and having lunch with friends. So I decided I could slip down to Bath for the day on the train without telling him, though I certainly meant to afterwards if I found any hard evidence of Marian's existence. I wasn't consciously being secretive.

The Royal Photographic Society has a museum, gallery and library all under one roof in the centre of Bath. The library's basically for members only, but I convinced them I was a serious researcher, so they let me in. I went through the index of every book they had on early photography looking for Marian's name. There wasn't a single mention of her. Thomas Wedgwood; Humphry Davy; Joseph Niépce; Louis Daguerre; John Herschel; William Fox Talbot: they were the names that kept cropping up, and I read enough to get a bluffer's grasp of how the invention came about and what they each contributed to it. There didn't seem to be room for Marian in any of the accounts. There weren't any obvious gaps she could fill or missing links she could explain. If I hadn't been so utterly certain of her existence, and her importance in photographic history, I'd have written her off there and then. In fact, I wouldn't have had much choice but to give up if the librarian hadn't asked me, as I was leaving, whether I'd found what I was looking for. I knew she wouldn't have heard of Marian, but I asked her anyway, just for the hell of it.

'I can't say I do,' she replied. 'But I do know a *man* called Esguard, strangely enough. It's an unusual name, so maybe he's a descendant of your Esguard. He's also interested in photography. In fact, he's a member of the society.'

You can imagine my reaction. I actually hugged the poor woman, I was so delighted. She said Milo Esguard was an elderly amateur photographer who'd been a regular user of the library until the last few years, when he'd got less and less mobile and had moved into a nursing home. A secretive and rather grumpy old chap, according to her, but with a charming side to him when he could be bothered to show it. She gave me the address of the nursing home: Saffron House in Bradford-on-Avon.

I wanted to go there straight away, but there wasn't enough time if I was to get back to London before Conrad came home, so I had to make another trip the next day. I took my car this time and got to the nursing home by late morning. It was a big old place up on a hill on the northern side of Bradford-on-Avon. The weather was exceptionally warm for April. Some of the residents were sitting out in the grounds having their elevenses, Milo Esguard among them. Except he wasn't actually *among* them. He'd rolled his wheelchair off to a distant corner of the lawn, where he was sitting reading the *Daily Telegraph* in a patch of sun, sheltered from the breeze by an overgrown rhododendron. The nurse positively encouraged me to go and speak to him. 'If you can cheer him up,' she said, 'we'll all be grateful.'

He was a big, heavy, white-bearded old fellow, done up in several woollies, mittens and a hat that looked as if it had been chewed by a dog. He was gruff and not at all welcoming. 'What do you want?' was his idea of a courteous introduction. He seemed to think I was some kind of social worker and took a lot of talking out of the idea, which was made more difficult by his come-and-go deafness. But his hearing and his temper both improved dramatically when I mentioned Marian. Then he became a different man, inviting me to pull up a chair and offering to arrange a cup of coffee. He had bright blue eyes and a twinkling grin, but whether the old sweetie or the old curmudgeon was the real him I couldn't tell.

He was amazed I'd heard of Marian and wanted to know how. My explanation didn't satisfy him at first. I think he may have suspected I was holding something back, which was understandable, because my story didn't make a lot of sense. But eventually he seemed to come round. That's when he began to open up. Still, he wasn't sure about me. That was clear. He didn't trust me and he didn't *dis*trust me. He was trying to make up his mind. I think what helped was how relieved, how overjoyed I was when he confirmed that, yes, Marian had really existed and, yes, she'd been a pioneer photographer. Or might have been. He implied her photographic achievements were basically just a family legend. His own researches had turned up nothing to verify them. What baffled and excited him all at the same time was that I knew about Marian quite independently. But his suspicious nature got in the way. I had to go back there twice the following week to win his confidence sufficiently for him to tell me as much as he ever did.

This is what it amounted to. Milo was a bachelor in his early eighties. Until recently, he'd lived in the same house in Bath as four previous generations of Esguards. His nephew Niall was now in occupation. He'd converted the place into flats after inheriting a half-share from his mother, buying out Milo and packing the old fellow off to the nursing home. A lot of Milo's conversation was devoted to character assassination of Niall. Anyway, the first Esguard to own the house was Milo's great-great-grandfather, Barrington Esguard, younger brother of Joslyn, who'd lived in some splendour at a country mansion in Dorset called Gaunt's Chase with his wife . . . Marian.

Gaunt's Chase dated from the family's golden era as bankers, speculators and East India Company men back in the seventeenth and eighteenth centuries. By Joslyn's time their fortunes were in decline. He was the last Esguard to live there. The house burned down in 1838. Joslyn died in the fire. As for Marian . . . nobody knew for sure. It was believed she'd deserted her husband by then. Why, and where she'd gone, was a mystery. But what about her photographic activities? Was the fire the reason no trace of them remained? Milo's answers to those questions were bound up with what he described, rather melodramatically I thought, as 'the tangled enigma' of his family's past. In truth, I realized later, that's exactly what it was.

The source of most of Milo's information was his grandfather, Hilton Esguard, who'd lived into his nineties. Hilton's source was his own grandfather, Barrington, who'd died when Hilton was in his teens, back in the 1860s. Barrington had actually known Marian, of course. He was a direct witness to events. According to him, Joslyn had frittered away the family fortune through gambling and unwise investments. He'd made the further mistake of marrying not for money but for love, or at any rate lust. He'd met Marian Freeman while visiting friends in Sussex, been instantly captivated by her, and had manoeuvred her into a marriage both of them came to regret. There were no children, something Joslyn regarded as virtual treachery on Marian's part. But childlessness at least left Marian ample time to pursue her scientific interests, themselves an affront to Joslyn's ideas of how a wife should behave.

This, then, was one strand of the legend. Marian

Esguard, amateur chemist and original thinker, hit on a method of preserving camera obscura images, a process she called heliogenesis, but which we would call . . . photography. And she did it some fifteen to twenty years earlier than Fox Talbot, working in secret at Gaunt's Chase. Secrecy was necessary because Joslyn was unlikely to approve of such unfeminine activities. Fortunately he was away more often than not, leading a rake's life in London. At some point, however, he found out and put a stop to it. Marian was forbidden to continue. Her response was to leave, though how she accomplished that against Joslyn's wishes wasn't clear. An additional complication, and a possible explanation, was that she had a secret admirer who'd begun to help her in her work and who aided her escape. Certainly it was an effective escape. Marian vanished and was never heard of again. This would have been around 1820, when she was in her early thirties.

Another strand of the legend concerned the fire at Gaunt's Chase. According to Barrington, Joslyn's hopes of recouping his financial losses suddenly soared when Queen Victoria came to the throne in 1837. Why wasn't specified, but Barrington alleged that the fire was no accident and that his brother was in fact murdered. The timing of the event – five days before Victoria's coronation in June 1838 – was supposed to be significant. A vague and hoary old conspiracy theory didn't interest me, of course. But the fire must have destroyed any physical evidence of her work Marian had left there. That was the real tragedy of it. It was a dead end in more ways than one. Barrington hadn't realized the importance of what his sister-in-law had been doing until Fox Talbot published his technique for photogenic drawing in 1839, by which time it was too late to scour Gaunt's

Chase for evidence that Marian had got there first.

Besides, Barrington Esguard was a frightened man, even in old age. That was the verdict of Milo's grandfather. Barrington was sure Joslyn had been murdered. He didn't want to share his brother's fate and, consequently, he didn't want to do anything to attract attention to the family. Marian's achievements, whatever they amounted to, were best forgotten.

But she could have publicized them herself, couldn't she? The question of where she'd gone when she left Gaunt's Chase, and what she'd done in the years that followed, was the most baffling mystery of all. Why did she abandon her work on heliogenesis? What could have stopped her? Milo didn't know. I was sure of it. He wasn't holding out on me about that.

I had the distinct impression he was holding out on me about something, though. I knew I wouldn't get anywhere by badgering him. He'd got to like me, and I'd grown quite fond of him myself. But he was still wary, still faintly suspicious. I couldn't work out why. What did it matter, after all, if I knew as much as he did? Where was the harm in it? Why wouldn't he tell me his old address in Bath, come to that? Was he afraid I might go round there and antagonize his nephew?

A week passed after my third visit, then he phoned me one day at home. I found his creaky old voice waiting for me on the answering machine when I got back from . . . wherever I'd been. '*There's something I can do for you, my dear, and something you can do for me,*' he said. '*About Marian. I've been thinking it over, and I reckon it's time, high time. Come soon, won't you? There's a lot to do and I need your help to do it.*'

I drove down to Bradford-on-Avon next morning. I could see at once there was a change in him. The decision he'd taken, whatever it was, had freed something in him. He talked faster and moved himself around in his wheelchair with greater energy than I'd seen him display before. He insisted we go out into the grounds to talk, though it was hardly the weather for it. His cloak-and-dagger streak was showing again. Once out of earshot of his fellow residents, though, I soon found out why.

'I've been trying to see my way round a problem that's been itching at me ever since I came here from Bentinck Place,' Milo announced, so revealing at last where in Bath the family had lived. 'Now I've realized *you're* the solution, my dear. I want you to retrieve something I left at the house when I moved out. I wasn't too well at the time and I couldn't risk Niall finding it, so I decided to leave it where it lay until I could go back later. But I'm not sure *later* is ever going to come. I need somebody fitter than me, somebody I can trust, to fetch it. Niall mustn't know, but that's not a problem because I still have a key to the front door and a pretty good idea of his comings and goings.'

It was then that I realized fetching whatever it was meant fetching it clandestinely, which Niall Esguard could well regard as burglary if he caught me in the act. Milo must have noticed the worried look on my face.

'Don't worry,' he said. 'The item belongs to me. I have every right to remove it. You'd simply be acting as my agent.'

'Why the subterfuge, then?'

'Because Niall has no proper regard for Marian's reputation.'

'So this . . . article . . . concerns Marian, does it?'

'Of course. I wouldn't ask you to take such . . .' He

97

smiled mischievously. 'I wouldn't put you to the bother otherwise.'

Then I asked the only question that really mattered: 'What is it, Milo?'

'It's what you're looking for, my dear. Evidence – if not proof itself – of Marian Esguard's genius.'

The old devil knew he had me hooked then. I didn't even care if he was exaggerating, which I reckoned he probably was. I had to see this . . . evidence . . . for myself. To do that I had to stake out the house in Bentinck Place, make sure Niall Esguard was off the premises, then let myself in with Milo's key and go straight to the cupboard tucked under the stairs leading to the first floor. At the end of the cupboard, I'd find that the space beneath the lowest three stairs had been panelled in. This was what Milo had found five years previously while clearing out some junk dating from his mother's days. The discovery had revived his suspicion that Barrington Esguard, if he *had* possessed evidence of Marian's work, would have been sufficiently worried in the wake of his brother's death either to destroy it . . . or to hide it. Behind the panel, where he'd subsequently replaced it, Milo had found a small wooden box with a sliding lid, the sort of thing that might have been designed to hold chess pieces or draughtsmen. But it had been used to store something else altogether.

'What was in the box, Milo?' I pleaded.

'See for yourself,' he replied. 'Then bring it back safely to me. It's time it saw the light of day.'

We agreed I'd make the attempt the following afternoon. Neither of us wanted to delay, and with Conrad in Tokyo, cutting one of his sharper deals, I could come and go as I pleased. Aside from fancying himself as a *rentier*, Niall Esguard was a semi-professional gambler;

it'd be a rare afternoon that didn't find him at one racecourse or another. He lived alone, and the tenants of the first-, second- and third-floor flats would probably be at work. Milo had thought it all out, you see. A clear run was what he predicted. I'm not sure I cared how difficult it was likely to be. My reluctance was mostly show. The temptation was simply too great to resist.

'I had to be sure I could trust you with this,' he said when he saw me off. 'And now I know I can. Godspeed, my dear.'

Bentinck Place is one of Bath's more dilapidated Georgian terraces, though its location – halfway up Sion Hill, with most of the city spread out below it – probably made it an exclusive development back in 1807, when Barrington Esguard bought number six as his seasonal residence. I couldn't stop myself imagining Bath as it must have been then: calm, refined, car-free and classically elegant. In fact, keeping watch on the Esguard house for an hour or so to make sure the absence of Niall's Porsche meant what I hoped, there were several stretches of time, probably no more than minutes in reality, when I felt I was almost back in 1807. If I screwed my eyes nearly shut, I could believe Barrington and his brother, maybe his sister-in-law, too, were about to step out, dressed in the fashions of the day, to savour the clear spring sunshine.

But nobody stepped out, real or imaginary. Eventually I realized I'd waited quite long enough. So, trying to look bold and casual all at once, I got out of my car, walked along to number six, opened the door with Milo's key and went inside.

It happened as I closed the door gently behind me, shutting out the noise of the world, and looked along the hall towards the entrance to Niall's flat and the stairs leading up to the other floors. The place was dowdily decorated, with chips out of the paintwork and stains on the wallpaper. The carpet showed a grubby track of footprints to and from the stairs. There was no furniture at all. It was a predictably featureless no man's land, shared between Niall and his tenants. But, as I glanced round, a sudden visual sensation hit me of the same hallway, with cream walls, polished floorboards, a blue and gold runner to the foot of the stairs, a console table, a mirror, a chandelier, a grandfather clock, an umbrella stand holding several walking sticks and parasols, numerous gilt-framed oil paintings and a shadow thrown across the ceiling by the fanlight behind me of a bonneted figure standing outside and raising a hand as if to knock—

It came and went in a flash. I don't know what you'd call it. A hallucination, maybe. It shook me, anyway. I had to lean against the door for a minute or so to let my heart stop thumping and my hands stop shaking before I could carry on. Then I tried to put it out of my mind and concentrate on what I was there to do. I hurried along the hall to the door of the cupboard under the stairs, pulled it open, switched on the light and looked in.

The cupboard was full of the usual sort of stuff: old coats, pots of paint, brooms, brushes, buckets and bundles of yellowing newspapers, plus, of all things, a surfboard. I cleared a path through to the back as best I could and soon found the panel blocking off the space beneath the lowest few stairs. It was cobwebbed at the corners, which was a relief, because it suggested nobody had examined it since Milo's departure. Milo hadn't said so specifically, but I had the feeling Niall wanted what was hidden there. If so, he presumably had a pretty good idea what it was. How hard he'd tried to wheedle the secret out of his uncle I couldn't tell, but he certainly wasn't likely to relish the thought of a total stranger taking it from under his nose. Except that I no longer felt like a stranger. Something close to *déjà vu* was clinging to me in that house. I'd never been there before, but everything about it seemed familiar yet different. It was as if I'd gone home to find somebody else living there. It touched a part of my memory that had been dormant so long I hadn't even known it existed, like having a dim childhood recollection stirred years later by a coincidental experience. And it was getting stronger – more intoxicating yet also more stifling – all the time.

I prised out the retaining nails with the pliers Milo had warned me to take along, pulled the panel aside and saw at once the small wooden box he'd described. I lifted it out with a sort of reverential slowness and slid the lid open just far enough to be sure there was something inside. It looked like nothing more than paper in the forty-watt half-light. I put the box down by the door and started the trickiest part of my task: replacing everything so that it looked undisturbed. I wanted to grab the box and run, but I knew I had to do a thorough job if Niall's suspicions weren't to be aroused.

As soon as I'd finished, I switched the light off, picked up the box, closed the door and started back down the hall. Then it happened again, only more intensely, more immediately. What I'd seen before was there again, in front of me, in colour and detail. And now in sound as well. The clock ticked. A floorboard creaked. A horse clip-clopped past outside. The shadow moved again. The person standing on the other side of the front door raised their hand to the knocker. I heard the creak of the knocker being pulled up. I closed my eyes and stretched

101

every fibre of my imagination to resist the sound I knew was about to follow.

And it didn't. There was a brief silence. Then I opened my eyes and everything was normal. But I didn't feel normal. I'd never felt *less* normal. I ran to the door, pulled it open and rushed outside. It was OK there. I was back in the real world. I slammed the door behind me and made for my car, trembling now from the sheer frightening novelty of the experience. I drove round the corner, then stopped to try to calm my nerves, which were pretty much shot. What *had* it been? Some sort of delusion? It was crazy. If you'd asked me to say what it had seemed like, I'd have said . . . like it had once been. Bentinck Place in the past. Yesterday rather than today. Or a lot of days before yesterday. And so *real*. So abundantly and authentically actual. As if, for those two split seconds, I'd truly been there. As if, but for my own fear wrenching me back, I could have heard the knocker fall and seen some capped and aproned maid approach the door and open it to the visitor whose shadow I'd glimpsed.

I could have examined the contents of the box there and then, of course. But I was reluctant even to touch it. I was frightened by what had happened, frightened by its power, its weird sucking falling pull at every part of me. I started driving again, heading for Bradford-on-Avon and any kind of explanation Milo could offer.

But he was past explaining anything. I think I sensed that as soon as I saw the ambulance turning out of the entrance to Saffron House, lights flashing and siren blaring. It could have been any one of the elderly and infirm residents, but somehow I knew it wasn't. I drove up to the house and got instant confirmation from the receptionist.

102

'Poor old Mr Esguard's had another heart attack,' she said, the 'another' deepening my dread. 'I told him only yesterday he was overdoing it.'

They took him to a hospital in Bath, where I spent the rest of that afternoon and most of the evening waiting for news, pacing up and down and drinking coffee, and wondering if it was my fault that he'd been 'overdoing it'. He'd been so animated the day before, perhaps *too* animated. Nobody had told me he had a weak heart, but even so I should have taken things more slowly. What did my fancies and fantasies matter compared with his life?

They wouldn't let me see him. He wasn't conscious anyway, and as a non-relative I didn't have many rights. A nurse asked me if I knew his next of kin. I said I didn't, but I should have realized the nursing home would be trying to contact Niall while I was sitting there, waiting and hoping. As it was, it never occurred to me that I was taking any sort of risk by staying put. Actually, it did occur to me, but only when a tall, thin, lank-haired man, who looked to be in his late thirties, sat down next to me in the waiting area and said, 'Mrs Moberly? I'm Niall Esguard.'

He must have been able to see the shock on my face. I'm always too transparent for my own good. Looking at him with his faintly pitted skin and his piercing eyes and his moist lips and his crooked nose, I felt that he could see not just straight through me but straight *into* me, where there was a secret he craved, cowering and pleading for protection.

'Sorry if I surprised you,' he went on in a husky whisky-and-cigarettes voice. 'They gave me your name at Saffron House. You've been seeing a lot of my uncle lately, apparently. Why's that, then?'

It was as much as I could do to speak, but I forced out something non-committal and got a ghastly little half-smile as my reward.

'Not been running any errands for him, have you?' Niall asked. 'Only he can be a devious old bugger. I wouldn't put it past him to talk a considerate lady like you into . . . a lot of trouble.'

'I can't imagine what you mean,' I managed to say.

'Just like I can't imagine what the two of you have in common. Unless it's something the *three of us* have in common.'

'What could that be?'

'Don't you know, Mrs Moberly?'

'No.'

'Sure of that?'

'Absolutely.'

'Well, perhaps I should . . . put you in the picture, then.'

'Picture?'

'Yes. Picture. As in photograph. Uncle Milo's quite an expert on photography. Its history. How it began. *Who* it began with. Some old squire out at Lacock in the eighteen thirties, so they say.'

'Do they?'

'Yes. But Uncle Milo's never been convinced of that. He's always . . . had an alternative theory.'

'Really? We've never talked about it.'

'Come off it. I bet you've never talked about anything else. According to—'

'Excuse me,' interrupted a nurse. 'Mr Esguard?'

'Yes,' Niall said to her, though he was still staring straight at me.

'The doctor would like a word with you, Mr Esguard. About your uncle.'

'Oh, right.' Niall hadn't much choice but to get up and put on a show of nephew-like concern. 'How is he?'

'Very poorly, I'm afraid. Would you come this way?'

The nurse set off. As he followed her, Niall turned his head to look at me and said, 'Don't run away, Mrs Moberly.'

But that's exactly what I did. As soon as he was out of sight, I rushed out of the hospital to my car and drove away. Niall Esguard had frightened me even more than Milo's heart attack. My life was beginning to be taken over by people and events, some here and now, some long ago, and I wanted it to stop. I wanted safe humdrum normality back again.

I didn't stop until I was back in London. I went straight home, thankful that Conrad wouldn't be there to demand explanations, and tried to think matters through. Niall knew my name, but nothing else about me. I'd given Milo my telephone number, but he'd made a point of memorizing it rather than writing it down. God, I was grateful for his sense of melodrama now. The last thing I needed was a creep like Niall on my trail. A conversation of just a few minutes had convinced me he had a vicious streak. He seemed to know Milo had been hiding something from him. And he seemed certain I was helping the old fellow.

He was right, of course. I had the box and whatever secret it contained. I'd intended to take it to Milo, confident he'd tell me the truth at last. But Milo was in no condition to tell me anything. I phoned the hospital and asked how he was. The answer was just what I'd dreaded. 'I'm afraid Mr Esguard died an hour ago without regaining consciousness.'

So that was it. Milo was dead. I sat staring into space, numb with the shock of it. Poor old Milo. I'd known him such a short time. Yet in some strange way I felt as if I'd known him all my life. I also felt responsible for his death, ludicrous though that may seem in any logical sense. If he'd been under more strain lately, it was because he'd wanted to be. He'd gone into this with his eyes open. Nevertheless, I couldn't help feeling I owed him something.

Facing up to whatever the box contained was just about the least. I knew it had to be done. Part of me was consumingly curious, in fact, though another part remained reluctant. But curiosity always wins over reluctance in the end. For reasons I couldn't properly have explained, I put the security chain on the door and unplugged the telephone before lifting the lid.

Sheets of paper. That's all there was in it. But not just any sheets. They were photographic negatives, measuring about six inches by four, developed on flimsy and obviously very old paper, variously creased, stained and torn. The dark areas appeared a muddy grey-brown, the light areas a pale, dirty yellow. There were seven in all: four outdoor shots of the same building from different angles – it looked like a substantial country house; two of the interior of a library, one focusing on a bookcase, the other on a handsomely mounted globe; and one of a man and a woman standing at the bottom of a broad flight of stone steps, the same flight that was visible at a greater distance in one of the house studies. There was one additional sheet, a positive print of the couple, with a tiny hand-pencilled caption added at the base. The print had a reddy-brown hue, but was strikingly sharp.

I can't remember in what order the realization hit me. I think the way the couple were dressed struck me first. The man wore riding boots over pale trousers, a high-buttoned double-breasted jacket beneath a long, loose duster coat, some sort of ruffled white shirt and stock, gloves and a narrow-brimmed top hat. He was holding a riding crop in one hand, slightly blurred, and leaning casually against an orb-topped pillar, his other hand clasping the lapel of his coat. He was clean-shaven, with a fleshy, faintly vapid face. I'd have put him in early middle age. The woman was somewhat younger, or at any rate looked it. She was standing stiffly upright, peering at the camera with a slight frown. She wore a pale, high-waisted, ankle-length dress and a short, darker-coloured jacket that reached no lower than her bosom. Ringletted hair could be seen beneath her frilled bonnet, held in place with a ribbon, one end of which was just a smudge, as if it had been disturbed by the wind during exposure. I didn't need a degree in costume design to identify her outfit as classic Empire line, which meant 1830 at the latest. The caption specified the date, anyway, along with the subjects, and location. 'Barrington and Susannah Esguard, Gaunt's Chase, 13 July 1817.' According to Milo, Barrington Esguard had been over eighty when he died, some time in the 1860s. That put his birth at around 1780 and his age in 1817 mid to late thirties, which wasn't far off what the man in the photograph looked.

The house was Gaunt's Chase, burned down in 1838. The couple were Milo Esguard's great-great-grand-parents. The photographer was Marian Esguard. And the date was more than twenty years earlier than it had any right to be. I was holding in my hand the proof, as Milo had promised, of Marian's genius.

And then, as I stared at the photograph, it happened again. Suddenly I was there, in the warm summer sunshine. At Gaunt's Chase in July 1817. I could see the shadow-etched pattern of the brickwork of the house, and the mellow cream glow of the stone facings. I could see Barrington and Susannah relaxing their poses and beginning to move. Barrington's coat was grey, his trousers fawn, his jacket green, his top hat a gleaming black. Susannah's dress was white, with a delicate floral pattern that had eluded the camera, her jacket turquoise, her bonnet grey. They smiled and moved away from the steps towards me. I could hear a dog barking somewhere and wood being chopped in the distance.

'What am I to believe we have just accomplished, Marian?' Barrington enquired in a sceptical tone. 'Beyond a certain stiffness of limb as a result of lengthy immobility.' He was talking to me, I realized, talking and looking and approaching.

'I wonder that Jos encourages you in this, my dear,' added Susannah. 'It is scarcely what I would have expected him to approve of as recreation for his wife.'

I could see and hear, and now I knew as well. I knew Barrington for the affable, pliable, empty-headed fool that he was and Susannah for everything such a man deserved in a wife. I knew them from long acquaintance. I was married to Barrington's brother, the altogether more intelligent, but vastly less genial, Joslyn Esguard. I'd been so for eight years, since he'd lured me away from the contentments of my agreeable existence in Chichester and condemned me to act out the part of his devoted wife at this wind-lashed home of his dubious ancestors on the Dorset uplands. My mind and my memory were aflood with all the jumbled events and circumstances of my life. They came to me as something quite natural and inescapable, as the sum of what constituted my past and present.

'I have not sought Jos's sanction, Susannah,' I heard

myself say. 'Nor do I intend to. My innocent little scientific explorations need not concern him.'

'Those stains on your hands must concern him, surely,' said Barrington as he drew closer. 'What did you say had caused them?'

'The substances I make use of to achieve the desired result.'

'I confess I am still somewhat uncertain what that result is. If this . . . contrivance . . . is, in essence, our dear old friend the camera obscura, what is to be gained by your squinting into it for minutes at a stretch whilst we impersonate statues?'

'It was a matter of seconds, Barrington, as you full well know. And what is to be gained is a more accurate picture of you and Susannah than the finest artist could achieve with oils and a brush.'

'So you say. But where is the picture?'

'Inside the camera.' I turned towards what Barrington had called my contrivance, a rectangular wooden box two feet wide by two feet high by eighteen inches deep, with a hinged top and a lens, now capped, fitted in the centre of the side he and Susannah had been facing. It was mounted on a modified artist's easel, having been constructed to my specifications by the estate carpenter, the excellent Mr Eames. 'But not yet visible.'

'When will it be visible?'

'Tomorrow. Susannah, you really must explain to your husband the great virtue of—'

It was gone. As suddenly and completely as I'd been there with them, I was back in the present, alone in the Mayfair apartment, cold electric light falling on the fragment of the past I held in my hand, traffic noise seeping through the half-open window to wash away the sights and sounds of another place and another life. I dropped the pictures back into the box and closed it, then slid it away from me across the table. What I'd seen and heard at Bentinck Place could just about be dismissed as tricks that my mind had played on me. But the force of what I'd just experienced was too great to resist. It was true. It was real, God help me, every bit as real as the empty room I sat in, or the bustling city beyond the window, or the table I was leaning on. For a few precious moments, I'd shared a life with Marian Esguard. Some part of me must always have done. That's how I knew what she'd achieved in the distant yet strangely close at hand pre-history of photography. And that part was growing stronger all the time. Nothing could stop it, even if I wanted it to. I'd been her. And she was becoming me.

I took a sleeping pill and went to bed. When I woke next day, it was nearly noon. To my surprise, I felt completely rested and refreshed. In daylight, it seemed possible to believe I'd somehow imagined what had happened, or at least that I could prevent it happening again. The person I'd been reasserted her right to an untroubled existence. I wasn't prepared to share it with a woman who'd died more than a hundred years ago. I wasn't going to let her take me over.

I showered and dressed, then put the box into a briefcase, walked down to our bank in Piccadilly and requested access to our safe deposit. With the box locked away securely, I treated myself to an expensive and solitary lunch. It had to stop, I told myself. It had already stopped, I willed myself to believe. I was going to forget Marian and revert to the frivolous life of Eris Moberly.

For a while it worked. I stayed in London, saw more of my friends and arranged a succession of dinner parties and evenings at the theatre. I made sure I was seldom alone and never at a loose end. Conrad jokingly complained that he couldn't take the pace I was setting. But I was running to stand still, drinking too much and eating too little. As spring moved towards summer, I felt more and more like a mouse on a treadmill in a cage with an open door. I could give up if I wanted to and step through the door into clear, cooling air. There was nothing to be frightened of. I was free of whatever spell Marian had cast over me. I was cured.

One day, as if to prove the point, I drove out of London down the A3, heading for a Persian rug shop in Guildford I particularly wanted to see. But I didn't stop at Guildford. I carried on south towards Chichester and, as soon as I saw its cathedral spire ahead of me across the plain, I felt hugely and bizarrely happy, as if I was returning home after many years' exile. I parked at the theatre on the northern edge of the city and walked down into the centre. Everything seemed only superficially ordinary. I looked at the modern shopfronts and the bland faces of the passers-by and sensed a reality beyond them. It wasn't at all threatening. I wasn't frightened of anything any more. I was completely at my ease.

I reached Market Cross and stood in its familiar shade for some time, gazing up at the cathedral. Then I walked down South Street, more slowly now, and turned into West Pallant, comforted by my recognition of the elegant Georgian house fronts lining the narrow street. There was Dodo House ahead of me, as I knew Pallant House had always been called by the locals on account of the poorly sculpted ostriches crowning its gateposts. No longer capable of noticing anything odd in such knowledge, I pressed on along East Pallant, passing the houses on its gently curving southern side, noting and remembering the double-pillared doorway of one and the gleaming area railings of another. Then, instinctively, I stopped, and turned and retraced my steps as far as number eight.

It was architecturally more modest than some of its neighbours, but otherwise a classical eighteenth-century red-brick townhouse. A brass plaque advertised it as the premises of a legal practice. The front door was hooked open to reveal a glass inner door, through which I could see the hall and stairwell. As I looked, something changed in my perception, like a filter being lowered across my sight and understanding. I climbed the steps and entered.

The hall was silent and empty, yet it teemed with memories. They came spilling out of the rooms around me and down the stairs to greet me, memories of a childhood and adolescence spent in this house with my brothers and sisters and our indulgent parents. Every detail was fresh and yet familiar, every facet of this small world within a world instantly recognizable.

I moved to the door of my father's study, knocked and entered. And there he was, turning slowly in his chair and laying down his spectacles and the medical journal he'd been reading on the escritoire beside him. Dear Papa, tubbier and older and balder than he'd once been, but still with that benign and crumpled grin that had delighted me as a small girl, and which continued to charm even his more ill-tempered patients. Dr Thomas Freeman, physician of Chichester and founder of the local dispensary for the indigent sick, looked at me fondly across his book-lined refuge from domestic disorder and laid his open hand characteristically across his chest.

'Marian,' he said. 'I had supposed you to be keeping your mother company at the milliner's.'

'She does not require my assistance to choose another few yards of ribbon, Papa,' I replied, with exactly the correct level of respectful sarcasm.

'No. Nor my sanction to commit me to the cost of it.' He chuckled. 'It is as well Annie has waited this long to marry. I have needed the years since you left us to put aside sufficient capital to fund the venture.'

'I believe Mr Drew is a good man,' I said, aware of the hint of contrast with my own choice of husband. 'You will not regret the expenditure, Papa.'

'Let us sincerely hope not. At least it has had the happy consequence of luring you from your seclusion in Dorset.'

'I required no luring,' I objected with a smile.

'And yet it *is* a rarity, is it not?' He rose, ambled across to me and softly pinched my cheek. 'Why do we see so little of you?'

'The journey is a troublesome one. And Jos can seldom spare the carriage. So, since he will not hear of me travelling by public coach—'

'He could bring you himself, my dear.' Father's grin faded. 'He *was* invited.'

'Alas, business required him to be in London.'

'Business? Does it really need to be so very brisk for a man of his means?'

'So he tells me, Papa.'

'And you remain a loyal wife. Yes, Yes.' He nodded solemnly and took a half turn towards the window. 'It does you credit, of course.'

'There is nothing for you to be concerned about.'

'I wish I could believe that. When I think of you, as I do more often than you can know, immured at Gaunt's Chase at the whim and mercy of a man who, from all I hear—' He broke off and sighed. 'You have always been the strongest of my children, Marian. I cannot but reproach myself with the thought that you have needed to be.'

'You need not reproach yourself, Papa. I thrive, as you see. My diet comprises something more than adversity. Of that you may be sure.' As I spoke the words, guilt stabbed at me, keenly and confoundingly. I was sparing Papa. But it seemed I was also sparing myself. 'There is, of course, a matter about which I would value your opinion. And I do not refer to my husband's character.'

'Perhaps that is as well.' Papa moved back to the escritoire, slid open a drawer and pulled out a dog-eared journal I recognized as a recent issue of *Ackermann's Repository of Arts*. 'I observe that Mr Ackermann supplies his readers with rather more than the latest fashion in bonnet trimmings these days.'

'He always has, Papa.'

'Well, well. Maybe so. At all events, I read the article you drew to my attention.' He opened the journal at a marked page. ' "A Singular Method of Copying Pictures and Other Objects, by the Chemical Action of Light." Most diverting.'

'And illuminating?'

He laughed. 'That, too. It certainly appears that the late Mr Wedgwood was a chemist of some originality. It is sad he did not live longer. Then we might have something more than Mr Ackermann's parlour games by which to remember him.'

'Parlour games? Can it be, Papa, that the true potential of Mr Wedgwood's discovery has escaped you?'

'I hope not. A pretty shadow-picture of a leaf or an insect's wing can be created by the action of light on a surface wetted with nitrate of silver, only to be erased by the further action of light, thus aptly reflecting the transience of every scene that passes before our gaze. What potential do you detect in this, Marian, that has eluded a scientist as eminent as Sir Humphry Davy for the better part of twenty years?'

'The camera obscura, Papa. That casts a picture, does it not, a picture that is something more than a shadow? Could not the image of that picture be preserved on a sheet of paper by the application of Mr Wedgwood's method?'

'I presume it might be possible to create such an image.' He frowned. 'But to speak of preservation is fallacious, my dear. See, we have Sir Humphry's word for it that all his late friend's ingenuity could not arrest the steady erasure of the image upon—'

'Hyposulphite of ammonia.'

He looked round at me intently. 'I beg your pardon?'

'Hyposulphites hold the key,' I continued excitedly. 'Their differential action on pure silver and silver salts should render the image permanent by washing away the remaining muriate of silver without affecting the metallic deposit. My experiments point unmistakably to that conclusion. And what holds true for Mr Wedgwood's shadow-pictures—'

'Could equally well be applied within a camera obscura.' Papa fairly gaped at me. 'Experiments, child? What *have* you been engaged upon?'

I felt myself blush slightly. 'Scientific research, Papa. The purest intellectual endeavour of mankind, as I recall you described it. Solitude and serenity of mind, taken together with an opportunity to convert an unwanted storeroom at Gaunt's Chase into a form of laboratory, have led me by trial and error to the conviction that I may stand close to a discovery of inestimable significance.'

'Hence the stains upon your hands about which your mother has complained.'

I shrugged. 'I have paid them no heed.'

'Has your husband?'

'He has seldom been in a position or condition to notice such trifles of late,' I replied with a straight face. 'Yet I must own he is bound to become aware of my researches eventually. I doubt he will think them fitting activities for a gentleman's wife.'

'I doubt that, too, Marian.'

'So I must make as much progress as I can before his objections intrude upon my work. Will you assist me, Papa?'

'How *can* I assist you when you are so far away?'

'By ordering these items for your pharmacopoeia.' I took a slip of paper from within the sleeve of my dress and handed it to him. 'And securing their delivery in time for me to take them back with me to Gaunt's Chase.'

Father put on his spectacles and perused the list. 'I thought your interest in chemistry ended when you entered upon womanhood, Marian.'

'It merely slept awhile.'

'And has clearly woken, refreshed and redoubled.'

'I must become proficient at handling the materials as well as the apparatus before the spring. Only then, when the supply of sunlight becomes abundant, can I hope to achieve any practical results. I have set Eames, our carpenter, to work on constructing a portable camera obscura suited to my purpose. He is a reticent and reliable man. I have also reserved a ream of the stationer's smoothest writing paper for my use. Thus I only now require—'

'A tame physician to help you smuggle this' – he flapped the list at me – 'this . . . alchemist's hoard . . . into your husband's house.'

'I am no alchemist, Papa.'

'No. But only because silver is not a base metal. What you propose to turn it into may prove more precious than gold.'

'And more elusive. I may not succeed.'

'I console myself with that thought, Marian. Your husband would not thank me for encouraging you in such an enterprise. In that sense, it would be best if it came to nothing. Perhaps, indeed, I should do what I can to ensure that it goes no further than it already has. On the other hand . . .' He tucked the list into his waistcoat pocket and smiled at me. 'Who am I to obstruct the purest intellectual endeavour of mankind? Or even womankind?'

'Dear Papa. I knew I could—'

'Can I help you?' A voice, sharp and insistent, sounded in my ear. And at its sound the study shuddered around me, vibrating and distorting in my sight and in my mind. My father was no longer there. *I* was no longer there. In its place, a brighter, emptier, starker room enveloped me. And the voice repeated, 'Can I help you?'

I turned and looked at a middle-aged woman in an office suit. She was standing close to me, peering into my face with a mixture of anxiety and irritation. I tried to speak, but couldn't find the words.

'Do you have an appointment with Mr Palmer?'

'I . . . I'm sorry?'

'This is Mr Palmer's office.' I glanced round. Clearly, it was exactly that, a 1990s solicitor's office, not an 1810s physician's study. 'Do you have some business with him?'

'No. I don't believe I do.'

'Then what is it you want?'

'Nothing. I'm sorry. Excuse me.' I brushed past her and made for the door.

117

A moment later I was in the street, walking fast and breathlessly back the way I'd come. My heart was racing, my thoughts whirling. It had lasted longer this time and been more intense, somehow more real even than before. Half of me yearned to go back to my father's house in my father's day and never return. The other half recoiled from the notion. He wasn't my father. I wasn't Marian Esguard. And yet I knew them both so well. I could learn nothing about Marian. I could only remember, could only rediscover what I'd already lived through with her – *as* her.

I went into the cathedral and sat in a pew for an hour or so, trying to confront the meaning of what was happening to me. I'd go back to London, of course, and maintain the pretence of normality for a few weeks. But then I'd give in again. Next time I'd go to Gaunt's Chase. I knew exactly where it was, even though Milo hadn't been more specific than 'somewhere in Dorset'. I knew and I couldn't forget. I'd go there and Marian would be waiting, with the life she'd led, for me to lead all over again. I'd go, and how long it would last this time, or how deeply it would draw me in, I had no way of telling.

I suppose that's when I decided to come to you. I'm either insane or . . . what would you call it? . . . possessed? I want you to stop me wanting this not to stop. I want you to tell me it's all very simple and you can make it go away. To be honest, I don't think you can. I don't think anyone can. But I'm told you're one of the best, so here's your chance to prove it. I'll do whatever you say. I'll try anything.

I certainly hope you can help me. Because, if not, I don't know what I'll do. After you, there's nowhere else to go. Except back to Marian.

Chapter Five

Daphne had agreed to meet me in Regent's Park during her lunch break the following day. We sat on a bench by the boating lake, a stiff March wind combing the bare trees around us. I handed her the tape and watched her slip it into her bag, then said, tiring suddenly of the thought of pussyfooting my way to the same point, 'You think she's mad, don't you?'

'She's ill and in need of my help, Ian. That's the only definition I'm interested in.'

'What about possession? Does your definition stretch to that?'

'No. Nor reincarnation. Nor calling up the dead. Nor corpse-candles and crithomancy. The human mind itself is quite complicated enough to account for Eris's fugues.'

'Fugues?'

'Episodes of altered consciousness, during which a person may become confused about his or her identity, often complicated by amnesia.'

'But not in Eris's case.'

'Strictly speaking, yes. Remember her description of

the fugues. Each one involved some memory loss, ranging from momentary in Bath to several minutes at least in Chichester. They would be classic dissociations but for the fixation on a specific alternative identity. A fixation I was unable to rid her of, despite lengthy remissions.'

'Are you saying she went on reverting to Marian?'

'There were two further fugues she reported to me, yes.'

'Did she record those experiences?'

'Yes.'

'Then I think I ought to hear those tapes, too.'

Daphne shook her head. 'There'd be no point. I wanted you to understand just how ill she is. Now you do. Dwelling on the symptoms can serve no purpose.'

'They're rather more than symptoms, though, aren't they? Niall Esguard's real enough. So was his uncle Milo. And his several-times-great-aunt Marian.'

'As far as I know.'

'Come on, Daphne. You went to Tollard Rising. You checked the facts. Marian existed.'

'Of course. But not *your* Marian. Or Eris's. She's a projection, a refuge, if you like, from a present-day reality Eris can't come to terms with.'

'That was your diagnosis?'

'Once I'd referred her to a neurologist and excluded physical causes, such as temporal lobe epilepsy, a psychological explanation was inescapable. Now perhaps you can see why hypnotic regression would have been so dangerous. I've no doubt we could have communicated with the Marian persona by that route, but in Eris's own mind that would have served to validate her delusions. My priority had to be the prevention of a degeneration into full-blown schizophrenia. In fact, such degeneration had probably already taken place, hence the false name and address. But I didn't realize that until it was too late.'

'Until she disappeared, you mean.'

'Yes. I misjudged the situation. Believe me, I've reproached myself for that since. Many times. I thought the problem was under control, but it wasn't. Not nearly.'

'Who are you saying I met in Vienna? Eris – or Eris-as-Marian?'

'I'm saying you met Eris in a fugue state. The likeliest explanation for her disappearance is profound amnesia consequent on that episode.'

'You mean she doesn't remember me?'

'It's possible.'

'My God, I never thought . . .'

'I can't be sure,' said Daphne, suddenly anxious, it seemed, to reassure me. 'She's probably very confused as well as very sick. That's why it's imperative we find her. And that's the reason I've breached confidentiality to the extent I have. I need your help, Ian. So does Eris. The woman you knew in Vienna – where do you think she might have gone?'

'I don't know,' I snapped, my voice rising. 'If I did, I'd have tracked her down by now, wouldn't I?' I felt Daphne's unruffled gaze rest on me. No doubt she was used to this kind of thing.

'I realize it's difficult. I guess we're both clutching at straws.'

'Well, there *is* more to clutch at than that. What about Saffron House?'

'I checked. Eris hasn't been seen there since Milo Esguard's death. She certainly didn't imagine that, by the way. The Royal United Hospital, Bath, last April.

121

Milo Coningsby Esguard, aged eighty-five, heart failure. His nephew Niall registered the death.'

'I'll start with him, then.'

Daphne looked at me in silent scrutiny, then said, 'I can't stop you, of course. I don't want to prevent you doing anything that might shed some light on Eris's whereabouts. But remember this. Marian Esguard certainly existed. But Eris's depiction of her – her *projection* of her – is a fantasy. That's why I haven't spoken to Niall Esguard. He isn't the man she describes, Ian. He's just a figure in her dreamscape. He isn't pursuing Eris. He's never threatened her.'

'Can you be sure of that?'

'What I'm saying is don't get caught up in her delusions. We're looking for Eris Moberly, not Marian Esguard. There aren't any pre-Fox Talbot negatives locked in a Piccadilly bank vault. There's no conspiracy at work. The only danger she's in stems from her own disturbed psyche.'

'Didn't you ever ask her to show you the negatives?' I turned to look at Daphne as I spoke, letting her see I meant to weigh her answer carefully. She knew the insides of people's heads better than I did, but Eris's fugues hadn't sounded like fantasies to me. They were too concrete, too specific in time and space, so much closer to memories than dreams. And the memory of the woman I'd fallen in love with was stronger than the scepticism I'd normally have brought to bear. Part of me was determined to believe every word she'd said – in Vienna *and* on the tape. 'I mean, that would have nailed the delusion once and for all, wouldn't it?'

'If I'd asked, she'd have found some reason to refuse. She'd also have interpreted my curiosity on the point as proof that the negatives existed.'

'Don't you harbour even the smallest suspicion that they might?'

'In my line of work I can't afford to harbour such suspicions, however slight.'

'I'll take that as a yes.'

'You shouldn't.'

'Let me listen to the other tapes, Daphne.'

'No.'

'They might hold some vital clue.'

'They don't.'

'Has it occurred to you that Niall Esguard might have something to do with her disappearance?'

'Absolutely not. We're dealing with an entirely self-generated psychosis. Eris visited Milo Esguard at Saffron House. And she probably met his nephew at the hospital. But what was said won't have been anything like her account of the conversation.'

'How can you be certain, since you haven't spoken to Niall Esguard?'

'The same way I can be certain you'll say he's lying if he doesn't confirm Eris's version of events.' Daphne frowned at me. 'Don't go down this road, Ian. It doesn't lead anywhere.'

'I'll believe that when I reach the end.'

'I'm beginning to regret letting you listen to the tape.'

'Don't. I'll only be doing what you, as a respectable professional psychotherapist, can't afford to do.'

'And what is that, exactly?'

'Turning over as many stones as I have to. Until I find the truth. Don't worry.' I forced a grin. 'I'll keep your name out of it. And whatever I learn I'll share with you. Doesn't that sound like a good deal?'

'All right.' She stood up and gazed out across the wind-stippled water. 'Since the need to find Eris by whatever means is something we have in common, I'm not even going to try to stand in your way.'

'What about those other tapes?'

She looked down at me. 'Prove you need to hear them. Then I'll consider it.' And with that she strode briskly away.

Two hours later, I was in Bath.

I knew the city reasonably well from an assignment for an architectural picture book a couple of years before. It's freighted with its own past more heavily than most places, on account of the massed terraces and crescents of Georgian town housing fixed in the pale local stone that can look as mellow and golden in the sunshine as it can seem drab and grey in the rain. I'd been back more recently in search of Marian, but found nothing. That seemed reason enough in my mind to suspect Niall Esguard of being up to no good.

Bentinck Place was as Eris had described it, a smart eighteenth-century terrace gone to twentieth-century seed, the design as impressive and the panoramic views as stunning as ever, but the structure well overdue for care and attention, with blackened frontages, rotting windows and rusting area railings.

I tried the only bell at number six that didn't have a name listed beside it, but got no answer. Niall Esguard didn't seem to be at home. These places usually have mews to the rear, however, and Bentinck Place was no exception. A high-walled cobbled lane plunged away down one side of the terrace, and I decided to check it before settling for the waiting game. It was just as well I did. Number six boasted a garage, the doors of which stood open to reveal a stylish old red Porsche with its bonnet up and its owner tinkering away while he sang along huskily to a country and western number on the radio.

I saw at once why Eris would have felt threatened by him. Even in an oil-smeared boiler suit he looked intimidating, cold hard eyes and a lean muscular frame conveying the unmistakable impression of somebody whose instinctive response to a problem was physical. Whether I posed a problem to him we were about to find out.

'Niall Esguard?'

'Who wants to know?' The stare was what did it. That and the squaring of his shoulders. He wasn't a man to be messed around and he believed in proclaiming the fact.

'My name's Ian Jarrett.'

'So?'

'I'm a friend of Eris Moberly.'

He stared at me for a second, then leaned into the car to turn off the radio. The silence seemed to deepen his deliberation as he stood erect and looked me up and down.

'I believe you met her at the time of your uncle's death last year.'

'Moberly?' he growled.

'That's right.'

'Yes.' He snapped his fingers. 'I remember. The woman who took to visiting Uncle Milo just before the end. I ran into her at the hospital the night he died. Friend of yours, you say?'

'She is, yes.'

'Mm.' Niall took a pack of Camels from his breast-pocket and lifted one out with his teeth, then added, 'I'd choose them less highly strung if I were you.'

'Would you really?'

'Not that—' He broke off to light the cigarette and savour the first drag. 'Well, I never knew what her game was. Maybe you do.'

'She's missing.'

'Is that a fact?'

'You haven't seen her since, by any chance?'

'No. She didn't show up at the funeral. The hospital was it. Bit of a surprise, really. I had no idea Uncle Milo got such glamorous visitors out at Saffron House.'

'Didn't they tell you about her?'

'No. She told me herself. Otherwise I wouldn't have known.'

'But you knew her name.'

'She introduced herself. Like a lot of women do when they meet me.'

'You and she don't seem to tell it quite the same way.'

'What's that supposed to mean?'

'It means she told me what you said to her. About your uncle's historical researches. And the inadvisability of giving him a helping hand.'

'She told you wrong.'

'I don't think so.'

'Pity we can't check with her, then.' He gave me a level stare. 'That would settle it.'

'What do you know about photographic history, Mr Esguard?'

'What do *you* know about it?'

'A little. Some original Fox Talbot negatives were auctioned recently. They fetched about ten thousand pounds each. For a genuine pre-Fox Talbot negative, you could be looking at ten times that.'

'Bit of a downer there aren't any, then. Fox Talbot started it all, didn't he? That I do know.'

'I have the impression your uncle thought otherwise.'

126

'He thought otherwise about most things. A contrary bugger, old Milo. Liked people to think he had aces up his sleeve, even when it was empty. *Specially* when it was empty, now I look back. As big a con artist as he was a piss artist. I probably tried to warn your friend not to take him seriously. Maybe she misunderstood. Not that it matters now, with the old boy dead and gone. But he could spin a yarn, no question. He could spin one with the best.'

'A yarn about your ancestor, Marian Esguard?'

Niall took a long deliberative drag on his cigarette, then said, 'Never heard of her.'

'Didn't your uncle ever mention her?'

'Might have. But it would have been in one ear and out the other.' He shrugged. 'I try not to store useless information.'

'A cache of negatives left by a previously unknown photographer active twenty years before Fox Talbot could be worth hundreds of thousands of pounds, Mr Esguard, possibly more. I wouldn't call that useless information.'

'I would.' He stepped closer and leaned against the end of a ladder hung horizontally along the garage wall, lowering his voice and cocking his head mock-confidentially. 'Unless I had the negatives, of course.'

'Which you don't?'

'How could I – when they don't exist?'

'Are you sure you haven't seen Eris Moberly since the night you met at the hospital?'

'Not really. I might have passed her in the street without recognizing her for all I know.' He grinned. 'You just can't say, can you?'

'I think you can.'

'Are you threatening me, Mr . . . Jarrett?' He was still

127

grinning. 'Or am I making the same mistake as Mrs Moberly?'

'What mistake would that be?'

'Reading too much into the things people say.'

'I mean to find her. You can read as much as you like into that.'

'But I don't read much, see. I prefer . . .' He pushed himself away from the ladder and glanced approvingly at the Porsche. 'Getting my hands dirty.'

'Dirty hands leave marks where they've been.'

'Unless the marks are washed off.' He looked at me through a plume of cigarette smoke, smiling faintly. 'Look, I don't want to be unhelpful. If Mrs Moberly is missing and you're trying to find her, well, that's . . .' The smile broadened. 'That's admirable, I suppose. The trouble is, I haven't a clue what she wanted out of Uncle Milo. And as for whether it has anything to do with her disappearance, well, your guess is as good as mine.'

'Not quite, I suspect.'

'Tell you what, though,' he went on, unabashed. 'If you're so sure Uncle Milo comes into it, I could put you on to somebody who knew him a sight better than I did. Somebody who actually listened to the crazy stuff he used to churn out. Somebody your friend might have spoken to, come to that, if she was as interested in my family as you seem to think.'

'Oh yes?' I said, my curiosity undeniably aroused. 'And who might that be?'

Montagu Quisden-Neve was the proprietor of a shabby genteel second-hand bookshop called Bibliomaufry. It formed the cramped bookend of a terrace of army-surplus stores, launderettes and tattoo parlours, overshadowed by the retaining wall and soaring six-

128

storey house-backs of one of Bath's bulkier Georgian crescents. According to Niall Esguard, Quisden-Neve had hung on every contradictory word of his uncle's photo-historical theories, before *and* after his move to Saffron House. He fancied himself as some sort of historian in his own right, apparently. So Niall had said, anyway. But I was aware that his priority might have been getting me off his back. I walked into Bibliomaufry that afternoon half expecting to find I'd been sent on a fool's errand.

The place was a dusty maze of books, shelved, stacked, boxed and piled. A plump, red-faced fellow in the trousers and waistcoat of a three-piece tweed suit, set off by a custard-yellow shirt and blancmange-pink bow tie, was bundling some old copies of *Punch* in coarse string at a desk somewhere near the middle of the maze. He had thick grey hair, worn long, which made him look like the ageing roué he quite possibly was.

'Mr Quisden-Neve?'

'The very same,' he replied, reddening still further as he fastened a knot in the string. 'The genuine article, indeed.'

'Niall Esguard said you might be able to help me.'

'Really? With what? A leather-bound set of the novels of Sir Walter Scott, perhaps?'

'I'm afraid not. It concerns his uncle.'

'There you have the advantage of me. Who *was* Scott's uncle?'

'I'm talking about Milo Esguard.'

'Ah. Poor Milo. I'm sorry.' He pushed the *Punch* bundle to one side and grew suddenly solemn. 'Not funny. I so often think I am, you know. But I find people seldom agree with me.'

'A friend of mine's gone missing. Her name's Eris

Moberly. She visited Milo Esguard several times during the weeks before his death.'

'As did I.'

'Anything you know might be valuable.'

'Eris Moberly?' He puffed at his cheeks thoughtfully, then slowly shook his head. 'I really don't think . . .'

'Let me describe her.' He listened patiently as I did so, but recognition didn't seem to dawn. 'Her friends are very worried about her,' I concluded. 'We fear she may have come to some harm.'

'That's good to hear, at any rate, in this dog-eat-dog society. If I disappeared, I frankly doubt anyone would bother to look for me. Other than my creditors, of course.' He ventured a grin, but swiftly dropped it. 'But then I'm not as well worth looking for as your friend sounds to be. More than a friend in your case, I take it. Excuse me, I don't mean to pry. It's just . . . your expression . . .'

'What about it?'

'*Haunted* is how I'd describe it. By love lost, or mislaid. In the shadows behind our eyes hides the past we run from, or else pursue. Don't you find that, Mr . . . ?'

'Jarrett.'

'Don't you? Honestly? Who are you really looking for? The damsel *disparue* – or yourself?'

'I'm looking for information, Mr Quisden-Neve. You either have some or you don't.'

'Yes.' He gave a pained little smile. 'And, alas, I don't. Milo never mentioned an Eris Moberly to me.'

'What about Marian Esguard?'

Quisden-Neve's eyes sparkled with sudden alertness. 'Marian Esguard. My, my, Mr Jarrett, there's clearly more to this than I thought. Exactly where does the mysterious Marian come into the problem of your missing friend?'

'I'm not sure. Except that she was the reason Eris went to see Milo in the first place.'

'Really? In that case it's still more unaccountable . . .' He tailed off into silence and rubbed his chin thoughtfully, then piloted his way through the book-stacks and past me to the door, where he slipped the bolt and turned the OPEN sign round to CLOSED. 'I usually celebrate the end of a bookselling day – or non-selling, come to that – with a glass of claret. Care to join me, Mr Jarrett? Then you can tell me all about Eris Moberly.'

I didn't tell him anything like all, of course, just enough to whet his appetite. We adjourned to his marginally less cluttered first-floor office, where he made a gulping assault on a ludicrously fine Pomerol while I related a carefully edited version of events. I claimed that Eris had shared her interest in Marian Esguard's putative photographic achievements with me, without explaining how she'd first come to hear of them. I'd thought little of her visits to Milo until her disappearance had left me with few other clues to follow. And, just to test the water, I added that Eris had continued to come down to Bath, ostensibly to see Milo, after his death, which I'd only just found out about.

'Fascinating,' pronounced Quisden-Neve when I'd finished. 'I really do wish Milo had introduced me to Mrs Moberly. Alas, he was a man who took pleasure in secrecy for its own sake. It was one of the reasons why he did so little to uncover the truth about Marian Esguard. He believed, on the basis of family rumour, and nothing more so far as I could ever discover, that she developed some sort of viable photographic technique

131

twenty years or so before Daguerre and Fox Talbot. In case you're wondering, however, I should make it clear that wasn't why I first cultivated his acquaintance.'

'Why did you, then?'

'Because Marian was married to Joslyn Esguard, and Milo was a repository of information about the husband as well as the wife. The photography question didn't interest me, not at first anyway, for the simple reason that I knew nothing about it. No, no, Joslyn Esguard was the lure for me.' He paused theatrically.

'Are you going to tell me why?'

'In view of the romantic nature of your quest, I suppose I must. For some years I've been pursuing a more scholarly quest of my own, with a view to publication and – who knows? – bestsellerdom.'

'A quest for what?'

'The answer to the mystery contained in the chart on the wall behind you.'

I turned and looked at the wall behind Quisden-Neve's office desk. Pinned up between a filing cabinet and a standard lamp was a large genealogical chart of the royal family from George I onwards, with as many fountain-penned additions and extensions as there were original printed entries, plus a spatter of asterisks, daggers and double daggers against various names, some of which were also boxed or underlined in red.

'Shall I explain, Mr Jarrett?'

'Why don't you?'

'Haemophilia is what it's all about. A hereditary disease which women can carry but only men can suffer from. As you may know, Queen Victoria was a carrier, as were two of her daughters, who, thanks to dynastic marriages, transmitted the disease to the Russian and Spanish royal families. One of Victoria's sons was also a haemophiliac. A peculiarity of the disease, by the way, is that none of the sons of a haemophiliac man will inherit it, but all of his daughters will carry it. None of this was known in the last century, of course. The genetic basis of the disease only became clear more recently. Victoria and Albert married off their children in blissful ignorance of the hereditary, not to say historical, consequences.'

'I don't quite—'

'Where did Victoria inherit the gene for haemophilia from, Mr Jarrett? That's the question. Neither of her parents, the Duke and Duchess of Kent, had any family history of the disease. Victoria was their only child, but the Duchess had been married before and had borne her first husband a non-haemophiliac son and a daughter whose subsequent lineage proves she wasn't a carrier. The chances of a mutant haemophiliac gene are about one in twenty-five thousand, on a par with being struck by lightning. Compare that with the absolute certainty that the daughter of a haemophiliac man will be a carrier.'

'But you just said—'

'The Duke of Kent wasn't a haemophiliac. Quite so. That raises the interesting possibility that he wasn't Victoria's father. Sexual mores at the time of Victoria's birth, especially among the aristocracy, were far from what we might term the Victorian ideal. Look at the chart. You'll observe that George the Fourth's only legitimate child, Princess Charlotte, died in November 1817, without issue. The cause of death was blood loss following the delivery of a stillborn son who, had he lived, would one day have been King of England. George was Prince Regent at that time, during his father's mad final years. None of his eleven surviving siblings had any legitimate offspring, though the illegitimate kind were two a penny. The King was past caring, but all that child-bearing must have seemed a cruel waste of effort to the Queen in view of the heirless outcome. By the close of 1817 all her daughters and most of her daughters-in-law were past the menopause, with no living issue to show for it. Hopes for dynastic continuity thus rested on her three unmarried sons: the Dukes of Clarence, Kent and Cambridge. Dutifully disentangling themselves in advanced middle age from their respective irregular unions, they all contracted hasty marriages to promisingly fecund Continental heiresses and did their overdue best to head off the prospect of the crown passing from one elderly brother to another. Kent won the race, fathering Victoria by the widowed Duchess of Leiningen, or at any rate seeming to. He was over fifty at the time and in poor shape. Significantly, even illegitimate offspring had previously been beyond him. Maybe his wife decided to improve his chances, so to speak. And maybe she had the misfortune to improve those chances with . . .'

'A haemophiliac?'

'Precisely. Which brings us to Joslyn Esguard.'

'You're saying Marian Esguard's husband was a haemophiliac?'

'If only it were that simple. That's what I hoped to learn when I first approached Milo, but he was able more or less to rule it out. His grandfather never even hinted at such a thing, and there's been no sign of the disease in the family in intervening generations.'

'What made you think of Joslyn Esguard in the first place?'

'Circumstantial evidence. When the idea occurred to me of basing a book on this apparently whimsical notion, which I'm certainly not the first to have entertained, I searched various archives for potential haemophiliac candidates and turned up a rather puzzling letter written by one Joslyn Esguard early in 1838 to Sir John Conroy, private secretary to the Duchess of Kent. Victoria was on the throne by then, her father was long dead and Conroy was rumoured to be rather more than a secretary to her mother. He'd previously been the Duke's aide-de-camp. Somewhat reluctantly, I'd already ruled him out as a candidate in his own right, but there wasn't much he wouldn't have known about the affairs of his royal mistress – pun very much intended – hence my interest in his correspondence.'

'What did the letter say?'

'Oh, see for yourself.' Quisden-Neve walked across to the filing cabinet, pulled open the bottom drawer, riffled through a bulging file and lifted out a flagged document. 'This is a photocopy of the original.' He passed it over for me to read. 'Joslyn Esguard's handwriting was scarcely copperplate, but I think you'll get the gist of it.' The writing was indeed a scrawl, but I could follow it easily enough. There wasn't, after all, much to follow.

> Gaunt's Chase,
> Dorset
> 12th Feb'y '38
>
> Sir John,
>   I am obliged to return to the issue raised in my earlier letter. I am armed with certain facts which I am prepared to make publicly known if we cannot reach an accommodation. I recommend your early attention to my requirements.
>
>   I remain etc., etc.,
>   Joslyn Esguard

'What *were* the facts, eh, Mr Jarrett? Queen Victoria was born on the twenty-fourth of May, 1819. That puts her conception at late August or early September, 1818. We know from the records that the Duke and Duchess were in residence at Kensington Palace during that period. We also know that the Duke visited his mother, who was dying, virtually daily, at Kew, leaving the Duchess to occupy her time . . . as she saw fit.'

'But not with Joslyn Esguard.'

'Not if my theory is correct, no. Yet clearly he knew something. The threat implicit in the letter is a scarcely veiled one. We shall never know for certain, alas.'

'Because of the fire at Gaunt's Chase in which Joslyn Esguard lost his life, five days before Victoria's coronation.'

'Yes. And four months after he wrote that letter. All of which is consistent with Barrington Esguard's claim that his brother was murdered. But if the fire *was* some sort of cover-up it was undeniably effective. The letter didn't take me anywhere along the haemophilia road. Instead, I found myself diverted by Milo down the un-related byway of Marian Esguard's possible role as a photographic pioneer. It promised to make my book still more commercially viable, I can't deny, which is why I pursued it as far as I could. Royal scandal and Regency feminism sounded like a winning combination to me. But I simply hit another brick wall. Milo had no evidence to back up the family legend, and I was unable to unearth any beyond a single tantalizing document.'

'What was it?'

'Another letter, written by Marian Esguard to her father, Dr Thomas Freeman, in the spring of 1817. I found it in the archives of the Chichester Infirmary, where Dr Freeman worked, addressed to him there rather than at the Freeman residence, which is odd in itself.' By now Quisden-Neve was once more burrowing through his files. 'Here we are. Marian had a more elegant hand than her husband, no question.'

Even in the form of a photocopy, a letter written by Marian Esguard carried with it a magical charge. I sat down and slowly read it through and, as I did so, I realized it had a significance that Quisden-Neve couldn't possibly appreciate.

Gaunt's Chase,
Sunday 20th April 1817

My dear Papa,

I shall burst with excitement if I do not tell you how much I have accomplished in the realm of scientific inquiry I have dubbed heliogenesis. I could not have made such progress without your assistance as my secret pharmaceutical supplier. The results, enhanced by the fine spring weather we have enjoyed here of late, have been quite, quite extraordinary, and I shall send you a sample, if you do not think it too indiscreet of me, as soon as I have one that will satisfy your exacting aesthetic standards. Hyposulphite of ammonia *is* the key. But the world beyond the door it unlocks is one I had never thought to see. The principle was purely a mental construction. The practice is real and true and visible. You will be astonished, as I already am. I hope you will also be a little proud. I shall write again soon.

Ever your loving daughter,
Marian

'Did Milo Esguard ever see this letter?' I asked when I'd finished.

'Sadly, no. He died before I came across it.'

'So he couldn't have told Eris about it?'

'Absolutely not.' Quisden-Neve retrieved the letter from me and slipped it back into the file. 'I'm always on the qui vive for rival researchers, Mr Jarrett. In this case, I'm happy to say nobody had got there before me. Only you and I are at all likely to be aware of what Marian Esguard wrote to her father in April 1817.'

By the time I left Bibliomaufry, Quisden-Neve having insisted I finish the bottle of Pomerol with him, it was too late to visit Saffron House, as I'd originally intended, so I booked into a hotel in the middle of Bath and phoned Daphne from there. I was excited by the contents of Marian's letter. To me it seemed inconceivable that Eris could have imagined an encounter with Dr Freeman that was clearly as close to the truth as it could be without having, in some sense at least, shared a genuine experience of Marian's. For some reason I wouldn't have cared to analyse, I wanted to prove Daphne wrong. I wanted to prove Eris wasn't deluded. I wanted Marian as well as her.

But Daphne was reluctant to accept my argument. And far more interested in the name of my informant than in the issue of what the letter did or didn't prove. 'You were told all this by Montagu Quisden-Neve?'

'Yes. Do you know him?'

'Not exactly. But Eris does.'

'No, no. You've got that wrong. Quisden-Neve's never met her.'

'Describe him to me.'

Before I'd got much further than the pink bow tie, she cut me short.

'She *does* know him.'

'How can you be sure?'

I heard Daphne give a long, thoughtful sigh. 'God, this is difficult. I wish . . .'

'What's difficult?'

'You'll have to listen to the second tape, Ian. As you wanted to. As I *didn't* want you to.'

'I won't try to talk you out of it, but why the change of heart?'

'You'll understand that as soon as you hear it. Until you do, I strongly advise you not to speak to Mr Quisden-Neve again.'

I couldn't focus my thoughts on anything that night except the second tape. Daphne had refused to give me even a hint of what it contained, except that Quisden-Neve figured somewhere. I had half a mind to confront him at Bibliomaufry next morning and demand an explanation, but I kept telling myself it would be better to know what I'd be demanding an explanation *of*, and that meant returning to London to take delivery of the tape. Daphne had said she'd drop it round to my flat after leaving her practice. My offer to collect it had been declined. That gave my suspicious mind still more to work on. Was she afraid I might try to force the third tape out of her as well? If so, her fear was well founded. That was exactly what I felt like doing. But she was my only real ally. I couldn't afford to alienate her. On the other hand, she couldn't afford to have me running round endangering her professional reputation. We both had plenty to lose and lots of reasons for trusting each other, even against our better judgement.

I slept poorly, racked by dreams of Eris-as-Marian, warm and close and insatiable, my eager demon lover running on before me. It wasn't the first time I'd had such dreams, and I knew it wouldn't be the last – until I found her.

As early in the morning as I dared, I drove out to Bradford-on-Avon and called at Saffron House. Milo Esguard was well remembered, by residents as well as by staff, but the name Eris Moberly didn't mean anything to anyone. Nor did my description of her. Milo received more visitors than most, apparently, despite his grouchy nature, but the only one to stick in their minds was a flamboyantly dressed bookseller from Bath. I gave up and headed back to London.

There was nothing to do at the flat but wait for Daphne to arrive and wonder what she'd meant about Quisden-Neve. He hadn't seemed to me to have the makings of a good liar. But perhaps that just made him a better liar than most. Perhaps flint-eyed Niall was on the level, whereas the silver-tongued Quisden-Neve wasn't. Either way, I was going to find out soon enough.

The doorbell rang just after five o'clock, and I pressed the entry button without checking it was Daphne. There wasn't anyone else it was likely to be, after all. Yet when I opened the door of the flat and looked out it wasn't Daphne I saw climbing the stairs towards me.

'Amy! What . . . ? What are you doing here?'

'Can I come in?'

'Of course, but . . .' She gave me a kiss, then walked past me into what I knew would look to her like a hovel. 'Why aren't you at school?'

'The Easter holidays began yesterday, Dad. Did you forget?'

'I must have done. I . . . When *is* Easter?'

'Next weekend. You really didn't know?'

'I've had a lot on my mind. Look, do you want some coffee?'

'Shall I make it?'

'All right. The kitchen's so small you shouldn't have any trouble finding your way round.'

In fashionably frayed jeans and a droopy black sweater Amy looked older than fourteen and older even than when I'd visited her at school two months before. Maybe I was responsible for that. Watching her put the kettle on and hunt down the coffee, the dried milk and the only two mugs there were, I had the chilling sensation that I was watching a girl I knew only slightly, the daughter of a friend perhaps, or a friend of my daughter, not the Amy I'd seen come into this world and grow and laugh and cry through all the years since.

'It's nice to see you,' I said, smiling stiffly at her. 'You should have phoned and warned me. I'd have . . . got some biscuits in.'

'What's going on, Dad?' she asked, flicking her hair out of her eyes as she spooned out the coffee. 'I mean, why are you on your own?'

'It's complicated.'

'Has she ditched you?'

'No.'

'Then why isn't she with you?'

'Like I said. It's complicated.'

'Mum thinks you made her up, this . . . Marian. Did you?'

'No. Of course not.'

'That's what I said.' The kettle boiled and she broke off to fill the mugs and hand me one. 'Mum told me you're seeing a shrink, though. Is that true?'

'In a sense.'

'Either you are or you aren't.'

'Then I am.'

'You're not making sense.'

'Just as well I'm seeing a psychotherapist, then.'

'I feel really shut out by this. You know?'

'I'm sorry, Amy. I wish I could explain.'

'You could try.'

'I can't. Not at the moment. There's too much happening.'

'Too much happening? What do you mean, Dad? Nothing's happening. Not to you, anyway. You're just . . . vegetating . . . in this dump . . . while Mum . . .'

'What about her?'

'She's seeing another man. I'm supposed to be meeting him on Saturday. She's really coy about it, you know? Like she's in love. Won't tell me anything about him. Not even his name. It's supposed to be some big secret.'

'Why are you telling me, then?'

'You know why.'

'Because you're hoping it's not too late for us to get back together.'

'Well? It isn't, is it?'

'I'm afraid it is.' The doorbell rang and I looked round, aware how eager I was going to sound to get off the hook. 'That's somebody I have to see.'

'Who?'

'Believe it or not, the psychotherapist your mother told you about.'

'So it *is* true.'

'Like I said. In a sense.' I walked across to the door release and pressed it. 'Listen, Amy, things are . . . diffi-

142

cult for me at the moment. But we could . . . go out one day . . . while you're home.'

'Which day?'

'Any one.'

'But *which* one?'

'I'm not sure. I'll have to . . .'

'Phone me?' she asked, anger and hurt tautening her expression.

'Yes. I'll phone you.'

'No you won't.'

'Of course I will.'

She walked across to join me by the front door and stared into my eyes, defying me to avoid her gaze. 'What's happening to you, Dad?'

'Nothing you need worry about.'

'What shall I tell Mum?'

'Nothing.'

There was a knock at the door. I reached for the handle, but Amy got there first and held on without turning it.

'You can still count on me when it matters, Amy.'

'It matters now.'

'I'll phone. In a few days. Honest.'

'Promise?'

'Cross my heart and hope to die.'

'Don't say that.'

'I just have.'

There was another knock at the door. Amy's face crumpled into angry confusion. Then she seemed to reach a decision, with all her mother's brisk expediency. ''Bye, Dad,' she said in a rush, kissing me lightly on the cheek and opening the door.

'Hello,' said Daphne, catching sight of her.

But Amy didn't reply. She brushed straight past her and raced off down the stairs, taking them two at a time. I watched her go in silence. And Daphne watched me. Then she stepped inside and I closed the door behind her.

'Your daughter?'

'You're not a psychotherapist for nothing, are you?'

'I won't be one much longer if I go on like this.'

'I take it that means you brought the tape.'

'Yes. But we have to talk about this, Ian. Everything's getting very . . . confused.'

'You don't need to tell me that.'

'But I do. Quisden-Neve is quite a spanner in the works. Without him, I could continue to regard Eris's fugues as text-book delusive experiences. Now it's not so simple.'

'It never was simple as far as I'm concerned. You have to face it, Daphne. Marian's letter makes a difference.'

'It's not just the letter. In fact, it's not the letter at all. Eris could have tracked that down herself. It could even have been the starting point for her fantasy.'

'Quisden-Neve seemed certain nobody had seen it before him.'

'Perhaps he was mistaken.'

'He's too experienced a researcher for that.'

'Then he must be lying.'

'Why should he be?'

'Why indeed?' Daphne moved unsteadily to the armchair and sat down, heavily clunking a set of keys onto the table in front of her. She looked much less self-controlled than the previous times we'd met. She looked, in fact, like a very worried woman. 'Have you got anything to drink by any chance?'

'Coffee?'

'I meant something stronger.'

'I'm afraid not. I just sleep here. Some nights I don't even do that. Stocking up a drinks cabinet doesn't seem to have crept to the top of my agenda yet. What about the coffee? My daughter made a cup and never touched it.'

'Forget it.' She raised a hand as if to ward something off, then let it slowly fall into her lap. 'Listen to me, Ian. Listen carefully. If these people – Niall Esguard, Montagu Quisden-Neve – turn out to be lying, now, to you, after the event so to speak, then it has to be because they have something to hide. And that means there has to be more to this than a dissociative disorder.'

'I've been trying to tell you that all along.'

'*But it doesn't make sense.*' Shocked by how loudly she'd spoken, she fell abruptly silent. We looked at each other. Then she opened her handbag, lifted out a tape and laid it on the table.

'Is that it?'

'Yes.' She fumbled in her bag, produced one of her slim cigars and lit it, the flame trembling along with her fingers. Then she sat back and crossed her legs. 'That's it.'

'When was it recorded?'

'Last October. She delivered it to me at a session on . . .' Daphne leaned forward to read the label on the tape. 'The fourth of November.'

'But you started seeing her back in . . .'

'June. That's right. Things began well and got better and better. I thought I had the case cracked.'

'What went wrong?'

'She went away on holiday with her husband in September. A month in Hawaii. It sounded like just what she needed to consolidate the progress she'd made over the summer. I was on holiday myself when she came back in mid-October. The fourth of November was our first session for seven weeks. I'd given her the tape to record any particular concerns that came into her mind during the lay-off. I never expected anything serious to crop up. I thought we were on top of it. I thought we had everything ironed out. Instead, there'd been a sudden regression. Worse than a regression, in fact. She'd jumped to another level of dissociation altogether. My first thought was that the holiday had brought her difficulties with her husband to the surface, and that she'd retreated into the Marian fantasy to avoid confronting them.'

'What difficulties, exactly?'

'You're missing the point. That was my theory *then*. That was my best guess. But it won't do now. It simply won't stand up.'

'Why not?'

'Because of Quisden-Neve.' She rose, strode to the window and yanked it up. The woodwork squealed. Cool air and traffic noise gusted in. 'I don't know what to think now. I honestly don't. What if . . . ?' She shook her head in dismay. 'What if it's all true?'

'True? In what sense?'

'Listen to the tape, Ian.' She turned and looked at me. 'Then bring it back to me. My practice, nine o'clock tomorrow, without fail. Can I have your word on that?'

'All right. You've got it.'

'Don't act on what you hear until we've discussed it. Promise?'

'I promise.'

'It's vital you do nothing . . . impetuous.'

'I won't.'

'But can I believe you? That's the question. There's something we can't get round, isn't there?'

'What's that?'

'Your love for her.' She stepped towards me and stared into my eyes. 'It worries me. It really does.'

'I'm doing this *because* I love her.'

'I know.' She nodded. 'That's what worries me.'

When Daphne left, I stood by the window and waited until I'd seen her walk away along the street. Then I sat down in the armchair, slid the tape into the machine and pressed the play button, as relieved to be alone at last as I was eager to hear Eris's voice once more. I wanted to be close to her, to see her and to touch her. But for the moment all I could do was listen. And for the moment that was good enough.

Chapter Six

I'm sorry, Daphne. I hoped it wouldn't happen again, and I know you did, too. I suppose we persuaded each other we had this thing beaten. Well, we didn't. It was just biding its time, gathering its strength maybe for when it lunged at me out of the dark. I'm talking as if it's some kind of ravening beast, aren't I, something outside myself? And that's what it feels like: something I'm just . . . incidental to. I know you said it all came from inside me, and I've tried to believe that, but it doesn't do any good. It didn't stop it coming back and it won't make it go away.

'Tell it calmly and sequentially,' I can hear you say. 'Chronological order sorts the real from the imaginary.' Well, I'll try. But don't rely on chronology too much, Daphne. I'm not sure I know what it means any more. Anyway, here goes.

Hawaii was great. It was so remote, so completely different from my normal life. Getting away from it all never sounded so appealing and never proved so wonderful. Out there, in the middle of the Pacific, I could be absolutely confident Marian wasn't going to catch up with me. Didn't I say something like that in that postcard of the Kilauea Crater I sent you? It was out of this world. Out of *her* world.

I didn't want to come back. I actually tried to talk Conrad into extending the trip. But he was already getting twitchy about being away from work so long, and he thought I'd flipped when I suggested staying on without him. There are some things he won't tolerate. We came back together, on schedule. And the very next morning it started to go wrong.

I got up late, a good few hours after Conrad had gone to work. I suppose the jet lag must have hit me. Anyway, I forced myself to go out and do some shopping. We were low on lots of things. When I got back there was a man waiting for me at the entrance to the apartment block. He was a paunchy, red-faced chap with a shock of grey hair, wearing a tweed suit, a bright yellow bow tie and a purple shirt. He looked like a cross between a country solicitor and a superannuated playboy.

'Mrs Moberly?' he said, stepping into my path and grinning. 'My name's Montagu Quisden-Neve. My card.' He handed me his card as he spoke. It described him as an antiquarian bookseller, with an address in Bath. 'We don't know each other, Mrs Moberly, but we do have a mutual acquaintance. Niall Esguard. Also his late uncle, Milo Esguard. Do you think I might come up to your flat and outline a small business proposition I'd like you to consider?'

I was too stunned to refuse. Even if I hadn't been, I'd have gone along with what he wanted. The mere mention of Niall Esguard terrified me. I'd thought I was safely out of his reach. But if this man Quisden-Neve could find me . . .

So I took him up to the flat. He carried my shopping

149

and burbled away about the weather and the charms of Mayfair, as if he was unaware how frightened I was. But I already had the impression the fruity-toned courtesies were an act. The bow tie and the double barrel didn't make him any softer centred than Niall Esguard. And once we'd got inside and he'd somehow manoeuvred me into pouring him a gin and tonic he soon made it obvious I had plenty to be frightened *of*.

'I'll come straight to the point, Mrs Moberly,' he said, still grinning like some obsequious car salesman. 'I was negotiating with dear old Milo at the time of his death for the purchase of some early photographic negatives, possibly the work of an ancestor of his, Marian Esguard. I see you've heard of her. It was frustrating to be denied such a historically interesting acquisition by the untimely intervention of the Grim Reaper, but none of us is immune from his attentions, so who am I to complain?'

'I thought you said you were going to come straight to the point,' I protested weakly.

'Quite so. I do beg your pardon. With Milo gone, I've been obliged to negotiate with his nephew, Niall Esguard. I believe you've met the gentleman, though "gentleman" is perhaps an inappropriate description. Niall is a believer in stripping matters to their essentials. He is a crude but effective operator in several substrata of life, a blunt-mannered individual whom only tiresome necessity prompts me to do business with.'

'I don't know what you're talking about.'

'Come, come, Mrs Moberly. Prevarication will not aid you. Niall believes you became his uncle's trusted confidante in the closing weeks of his life, and so do I. Since the negatives were not among Milo's effects, it follows that he gave them up for safe-keeping. To you, I rather think. Such is Niall's conclusion, at all events.

One he would be keen to discuss with you, if only he knew where to find you. There, of course, I have the advantage of him. For I *do* know where to find you. Indeed, I *have* found you.'

'How did you trace me?'

'Simplicity itself, my dear. But the sort of simplicity alien to Niall's smash-and-grab mentality. I gleaned your name and address from the library users' book at the Royal Photographic Society in Bath. It was foolhardy of you to record the purpose of your visit so openly, if I may say so. "Marian Esguard." Rather a give-away, I fear. But perhaps you had no reason at that time to place a premium on secrecy. Still, you should have gone back later and erased the entry. I would have done, in your shoes. And very elegant shoes they are, too. Made in Milan, I would guess. I find you can tell the product of a Milanese last at a glance, don't you?'

'What do you want?'

'I want the negatives. Please don't trouble to claim you don't have them, or that they don't exist, or that you have no idea what I'm referring to. We both know what they are, though I suspect you may not have taken steps to establish their monetary worth, which is perhaps just as well. It is also irrelevant, since I'm not offering to buy them from you. What I *am* offering to do is say nothing to Niall Esguard concerning your whereabouts and, purely as a gesture of goodwill, to cover your tracks in Bath rather more effectively than you managed to. In return, of course, for your surrender of the negatives.'

'I—'

'Say no more, Mrs Moberly. I have the distinct impression you're about to indulge in a pointless series of denials, which will only embarrass you as well as me. Since I assume the negatives are not stored here, I will give you a few days to reflect on your position and to retrieve them from whichever bank vault they currently rest in. I shall be returning to the capital the day after tomorrow. Join me for tea at Richoux in Piccadilly at three o'clock that afternoon. And bring the negatives with you. That, my dear, is all you need do to bring this matter to a painless conclusion. But you *do* need to do it. The requirement, I fear, is strictly non-negotiable.'

I was in a state of shock when he left. I didn't know what to do or where to turn. He'd found me so *easily*. The idea that I could opt out of Marian's life – and opt *her* out of *mine* – was in ruins. And, worse than that, I felt I'd somehow let her down. She wouldn't have wanted either Niall *or* Quisden-Neve to have the negatives. They were hers and, in a sense, mine. They ought never to be theirs. But how could I avoid handing them over? In the simple, logical twentieth-century world I inhabited, what the hell was the problem with giving up a few old pieces of paper in exchange for my peace of mind? Well, that *was* the problem. It wouldn't be at peace. I knew that even if I knew nothing else. On the other hand . . .

I can't account clearly for what I did next. I suppose on some level I felt I had to get as close to Marian as possible before I decided what to do. On another level I had to get out of the flat and out of London. It was choking me. I wanted to run away and hide. And, if I ran, there seemed only one direction I could run *in*.

So I started driving, south-west out of London along the A30, past Windsor Great Park, down through Camberley and Basingstoke and Salisbury in buttery autumn light, until I reached Cranborne Chase and the wide-open rolling hills round Tollard Rising. It was my first visit, the first I'd dared to make, but everything had that feeling of vague familiarity I'd known it would have. The lie of the land; the shape of the buildings; the folding together of field and sky: I recognized them all. I'd waited for them, just as they'd waited for me.

I parked the car on Charlton Down, with the landscape of the past and the present fusing in the mellow late afternoon below me. Then I clambered over a barbed-wire fence that had once been a fragrant hedgerow and struck out across the swelling breast of the down, knowing the exact moment when the roofs and chimneys of Gaunt's Chase would have come into view – *if* it had still been standing. Sheep scurried away as I walked dead straight through the dull, green, flowerless pasture. The wind was cool, the sunlight weakening at the merest hint of dusk. I was still in the real world, defying that other world to show itself, rushing to prove the truth or falsehood of what had hovered at the edge of my mind's eye for far too long. I thought momentarily of Quisden-Neve, then of the negatives I'd seen in the box. I remembered one weirdly tinted shot of the house taken from just the angle at which I'd see it first if—

And as swiftly and simply as the blinking of my eye it was done. I was there. And it *was* the real world. The grass was a richer green, spattered with meadow flowers. The turf yielded like a cushion beneath my feet. When I looked down, I saw the polished toes of my half-boots sinking into it with every step, and the hem of my ankle-length pink-and-yellow dress swaying as I walked. There was no surprise in any of this, no shock or wonderment. It was as natural and fitting as arriving home and opening the door and going in.

I glanced ahead and saw Gaunt's Chase, unrazed and unaltered in its parkland setting on the gently sloping westward face of the down. The house was shimmering faintly in a heat haze and I was aware, as if remembering a briefly forgotten practicality, that it was a summer's afternoon in the year 1817, the sunlight falling warmly on my back as I returned, neither hurrying nor dawdling, from a walk to my favourite vantage point, where so much of Dorset and Wiltshire stretched itself in my hilltop gaze that the limitations and confinements of my domestic existence could seem like contemptible trivialities.

Marian's life became mine once more in that instant. Every memory of her past and every fact of her present burst into my mind like so much half-expected fore-knowledge. I was thirty years old, plain by the standards of the day and too slim to be flattered by the bosomy fashions, too energetic and intelligent to be content with rural isolation, but nonetheless subject to the variable and sometimes brutal moods of a husband who came and went as he pleased and behaved accordingly. My contentment, amounting almost to happiness, was thereby explained, for Jos was in London, at the house in Berkeley Square, which I'd not visited since the earliest years of our marriage. And though Gaunt's Chase could never truly be home to me, because every brick and pillar bore some imprint of its owner, it was, in his absence, a place where I could live at ease with myself.

Besides, there was more to life than fashion and a fond or faithful husband. There was science – and my dream of heliogenesis. The warm summer sun was the agent of something altogether astonishing. Since the spring, I'd achieved more than I'd ever have thought possible when the idea first came to me. And in the last few days those achievements had accelerated beyond my wildest expectations. I was excited and impatient to share my new-found knowledge with the only person in the locality I trusted not to abuse my confidence.

So I was already thinking of him when I saw the figure moving towards me along the edge of the beech hanger north-west of the house. Then I recognized who it was and felt my heart jump with a girlish anticipation I was tired of rebuking myself for. I had scant cause to be grateful to Jos, when all was said and done, but the society of Lawrence Byfield was one blessing he *had* conferred on me, albeit unwittingly. When, earlier in the year, he'd mentioned giving a London acquaintance of his the use of Legion Cottage while he convalesced from an illness, I'd feared Mr Byfield would turn out to be as rank a scoundrel as my husband's liking for him implied. To my amazement, however, he'd shown himself in the months since to be a man of honour as well as charm, of discernment as well as humour. At first I'd distrusted my own liking for him. I remembered my susceptibility to Jos's flattering attentions during our courtship, and the loveless marriage it had misled me into. I knew from bitter experience how a certain kind of man enjoyed deceiving women into thinking well of him, just as he enjoyed the moment when he chose to reveal his true character. Besides, Jos counted Mr Byfield as a friend, and I secretly regarded any friend of my husband as an enemy.

But I had been obliged to reconsider. Lawrence Byfield was a good man, accounted odd by some because of his unfashionable beard, his pale and sometimes strained expression, his incapacity for idle chatter, his contempt for gossip and the gravity of his manner, which the unperceptive mistook for arrogance. Then there was his limp, which colourful rumour attributed to a knee wound suffered in a duel, and the unspecified illness from which he was recovering. His unwillingness to volunteer either explanations or clarifications was held against him. But not by me. I admired his restraint as well as his reserve. I found in him the first human mystery ever to fascinate me. Above all, I detected in him a nature akin to my own. He had the wit to see how matters stood between me and Jos. I had the impression he knew my husband as well as I did, if not better. He understood very clearly what marriage to his friend was likely to involve.

He never said as much. He never spoke a word that would bear such a meaning. But in the way his eyes rested on me, in the warmth of his smile and the tenderness of his solicitations, I could detect an anxiety on my behalf that was as delicate as it was diligent. Jos left me more completely to myself during Mr Byfield's tenancy of Legion Cottage than he ever had before. I sometimes wondered if it was *because* of Mr Byfield's tenancy, preposterous though the notion was. His presence on the estate seemed to act as a guarantee of my well-being. Jos grew inhibited in his company and took to spending more and more time in London, where Mr Byfield, on account of his health, could not join him. I was grateful for this, and so, I sometimes suspected, was Mr Byfield.

The spring and summer of 1817 were thus happy seasons for me. I progressed from the experimental application of my heliogenic theories to something approaching the perfection of a new and revolutionary pictorial technique. Each week seemed to bring some new insight, some new refinement of the craft. It was truly magical to see the pictures that I made by the manipulation of sunlight and darkness and chemically treated paper. I wrote to my father and told him of the significant strides I was making. He replied in tones of incredulity I could well understand. He'd not seen the pictures. But I had. And so had Lawrence Byfield.

I first mentioned my heliogenic researches to him one warm afternoon in late April, when I found him attempting a watercolour painting of Gaunt's Chase from the far side of the park. I wanted to impress him, I later realized. He was the only person in the whole of Tollard Rising I *did* want to impress. So I goaded him with the claim that I could produce a better and more accurate picture without the aid of paints and brushes. He took me up on the challenge and called the following day to view the result, unaware of the procedure I'd planned to follow and of its scientific basis. When I showed him the picture, he was clearly taken aback.

'But . . . what is it?' he said in amazement.

'It is a heliogenic drawing,' I replied self-importantly. 'A bringing together on paper of the reaction to light of nitrate of silver and the pictorial properties of a camera obscura.'

'You did this?'

'I made it, certainly.'

'How?'

'As I just told you, Mr Byfield. To be more specific, I trained a modified camera obscura on the part of the house you see pictured, having secured at the back of the camera a sheet of paper soaked successively in solutions of common salt and nitrate of silver. I then removed the sheet of paper from the camera in the darkened basement room I work in, observed the felicitous result, and sealed it against the depredating effects of daylight by applying a solution of hyposulphite of ammonia. I had the advantage of yesterday afternoon's strong sunlight, of course. In cloudy weather I doubt—'

'It's a miracle.'

'No, no. A remarkable achievement, I think, but not a miracle.'

'I've never seen anything like it.' He shook his head at me and smiled. 'But that, perhaps, should not surprise me.'

'Why not?'

'Because, Mrs Esguard, I've never met anyone quite like you.'

From that day on we grew to be friends and, in a sense, colleagues. Though I never acknowledged as much to myself, it was my eagerness for his company, and his for mine, that drew us together, quite as much as his scientific curiosity. There was no danger, of course, that he would object to a mere woman carrying out such work. His openness of mind on that score was implicit from the start. Yet some, notably Jos, *would* object. So it was that a secretive element was part of our friendship from the start. We were, in effect, colluding in the deception of my husband, and the reputable, intellectual reasons for doing so made it easier than it otherwise would have been to entertain other reasons that were neither reputable nor intellectual.

My pleasure at seeing him riding towards me on Pompey that afternoon of early August would therefore have been considerable, whatever the circumstances. They were heightened, however, by my exultant mood, a mood stemming from a discovery I had made just two days before, which promised to elevate my researches to a wholly new level of significance. And what is a discovery worth if it cannot be disclosed to a friend so that he too may relish the joy of it?

He saw me almost as soon as I saw him and waved in greeting, then altered his route and trotted slowly across to meet me.

'Good afternoon, Mrs Esguard,' he said as he drew up in front of me, courteously correct as ever. 'You look, if I may say so, the very picture of good health.'

'The climb to Charlton Down is an invigorating one, Mr Byfield,' I replied.

'I must undertake it more often if it is likely to prove such a tonic as your appearance suggests.' He dismounted, wincing slightly as his right leg touched the ground. 'But I suspect there may be more than fresh air and exercise to this . . . beaming contentment of yours.'

'There may be, yes.' I patted Pompey's muzzle. 'I cannot deny it.'

'Some new heliogenic miracle, perhaps?'

'Am I so very transparent?'

'Only to one who knows your secret.'

'Well, well.' I blushed. 'It is true. I have chanced upon a quite remarkable enhancement of the heliogenic process.'

'I doubt chance played a more important role than reason.'

'Let us settle for trial and error.'

'Let us by all means, if it will appease your modesty. Where have trial and error taken you, might I enquire?'

'To an appreciation of the unique properties of gallic acid.'

He smiled. 'And what are those properties?'

'Its silver salt is astonishingly potent, Mr Byfield.' My voice quivered with excitement. 'It actually strengthens the image *after* formation, so much so that a faded picture, indeed a picture in which nothing is visible at all, may be rescued from oblivion by the gallate's deposition of silver on the original base. You recall my failed portrait of Barrington and Susannah?'

'I do.'

'It is failed no longer. It is as bright and sharp as day. Will you not come and see? I have already printed a reverted copy. It is in my laboratory.'

'I can scarcely believe what you are saying. You have . . . restored the picture?'

'I have done more than that. I have released the true image from its hiding place.'

'It sounds miraculous.'

'I have reproved you for likening me to a miracle-worker before, Mr Byfield. All I am doing is liberating the possibilities of science.'

'And thereby plucking the light from the air as a lepidopterist would net a butterfly. If that is not a miracle, then it is certainly an act of genius. I would be honoured to be shown the rescued portrait of your brother-in-law and his wife. Indeed, I positively itch to see it. Unfortunately, I told Fowler I'd collect Pompey's new bridle this afternoon, and I don't want to keep the poor fellow waiting. Neither does Pompey, do you, boy?'

Pompey shook his head in apparent comprehension and I smiled at both of them. 'Call on your way back, Mr Byfield. There are hours of good viewing light left to us.'

Thus was it settled. Mr Byfield rode on to Fowler's saddlery in Tollard Rising, whilst I returned to the house and my favourite domain: the room in the basement I called my laboratory. A whole wing of the basement had fallen into redundancy since Jos's father's day, on account of the reduction in the size of the household. There had once been a steward as well as a butler, for instance, each with his own pantry. I had set up my laboratory in one of the rooms vacated as a result of the mergence of the two offices. It was a plain but airy chamber, where I could work undisturbed amidst my ever-expanding stock of paper, chemicals and printing equipment. I kept the room locked when I was not there to prevent the servants upsetting an experiment. I confess I also wanted them to know as little as possible of what I was doing. I harboured the fear that Jos's disapproval would be aroused more by the success of my work than by the work itself. It had often given him pleasure to let me think myself free, before twitching on the rein to remind me that he would never let go.

But Jos had been in London for months and given no hint that he meant to return before the autumn. I had attempted to obtain a picture of his brother and sister-in-law during their impromptu visit partly as an act of defiance, in the hope that I might one day flourish it beneath Jos's contemptuous nose. It was perhaps as well that the results had been so disappointing, for Barrington left with only my discomfiture to mention, something Jos would have relished. Thanks to my recent discoveries involving gallic acid, however, it seemed that I had my trophy without the hazard. I was triumphant and could not resist displaying my triumph to Mr Byfield, the one man who might appreciate it in all its aspects, even if he was too delicate to reveal as much.

I had left the reverted portrait of Barrington and Susannah in its printing frame, one of a dozen or so Eames had constructed for me, with many a puzzled scratch of his aged head. It was standing on the bench that ran the length of the wall facing the door, immediately beneath the high window that was the only source of natural light in the room. I closed the door behind me and walked across to examine it, marvelling at the clarity of the image. Then I moved further along the bench, drew out a stool from beneath it and sat down. I opened a drawer, took out my notebook, pen and ink, and began the painstaking but deeply satisfying process of recording my latest findings.

Time passed as I sat there, engrossed in the day-by-day chronicle of my discoveries. Two hours or more elapsed. The light changed. Late afternoon became early evening. I felt as peaceful as I was elated, possessed by a strange joyous calm.

Then there came a knock at the door. It did not open. The servants had been instructed always to wait for a response. I closed the notebook, walked across to the door and pulled it open. One of the maids, Jane, was standing outside with Mr Byfield. I thanked her and invited Mr Byfield in. He strode directly to the printing frame and looked at the picture.

'It's utterly astonishing,' he said after a moment. 'Such a transformation!'

'I will admit to you, Mr Byfield, that with this one picture I have surpassed my highest hopes for the success of heliogenesis.'

'I do not wonder at it. And the magical ingredient is . . . gallic acid?'

'It is.'

'A substance quite unknown to me, I confess.'

'It occurs naturally, in oak-gall. Sir Humphry Davy wrote up his method for its extraction in the very same volume of the *Journals of the Royal Institution* that contained his essay on the late Mr Wedgwood's camera obscura experiments fifteen years ago, a volume which naturally I have pored over many a time. Without it, I doubt I would have thought of including gallic acid in my trials. I thank the good Lord, as well as Sir Humphry, that I did, because it may yet bestow further rewards upon us. Where gallic acid can restore it can also accelerate. Do you not see, Mr Byfield? It is logical to suppose that if I treat my camera paper with a solution of the acid *before* attempting to obtain a picture, the acid's reaction with the nitrate of silver in which I already wash the paper will increase the receptiveness of the surface many times over. Moving objects will be within my compass. Bright sunlight will no longer be essential. A bird in flight; the sky at night; a candle burning in a darkened room: there is no limit to what might be achieved.'

'Are such things really possible?'

'I believe they are.'

'Then coincidence has proved itself a blessed ally.' He turned from the picture and smiled at me. 'Yet again.'

'You have some other fortuitous event in mind?'

'I do. Can you not guess to what I refer?'

'No.'

'Why, the happy chance of my meeting you, Mrs Esguard. Believe me when I say that I count that one of the greatest blessings ever bestowed upon me.'

I blushed and looked away. 'For shame, Mr Byfield.'

'There is no shame in this, Marian.' He grasped my hand and held it to his chest. I stared at him, amazed, but in no way affronted. He had only said what I had often thought myself – and prayed he might also think. 'You feel it, too, do you not?'

'I cannot deny it.'

'Some would call the sentiment improper.'

'So, no doubt, would I . . . if I did not share it.'

'I hoped you did.' He raised my hand gently to his lips and kissed the knuckles. 'And feared it also.'

'What are we to do, Lawrence?'

'I—'

The door flew open behind us, crashing against the edge of the nearest table like a thunderclap. I whirled round, to be met by a sight that froze my thoughts as well

163

as my limbs. A man dressed in dusty riding clothes was standing in the doorway, glaring at us. He was tall and broad-shouldered, with an unruly mane of greying hair, a crooked nose, hollow cheeks and deep-shadowed eyes. It was the face of one who at thirty had been handsome and well aware of it, but who at forty wore with scorn the visible ravages of the life he had chosen to lead. It was the face of my husband, Joslyn Esguard.

'You look uncommonly displeased to see me, Marian,' he said, striding into the room, the leather of his riding boots creaking audibly. 'You, too, Lawrence.' As he stepped between us, I realized to my dismay that Mr Byfield was still holding my hand. I pulled it away, conscious of Jos watching me and studying my expression as I did so. But I could not bring myself to return his gaze, aware though I was that a wholly innocent wife should never flinch from looking her husband in the eye. 'Can it be that my arrival is . . . untimely?'

'Not at all,' said Mr Byfield.

'You think it the reverse, then? Timely in the extreme? Well, perhaps you are right. Perhaps I have returned not a moment too soon.'

'What can you mean, Jos?' I asked, nerving myself at last to look at him. 'Mr Byfield and I—'

'Must say goodbye,' Jos interrupted, his voice rising. 'For I am master here. And I have no intention of playing the cuckold. You, sir.' He turned to Mr Byfield. 'Oblige me by leaving my house this instant. And quitting Legion Cottage tomorrow.'

'You cannot be serious.'

'Never more so.'

'You are labouring under some gross misapprehension.'

'You deny seeking to engage my wife's affections?'

'I most certainly do.'

'Then I will make you an offer, sir. I will call at Legion Cottage at noon tomorrow. If you are still there, we will discuss how you may give me satisfaction in this matter.'

'Good God, Jos, do you know what you're saying?'

'As clearly as I know what you and my wife were about when I opened that door. And what it would have led to had I not.'

'Jos—'

'*Be silent, madam,*' he roared at me. 'Now, sir, will you leave of your own free will? Or shall I be forced to have you thrown down the steps by the servants? For myself, I'd prefer the latter. But never let it be said that I deny any man the opportunity of a dignified withdrawal.'

Mr Byfield looked at me uncertainly, as if for guidance. I shook my head, urging him to comply, begging him with the force of my gaze to leave before a bad situation grew infinitely worse.

'Well, Byfield, what's it to be?'

'It *is* your house, Esguard, as you say, and if you insist, then naturally I shall leave.'

'I do insist.'

'And Legion Cottage is undeniably in your gift. I would appear to have little choice but to accede to your intemperate demands. As to your aspersions upon Mrs Esguard's—'

'Leave me to deal with my wife as I see fit, sir. She is none of your concern.'

'But she is, sir.' Mr Byfield lowered his voice and fixed Jos with his gaze. 'I shall not depart from this neighbourhood whilst I have the slightest doubt as to her well-being.'

'Then you'll suffer the consequences.'

'So be it.' The two of them stared at each other,

breathing hard. Then Mr Byfield turned to me and nodded. 'Your servant, ma'am.' So saying, he strode to the doorway and stepped out of the room.

Jos followed him, bellowing down the passage for attention. As he did so, Mr Byfield glanced back at me over his shoulder. His look was one of helpless rage and longing. He must have seen the same look on my face. I raised my hand in the faintest and fondest of farewells and there was an answering flicker of his gaze. Then he moved out of sight.

'Show Mr Byfield out, girl,' Jos snapped at Jane as she came scampering up. 'Then return here.'

'Yes, sir,' came the breathless reply.

As Jane made off after Mr Byfield, Jos turned and ambled back to where I was standing by the bench. He smiled with mock amiability and glanced round at the printing frame, the camera on its pedestal, the stacks of paper, the phalanxes of chemical bottles. He took it all in, nodding slowly, his lip curling in scorn. Then he said, 'What have you been about, Marian? What is all . . . this?'

'Some amateur chemistry. Nothing more.'

'I would call this . . .' He pointed to the picture of Barrington and Susannah. 'Rather more than chemistry.'

'It is nothing that need concern you.'

'No?'

'Some . . . inconsequential experiments. That is all.'

'Barrington wrote to me, describing your "inconsequential experiments" as best he was able. I didn't care for the sound of them.' He peered closer. 'I care even less for the look of them. A hundred years ago, I warrant they'd have burned you as a witch.'

'Perhaps so.'

166

'You have been a poor kind of wife to me, Marian. You defy me in everything.'

'I cannot imagine what you mean.'

'Oh, I think you can.' There was a tap at the door. It was Jane. Jos looked round at her. 'What is it, girl?'

'Mr Byfield has . . . left, sir.'

'Good. You may go now. Close the door behind you. We shall not wish to be disturbed.'

'Yes, sir. Cook wonders if—'

'*Go, damn you.*' And go she did, in a fluster of meek obedience.

'There is no need to—'

He punched me in the midriff with a sudden savage swing of his fist. I groaned and fell forward, quite winded for the moment, then leaned slowly against the bench. 'I have been negligent in my management of you, Marian,' he rasped. 'But be assured I shall mend my ways. And yours with them. You have the key to this room, I'm told. Where is it?'

'The . . . the drawer . . . there.' Nausea had swept over me. I signalled desperately along the bench.

'Thank you.' He fetched the key. 'No doubt you can guess why I did not strike you in the face, as I was tempted to. A visible bruise might provoke Byfield into challenging me. And I do not wish to kill him, though you may be sure I will if I have to.' He walked to the door and locked it, then slipped the key into his pocket and turned to look at me. 'I heard no crack. I think you have escaped without a broken rib.' He stepped closer. 'On this occasion.'

'Jos . . . For pity's . . .'

'Turn round.'

'What?'

'You heard me. Turn round.'

'Why?'

'Obey me without question.' He grabbed me by the jaw, crushing my cheeks against my teeth, and stared at me, his eyes daggering into mine. 'Or it will be the worse for you. Now.' He released me. 'Turn round.'

Trembling, and wincing from the blow to my midriff, I turned and faced the bench.

'I shall be paying you close attention while I'm here, Marian. And when I return to London you will be accompanying me. There will be an end of "amateur chemistry" and of all the latitude I have mistakenly allowed you. It is time, I think, to remind you . . .' His arms suddenly encircled me. He grasped my breasts in his hands and squeezed them painfully. I felt his breath on the back of my neck. 'Of your obligations to me as my wife.'

'Jos. Stop this. Please.'

He let go and stepped back. 'Bend over, madam. *If you please.*'

'Not here. Not like this.'

'Do as I say or there will be worse than a bruise to remember this day by. Bend over.'

I did as I'd been told, leaning forward over the bench until my forehead touched its rough wooden surface, my hands supporting me on either side. As Jos hoisted up my dress and shift, I prayed he would stop. But I knew with a certainty born of our long and loveless acquaintance that he would not.

'If you will play the whore, madam, you must expect to be served as such.'

I heard him fumble with his clothing. In that moment I wanted only to run and hide, to flee far and for ever from this brutish man who neither loved me nor understood me, and evidently did not want to. What he meant

168

to do was not driven by lust, nor even by loathing. It was his reassertion of his ownership of me. The knowledge of that would make the experience of it even worse. I braced myself, clenching my teeth as he grasped my hips and raised me to meet his thrust. I clamped my eyes shut, trying to remember my walk back across the park from Charlton Down a few short hours before, struggling to plant a picture of it in my mind as a defence against—

I was running fast across the field, back towards the car, dusk turning the sheep to spectral blurs around me. There was the fence ahead, only the posts visible in the twilight. If I looked back now I wouldn't see the chimneys of Gaunt's Chase standing stark and black against the deepening grey of the sky. The house had vanished. But the things done in it remained. I remembered them and they remembered me.

I scrambled through the fence, cutting my hands on the barbs and tearing a hole in my trousers. Only when I was inside the car, encased in twentieth-century steel and man-made fibre, did I feel safe. I turned the radio on and tuned in to Radio One, loud and blaring and aggressively modern. If I could somehow jam the signal, maybe it would stop. Maybe it would just go away. I felt so drained by it, so bewildered and yet so weary. I reclined the seat and lay back, letting the beat of the music dull my senses. I closed my eyes, praying I'd see nothing but the velvety blackness of sleep. And my prayer was answered.

But when I woke, suddenly, to complete alertness, I wasn't in the car. I was in the bedroom at Gaunt's Chase, morning sunlight stretching across the coverlet towards me. Memories of the night before pounced and sank in their claws. I flinched and closed my eyes, then opened them again and turned my head. Jos lay on his back beside me, snoring heavily. The smell of him – stale brandy, cigar smoke and horseflesh – hit me like a blow to the face. I felt sick and the sensation instantly sharpened the recollections of what he'd done to me. I had been sick before he'd finished with me. I could still taste it in my mouth. I hated him more than I thought it possible for one human to hate another. If a knife had lain on the table beside me, I would have taken it and cut his throat and watched the blood spurt out of him with pleasure.

But there was no knife. And there was nothing to be done but deal with the world as Jos had remade it for me. I slid out of the bed, washed myself as best I could from the ewer and dressed hurriedly, watching him all the time for fear he might wake. But he slept on, as if with an untroubled conscience.

I found his waistcoat, stained with port, where he'd flung it down. I took the key to the laboratory from the pocket he'd left it in and slipped out of the room, opening and closing the door with exaggerated care. Then I hastened down to the basement, using the back stairs. I was relieved to meet none of the servants on the way. I did not want to see anyone. Nor did I want anyone to see me. How much they knew or had guessed I did not care to contemplate. But I had to see my laboratory. I had to be sure it was as bad as I remembered.

It was, if anything, worse. There wasn't an unbroken chemical bottle to be found. The cameras were smashed beyond repair. The pedestals and printing frames were so much matchwood. My work lay in ruins. I gathered up a few scattered heliogenic pictures, put them back in their portfolio and wondered how best to keep them safe.

In the end, I decided to put them at the back of a cupboard beneath the bench. The laboratory was probably the last place Jos would look, if look he did, now that he had done his best to lay it waste. Then I went back out, fastened the lock, placed the key beneath the door and flicked it into the room. I heard it slide some distance across the floor and contented myself with the thought that Jos would have to use a battering ram next time he wanted to enter. As for the key, he would search me in vain for it. I would suggest he had simply mislaid it, a possibility he would be poorly placed to deny.

I met Briggs on my way out of the house and bade him as calm a good morning as I could summon. Then I struck out across the park, trying to draw some comfort from the sweet summer air. But there was no comfort to be had that day, only the bleak satisfaction that is to be derived from not adding to a pile of sorrows.

Legion Cottage lay in a dale beyond the beech hanger, a plain but homely little house where I had often, of late, dreamed of leading a happier and simpler existence than the one fate had allotted me. I hesitated before knocking at the door and did not, in the event, need to screw up the courage to do so, because Mr Byfield opened it of his own accord. He looked haggard and hollow-eyed and I prayed my face did not reveal my thoughts as clearly as his did.

'I saw you approaching,' he said. 'Will you come in?'

'Thank you,' I said, stepping into the hall. 'I'm sorry . . . to call so early.'

'Do not be. I am relieved to see you. It is a weight lifted from my mind. You are . . . well?'

'I am.'

'I own I was fearful what Jos might do when I left.'

'He did nothing. He only said that he would act if you were not gone by noon today.'

'How can I go? Do you not understand, Marian? I love you.'

'If you do, then you *must* go. If you stay, Jos will kill you.'

Mr Byfield almost smiled at that. 'He may try.'

'I know him, Lawrence. All too well. He would find a way. And it would not necessarily be gentlemanly. He puts on honour and takes it off like a glove, according to the weather.'

'I'm not afraid of him, whatever the weather.'

'Then I must do your fearing for you. Do as he told you. Leave this place.'

He took my hand and held it to his chest. 'Do you want me to leave?'

I nodded. 'Yes. Most certainly.'

'Come with me, Marian. We could go abroad, beyond scandal's reach as well as Jos's.' He bent towards me, intending, I think, to kiss me. But I pulled away. 'I will not abandon you to such a man, wife though you are to him, and friend though he is – or was – to me.'

'You must.'

'It cannot be endured.'

'Yet it cannot be cured. I *am* his wife.'

'You should not be. He does not deserve someone as fine as you.'

'But life does not always treat us as we deserve. You must go and I must stay. That is the way of it.'

'Is there no hope for us, Marian?'

'There is always hope.'

'May I write to you?'

'Under no circumstances. It is the very thing Jos will be on the watch for.'

'Then *you* must write to *me*. They will hold post for me at my club in London – Boodle's, in St James's Street. Should your existence here become unbearable, you can call upon me to do as much to aid you as you require. As much, indeed, as you will allow. Say you will do so if he drives you too hard and I will go. Not gladly, it is true. Very far from that. But I *will* go.'

'Very well. You have my word. And my thanks. To know there is someone I can turn to at direst need . . .'

'The offer is not lightly made.'

'Nor would it be lightly taken up, I assure you.'

'I could wish that it would be. But it is not in your character to yield easily. You should know, however, that it is not in mine either.'

I looked at him for several silent seconds, and he looked at me. Our understanding was sealed in that interval, beyond the reach of words.

'I must go, Mr Byfield.'

'And so, it seems, must I, Mrs Esguard.'

'Goodbye, sir.'

He reached out and laid the backs of his fingers gently against my cheek in as much of a farewell caress as he thought I was likely to permit. 'Until we meet again,' he murmured. Then his hand fell away and I opened the door and walked out into the fragrant, heedless morning.

There was no need to hurry back to Gaunt's Chase. Jos would sleep a while yet. It would probably be a good deal later than noon when he stormed into Legion Cottage – and found it empty. I made my melancholy way up to the summit of Charlton Down and gazed out at the unconsoling beauties of the Nadder valley, where the sunlight picked out the course of the river like some shimmering serpent coiled amidst the rolling woodland and the church steeples and the golden swathes of ripening wheat. I sat down and closed my eyes, and let the breeze stirring my hair be my only reminder of where I was and whither I was bound to return. I lay back on the turf, listening to a skylark chirring somewhere above me. On it went, singing for the simple joy of its precious life. On and blithely on.

Then it stopped, as suddenly and completely as if a hand had closed round its throat. The wind stopped, too. Its susurrant passage through the grass ceased in the same instant. There was a moment of utter silence. Then I opened my eyes.

And I could see the sky before me through the windscreen of the car. I was shut away from birdsong and breeze. It was morning. I'd slept there through the night, as the stiffness of my limbs and the low whisper of music from the radio confirmed. It had been on so long the battery must have run down. I sat up, shivering in the chill. Then I realized I was no longer afraid. I'd been through the worst of it. This was the other side.

I tried to start the car, but the engine couldn't raise more than a pitiful moan. I began looking for my mobile phone, then remembered I'd left it at home. Conrad would be beside himself with worry. The police might be looking for me by now. Everyone was going to be very angry when I explained that I'd driven to Dorset on a whim and spent the night in the car for no halfway credible reason. Draining the battery wasn't going to sound very clever either. In fact, my behaviour was going to seem at best irrational, at worst . . .

But I couldn't just stay there, worrying about the recriminations that were waiting for me. I got out, flagged down the first car that came along and begged a lift into Shaftesbury. I booked into a hotel there and phoned Conrad, cobbling together a story that jet lag had caught up with me after I'd driven into the countryside to blow away the cobwebs. He was too glad to hear from me to subject my account to much analysis. The police hadn't wanted to know, apparently. They'd annoyed him by suggesting I might have left him. He was going to be angry with me later. I could sense it. But for the moment he was just grateful I was all right. Pressure of work meant he couldn't come and fetch me, but he promised to contact a local garage and phone me back. By the time he did, I'd had a bath and some breakfast and was feeling more like my normal self. But it was only an act. Part of me was sure of that and still is. Marian and I are woven together. Look at me closely and all you see is a single thread. Step back and you see the pattern she and I can only glimpse. I don't know what it is. I don't know what it means. But it's there.

The garage picked the car up for me and delivered it to the hotel, complete with new battery, later that morning. I drove straight back to London, keeping my eyes on the road and my mind fixed on Conrad and our life in the here and now. It worked. Marian stayed out of sight. She followed me, of course, but at a safe distance. It was up to me whether I closed the gap between us. The when and the how were still in my control. But I couldn't escape her. And nor, I suppose, could she escape me.

I didn't have to wait at home long before Conrad arrived. True to form, he'd stopped being relieved and started getting resentful. What the hell did I think I was playing at? Did I have any idea what kind of a night I'd put him through? Et cetera, et cetera. I had to do a lot of grovelling. I didn't mind. In fact, it was good for me. It meant I didn't have to think about what had really happened. The effort I had to put into selling Conrad my cover story almost convinced me it was true. We went out to one of his favourite restaurants for a smoothing of ruffled feathers. We could have been back in Hawaii, so remote and unlikely did my experiences in Dorset seem.

But it was only the fleeting effect of wine and good food and the company of a husband who firmly believed I was nobody but Eris Moberly. In the morning, when Conrad went to work and I was alone again, the memories returned. And with them the recollection of Quisden-Neve's stark ultimatum. Give up the only tangible evidence I had of Marian's achievements or have all the forces tugging at my life implode. What was I supposed to do?

I went down to the bank and took the box out of the safe deposit. I sat in Green Park, just staring at it, trying to think of some way out of the dilemma. It can't all be a delusion, can it, Daphne? That's the point. Not when creeps like Quisden-Neve try to blackmail me into handing over a box of old negatives. I can't invent a fantasy that just happens to be true. I can't imagine Marian Esguard if she really existed. I can only . . . meet her. I can only . . . find herself inside me.

That's when I decided what to do. Let go of her. The negatives were what had started it all. Without them I might be released. If I gave them up, maybe she'd give me up. Maybe Quisden-Neve was doing me a favour. Locking them in a bank vault wasn't enough. They had to be out of my reach. And Quisden-Neve would make sure they were.

I drank most of a bottle of wine with a frugal lunch at the Park Lane Hotel, then walked down to Richoux for our appointment. He didn't look in the least surprised to see me, damn him. He looked, in fact, like a man

176

utterly confident in his own tactics. As he had a right to be, I suppose.

'Well, well, well,' he said, picking his way through the box. 'These really are quite extraordinary. There's barely any degradation. Thank you, Mrs Moberly. I'm most grateful.'

'So am I,' I murmured in reply. And that did surprise him.

'I beg your pardon?'

'You're welcome to them. And everything that goes with them.'

'What might that be?'

'You have no idea, do you? Well, that's probably just as well. Have them with my compliments. I reckon I'm better off without them.'

He looked puzzled. But his pleasure at a scam well worked soon blotted out anything else. He was like a schoolboy who'd stolen a stamp collection. Suddenly he wanted to be alone, to ogle his haul. So I left him to it.

'I have your word I'll hear no more of this?' was my parting shot.

'You do, Mrs Moberly. You have, indeed, my cast-iron copper-bottomed guarantee.'

Quisden-Neve's guarantee wasn't worth much. But it's held so far. Nothing's happened since. It's only a week or so, of course. There's no way to tell if it's permanent. Sometimes I don't want it to be. At other times I dread the very thought of another fugue. It's as if, any second, a chasm could open beneath my feet and I'd fall and fall and never stop falling. I keep expecting it to happen, but it doesn't. Am I free of her, Daphne? Or just fooling myself? And why did she ever get a hold on me in the first place? If you can't tell me and make me believe it, I can't be sure she won't reclaim me.

That's the worst of it. If you can't convince me – absolutely and completely – I'll go on waiting. For the first crack to appear in the ground. For the past to swallow me. For the person I am to become the person I was.

Chapter Seven

I'd listened to the tape three times by dawn. I'd listened long and hard enough to feel I was almost living Eris's experiences with her, both as Eris and as Marian. I was sure now it was all true. Daphne could theorize about fugal delusion as often and expertly as she liked. It wouldn't make any difference to me. This had to be the real thing. Possession, reincarnation, or some other strange overlap between two women's lives. Marian Esguard had lived. And part of her lived still in Eris Moberly. That was why Eris was in danger *and* why she'd gone missing. That was why she needed my help so desperately. Nobody else, not even her psychotherapist, seemed able to understand that. But I did. What's more, I had a way to help her at long last. I had the lies and evasions of Montagu Quisden-Neve to ram down his Pomerol-rinsed throat.

Daphne would have to wait for the tape. She'd foreseen the possibility clearly enough. I reckoned she'd only made me promise to return it as a means of covering her back. She wanted me to confront Quisden-Neve – *and* Niall Esguard. And she wanted to be able to deny it. So

I decided to do her the favour she'd lacked either the nerve or the honesty to ask me. By nine o'clock, the time I was supposed to be reporting to her practice in Harley Street, tape in hand, I was in Bath, sitting in my car a few doors up from Bibliomaufry, waiting for the proprietor to put in an appearance. Nine thirty was opening time, according to the sign in the window, but I didn't take Quisden-Neve for the punctual type. He could easily be late. Still, when he did arrive, I'd be waiting. And I'd be angry. The longer I waited, in fact, the angrier I was going to be. Part of me enjoyed the feeling as it grew inside me. There was some grim relish to be had in knowing I'd been deceived, because deception assumed a motive. And a motive, whatever it was, meant Eris wasn't mad. She needed my help, not my doubt and disappointment. She needed me to trust my instincts as well as my memories. And I was glad to do just that. I was actually happy to do it, happier than I'd been for a single moment since I'd waved to her across the Ringstrasse in Vienna – and seen her face for the last time.

A taxi overtook me and slowed to a halt outside Bibliomaufry. Sudden concentration snatched me back from my reverie. I leaned forward and peered at the taxi's rear window, but I couldn't see a passenger. Then the driver tooted his horn. I glanced across the road to see if he was picking up somebody from the other side, but nobody was waiting and nobody appeared. Then, to my horror, the door of Bibliomaufry opened and Quisden-Neve bustled out, carrying a raincoat and a Gladstone bag. I swore and made to get out of the car, but a horn blared as a lorry sped past, and I recoiled, swearing again when I saw Quisden-Neve was already clambering into the cab. It was too late to do anything but follow. The old devil had been too clever for me.

The taxi headed south down Walcot Street to Pulteney Bridge and on past the Abbey. It looked as if the railway station was our destination, but if Quisden-Neve knew I was following him, which I suspected he did, he had to be aware his ploy wasn't going to work. He just didn't have a big enough lead to shake me off.

The station it was. I hung back as the taxi pulled up outside. Quisden-Neve climbed out, paid the man off and rushed into the booking office, glancing at his watch as he went. I moved in behind the taxi and reversed into a parking bay, gaining a clear view through the station doorway as I did so. For a tubby man, Quisden-Neve moved fast. Already he was halfway up the stairs to the platform. I jumped out and followed.

There was a train standing in the station. Doors were slamming and whistles shrilling as I reached the top of the stairs. And there was Quisden-Neve's tweed-covered backside plunging into a carriage ahead of me. I raced across the platform, wrenched open the nearest door and flung myself in. The next second we were moving.

The train was crowded. Half the passengers were still taking their seats and stowing their luggage. It took several minutes to get as far as the carriage I reckoned Quisden-Neve had entered, and there was no sign of him. Maybe he'd headed further down the train. I struggled on through the ruck.

Then I saw the Gladstone bag and the raincoat, dumped in a seat as some kind of claim. 'Excuse me,' I said to the woman sitting between them and the window. 'These look like they belong to a friend of mine. We seem to have missed each other. Perhaps you saw him get on at Bath. Middle-aged. Grey hair. Lots of tweed.'

'Yes. He was here. But only for a second. He went that way.' She pointed towards the front of the train. 'To the buffet, I expect.'

'Right. Thanks. By the way, I know this'll sound stupid, but where are we going?'

'London,' she replied, looking as if it did indeed sound stupid.

'Of course. And the next stop?'

'Chippenham. In about five minutes.'

'Thanks a lot.'

I pressed on, the going getting easier as people settled in their seats. But Quisden-Neve remained elusive. I reached the buffet and he wasn't there. I checked the first-class carriages beyond, drew another blank and turned back. There were the loos to be checked as well, of course, but I couldn't hang around outside every engaged one. Besides, he might be planning to slip off at Chippenham. We'd be there any minute. I heard the announcement as the thought entered my mind. 'This train will shortly be arriving at Chippenham.' We began to slow. The housebacks of the town were already visible through the window. 'Chippenham will be the next station stop.' I glanced into the first unengaged loo I came to. It was empty. The loo in the vestibule of the adjoining carriage was also unengaged. I crossed to it and pushed at the door, but it only opened halfway. There was some kind of obstruction behind it. I pushed harder and leaned round to see . . .

He was there, in front of me, his tweedy bulk swaying crazily in my face. I started back and gasped, colliding with a man behind me. The tilt of the train swung the door open. I gaped, and sensed the other man gaping, at the reflection in the mirror of Quisden-Neve, hanging like some huge swollen doll from the coat hook on the loo wall: head lolling, face purple. Something – some ligature of wire or rope – held him by the throat and was looped round the hook.

'Help me get him down,' I cried, gesturing to my dumbstruck companion. 'He might still be alive.'

'Bloody hell,' was the only answer I got. We were pulling into the station now. 'I'll call the guard.'

Ignoring him, I stepped into the loo, grasped Quisden-Neve by the shoulders and tried to heave him off the hook, but his weight was too much for me. It felt like dead weight, too. My mind was a chaos of wrestling thoughts. What had happened? Had he killed himself? Or been strangled, then hung on the hook like some carcass in an abattoir? It would have taken a stronger man than me to do it. And why in God's—?

The ligature snapped as the train came to a halt, the strain finally proving too much for it. Quisden-Neve hit me like a falling sandbag, jamming me against the basin, his sightless eyes staring into mine. Then he slid onto the floor and flopped out into the vestibule just as the train door opened. I heard a woman scream. Then another. I couldn't blame them. I felt like screaming myself.

'OK, people,' said the guard, bustling up from the carriage behind me. 'Stand back.' He stooped over Quisden-Neve and felt beneath his ear for a pulse. Then he glanced up at me. 'You the gentleman who found him?' I nodded. The guard rolled his eyes sadly. 'They always think of new ways to top themselves.' He looked out at the people on the platform. 'There's going to be quite a delay, ladies and gents. Why don't you go and sit down?'

They began slowly to disperse, as did the crowd that had formed in the vestibule, muttering to each other as they went. 'He is . . . dead, isn't he?' I asked numbly.

'Looks that way to me, sir. But if you want to try mouth-to-mouth . . .' He ventured a smile. 'I never took the lessons myself.'

'Nor me.' I turned and looked out through the window. God, what was going on? Quisden-Neve was no candidate for suicide. But if he hadn't killed himself . . .

My eyes suddenly focused on the car park beyond the platform. A man in a leather jacket and jeans was standing beside a car near the fence closest to the station. It was an old red Porsche. And the man was Niall Esguard. As I watched, he opened the door, tossed what looked like a Gladstone bag into the back, then climbed in and began to reverse out of the parking space.

'Hold on, sir,' said the guard as I plunged past him. 'The police will be wanting a statement and all sorts.'

'I'll be back in a minute,' I shouted to him as I jumped down onto the platform. Then I made for the footbridge. The Porsche was already cruising out of the car park. Pursuit was pointless. But so was getting trammelled in the bureaucratic aftermath of Quisden-Neve's death. A post-mortem would probably show what I already knew: he'd been murdered. And I knew who the murderer was. Even though I couldn't prove it. Or suggest a motive. To do that, I had to get back to Bath. Without delay.

I headed for the station exit and climbed into a taxi, reasoning things out as I went. Quisden-Neve must have been expecting to meet Niall on the train, otherwise he wouldn't have left his seat so quickly. For his part, Niall must have planned to get off the train at Chippenham, because he'd left his car there, so he'd clearly set Quisden-Neve up from the start. They'd been in this together. But Quisden-Neve had grown too demanding – or he'd had his conscience pricked by my

184

visit. Either way, he'd suddenly become expendable.

'Where do you want to go, sir?' asked the taxi driver.

'Bath Spa railway station.'

'Haven't you just come from there? I thought that train—'

'Step on it, will you? I'm late.'

'Oh, overshoot job, was it?' He started the engine and pulled out of the rank. 'Fall asleep?'

'You could say that.' I glanced up at the reflection of myself in the rear-view mirror. 'But I'm awake now. Well and truly.'

Going back to Bibliomaufry was neither logical nor sensible. If there was anything to be found there to my advantage, Niall was going to have removed it by the time I arrived. The most I could hope to accomplish was to catch him in the act, and I had the memory of Quisden-Neve's bloated, lifeless face fixed starkly enough in my mind to suggest how dangerous that might be. Besides, if I was seen breaking in, and the police matched my description with that of the vanishing witness at Chippenham, I could be storing up enough trouble for myself to spare Niall the effort of lifting a finger against me.

In the event, I didn't need to break in. The back door, accessible across an overgrown patch of garden, was standing ajar, consistent with Niall's having taken Quisden-Neve's keys from his pocket and been and gone already by the most discreet route. The state of the first-floor office told the same story. Several drawers were sagging open and it looked as if Niall had been through the filing cabinet as well. The drawer where Quisden-Neve had stored the letters from Marian to her father and from Joslyn Esguard to Sir John Conroy held only empty pockets. And the negatives? A small safe stood in one corner. It, too, was open and empty. Niall had been swift and thorough. Whatever I might have found, he'd found first.

I picked up the telephone and dialled 1471. The computerized voice gave me a Bath number as that of Quisden-Neve's last caller, at a quarter to nine that morning. I pressed 3, listened to it ring, then heard an answering machine cut in. 'I can't take your call right now. If you—' It was Niall Esguard. As I suppose I'd known it would be.

Then I noticed the desk diary lying beside the telephone. I leafed through it to today's date, wondering if there'd be any appointment recorded. Somehow I didn't think so. But I was wrong. One o'clock was circled, followed by the name and address of an Italian restaurant in Covent Garden. And the name of somebody who wouldn't be meeting Montagu Quisden-Neve after all. Not that she'd be wanting for company. Nor for conversation. We were going to have a lot to talk about. Starting with why Quisden-Neve should even know her – let alone be having lunch with her.

Nicole looked almost as surprised to see me weaving towards her between the tables of Bertorelli's restaurant two and a half hours later as I'd felt on seeing her name in Quisden-Neve's diary. It didn't stop her looking good with it, though. She'd lost a little weight since I'd last seen her and gained a distinct touch of glamour. She had more of the fashion editor about her now than the news reporter. I'd been the one to end our affair. But she'd been the one to recover from it first. And she'd gone on recovering – ever since.

'Ian! This is a coincidence, I must—'

'It's no coincidence.' I sat down opposite her. 'You're waiting for Montagu Quisden-Neve, right?'

'Yes.' She smiled nervously. 'How did—?'

'He was found dead on the train up here from Bath this morning.'

'Dead?'

'Strangled. It could have been suicide. But I reckon they'll settle for murder in the end.'

'Wait a minute. I don't understand. You're telling me Quisden-Neve's been murdered?'

'That's what I'm telling you.'

'How do you know?'

'I was on the train. I saw him. I *found* him, as a matter of gruesome fact.'

'You *found* him?'

'I was looking for him.'

'Why? What have you to do with the man?'

'It's a long story. But tell me a shorter one, Nicole. What have *you* to do with him?'

'What business is that of yours?'

'I don't know. That's why I'm asking.'

'Well, ask nicely, then. I don't see why—' She broke off as a waiter hove alongside. She ordered a second gin and tonic. I ordered a double. The interruption imposed a fleeting calm between us that almost amounted to a truce. 'Keep your voice down, Ian, please. You rush in here, shouting about a murder on a train. What are people going to think?'

'I don't care. Just tell me about Quisden-Neve.'

'There's nothing to tell. I've never met him. And it seems now I never will.'

'Why were you going to have lunch with him?'

'I'm a journalist. I have lunch with all kinds of people. I even used to have lunch with you.'

'Why Quisden-Neve?'

'I was following up a lead.'

'What about?'

'I don't have to answer your questions. Certainly not when you won't answer mine.'

'Would it help if you owed me a favour?'

'It might. But I don't.'

'You do, actually.' I showed her the page I'd torn from Quisden-Neve's diary. 'When the police realize they're dealing with a murder, this sort of titbit could get you a lot of unwelcome attention. I thought you might prefer to forget all about your appointment with him in the circumstances. Now you can.'

She looked at me long and hard, then took the page from my hand. 'He was definitely murdered?'

'No question.'

'Why?'

'No idea. What about you? This lead, perhaps?'

'Maybe.' She gave an evasive little moue. 'If he really had something.'

'Something about what?'

'You're better off not knowing.' She set light to the diary page with a match from the complimentary box on the table and let it burn out in the ashtray. 'Sounds like it could be getting serious.'

'You could never be frightened off a story, Nicole.'

'I'm older and wiser.' The gins arrived. She took a sip. 'Unlike you.'

'Says who?'

'Faith. She phoned a couple of months ago. Accused me of starting it up with you again. Took a lot of dissuading. I gathered you'd left her.'

'You gathered right.'

'Who for?'

'You don't know her.'

'Must be somebody pretty special, that's all I can say. I never coaxed so much commitment out of you.'

'Life turned sour on us, Nicole. You know that.'

'Didn't it just? Well, it still doesn't seem to be doing you many favours, Ian. I've seen you look better. Actually, I can't remember seeing you look worse. Not even after the accident.'

'Tell me about Quisden-Neve.'

'No. It worries me, you knowing him. It makes me feel uncomfortable.'

'Please, Nicole. I'm begging you.'

'My God.' She looked at me with a shocked expression. 'You really are desperate.'

'Oh yes. More desperate than I've ever been.'

'All right, then. As long as it goes no further.'

'You have my word.'

'And I know what that's worth, don't I?' She held up her hand to forestall my protest. 'OK. It's no big deal. Well, maybe it is, if getting yourself murdered is anything to go by. Quisden-Neve phoned me a few days ago. He'd read a piece I'd written for one of the Sundays about Nymanex. Heard of it? Read it, maybe?'

'No. On both counts.'

'Nymanex is a sky-rocket financial services company. Come from nothing. Going as high as the market will let it. Flash Docklands HQ. Even flashier profits. A bit iffy round the edges. No-one's quite sure how they started. Nor how close to the wind they're sailing. There's a lot of money sloshing around. But some of it – whisper it if you dare – could be anonymous clients' laundry.'

'They're crooked?'

'Or their rivals are jealous. Or both. Who knows? Well, Quisden-Neve claimed to. Hence lunch. He said

he had information about the early life, and by implication criminal career, of Nymanex's chairman. Since
Conrad Nyman's every bit as mysterious as the company
he founded, I thought I'd better—'

'What did you say his name was?'

'Nyman. Heard of him? Well, I can't say I'm—'

'His *first* name.'

'Conrad.' She stared at me. 'What about it?'

I'd always associated Docklands with photographic
assignments: the running battle between Rupert
Murdoch and the print unions at Wapping; the phallus
of the Canary Wharf tower rising from the wastes of the
Isle of Dogs; river light falling on the prettified ware-
houses and the heron-like clusters of cranes and gantries.
It was strange to drive into it along West Ferry Road on
a bright spring afternoon with no camera bag in the car
beside me and no concern for weather or angle or point
of view. Being a photographer, which I'd once have said
was central to my personality, was falling away behind
me somewhere, in the past that Eris and Marian between
them had exiled me from.

Yet photography was part of what was happening to
me and part also of what had happened to them. The
mystery of what Marian Esguard had or hadn't accomplished back in 1817 was wrapped around the enigma of
Eris Moberly. It held the answer. I just wasn't looking
hard enough, or in the right place, to see it for what it
was. But I would in the end, I felt certain. Because it was
there. And it couldn't stay hidden for ever.

Nymanex Ltd occupied the top floor of one of
Canary Wharf's lesser summits, a gold-tinted steeple
of glass overlooking what had once been a basin of
West India Docks. The secrecy Nicole had described

was nowhere to be seen, but money was a different matter. Green-veined marble, swirl-knotted hardwoods and co-ordinated silks had been thrown about the place with profligate zeal. It seemed more like a luxury hotel than a working office.

I didn't blame the receptionist for looking at me doubtfully when I asked to see her ultimate supremo on an urgent personal matter. I could only hope the simple message I persuaded her to convey to Conrad Nyman's secretary would open as many doors as it needed to. 'Tell him it concerns Eris.' Was she his wife? Nicole hadn't known for certain if he was married or not, but she'd thought probably not. I couldn't risk assuming anything, except what was by now an article of faith for me. He was Eris's Conrad, in some way, shape or form. I wasn't reeling in a string of coincidences. There was a meaning and a connection between everything.

That much was swiftly confirmed. Eris's name acted as an open sesame. I was shown through to the secretarial suite. Nyman's personal assistant, Anunziata, who looked as if she could, and quite possibly did, model for *Vogue* in her spare time, explained that the great man was in a meeting he couldn't leave, but she *had* spoken to him and he'd be happy to see me if I could wait twenty minutes or so. Her air of breathless discretion suggested she knew who Eris was and why her boss would be anxious to discuss her with a stranger, but I knew better than to probe. It was Nyman or nobody.

I leafed through a glossy brochure about the way ahead in financial services – the Nymanex way, naturally – while I waited. There was no sparkle-toothed portrait of the chairman, which I thought unusual, but hardly suspicious. All in all, I didn't catch the slightest whiff of the shady dealings Nicole had hinted at. But I wasn't exactly an expert. And Anunziata's perfume was potent enough to blot out a midden-load of odours.

The meeting broke up on schedule in a march-past of suits. Anunziata went into Nyman's office to confer with him, then came out and said he was ready to see me. I walked into a room of empty pastel vistas, with high windows that opened on to a balcony, where Nyman was waiting to greet me against a backdrop of sunlit tower blocks camped along the curving shore of Limehouse Reach.

He was a strikingly handsome man, probably in his early forties, with blue eyes, grey-blond hair and rugged features, dressed more for the weekend than for the office, in blazer, open-neck shirt, cream trousers and soft leather loafers. He looked the outdoor type, a yachtsman perhaps, or a horseman, certainly not a City wheeler-dealer. He was sniffing the clear cool air like somebody ill at ease in a world of tinted glass and tubular steel. But there was a glint in his gaze as well, a hard steady set of caution about him. He was nobody's fool. And he was unlikely to suffer them gladly.

'Mr Jarrett.' He shook my hand firmly. 'I'm Conrad Nyman.'

'Good of you to see me.'

'I could hardly refuse, could I? Do you want to sit down, by the way?'

'No. Out here's fine. It's a wonderful view.'

'But you didn't talk your way in here to admire it.'

'I didn't talk my way in at all. I just . . . asked.'

'True enough. So ask some more.'

'Is Eris your wife, Mr Nyman?'

He smiled. 'No. I'm not married. Never have been.'

'Ever met a man called Montagu Quisden-Neve?'

'No.'

'Or heard of a woman called Marian Esguard?'

'I don't think so.'

'But you do know Eris. Eris Moberly, that is.'

'I do.'

'May I ask how?'

'No. But only because I think it's my turn now. How do *you* know her, Mr Jarrett?'

'I met her in Vienna in January. We . . . Well, we agreed to keep in touch back in England. But she vanished without trace.'

'January, you say? That's odd.'

'Why?'

'Because January's about when I stopped hearing from her. But go on. What brought you to me?'

'In Vienna, she called herself Marian Esguard. Back here, Eris Moberly. I traced her psychotherapist, who mentioned Eris had claimed to be married.'

'To me?'

'To somebody called Conrad. The connection's tenuous, I admit, but you're the first Conrad I've come across in my search. I know Eris had dealings with an antiquarian bookseller, Montagu Quisden-Neve, who subsequently offered to supply information about you to a journalist I happen to know, Nicole Heywood.'

'Ah, Ms Heywood. Author of a prickly little piece about my company. She's in this as well, is she?'

'I don't know what *this* is. I'm only interested in finding Eris Moberly. I came here on a hunch. To see what would happen if I dropped Eris's name into your pond. And what happened was that you bit.'

'Yes. So I did.' He smiled again and leaned back against the balcony railings. 'What do you do for a living, Mr Jarrett?'

'I'm a photographer.'

'Where's your camera?'

'I'm resting.'

'That's good. I hate cameras, you know. I hate being observed. I don't mind the kind of thing Ms Heywood does. That's par for the course in this game. But spyholes and zoom lenses? I don't like those at all.'

'I'm not a paparazzo, Mr Nyman.'

'Weddings and christenings more your game?'

'No. Architecture.'

'Really? What do you think of this building?'

'Nothing. Right now, I don't think about much except finding Eris.'

'Are you in love with her?'

'Does that matter?'

'To you, I imagine it must. To me, it could be the answer to a prayer.'

'In what way?'

'She's been pursuing me, Mr Jarrett. For most of the past year. She phones. She writes. She calls at reception. She follows me into restaurants and bars. It's all harmless enough in its way, I suppose, but it's pretty damned wearing. She's become obsessed with me, imagining a mutual attraction that in reality is strictly one-way. The poets had it dead wrong about unrequited love. It's every bit as hard to bear for the loved as for the lover. I just can't shake her off. Or I couldn't, until this past couple of months. Maybe . . . well, you don't have to tell me about your relationship with her. That's none of my business. She's an attractive woman.'

'But she didn't attract you?' My pride was hurt by what he'd said. 'Is that it?'

'I have the impression you don't believe me.'

'The woman I met in Vienna—' I broke off, disabled by the truth of Daphne's diagnosis. The woman I'd met

194

in Vienna had only existed in Vienna. Back here, she was a stranger to me. 'I don't recognize your description of her.'

'Would you recognize her writing?'

'Of course.'

'Come inside, then. I have plenty of examples of it.'

He led the way back into his office and moved towards the desk that formed, along with a conference table, a broad T of polished wood at the far end of the room. A huge, starkly framed oil painting – some sort of sombre Nordic landscape – shared the wall behind the desk with wooden filing cabinets. The desk itself was empty, save for a week or so's worth of the *Financial Times*, held down by what looked suspiciously like a genuine gold ingot. Nyman slid into an over-designed swivel chair behind the desk, opened a deep drawer and lifted out a file.

'I'm not married, as I said, but there is . . . someone in my life. I wouldn't want them to see this stuff, so I keep it here.' He laid the file on the desk and piloted it round with his finger to face me. The initials E.M. were written on the cover in thick black ink. 'I threw the first few letters away. Then, when she didn't let up, I decided to keep them, just in case things turned ugly. Which they never did, I'm glad to say. Unless that's what they're doing right now.'

'Like I told you, I'm just trying to find her.'

'She's no longer in Bath?'

'Was she ever?'

'Certainly. She wrote from an address in the city. Most of the letters were posted there.' He frowned at me. 'You didn't know?'

'She told me she lived in a village in Dorset. Her psychotherapist thought she lived in Mayfair.'

'With me, no doubt.'

'With Conrad Moberly.'

Nyman sighed. 'She's a seriously mixed-up woman. I know you don't want to hear that, but it's the truth. See for yourself.'

He flipped open the file. I sat down in the nearest chair and looked at the topmost letter. The writing was familiar. I took the envelope containing the postcard of the church at Tollard Rising out of my pocket and compared the hands. They were unquestionably the same. The letter was headed 33 Inkerman Avenue, Bath. I glanced through it, disbelief souring into dismay as I read. 'You have to understand, Conrad, that we were meant for each other . . . I'll persist in this because I have to make you understand . . . I love you and I know that secretly you love me. You just have to have the courage to admit it. I'll give you the courage. I'll give you everything.' I leafed through several more in the same vein. 'You say you don't want to see me, but I know that's not true. You're denying what you truly feel, Conrad. You have to stop doing that.' And several more after that. 'I'll meet you anywhere you like, under any conditions. Just give me a chance to explain. That's all I ask. It's not much, is it? . . . Don't you want children, Conrad? I do. But they have to be yours. Yours and mine. Nobody else will do.' At the end of each letter was the same message. 'With all my love, Eris.' I flipped through them until they were a blur. But still they read the same. 'With all my love, Eris.' Over and again. 'With all my love, Eris.'

I closed the file and sat back in the chair, breathing deeply to hold nausea at bay. Shame and shock were churning inside me. I didn't know what to think and I couldn't think what to say. Eventually, as if taking pity on me, Nyman retrieved the file and put it away. 'You had no idea about any of this, did you?' he enquired gently.

'No. None at all.'

'It's definitely her writing? The writing of the woman you met in Vienna, I mean?'

'I . . . think so. I . . . can't be . . . absolutely certain.'

'Would a photograph help?'

'You have one?'

'A still from the reception security video.' He took an envelope from the drawer, opened it and slid the contents across the desk for me to see. It was a fuzzy black-and-white print of a picture taken from near ceiling level of a smartly dressed woman crossing what I recognized as the Nymanex reception area. And I recognized the woman as well. Instantly and unmistakably.

'Could I keep this?'

'Why not? I can easily get another copy. If I need to.'

'Let's hope you don't.'

'I've heard nothing from her since before Christmas. I assumed it had worked itself out somehow. I don't want to be hard on her. Or you. One hears of such things. Sometimes one experiences them. She never threatened me. It was only ever unwelcome attention. I wasn't going round in fear of my life. And it sounds as if she was doing her best to get a hold of herself even before she met you. This psychotherapist you—'

'She knows nothing of this. Not a thing.'

'What was Eris seeing her about, then?'

'Something else altogether.'

'Obviously, but—'

'Did she ever tell you she was in danger?'

'Well, yes, as a matter of fact she did. There was a letter in which . . . Hold on.' He leafed through the file, then took out a single sheet and passed it to me. 'She tried to talk to me when I left here one evening last October, but I wouldn't let her. That arrived a few days later. Read the second paragraph.'

'"I'm in trouble, Conrad. I need your help. I'm involved in something I don't completely understand. Let me explain it to you, please. I have to explain. You have to help me."' I handed the letter back. 'What did you do?'

'I ignored her. As usual. What should I have done? Are you saying she really was in danger?'

'I think it's possible, yes. Did she ever mention photography to you?'

'Photography? No. Well . . .' He tapped his forehead thoughtfully. 'Actually, I suppose she did. The first time I met her. Greenwich Park, one day last spring. Not long after Easter. I'd had a meeting at the Maritime Museum. Some sponsorship wrangle. I felt like a walk afterwards, so I took a stroll in the park. The weather was beautiful. Dashing back here didn't exactly appeal. Wish I had done, though. Would have saved me a lot of bother. I sat down on a bench up near the Royal Observatory. She – Eris, I mean – was already sitting there. We struck up a conversation. I probably flirted with her. A little. As you would. Pretty girl, spring sunshine. It didn't mean anything. So I thought.'

'What about photography?'

'Ah yes. Well, she said she'd been to the observatory to see some special kind of camera they have there.'

'A camera obscura?'

'That's right. I suppose you'd know all about such things in your line of work. I don't, of course. Cameras make me uneasy, as I told you. As I would have told Eris, if she'd given me the chance. She had a camera with her. The standard point-and-press job. She produced it quite suddenly from her bag and took a picture of me. Bizarre behaviour, really. It disturbed me. I didn't like that at all.'

'She took a *photograph* of you?'

'You sound incredulous.'

'I am. It's so . . . out of character.' It was also the mirror image of my own first meeting with her, in Vienna, when I'd been the photographer and she the unwilling subject. 'In my experience, she was almost as camera-shy as you seem to be.'

'Really? You surprise me. Anyway, that's what happened. I made it obvious I didn't like her taking such a liberty. She apologized and offered to let me have the negative as well as the print when she had the film developed. I said she needn't bother, but she insisted. In the end, I told her to send it to me here when it was ready. That was my big mistake. It meant she knew where to find me. The first letter came with the picture. No negative, however. She said I could collect that when we next met. For dinner, she suggested. Well, I didn't like the sound of any of it, so I didn't reply. But she wouldn't take no for an answer. Her . . . campaign, I suppose you'd call it . . . started there.'

'And ended in January?'

'Christmas, actually. But, tell me, what danger do you think she could possibly be in?'

'I don't know. But danger there undoubtedly is.' I was angrier with myself than I was with him, but still I felt the need to strike back on Eris's behalf, to prove there was more to all this than a futile infatuation. 'You remember I mentioned a bookseller called Quisden-Neve?'

'Yes. Ms Heywood's informant. I was going to ask—'

'He died this morning. Found strangled in the loo on a Bath-to-London train.'

'Nasty.' But, nasty or not, Conrad Nyman didn't bat an eyelid. 'Well, I suppose I don't have to worry about what information he had now.'

'Let's hope the police don't think of that.' It was unlikely they would. But they didn't have my incentive. Suddenly, from the depths of self-pitying disillusionment had come a redeeming surge of hope. The photograph of Eris proved nothing by itself. Only the letters substantiated Nyman's account. And their authenticity depended on the postcard. I'd never seen Eris write a single word. I had no way of being sure they were genuine. Niall Esguard had murdered Quisden-Neve. That, at least, I didn't doubt. But why? For reasons of his own? Or to prevent Quisden-Neve from blackening somebody else's name – somebody who could well afford to pay Niall to do his bidding? 'You said you'd never heard of Marian Esguard, didn't you?'

'Did I? Well, it's true. I haven't.'

'What about Niall Esguard?'

'No.'

'Milo Esguard?'

'No again.'

'Joslyn Esguard?'

'Definitely not. Is this some kind of weird guessing game, Mr Jarrett? If so, let's cut to the chase. The only Esguard I know – or know *of* – is a young woman called Dawn, *not* Marian.'

'What?'

He smiled faintly at my confusion, painfully apparent as it must have been. 'I had my security officer run a check on Eris, just to see if she posed a serious threat. The address in Bath turned out to be genuine enough. She lives there – or did last year, anyway – with Dawn Esguard. That's really all I can tell you. If you want to know any more, I suggest you call round there and ask them as many questions as you like. Who knows, you may even get some answers. I certainly hope so.' His smile broadened. 'For your sake.'

It had been dark for an hour or more when I reached Bath for the second time that day. Inkerman Avenue was a long straight road of Victorian terraced houses halfway up Twerton Hill. Number 33 was no different from any of the others, a tiny, walled front garden separating a modest bay-windowed frontage from the pavement. Lamplight shone through the thin ground-floor curtains, and the subdued beat of rock music reached my ears as I approached. It seemed certain somebody was at home. But who? I rang the bell and, hearing footsteps in the hall, wondered for a crazy second if Eris was about to open the door, smile at me and blithely announce, 'Oh, so you finally made it.'

But the woman I saw standing in the narrow porch as the door swung open wasn't Eris, or anyone like her. She was about the same age, and prettier by conventional standards, but there was a hardness to her mouth and eyes and the set of her jaw. She had short, spiky blond hair and was wearing a loose belted shirt over leggings and pixie boots. Her right hand was resting on the latch, and I couldn't help noticing, as a trio of bangles settled around her forearm, a pronounced scar across her wrist, the sort of scar that might be left by an attempt to slash the artery.

'Dawn Esguard?'

'Yeh,' she replied cautiously.

'My name's Ian Jarrett. I'm a friend of Eris Moberly.'

'Is that right?'

'Does she . . . still live here?'

201

'No. Left last Christmas. But if you're a friend of hers . . .'

'Have you seen her since then?'

'No. She cleared out of Bath altogether, didn't she?'

'Did she? Could I possibly . . . step inside and' – I shrugged – 'talk to you about her?'

'Why'd you want to do that?'

'Because I'm worried about her. I think she may have come to some harm.'

'Eris? No chance.'

'She's missing. Nobody seems to know where she is.'

'What does her husband say?'

'I don't know. I'd ask him, if only I could find out who the hell he is.'

'His name's Conrad, isn't it?'

'That's a very good question. Ever met him?'

'No.'

'Neither has anyone else.' I gave her what I hoped would look like a reassuring smile. 'See what I mean?'

'All right. You can come in. But I haven't got much time.' She moved aside, and I stepped past her into the hall. The rock music seemed to be coming from upstairs, but she directed me into the sitting room, where an oversized black leather three-piece suite, a vast old sideboard, a table bearing the remains of a meal, an ironing board piled with clothes and a TV switched on with the noise turned down were tangled in a sullen stand-off for floor space. 'Sorry about the mess,' she said, following me in. 'End of the week. You know how it is. What's this about Eris, then?'

'She's gone missing. And I'm trying to find her. But, so far, all I've found is that I know much less about her than I thought. Her name, for instance.

202

She introduced herself to me as Marian Esguard.'

'Esguard? That's weird.'

'Your name.'

'My husband's, you mean. Ex-husband's, anyway. I don't know why I go on using it. Except, well, it's more interesting than Smith, isn't it?'

'Who is your ex-husband? Not Niall?'

'Yeh. You know him?'

'Met him. Recently. While I was looking for Eris.'

'They don't know each other.' She frowned doubtfully. 'Do they?'

'It seems they do.'

'That doesn't make any sense.'

'Little does in Eris's life, it seems. Have you heard of Marian Esguard? The real one, I mean.'

'Don't think so.' She thought for a moment. 'Hold on. Niall's uncle, old Milo, he sometimes rambled on about his ancestors. Marian could have been one of them. I didn't pay much attention. I had enough trouble with *this* generation of Esguards, without worrying about—' She broke off to light a cigarette. 'Eris did ask about the name. And the family history. The full works. She even went to see old Milo out at Bradford. Maybe that's how she met Niall.'

'How exactly did you come to know Eris, Mrs Esguard?'

'Took her in as a lodger this time last year. It's not easy to make ends meet, especially when that bastard Niall . . . Anyway, Eris answered my ad in the paper. She suited me. Quiet, reliable, a good payer. She said she was doing some sort of part-time photographic course at the university. Must have been *very* part-time, though, because she was forever going up to London, and not just for the weekend.'

'When she wasn't quizzing you about your ex-husband's family, you mean?'

'Yeh. Well, she said it was an unusual name, see. Said there was an early photographer called Esguard who she'd come across in her studies. That's why I sent her to see Milo. He'd have known if anyone did. But she can't have got much out of him before he died. It was round the same time I heard he'd snuffed it.'

'When you were married to Niall, did you ever visit Bentinck Place?'

'Once or twice. To see Niall's mum, when she was still alive. And Milo, of course. He was living there then.'

'Did Eris ask you about the house? Its history? Its . . . design?'

'She might have done.'

'And this *is* Eris, is it?' I showed her the photograph from the Nymanex security video.

'That's her, yeh.'

'This her writing?' I held out the envelope containing the postcard for her to see.

'Could be. She wasn't exactly in the habit of writing to me. Hold on, though. She did send me something.' Dawn crossed the room, leaned over the back of the couch, poked around in the sideboard, then lifted out a small cardboard box. 'A slice of wedding cake,' she announced, bringing the box back with her for me to see. 'I kept this for pins and stuff. But the label's still on it. My name and address, in her writing.'

'It looks the same.'

'Does, doesn't it?'

My eye drifted from the label to the stamp and its distinctive motif. 'This was posted in Guernsey,' I said, almost as much to myself as to Dawn.

'Yeh. Well, that's where they went to live after the

wedding. Eris never said what this fiancé of hers, Conrad, actually did. But, just from the way she talked about him, I got the impression he was in the mega-bucks league. And Guernsey, well, that's a . . . what d'you call it?'

'Tax haven.'

'Right. And who needs a haven if they don't earn it in the first place? Some girls get all the luck.'

'Did Eris leave a forwarding address?'

'No. She didn't. And, in case you're wondering, I haven't been invited over to Guernsey for a posh weekend. I was never really Eris's type. You know?'

'I suppose I do.'

'I haven't seen or heard from her since before Christmas. Sorry.'

'Me, too. But thanks anyway.' It was clear she wanted me to go and equally clear I'd learn nothing by staying. I walked slowly out into the hall and turned towards the front door. As I did so, I noticed a copy of the local evening paper lying on the telephone table, folded so that a headline running across the bottom of the front page was visible. BATH BOOKSELLER FOUND STRANGLED ON LONDON TRAIN. I stopped beside the table and glanced down at it.

'*Montagu Quisden-Neve, respected and popular proprietor of the noted Bath antiquarian bookshop, Bibliomaufry, was found dead this morning aboard . . .*' My eye raced ahead. '*It is not yet clear how Mr Quisden-Neve met his death. The results of a post-mortem are expected tomorrow. Police are, however, treating his death as suspicious, and are particularly anxious to contact one of the two men who discovered the body and who left Chippenham station prior to the arrival of investigating officers.*' There was no description. That was one mercy. But there was an ominous closing quote. '"*It is vital we eliminate this man from our inquiries,*" *said a police spokesman.* "*It is in his own best interests to come forward.*"'

'Take it if you want,' said Dawn. 'I never have time to read the thing.'

'No. No thanks. That's all right.' I turned to look at her. 'Your ex-husband, Mrs Esguard. Niall.'

'What about him?'

'Would you say he had a . . . capacity for violence?'

'Yeh. I would. Lots of capacity.'

'Do you think, in certain circumstances, he might be capable of murder?'

'Why do you think I left him? Of course he's capable of it. I've known a bloke come up behind Niall in the pub and tap him on the shoulder and get a glass shoved in his face just for surprising him. It's what I always tell people. Don't *ever* push your luck with Niall. The truth is, see, you won't have any to push. Know what I mean?'

'I think I do. But, just supposing I wanted to prove your point, which pub would I be likely to find him in?'

The Black Dog wasn't the sort of pub a Bath tour guide would be likely to recommend to foreign visitors. The décor was a baleful mix of bottle-brown and ash-grey, the clientèle were either grim-faced and narrow-eyed or loudly drunk, and the barman, addressed by all as Darren, looked as if he'd just fought the losing half of a boxing match. I'd banked on there being some degree of safety in numbers, but, glancing round at this band of potential witnesses to my brutal murder, I reckoned it would be pretty minimal. Perhaps it was just as well there was no sign of Niall. Nor had there been all day, according to Darren.

'You expecting to find him here, were you?' he added gruffly.

'Sort of. A mutual friend said he uses the place.'

'Yeh, well, he does. But not tonight.' Darren smiled as broadly as his split lip allowed. 'He's out of town.'

'Who's the mutual friend?' enquired the thin, greasy-haired occupant of the nearest patch of bar.

'Quisden-Neve,' I replied, deciding to be provocative just to see what came of it.

'Neasden-Quiff? Bloody hell. I heard he'd—'

'Why don't you shut it, Albert?' Darren cut in. 'Do us all a favour.'

'I expect you were about to say you'd heard he was dead, Albert,' I said, turning my back on Darren as best I could. 'Is that right?'

Albert shrugged. 'It was in the paper.'

'Did Monty use to come in here?' I asked, trying to make him sound like an old friend of mine.

'Off and on. You'd not forget him in a hurry, would you?' Albert loosed a chain-smoker's laugh at me.

'Did he drink with Niall?'

'When he came, yeh. No secret, is it?'

'Not to me, no. What with them being business partners in a manner of speaking.'

'Thought as much.' Albert leaned confidentially towards me. 'Ever since that Neasden-Quiff came on the scene, Niall's had . . . more calls on his time.' He winked. 'That's what all this travelling's about, ain't it? Hobnobbing. Greasing palms. Taking a cut. Niall's going up in the world. I cottoned on to that long before these dozy buggers.'

'I think you're probably right.'

'No wonder he's always hopping over to the Channel Islands. Salting away the proceeds, ain't he?

207

It'll be bloody Switzerland next, I shouldn't—'

'Which island?'

'What?' Albert seemed confused by my sudden urgency.

'*Which* Channel Island does he visit?'

'Well, I don't—'

'Guernsey?'

'Could be.' Albert summoned the considerable effort required to think. 'Yeh, that's the one. Guernsey.'

The ground floor and basement of 6 Bentinck Place were in darkness. Niall Esguard was off on one of his regular jaunts to Guernsey, where his ex-wife's former lodger, Eris Moberly, was supposed to be leading an affluent married life. And Guernsey had other connotations, too, which my mind was too weary to do more than reach towards. A haven could be a hiding place. And a hiding place could be a prison.

The truth was that I still didn't know enough to understand what the things I'd discovered meant. I needed more to go on. And the only place left to try was inside Eris's head. I had to hear the third tape.

I walked back to the car and phoned Daphne from there. She was, as I'd anticipated, angry. But not angry enough to make me doubt that, secretly, she was willing me on. She'd evidently not heard about Quisden-Neve. She'd have been frightened as well as angry if she had. As it was, reluctantly but inevitably, she yielded to my pleas.

'Let's just put back our appointment by twenty-four hours, Daphne. Nine o'clock tomorrow morning, at your practice. I can be there.'

'Why weren't you there *this* morning?'

'Problems with my daughter.'

'Are you sure you didn't go to see Quisden-Neve?'

'Of course not.'

'All right. But don't let me down again. I've been worried about you all day.'

'There was no need. I've had a really quiet time of it. See you tomorrow.'

I drove back to London. The motorway was empty and I made it to Chiswick by eleven o'clock. All the way, I'd told myself to head straight for the flat and get some sleep. But something – curiosity, conscience or some collision of the two – prompted me to take the North Circular to Finchley, then drive cautiously up through Whetstone to Barnet. It was a route I'd not followed in five years. I'd have expected to feel more, to be assailed by chilling memories, as I passed the very spot on Barnet Hill where I'd struck the shadow that turned out to be a flesh-and-blood human whose life ended in that moment. But Eris's disappearance had laid a dead stranger's ghost. I could remember now, without flinching.

It was late to be paying calls, social or otherwise. But I knew Nicole's habits. Pushing midnight was actually a good time to find her awake and alert. It was one of her feline characteristics, along with physical grace, claws that could sink in without warning and inexhaustible self-sufficiency.

She answered the door in a maroon silk bathrobe and looked strangely unsurprised to see me. 'Funny how you can tell people by the way they ring a bell, isn't it?' she said by way of greeting. 'Even after five years.'

'Can I come in?'

'I don't think that's a good idea.'

'It's important.'

'So's my guest. He isn't going to be impressed by you blundering in.'

'Ah. Right.'

'To be honest, Ian, no-one would be. You looked a mess at lunchtime. Now you're more of a wreck.'

'About lunchtime . . .'

'Get to see Nyman, did you?'

'Yes.'

She seemed genuinely surprised. 'Really?'

'Yes. That's why I'm here. Would Nymanex have interests in Guernsey?'

'I expect so. Plus Jersey and the Isle of Man. Probably the Cayman Islands, too. A lot of their clients are tax exiles.'

'Is Nyman himself likely to go to Guernsey a lot?'

'I don't know. Probably not very often.'

'But sometimes?'

'I suppose so. What of it?'

'It's a connection.'

'With what?'

'I'm not sure.'

'And I'm not sure I want to stand here listening to you explain why you're not sure.' Her surprise had subsided now. 'If you'll—'

'There's something sinister going on, Nicole. I'm trying to warn you to be on your guard.'

She looked at me in mild puzzlement. 'Sinister? What the hell does that mean?'

'It means you should be careful. Somebody murdered Quisden-Neve. They mightn't stop there.'

'I only have your word for it that he *was* murdered.'

'Don't you believe me?'

'I believe you're speaking the truth as you see it.' She

sighed. 'And I believe you're right. I *should* be more careful. Especially about who I answer the door to late at night. Good night, Ian. And thanks for calling. Next time, phone first. It'll save you the journey.'

During a sleepless stretch of the night, a troubling thought came to me, keeping its distance like a wolf beyond the campfire's glow, but impossible to ignore. If the search for Eris was driving me mad, I'd be the last to know. I alone would believe the events I'd experienced. To Daphne and Nicole, to Faith and Amy, they'd just be a jungle of delusions I'd marched off into, never to return.

The thought recurred as I sat in Daphne Sanger's consulting room next morning and recounted what had happened since I'd listened to the second tape. She had to be told about Quisden-Neve, about Conrad Nyman and Dawn Esguard, about all the teeming uncertainties I'd prised out of the blank wall of Eris's disappearance. But would she believe me? Or was she already doubting me, just as she'd doubted Eris?

A shriller complaint about my irresponsibility would ironically have done something to set my mind at rest. Instead, she was almost philosophical about my broken promise and the avalanche of events it seemed to have triggered.

'You should have come to me first, Ian. You really should.'

'I know. I'm sorry. I just . . . reacted.'

'And why didn't you tell me any of this last night?'

'I didn't want to worry you.'

'Well, I am worried. With good reason. Most of all because I haven't a clue what's going on. Quisden-Neve. Niall Esguard. What in God's name are they up to?'

211

'*Were*, in Quisden-Neve's case. Either way, I don't know. Any more than you do. Except there's more to it than the dissociative disorder you thought you were treating.'

'Obviously,' she snapped, lighting a cigar to calm herself. 'You mean to go to Guernsey?'

'After I've heard the third tape.'

'Ah. The third tape. I wondered when we'd come to that.'

'I have to know what I'm dealing with.'

'It won't tell you.'

'I still have to hear it.'

'Yes. I suppose you do.' She stood up and paced the room, puffing at the cigar, then turned to face me. 'I shouldn't be encouraging you, of course. You've given me ample proof of your unreliability. And now a man's died. I ought to be telling you to go to the police and give them as much help as you can. I ought to go to them myself, come to that.'

'Why won't you?'

'Because they wouldn't believe *me*, let alone you. The whole business is too . . . tenuous, too . . . bizarre. Besides, I feel partly responsible for what's happened. If I'd told you everything from the start, you'd have been wary of Quisden-Neve when you first encountered him. Then he might still be alive. Even though we don't have any way of knowing why Niall should have wanted to kill him.'

'To shut him up. Why else?'

'I don't know. But there may be other reasons. There may be ramifications to this we have absolutely no appreciation of. I can assure you the third tape doesn't answer any of the questions you've succeeded in raising.'

'I'd like to satisfy myself on that point.'

'Yes, yes. All right.' She waved her hand irritably, the smoke from her cigar describing a tetchy zigzag in the air. 'You've convinced me. I'm not trying to argue. But we can't go on like this. Don't you see? It's all getting dangerously out of control.'

'Maybe that's inevitable, if we're to find Eris.'

'Maybe.' She nodded thoughtfully. 'Maybe so.'

'Daphne, why don't you just give me the tape and trust me to deal with the consequences of whatever I learn in Guernsey?'

'Because that's the easy way out. And I've been taking the easy way out for too long.'

'What do you suggest, then?'

'I suggest you listen to the tape, here, right now, with me. Then we can discuss what to do for the best.'

'What about your clients?'

'It's Good Friday. I don't have any. So we'll play the tape, Ian. Afterwards we'll agree a course of action.'

'And then?'

'We'll carry it through. Together. You and me.'

'You mean—'

'I mean this is going to be a team effort from now on.'

'Hold on. I'm not sure—'

'Those are my terms.' She stabbed out the cigar in an ashtray on her desk and stared, almost glared, at me. 'Take them or leave them.'

'Right. OK.' I smiled ruefully. 'I'd better take them, hadn't I?'

'I think so, yes.' She sat down beside me, instantly growing gentler in her manner, yet more solemn at the same time. 'You have to understand that the fugue Eris described on the second tape had a profound effect on her. Previously, she'd gone along with my suggestion that there was an identifiable, explicable and, most important of all, *treatable* psychological explanation for her dissociative experiences. Subsequently, she could never quite bring herself to believe that. The fugue life was real to her. As real as her other life, in many ways.'

Now wasn't the time to tell Daphne that it seemed equally real to me. 'You mean she no longer regarded the Marian persona as delusory?'

'Not in any way. The vicarious trauma of the rape, in particular, seemed to fix Marian deep inside her.'

'But that didn't mean more frequent fugues?'

'No. Fear kept them at bay, I think. Fear of what she might experience if she reverted to Marian again.'

'Yet she did revert?'

'Ultimately, yes. I'd taught her various mental disciplines to help her focus on everyday practicalities. Our sessions had degenerated into little more than holding operations in that sense. My approach was based on the theory that if we could achieve a fugueless period of some length – three months was the target – then Eris would have the confidence she needed to address the true origin of the fugues, which I remained certain lay strictly in the realm of psychopathology.'

'You never wondered if she was right to believe in their reality – however you define it?'

'Of course not.'

'But now, with all that's happened since?'

'Now is different. And totally outside my professional expertise. That's why I'm trusting you with so much that Eris believed – and had every right to believe – would go no further. I can excuse myself on the grounds that she deceived me. About her marriage, about every detail of her life. But the question remains: *why* did she deceive me?'

'You never made the three months, of course.'

214

'No. Our last session before Christmas was on the sixteenth. She told me then that her husband had arranged for them to spend most of the holiday at the same hotel near Bath where they'd gone at Easter. He was hoping it would cheer her up, apparently. He'd noticed how depressed she'd been. Thought the break would do her good. So it might have done, somewhere else. But going back to Bath struck me as unnecessarily risky. I advised Eris to talk him out of it. She said she'd tried, but he was adamant he knew what was best for her. Besides, she was confident she could get through the trip unscathed. That surprised me, so much so that I took it as evidence that we really were making progress. I should have seen her confidence for what it was, of course: a subconscious yearning to return to Marian's life. Our next appointment was for the sixth of January, and I was naturally apprehensive about the condition I'd find her in. I'd given her a tape to record her experiences during the gap between sessions as I had during the previous lay-off.'

She rose, crossed to the desk and removed a small padded envelope from one of the drawers. A franked stamp and handwritten address were visible on the side she showed me. 'It arrived on the seventh. The day after our appointment. Which Eris didn't keep. The sixteenth of December was the last time I saw her.' Daphne let the tape slide out of the envelope onto the desk. 'When I'd heard what's on the tape, I knew why she hadn't come to see me. And why I had to find her. But, as you know . . .' She raised her spectacles clear of her nose with her fingers and massaged the bridge. 'I'm still looking.'

Chapter Eight

Sorry I couldn't face you with this, Daphne. It's not that I distrust you. I distrust myself. I look on you as a friend now. I remember you warning me not to do that, but some things can't be helped. The result is I've started wanting to spare your feelings. I know you still believe we can get on top of this thing, but I don't. I'm not sure I ever have. Now I'm certain, though. What's worse, I don't really want to try any more. I can either give in to it or run away from it. Those are the only choices. So I reckon you may as well be spared the agony of trying to find some other way that doesn't exist. But I know you'll want to hear what brought it all to a head, and it really does help to talk about it. There's no-one I can talk to apart from you. That's what I'm doing, even though you're not sitting across the room from me as I speak. But you'll listen. I know you will. And you'll understand. I hope.

We went down to Somerset on Christmas Eve and everything seemed fine to start with. The weather turned cold and there wasn't much incentive to leave the hotel fireside. Conrad threw himself into the parlour games that were organized for guests and took me on occasional tramps round the local lanes. But he didn't suggest revisiting Lacock or going into Bath, and I didn't either. Apart from anything else, I was afraid I might bump into Niall Esguard. I felt safe in the vicinity of the hotel and planned to sit it out there until we went home.

If Conrad had stuck close to me, I'm sure that's what I'd have done. But he'd booked himself a day's hack on the Mendips, courtesy of some arrangement the hotel had with a local riding stable. Since I've never ridden, that meant I had the day to myself. It was a long day, too, because Conrad wanted me to drive him down to the stables for an eight o'clock start and pick him up again at four. The place was near Shepton Mallet and on the way back to the hotel – navigation's never been my strong point – I took one wrong turning after another and found myself on the Bristol road. I turned east off that and the signs started reading closer and closer to Bath, so I pulled into a lay-by and tried to make sense of the map.

It was early on a Sunday morning in the middle of a long holiday, so, as you can imagine, there was nobody else about. I got out of the car to try to get my bearings. There was a wooded hill away to my right that I thought was probably the one named on the map as Stantonbury Hill, but the sun was in my eyes and I couldn't really be sure of anything. It was so bright and low in the sky that it blinded me for an instant. I turned away and blinked, waiting for my sight to clear. As it did so, I realized the colour of the fields was suddenly sharper, the hedgerows and patches of woodland a mellow gold, as if they were in full autumn leaf. The sunlight that had dazzled me was noticeably warmer on my back. The chill was gone from the air, the frost from my breath. The car had vanished and the road had changed. The white-lined tarmac had become a dusty earth-and-flint lane. I felt a flutter of something like a ribbon at my throat.

And at once I realized I was in Barrington's barouche, returning to Bath from a drive into the country west of the city. Barrington himself sat opposite me; the splayed girth of his long yellow coat seemed to magnify his bulk, which had surely increased even since the summer. His plum-coloured waistcoat was stretched to bursting point over his stomach, which his slouched posture did not show to advantage. Every burrow in his pocket for his snuffbox was a struggle. I could not help wondering whether Susannah, who was sitting beside me beneath an excess of travelling rug, found the prospect an edifying one. If not, it would have explained the determination with which she gazed at the hilltop to our right.

'We had an altogether delightful picnic with the Aislabies hereabouts in June, did we not, my dear?' she remarked.

'What?' Barrington's attention appeared to have been elsewhere. I had the discomforting notion it had been fixed on me.

'The Aislabies. In June. Yonder. Was that not where Mr Aislabie pointed out to us the course of the Roman dyke?'

'Wansdyke,' Barrington specified.

'Quite so. Mr Aislabie knows much of such matters, Marian,' Susannah continued, turning towards me. 'You will find him to be a very well-informed gentleman.'

'I'm sure I would,' I said. 'If I were ever to meet him.'

'Oh, but you shall. The Aislabies are of the party this evening.'

'I did not know you were to have company this evening.'

'You must remember this is Bath, my dear, not Tollard Rising. Company of a sociable and stimulating nature is the guiding purpose of the city.'

'Yes,' said Barrington in a sour tone. 'Of sociability and stimulation there is no end.'

'Exactly,' said Susannah, not apparently detecting the slightest hint of sarcasm in her husband's voice. 'And I can conceive of no better tonic for your oppressed spirits, Marian. We are pleased to have this unexpected opportunity to share with you the benefits of life in Bath. Are we not, Barrington?'

'Uncommonly' was his grudging reply, merging with a snort as he inhaled enough snuff to quench a candle.

It was obvious to me, as it must have been to Susannah, that Barrington was anything but pleased to be acting as my host. I was in no position to complain, since I was an equally reluctant guest. I had been wished upon them by Jos in circumstances that were embarrassing and disagreeable to all three of us. Jos's resolution to govern me with a close and strict hand had endured for less than three months, though what I had suffered during those months had made them seem more like years. I had to guard my memory not to dwell upon the cruelties and indignities he had inflicted upon me at Gaunt's Chase in the weeks following Mr Byfield's departure from Legion Cottage. There were things he had done to me which I knew now were things he had always longed to do and which he falsely justified on account of my supposed misbehaviour. All he had accomplished, however, was to free me of any sense of obligation to him. Abomination reaps its own reward. I no longer regarded myself as his wife.

Tiring of the effort involved in torturing me, Jos had decided to return to London, but not, as he had originally threatened, with me. There were corners of his life he still did not want me to glimpse, even though, had he but known it, my opinion of him could sink no lower. I had hoped, with little confidence, that he would leave me to my own devices at Gaunt's Chase. Then, little by little, I might reassemble my heliogenic laboratory and return to the researches which, since their abandonment, had sometimes seemed as distant as dreams. But Jos had no intention of restoring any degree of liberty to me. I was consigned to his brother and sister-in-law for safe keeping, until such time as he wished to reimpose direct supervision of me.

What Jos had told Barrington, and what Barrington had told Susannah, I had no means of knowing and no wish to enquire. The truth of my position in their house – that of a comfortably accommodated and courteously treated prisoner – was apparent from the first. I had been there for just over a fortnight without succeeding in having a waking hour to myself. The servants had clearly been instructed to warn their master or mistress of any attempt on my part to leave the house unaccompanied. A secret rendezvous with Mr Byfield was what they feared, of course. His name was never mentioned. The reason for what Susannah termed my 'oppressed spirits' was never alluded to. But it was understood plainly enough.

As gaolers, however, Barrington and Susannah lacked the vital ingredient of zeal. They embarked upon the role conscientiously enough, but tired rapidly as one week stretched to two and beyond. Barrington had become first bored, then discontented. Susannah had grown excessively talkative and short-tempered with the servants. I irked them and they irked me. We were united by an unspoken desire to be free of each other. And in that desire lay my opportunity to test the strength of the shackles Jos had sought to fasten round me.

'We shall be returning to Bath by way of Weston, I take it,' I remarked in what I judged to be a casual manner.

'Indeed,' said Barrington.

'Miss Gathercole lives by the churchyard there, does she not?'

'I believe so.'

'She entreated me to call for tea if ever I was in the neighbourhood.'

'She did?'

'I said that I would be charmed to do so.'

'Good God.'

'She is a meek and solitary creature, Barrington. We can surely show her some small consideration.'

'She is a liability as a whist partner and a sore test of patience as a conversationalist. I do not know what greater consideration I can be expected to show her than that of refraining from the direction of her attention to such pitiful truths.'

'It would be embarrassing not to take up her invitation.'

'I could bear such embarrassment with fortitude.'

'But I could not.'

'Go then.' The words were out of his mouth before he could weigh them against his obligations to Jos.

'If you will set me down by the church, I will devote an hour to Miss Gathercole and enjoy a bracing walk back to Bentinck Place across Sion Hill. It is a fine afternoon. I feel I would benefit from the exercise and I am sure Miss Gathercole would appreciate the company.'

'No doubt.' Barrington wrestled his hunting watch out of his waistcoat pocket and consulted it. 'Well, well, there's time enough, certainly.'

Susannah cleared her throat ostentatiously. 'My dear, should we not—?'

'Damn it, let her go if she will. Where's the harm in it?' He smiled at me awkwardly, aware he had come dangerously close to acknowledging the delicacy of his position as my custodian. 'Pay your charitable call, Marian, by all means. I would not wish to come between you and a kindred spirit. A twittering spinster is, I feel sure, just the counsellor you require at this passage in your life.' His smile broadened disingenuously. But I knew better than to rise to his bait. What was Barrington's lumbering satire compared with the torments his brother had devised for me? And what did it matter anyway, when I had achieved no less than I desired?

We were approaching the village of Corston and were within sight of the outskirts of Bath. The autumn sun flattered the pale stonework of the buildings and would have enchanted those disposed to be enchanted, as I had certainly been when I first visited the city as a girl of fifteen in the company of my parents. But I had not heard the name Esguard then, nor learned how much more bitterness there was than sweetness in the world. The vista left me unmoved.

As doubtless it did my brother-in-law, not least because he had his back to it as we approached and was listening, though scarcely attentively, to his wife's third discourse of the day on the recent tragic death in child-birth of Princess Charlotte. This had occurred the previous week, at Claremont House in Surrey. The child she had borne, a son, was also dead. The Queen, who had been in Bath partaking of the waters, was reported to have returned to London. It was a lamentable business, but it had given me some grim comfort. I would never bear Jos a son, nor die in the attempt. God had cursed him with a barren wife, so he complained. But, if he was right, then I could only regard it as a blessing. I wanted no child of his, nor any child of mine to have such a father.

'It is as melancholy an event as can be imagined,' doled Susannah. 'The Prince Regent is left not merely bereft, but without an heir.'

'He'll find some way to assuage his grief,' growled Barrington. 'And there's always an heir, if one searches hard enough. The failure of one line is the success of another.' He looked at me and I could not help blushing. It seemed clear he intended some reference to the advantage his odious son Nelson would ultimately derive from my childlessness. 'Thank God I married a robust woman.'

'Barrington, please!' objected Susannah.

'I'm complimenting you, madam,' he retorted with a smirk.

'How is dear Nelson?' I enquired, well knowing that the infrequency of his letters was the despair of his mother. 'I have heard so little of his exploits since my arrival.'

'His schoolmasters seem pleased enough,' was Barrington's grudging reply.

'How proud you must be of him.' The sentiment was genuine. I imagined Barrington would indeed be proud of a son who was maturing as rapidly as Nelson was into a prig and a bully.

'Nelson's a fiery little fellow,' said Barrington, a paternal gleam lighting his eye. 'He has the Esguard up-an'-at-'em.'

'How gratifying.' And now it was my turn to give a disingenuous smile.

I sustained the cut-and-thrust of our conversation all the way to Weston, calculating that it would encourage Barrington to be rid of me. So it proved. His expression as he helped me down from the barouche outside the church suggested that his subservience to Jos's whims was being sorely tested.

I watched them pass out of sight along the road into Bath before approaching Miss Gathercole's cottage, one of a terrace adjacent to the churchyard. Her insistence, conveyed at a whist party three nights previously, that I should take tea with her could indeed have been the desperation of the lonely. I had detected some greater significance to it, however, some depth of meaning which spoke of an altogether more subtle and perceptive character than Barrington and Susannah believed her to possess. It scarcely mattered if I was wrong. This interval of liberty would be a joy, however I spent it.

The door was answered not by Miss Gathercole herself, nor yet by some maid-of-all-work, but by a stockily built fellow in a pea-jacket. He had a broken nose, a scar over his right eyebrow and swollen knuckles. He also had a direct and challenging manner that marked him as neither servant nor gentleman. 'Would you be Mrs Esguard?' he asked before I could get out a word.

'I would, yes.'

'Step inside, ma'am. You're expected.'

A short, narrow passage, which he seemed more or less to fill, led to the rear of the cottage. A door to his right, towards which he extended his hand, gave on to a small sitting room, in which I could see Miss Gathercole in a chair by the crackling fire, smiling at me in welcome.

As I stepped into the room, I realized that someone was sitting in the chair on the farther side of the fire. He rose as I entered and bowed towards me. For a second I hardly dared believe the evidence of my eyes. My astonishment must have been apparent, for Mr Byfield gave me a warm and reassuring smile before stepping forward to take my hand.

'I cannot tell you how good it is to see you again, Mrs Esguard,' he said. 'I can only hope that you know without the need for me to say.'

'It is an inestimable pleasure for me, too, Mr Byfield,' I responded.

'That is fortunate,' put in Miss Gathercole, as she rose and joined us in the middle of the room, 'since I find that I have to leave you for a while. I do beg your pardon, Mrs Esguard.' She smiled at me like the kindest and most indulgent of dimple-cheeked aunts. 'You have happened to arrive just as I am compelled to attend to urgent business elsewhere. I trust you will excuse me.'

'Yes. Why, yes, of course, Miss Gathercole.'

'Mr Byfield will, I am sure, entertain you in my absence.'

'Rest assured I'll do my best.'

'May I take Poulter for the fetching and carrying?'

'Please do. And work him hard, Emily. He's like a horse too long in the stable at present. All huff and no puff.'

Miss Gathercole laughed and went out, closing the door behind her. I saw her pass by the window a moment later, accompanied by the barrel-chested Mr Poulter.

'I am no stranger to Bath, Marian,' said Mr Byfield, detecting the puzzlement in my gaze. 'Emily and I are old friends. Your brother-in-law probably regards her as a person of no consequence.'

225

'Yes, he does.'

'So people of unsuspected depths often appear to the shallow and foolish.'

I smiled. 'I feel sure that is true. And Mr Poulter?'

'A retired pugilist whose services I have had need of these past months.'

'Why, pray?'

'Because your husband has set some dubious folk on me, against whom I have been obliged to protect myself.'

'He has done *what*?' My grasp on his hand tightened. 'Lawrence, I had no inkling of this. I thought your departure from Tollard Rising was sufficient for Jos's purposes. Had I realized he meant to—' I broke off and stared at him, aware, as he must have been, of the tension between us that communicated more certainly than any words the strength of our mutual attraction.

'Had you realized, you might have written to me? Is that what you were about to say?'

'I did not write because . . . there was nothing you could do for me.'

'There is nothing I would *not* do for you.'

'You cannot *un*marry me.'

'Has Jos not done that already, Marian, in the only sense that truly matters?'

'I am pledged to him in the sight of God.'

'As he is to you. But can you stand here and tell me he has honoured his vows?'

'No,' I replied in scarcely more than a murmur. 'I cannot.'

'Just as I cannot stand here and tell you I do not love you.'

'Lawrence, I—'

'Do *you* love *me*, Marian?'

A silence fell. We looked at each other and I saw in

his face the mirror image of a passion I had sought too long to deny. 'Yes,' I said, nodding in slow and certain acknowledgement of the truth of what I was about to declare. 'I do love you.'

He took me in his arms at that and kissed me, as I wanted him to, as I would not, for all the world, have had him do other than. 'I will not let us be apart any longer,' he whispered as he held me. 'I will not let you renounce our love.'

'I could not renounce it, Lawrence. Not now.'

'I have been in hell these past months.'

'I too.'

'Then let us make a heaven for ourselves.'

'How can we?'

'We will go abroad. I am a man of modest but independent means. We will not starve.'

'I should not care if we did. So long as we starved together.'

He laughed. 'You are a brave woman, Marian.'

'That is not what people will say of me.'

'Do you care what they will say?'

'Once I would have done. But no longer.'

'I hate the thought of Jos so much as touching you.'

'If we go quickly, he never will again.'

'Emily tells me you are to attend the ball at Midford Grange on Thursday.'

'Susannah has spoken of it, yes.'

'That will give me time to arrange a passage to the Continent from Bristol. I shall send Poulter with a phaeton to wait for you at the house. He will go unnoticed among the other drivers. It should be a simple matter for you to meet me, and we can travel on together. We will be long gone before Jos hears of it, you may be sure.'

227

'Can it be so easily accomplished?'

'If you are willing to depart with nothing but the gown you wear to the ball, I believe it can.'

'So long as I depart with you, Lawrence, I am willing to relinquish all material possessions.'

'You will have to relinquish your good name also, Marian. Remember that. They will call you an adulteress.'

'I do not care.' All the pretence and misery Jos had forced upon me stood renounced in that instant. In admitting my love for Lawrence Byfield, I was taking a step into the unknown. And I was rejoicing as I did so. 'I am yours,' I declared, returning his ever more frantic kisses. 'Body and soul.'

'Emily and Poulter will not be back . . . for an hour at least.'

'Nor need I be . . . at Bentinck Place.'

'One hour, then.' He stared deeply into my eyes. 'As a foretaste of all the hours to come.'

'Yes.' I smiled at him. 'Let it be so.'

And it was so. He took me up to a small room beneath the eaves of the cottage, where a fire was burning. There, as the November afternoon greyed towards dusk, I gave myself to him as I had never, from the very first, given myself to my lawful wedded husband. There was passion where before there had only ever been brutality. There was love and all the physical fruits of it compressed into an hour. I had often dreamed how such things would be between two people joined in tender consent. To learn the answer was to clasp a magical truth and to glimpse the emptiness of Jos's soul. All the forced serving girls and hired whores in the world would fail him in this. He could never know what Lawrence Byfield showed me that afternoon: the rapture of giving and receiving;

the bliss of union, as like the angels in heaven as the beasts in the field.

I left the cottage while our enigmatic hostess was still absent and walked slowly up across Sion Hill towards Bentinck Place, composing myself as I went and praying there was nothing in my manner or appearance to betray the convulsion of my emotions. For three days more, I would have to act the part of Barrington and Susannah's reluctant and oppressed house guest. Then freedom and happiness would be mine. It was not long to wait, though it seemed an eternity. It was hardly any time at all, set against—

And just like that, as abruptly as an interrupted sentence, I came to myself as Eris again. I was most of the way across High Common, with the foreshortened arc of the housefronts of Bentinck Place already in sight. I stopped in my tracks, frozen by panic and confusion. How had I got there? What was I doing? I stumbled to a nearby bench and sat down, breathing shallowly and sweating despite the chill of the morning. I looked at my watch and saw it was nearly noon. More than three hours had passed since I'd got out of the car: three hours and quite a few miles. I must have walked into Bath without realizing it. I certainly felt tired enough to have done so. Of course, I *had* realized it in a sense. The ride in the barouche and the stop at Weston were crystal clear in my mind. It wasn't like remembering a dream. It was actually the opposite. Sitting there on that bench, I felt like a dreamer aware they're dreaming, aware of the waking world they can return to if they simply open their eyes. It took no effort. The effort was all the other way.

But Bath was a dangerous place for Eris Moberly to be. That much I knew. The truth of it was something to grasp and hold on to. I had to get away. The longer I remained, the greater the chance, remote though it logically was, of encountering Niall Esguard. Perhaps it was approaching Bentinck Place that had shocked me out of the fugue. I decided to head for the railway station. I'd be able to get a taxi there. I got up and began walking fast downhill, across Weston Road and on through the park below the Royal Crescent to Queen Square. There was a slow-moving queue of traffic along the north side of the square, and I stood at the edge of the pavement, waiting to cross. For a second, I looked up at the elegant buildings around me. It really was no more than that – a momentary lessening in my concentration. But it was enough. The noise of the traffic ceased, the cars vanished and the square was quiet and empty. Nothing moved. Nothing told me for a fact what I knew for a certainty. This was Bath as it had once been. And I, too, was as I had once been.

'Mrs Moberly?' I heard somebody say. Fear gripped me with transforming force. I turned, the world reverting around me to the present as I knew it. And there, in front of me, was Montagu Quisden-Neve, muffled up in an overcoat and fedora, with a red-and-white polka-dot bow tie lurking garishly in the shadow of his upturned collar. He treated me to his faintly lecherous man-of-the-world smile. 'Upon my soul, it *is* Mrs Moberly. What are you doing in Bath, my dear?'

'I . . . I don't . . .'

'Are you quite well?'

'I'm not . . . not sure.'

'Did you come here to see me?'

'No.' I began to recover my composure. 'Of course not.'

'Why, then, may I ask?'

'I don't think it's any of your business.'

'I must beg to differ with you there, Mrs Moberly.'
He stepped closer and lowered his voice. 'It would no
more be in my interests than it would be in yours to have
friend Niall come across you roaming the streets. He *is*
still anxious to find you, remember. I frankly fail to
understand what you can be thinking of.'

'Another world.'

'I beg your pardon?'

'I'd be happy to take your advice and leave the city
straight away, actually.' An idea had come to me. 'Any
chance of a lift?'

'You don't have a car?'

'It's in a lay-by, out beyond Corston.'

Quisden-Neve frowned. 'You walked in from there, I
suppose.'

'As a matter of fact, I think I must have done.'

His frown deepened. He glanced at his watch. 'This
really is . . .' Then he sighed, evidently conceding a
pragmatic point to himself. My presence in Bath really
was a problem he could do without. 'Very well. My car's
just round the corner. I suppose I have little choice but
to act as your chauffeur. Shall we?' He led the way along
the north side of the square, setting the stiffish pace of
someone who suddenly felt conspicuous.

His car, a flashy old Jag going to seed at about the
same rate as its owner, *was* just round the corner, in Gay
Street. He moved a dusty stack of *Illustrated London News*
to make room for me in the passenger seat, then we were
away, back round Queen Square and out along the
Bristol road.

'Your husband should take better care of you, Mrs
Moberly,' he said as we flashed past Weston church and
the terraces of Victorian housing that had long since
replaced the surrounding cottages. 'Wandering around

the countryside is no occupation for a lady like you.'

'You don't know what I'm like.'

'True enough. But even so—'

'Sold my pictures yet?'

'If you mean the Esguard negatives, I don't recall saying I was going to sell them.'

'You still have them, then?'

'I see no profit in discussing the subject. Your best course of action is to forget about them altogether – and to avoid visiting Bath.'

'What if I can't?'

He looked at me askance. 'Try harder.'

'Why weren't there any more?'

'What exactly do you mean?'

'I mean, why was 1817 the beginning and end of it?'

'Perhaps it wasn't.' He grinned his eager collector's grin. 'Perhaps she carried on the work, wherever she went after leaving her husband.'

'And where might that have been?'

He shrugged. 'Who can say?'

'Lawrence Byfield spoke of going abroad.'

'It would have been the obvious thing to do, but—' He suddenly stamped on the brakes and skidded to a halt. A car behind us blared its horn, then overtook noisily, the driver shouting and gesturing at us. But Quisden-Neve didn't even notice. 'Just a moment,' he said, staring at me. 'You know about Byfield?'

'Apparently.'

'So Milo told you everything.'

'What if he did?'

'Did he tell you where they went?'

'Did he tell *you*?'

'Of course not. Otherwise—' There was more blaring of horns. This time Quisden-Neve did notice. He drove on. 'I had Milo's solemn assurance that I was the only person he'd ever told about Byfield. He only told *me* because he was too ill to carry on ferreting about looking for clues as to where Byfield and Marian might have gone, assuming they did run off together, which wasn't by any means certain. I agreed to conduct enquiries on his behalf on the strict understanding that the information would go no further.' He slapped the steering wheel in irritation. 'Milo didn't play fair with me, he really didn't.'

'Perhaps you didn't play fair with him.'

'On the contrary. I didn't explain my parallel interest in Byfield to him, it's true, but then why should I have done? It was scarcely germane to the issue.'

'What is your "parallel interest"?'

'Nothing that need concern you. Let us return to what Byfield spoke of doing. How is anyone, even Milo, to know? He had the name, passed down from Barrington, as a candidate for the role of Marian's lover. The name and nothing more. Yet you seem to be implying he knew what might have been in Byfield's mind and hence in Marian's.'

'I'm implying nothing.' We were through Corston now and in sight of Stantonbury Hill. 'The lay-by's just round this next bend. You'd better slow down.'

'Why don't we both slow down?' He eased his foot off the accelerator and turned to give me what I think he intended to be a reassuring smile. 'I for one am always willing to be open-minded about situations where co-operation may be genuinely and mutually beneficial.'

'I thought you wanted me out of Bath.'

'I recommended it.' We rounded the bend and saw the car in the lay-by ahead. Quisden-Neve pulled in behind and turned off the engine. He pursed his lips thoughtfully, then said, 'If you know where they may have gone, Mrs Moberly, I'd be prepared to offer you a share in the proceeds in exchange for the information.'

'What proceeds?'

'The negatives, if proved to be genuine, will fetch a small fortune at auction, boosted by publicity, of course. My book will bring in a lot of that.'

'Your book?'

'About Marian Esguard. And how she ties in with another research interest of mine. *If* she ties in. I have to trace her movements, and hence Byfield's, after 1817 to nail it down. If you could point me in the right direction . . .'

'I can't.'

'Are you sure?'

'If Milo knew, he didn't tell me.'

Quisden-Neve clicked his tongue. 'A pity.'

'So perhaps you'll excuse me.' I turned to open the door. As I did so, Quisden-Neve grasped me firmly by the elbow. I looked back at him levelly. 'I don't think we have anything else to say to each other.'

'I disagree, Mrs Moberly. There's a great deal of money at stake here.'

'I'm not interested.'

'Come, come. We're all interested in money. But greed can sometimes blind us to the need to share it with others if any is to be made at all. I'm offering you what would effectively be a partnership.'

'Thanks, but no thanks.'

'Don't rush into the decision. And don't make the mistake of supposing it's straightforward.'

'It feels straightforward to me.'

'You're forgetting the muscular Niall. If you won't help me, I may be compelled to help him.'

'We made a deal about that.'

'Overtaken by events.' He grinned. 'Returning to Bath really was rather foolish, you know.'

'Let go of me.'

He did so. But his grin remained. 'Enjoy the rest of the holiday with your husband, Mrs Moberly. And think about what I've said. Give me a call early in the New Year. You still have my card?'

'You won't be hearing from me.' I opened the door and climbed out.

'In that case,' he called after me, '*you'll* be hearing from *me*.'

I slammed the door and caught one last glimpse of his grinning face through the windscreen. Then he started up, pulled out into the road in a raking U-turn and sped away. I watched him go as the realization seeped into me that he meant exactly what he'd said. He sensed I knew more about Marian than I was willing to reveal. And I wouldn't be rid of him until he'd found out how much.

I suppose that was when another realization dawned on me. I couldn't go on as I was. There was just too much crowding in around me, too much of everything for my mind to hold. I had to find a way out, just as Marian had back in the autumn of 1817. I had to run where no-one could follow.

I got into the car and looked at the map. Midford lay a few miles south of Bath, an easy evening's journey for the sake of a social gathering. I drove to it by as circuitous a route as I could manage, avoiding Bath itself. The village didn't amount to much: a pub and assorted cottages huddled in the shadow of a disused railway viaduct. That wouldn't have been there in 1817, of course. It was hard to imagine what would. I asked in the pub, however, and got immediate recognition of the name Midford Grange.

'Take the turning for Combe Hay and it's first on the right. They're doing it up nice, so they say. You thinking of buying one of the flats?'

I implied I was and drove round to take a look. The Grange was a middling country house of steep gables and tall chimneys, partly obscured by scaffolding, set in neglected grounds bounded by a crumbling wall and rook-infested woodland. An estate agent's board proclaimed its imminent conversion into six stylish self-contained country apartments. In the grey winter light, it looked cold and dismal. But Marian would have come there, as I knew I had to, by night and the glow of welcoming lamps.

I drove back to the hotel, had something to eat, then slept for two soothing hours. I felt calm now, and absolutely certain about what I had to do. I collected Conrad from the stables on schedule and let him talk me through his day over tea at the hotel, as darkness fell. Then he took himself off for a bath before dinner, leaving me by the lounge fireside. But I didn't stay there for long.

Nobody paid me any attention as I walked out to the car and drove away. I was at Midford within twenty minutes. Already, nightfall was having its effect. The village felt different somehow, more remote, more watchful. I parked at the pub, put on the thornproof coat from the boot, took the torch and crowbar from Conrad's toolkit, and walked round under the viaduct and down the lane to the Grange. The gates were closed and padlocked, but several stretches of the boundary wall were semi-ruinous. I scrambled over one into the thin end of the wood, and hacked my way through to the edge of the lawn surrounding the house.

The building was even darker than the starless sky, a slab of solid inky black. Plastic sheeting was flapping somewhere in the wind. There was no sign of life, least of all the life of times long past. But I knew Marian too well to doubt she'd come to me if I gave her the chance. I crossed the lawn and trailed the torch beam round the scaffolded section of the house to the source of the flapping: a run of new ground-floor windows not yet glazed, shrouded against the weather. One corner of the plastic sheet had worked itself loose. I loosened it further with the crowbar, then clambered in over the sill.

I was in a small square high-ceilinged room, plastered and floorboarded and fancily corniced, smelling of wood and cement and newness. I walked out into a hallway and into the next room. It was larger and rectangular, with a fireplace and French windows at the far end. It looked as if the builders had done a fair job of sweeping away all traces of the original design. I switched off the torch and let the darkness soak into my eyes. Nothing happened. The smell didn't alter. The plastic sheeting still flapped. The present held me firm. A sudden fear gripped me that I might have lost Marian for ever. It was a fear that felt like grief, like a surge of pain. I closed my eyes and took a long, deep breath.

'Do you think it possible that the gravity of your manner deters potential dancing partners, Marian?'

Barrington's voice, low and simpering, came to me a fraction of a second before I opened my eyes and started back in amazement at the life and colour and noise that had suddenly filled and somehow enlarged the room. Chandeliers ran the length of the ceiling, ablaze with candlelight. The walls were covered with vast gilt-framed oil paintings of old men in wigs and hunting dogs and sloe-eyed ladies in sylvan settings. Between them pairs of dancers performed their measured steps and gestures, facing each other in the longways formation I had often seen before. The ladies' gowns shimmered and the gentlemen's shoes clipped on the polished floor. At the far end of the room, on a dais set up before the French windows, an orchestra played. Liveried servants and those sitting out the dance lined the walls. Glancing round, I could see the eager sparkle in the dancers' eyes and sense the pleasure and the care they were taking. The gentlemen wore black or maroon tailed coats, with fancy waistcoats and paler breeches; the ladies elaborate ballgowns, with puff sleeves, jewelled bandeaux and long white gloves. I was aware that my own gown was relatively plain and darker than most. But I was also aware that I had chosen it with more of a mind to travelling than to dancing.

'Ignoring those who choose to speak to you could, of course, be equally effective.'

I looked round to confront Barrington's narrow-eyed gaze. A peacock would have envied him his waistcoat, though possibly not the tightness of its fit. 'I do beg your pardon,' I said. 'My mind was quite elsewhere.'

'Evidently. And where, may I ask, was it dwelling?'

'I really am . . . not sure.'

'Perhaps you are pining for dear Jos.'

'Perhaps so,' I responded, paying him back smile for smile.

'He can be a neglectful fellow, he really can.' Barrington stepped closer and lowered his voice. 'I would not leave my wife to languish in my brother's house. Of that you may be certain.'

'But Jos has so many more demands upon his time than you.' Seeing Barrington cock his eyebrow, I added, 'So he tells me.'

'I look upon you as my sister, Marian. It is only fair to tell you that Jos is not so busy as he sometimes claims.'

'You must be mistaken, Barrington. If he were not, why would he so often have to exile himself from Gaunt's Chase?'

'I think you are intelligent enough to know why. Indeed, I think you are quite possibly the most intelligent woman I have ever met.'

'I could almost believe you mean to flatter me.'

'Not at all. I state the simple truth. For evidence, I need look no further than your experiments with the camera obscura.'

I glanced away. 'Jos does not wish those to be spoken of.'

'But Jos is not here.' Barrington paused and we both pretended to watch the dancing. Then he said, 'And he has no jurisdiction over what I permit to be done under my own roof. I could obtain whatever equipment you need.'

'Why might you do that?'

'Because I am a more considerate fellow than you suppose.' He took my arm, prompting me to look round at him. 'And because I have an open mind where scientific enquiry is concerned. There are many, my brother among them, who believe women should confine their energies to childbirth, embroidery and the occasional quadrille.'

'But you are of more enlightened stock?'

'I am, since you ask. I see you for what you are and the world for what it is. You are a married woman, whom the world will ever discount on the strength of your husband's unreasoning censure. But you need not allow your discoveries to wither because of it. There is a way to make them known through the agency of one whom the world will not discount.'

239

'You are referring to . . .'

'Myself.' He beamed, as if bestowing upon me the grandest of favours. 'Jos spoke of a portrait of Susannah and me. He described what only someone who was there at the time could describe. Yet he was not there. He spoke of witchcraft, thus revealing the anachronistic cast of his mind, whilst my own thoughts turned to something altogether more in keeping with the temper of the age.'

'And that is?'

'Commercial opportunity. The profit that so often rewards the pioneer. In such a case as this, we could be speaking of as much as you need to purchase your freedom from what I judge to be a deeply uncongenial existence. There would, I feel sure, be more than enough for both of us. Look at the portraits around this wall. Consider the legion of artists and draughtsmen and silhouettists the fashionable world maintains. I know nothing of the science of what you have been about with your camera and your chemicals. I do not need to. That is your province.'

'Whilst yours is . . .'

'Presentation and exploitation. On your behalf. In your place, so to speak.'

'Fame as well as fortune, in fact.'

'Possibly. But I would be accepting the risk of your failure. A good deal of Jos's wrath would be directed at me were he to learn that I was acting as your patron.'

'You have thought this through, I do see.'

'Oh yes. I speak only because the time is ripe.' The dance had come to a close in the last few minutes. The ladies and gentlemen broke up into smaller groups. The orchestra fell silent. Susannah detached herself from her partner and bore down upon us, gown

240

billowing like a galleon in full sail. 'I sometimes think you married the wrong brother, Marian,' Barrington continued musingly. 'I really do.'

'Susannah is enjoying herself. You should partner her in the next dance.'

'I suppose I should.'

'Whilst I give thought to your . . . interesting proposition.'

'You do find it interesting, then?'

'How could I not?'

'Such an invigorating evening,' declared Susannah as she joined us, flushed and breathless. 'And so much more elegant than anything put on at the Assembly Rooms. Do you not agree, my dears?'

'You are certainly an adornment to the proceedings, Susannah,' I replied. 'Your husband was only this minute sharing with me his resolve to take the floor with you for the next dance.'

'Indeed,' mumbled Barrington.

'Provided it is not a waltz.'

'There is no fear of that at Midford Grange.' Susannah's eyes danced in anticipation. 'But why are you so idle, Marian? I can scarcely believe you are in less demand than me.'

'I confess I am.'

'You should smile more, my dear. You should practise a little gaiety. Am I not right, Barrington?'

'Perhaps Marian's gifts lie in another direction.'

Susannah frowned, momentarily discomposed by the notion that her husband recognized me as possessing any gifts, in whatever direction. Then the orchestra struck up the next dance and she was wreathed in smiles once more. 'Come, then, Barrington. Let us stretch those calves of yours.'

A quiver of something close to distaste passed over Barrington's face. Then he grinned, gave Susannah his arm and guided her out into the throng. I studied him as they went. A more percipient man than I had supposed, he no doubt thought time was his ally in the campaign to recruit me as his partner in commerce. Little did he know that the time was already past. I was about to leave his life for ever. He might be right that the world would look more reasonably upon my heliogenic discoveries if they were presented by a man. But that man would not be Barrington Esguard. I had no need of a patron when I was about to acquire a loving protector.

The dancing had recommenced. Nobody's attention was on me. I turned, moved slowly down the room to the door and slipped out into the hall, then walked steadily but unhurriedly across the marbled floor, past the grand staircase to the main entrance.

'I believe I will take a breath of air,' I remarked to the footman standing by the doors.

'It's a cold night, ma'am.'

'Even so.'

He nodded, opened the doors and stood back as I passed. I heard them close behind me as I descended the steps to the drive and felt the chill strike my face and bosom. The stars were out. The whinnying of horses and the chinking of harnesses carried clearly through the still air. Glancing to my left, I saw a phaeton standing near the angle of the house, facing away from me, its lamps lit. I walked towards it.

'Good evening, ma'am,' said Poulter as I drew alongside. He jumped down, wrapped a cloak round my shoulders and helped me up, then climbed back into his place and tightened the reins. 'Shall we be on our way?'

'We shall, Mr Poulter.'

I did not look back as we headed down the curving drive and out through the gates. The ball would go on without me. Eventually, I would be missed. But by then . . .

'Have we far to go, Mr Poulter?'

'Half a mile or so, ma'am, no more. I'll be leaving you there.'

'Then let me thank you now for playing your part in this.'

'There's no call for thanks. I'm no more than hired help.'

'Do I detect disapprobation in your voice?'

'I should hope not. I do as I'm bidden. And I don't pass judgement. Bid me turn back to the Grange and I'll do it. Bid me go on and I will.'

'Then let us go on.'

'Very good, ma'am.'

We continued in silence down a narrow, high-hedged lane that wound away into the countryside south-west of Midford. I took it to be a discreet if indirect route to the Bristol road. There was no highway in sight, however, when we stopped in the lee of a small wood. Poulter uttered a word of instruction to the horses and they stood where they were. Nothing moved. The night and everything in it held its breath.

'Is Mr Byfield to meet us here?' I asked at length.

'This is the meeting place,' Poulter replied.

'Can he have been delayed?'

'There's no delay.'

'Then where is he?'

'He's here, Marian,' said a voice beside and below us. But it was not Lawrence's voice. A darkly clad figure appeared out of the shadows at Poulter's elbow, and I found myself looking down into Jos's bloodshot eyes and smirking face.

'You should have bidden me turn back, ma'am,' murmured Poulter. Then he handed the reins to Jos, jumped down and vanished. Jos had climbed up into his place before I could even think of jumping down myself. His face was suddenly close to me. His free hand snaked round my shoulders, twitched back the hood of the cloak and clasped the nape of my neck as in a vice.

'Good evening, Marian,' he rasped, his tainted breath steaming in the air between us. 'Mr Byfield is indisposed. I trust your husband is an acceptable substitute.'

'Jos, I—'

'Be silent, madam.' His grip on my neck tightened painfully, then eased fractionally. 'Listen to what I have to tell you. Listen very carefully. Your life may depend upon it. The play is at an end, Marian. Your leash has run to the collar. It is time for my oh-so-clever wife to understand the limits of her cleverness. You have been entertained by actors too long. Now the playwright takes the stage. Did you suppose I invited Mr Byfield to take his ease at Gaunt's Chase out of solicitude for his health? No, no. Even then he was answering to my purposes.'

'It cannot be.'

'Did I not tell you to be silent?' His hand tightened round my neck once more. 'You have never obeyed me, Marian. You have defied me at every turn. And you have had the arrogance to suppose that you needed neither my love nor my mastery. What recourse did you leave me but to hurt you in the only way you can be hurt? I found you the lover you thought yourself too superior to need. I found him for you, and now I have taken him away. Fear not. He is well. As well as ever. And richer, thanks to what I have paid him to cuckold me. He has

244

gone abroad, as he spoke of doing. But he has gone alone. Though doubtless he will not remain so. Byfield bestows his affections on womankind with an admirable lack of discrimination, as your own case amply demonstrates.'

I tried to tell myself that he was lying. I tried to believe that Lawrence had been waylaid, betrayed perhaps by Poulter. But with every word from Jos my certainty faltered.

'You are my chattel, Marian. Mine to do with as I will. Your independence of spirit is at an end. You may still hope for rescue or escape. But there will be neither. Byfield is gone. The future he held out to you will never be. It never could have been. All he did was help me break you. That was all he was required to do. You let him have his way with you. But it was *my* way. Well, now that you know the pleasures of love, I will make sure you never experience them again. Denial is the whip I will take to your back, when I do not take the whip itself.'

He relaxed slightly, some of his venom already spent. 'You have chosen this outcome, madam. I have not forced it upon you. I require a meek and obedient wife. Henceforth, that is what you will be. We will return to Midford Grange and you will dance with me. And you will smile and dote upon me and do whatever I tell you to do. That is how it will be. And that is how it will continue to be. So, speak a word, if you please. But take care to make it a compliant one. Shall we go, madam?'

My mind raced to accept and address this sudden overturning of everything I had yearned for and believed attainable. I would have wept were it not for the depth of the hatred I bore Jos. It is a terrible thing to admit, but the power of that hatred sustained me in the instant of my shattered dreams and sundered hopes. I knew only one thing for certain. I could not, would not, accept Jos's terms. He had broken me, it was true. I would never be whole again. But he could not bridle me. I would rather die than admit defeat at his hands.

'Well?' he snapped.

'No,' I answered, quietly but firmly.

'What?'

'I refuse.'

'You cannot.'

'But I can.' I fixed him with my gaze. 'Listen to me, Jos. Now we will talk of *your* life. And a promise I will make you. A solemn vow. If I go with you to Midford Grange, I will do so as the very model of what a wife should be. And I will sustain the performance as long as I have to. Until fate hands me my chance.'

'There will be no "chance".'

'Oh, but there will. There is bound to be. When you are sleeping, or drunk, or careless, or paying me no heed. When you have forgotten my promise. Then I will strike. I will kill you, Jos, if you do not let me go. I give you my word. I will kill you and be hanged for it. But you will not be there to see me hang. You will be dead.'

He said nothing. He went on staring at me in the shadows cast by the phaeton's lamps. The horses stirred and I heard the reins creak as he restrained them. Then he gave a low, mirthless laugh from which some edge of confidence was lacking. 'You cannot expect me to believe such nonsense.'

'Believe it or not as you please. It is the truth. You have taken everything from me, as you intended. But everything encompasses fear and self-preservation and a Christian conscience. You have deprived me of those along with every ounce of hope. So the consequence is this. If you force me to remain with you, I will find a way to take your life. You would do better to kill me now. But can you trust Mr Poulter so far as murder? I doubt it. Let me go, then. I promise you will never see me again.'

Silence intruded once more. Our thoughts, our memories, our knowledge of each other contended in the cold and motionless air. I was defeated. And he was confounded. He had succeeded too completely. He had outwitted himself.

'What is your answer, Jos?'

He gave none. None, that is, that he had not already given. I realized as I waited that he was no longer touching me. I slowly lowered myself to the ground on the far side of the phaeton from him. He made no move. I stepped back. Still he said nothing.

'Goodbye, Jos.'

'Be sure I never *do* see you again, madam,' he said, in the tone of one forcing out the words. Then he flicked the reins and the phaeton moved forward. 'Get on, damn you,' he shouted at the horses. I heard him rattle out the whip and give them the feel of it. They started and broke into a canter. The phaeton swayed away along the lane. As it turned a bend and vanished from view, I sensed a presence at my shoulder.

'This isn't what was foreseen, ma'am,' said Poulter.

'Where is Mr Byfield?'

'Gone abroad. I was given no hint of his destination.'

'He and my husband . . . have been acting in concert?'

'I wish I could say otherwise.'

'Whilst you and Miss Gathercole . . .'

'Have much to be ashamed of. But what else should we expect when we go to the market and sell ourselves to the highest bidder?' He sighed. 'Can I see you on your way somewhere, ma'am?'

'I do not think so.'

'I'm loath to leave you here.'

'Then you should not have brought me.'

'I have a hired mare tethered in the wood nearby. She's from the inn at Saltford, up on the Bristol turnpike. Take her back if you want. She'll give you no trouble. If you can manage the saddle, that is. It's not—'

'I can ride astride if needs be, Mr Poulter.'

'Indeed, ma'am. Well, there's nothing to pay at the inn. And most of the London coaches pick up there. If you're set on leaving the area by the swiftest route . . .'

'I could do no better?'

'You could not.'

'I accept, then. You'll understand that I don't feel inclined to thank you.'

'I understand, ma'am. Let me show you where she is.'

I followed him through the gloom to the corner of the wood. The mare neighed at our approach. Poulter untied her, led her out into the lane and helped me to mount. I gathered the cloak around my legs for modesty's sake and waited while he adjusted the stirrups. Then he stepped back.

'If you follow this lane, it'll bring you out on the heights above Bath. Bear left at the Odd Down cross-roads and you'll be able to cut across to the turnpike without touching the city.'

'You seem to know my requirements well.'

'I've helped to wish them on you, ma'am, have I not?'

'So you have.'

He tipped his hat. 'Good luck.'

'Goodbye, Mr Poulter.'

With that I rode away into the night. The stars and a three-quarter moon were bright enough to light my path. Jos was a mile or more away by now, the gap between us stretching into permanence. I was alone and free at last to weep tears of anguish for the love I had wasted on Lawrence Byfield and the treachery he had found it possible to practise against me. Was it all pretence, then, the wooing and the winning? Was there nothing heart-felt and wholesome in the things we had done? I knew, even as the tears ran down my cheeks, that I would have to learn the answer. As I rode on, the knowledge hard-ened my distress and transmuted it into the steeliest resolve. Wherever he had fled, I would follow. However long it took, I would find him. And then I would call him to account. I pulled my handkerchief from my sleeve, closed my eyes and wiped the lids dry.

And when I opened them I was walking down a tarmac lane, with the amber glow of city lights visible beyond the horizon. I still held the torch in my hand. When I switched it on, its beam showed only an empty stretch of hedge-flanked road ahead. On instinct, I turned round and started back the way I seemed to have come. Soon, I reached a junction, a finger-post pointing to Midford one way, Combe Hay the other. I headed for Midford, walking fast to stay warm. I began to recognize the lie of the land, or to feel that I did. I pressed on and came to the padlocked gates of Midford Grange. I walked straight by.

Within minutes, I was back in the village. The pub was in darkness. Looking at my watch, I saw it was already past midnight. Conrad would be beside himself. I got into the car and drove away as quietly as I could. The night was neutral between past and present, a dark gulf of infinity that I seemed to speed through with neither starting point nor destination. Marian's despair lingered in my memory like an unassuaged loss. I knew what she'd meant to do, and now it seemed so clear and simple in my mind that I could only do the same. Beyond a certain point, there's no turning back, no possibility of returning to what you've left behind. She understood that. She made me understand it, too.

I reached the main road and paused at the junction, staring at the sign ahead of me. The hotel lay to the right. A minute or so passed. Then a car came up behind me. The driver waited for a second, then sounded his horn. That's when I made my decision. I turned left and drove away, tears filling my eyes as I accelerated.

It was as simple as that, Daphne. A twitch of the indicator, a turn of the wheel. And it was done. I drove on through the night to London and dropped the car off not far from the flat. But I didn't go home. That would have tested the strength of my resolution too soon. I have to face this in my own way, you see. I can't be helped. I don't exactly know what I'm going to do. I'm not sure whether I'm fleeing her or following her. It's one or the other. Or perhaps it's both. Somewhere out there I'll find her. Or I'll lose her in whatever life I find instead. Don't come looking for me. You've done all you can. Now it's up to me. There has to be an answer. Hers or mine. There has to be some way of dealing with this. That's all I'm really aiming for now. A way to go on. A future. Survival. My own life and nobody else's. Freedom. What price, though? That's the question. If I learn the answer, I'll let you know. That's a promise.

Chapter Nine

'Tell me again why you think we'll find her here,' said Daphne as we stood on the foredeck of the Weymouth–Guernsey car ferry, moving into St Peter Port through a light Channel mist early the following morning.

'There was a Guernsey stamp on the package she sent Dawn Esguard,' I replied, my mouth tightened by the stubbornness with which I'd repeated the same line of reasoning over and over again. 'And Niall's been coming here a lot lately. Plus Nymanex are bound to have a base here because it's a tax haven, so we can assume Conrad Nyman's no stranger to the island. Too many coincidences not to mean something, I reckon.'

'Unless Niall's just following the same false trail as us. And Nyman's just an innocent businessman.'

'That's what we're here to prove. One way or the other.'

'And besides . . .' She let the thought drift away behind us. But the echo of it remained. There *was* nowhere else to look.

'You didn't have to come,' I reminded her.

'Didn't I?' She looked at me, narrowing her eyes thoughtfully. 'Oh, I think I did.'

'Why?'

'Because neither of us can give up while there's still a chance.'

'Even though you don't think it's much of one?'

She nodded. 'Even though.'

Daphne was right, reluctant though I was to admit it. Guernsey was a small island, but that didn't make it a hard place in which to hide. Tax havens are accustomed to privacy, if not downright secrecy. And Guernsey over a fine Easter weekend had also attracted its fair share of early-season holidaymakers. We'd found hotel rooms and ferry berths difficult to come by. Half the known yachting world seemed to have gathered in the harbour at St Peter Port and the town itself was crowded with tourists, trippers, shoppers and any number of people who might have their own very particular reasons for being there.

Like Daphne and me, for instance. Though we'd joined forces, you couldn't exactly say we'd opened our hearts to each other. We were both a little too ashamed of our failure to second-guess Eris in the past to manage complete honesty. If Daphne had been a more perceptive psychotherapist and I'd been a more attentive lover, Eris's struggles with her real enemies, as well as her imaginary demons, could have ended long since in . . . what? There was the thorn I couldn't dislodge from my flesh, any more than I suspected Daphne could. Marian Esguard was real. Had been, for sure. What was she now? *Where* was she now? She'd ridden away into the Somerset night and Eris had gone after her. That was all we really knew. And even that we hardly knew for sure.

252

The scale and relative hopelessness of what our search involved soon became apparent. We had the Nymanex video still of Eris to show around, of course, but just how many shops, cafés, pubs and hotels could we try without driving ourselves into the ground? Over the next three days we went a long way towards finding out. And I doubt we made any real impression on the task we'd set ourselves. Even at the pub slap-bang opposite Nymanex's discreet brass-plaqued office in St Peter Port's financial district, nobody had heard of Conrad Nyman, far less Niall Esguard. And the picture of Eris drew only blank looks. We circled the narrow traffic-choked lanes of the island, hoping to hear or see something, to strike a chord, to jog a memory. But there was nothing. We were strangers looking for strangers, surrounded by people with better things to do.

By Wednesday, we'd begun to lose patience with each other as well as with what we were doing. Nymanex's office was open for business after the Easter break and, since it offered the only shred of a clue we had to follow, I called in and tried to make an appointment with Conrad Nyman, to test my suspicion that he was some-times to be found there. It was pretty obvious the receptionist thought I was mad. 'We're just an out-station, sir. Mr Nyman's based in London.' Nor did Eris's picture ring any bells.

'Nobody knows her, Ian. Nobody's *seen* her. It's the same answer every time. If she was on Guernsey, I don't think she stayed long.'

'Then why is Niall here?'

'We don't know for certain that he is.'

'He's looking for her. Don't you see, Daphne? He's hunting her down. We have to get to her first.'

'Fine. Just tell me how.'

'By not giving up.'

'Can we at least take a break? I need some air. Let's drive to the coast. Stretch our legs.'

'You go.'

'No. *We'll* go. I'm giving you sound professional advice, Ian. Step back from this for a few hours. I think we need some perspective. How about a seaside stroll? It could work wonders.'

'You make it sound like a prescription.'

'In your case, it is.'

I went in the final analysis because I was too tired to think of anything better to do. We drove down to Icart Point on the south coast and walked a couple of bracing miles along the cliff path. The views stretched across the sea to Jersey and a hazy hint of Brittany beyond. Some perspective really was needed. But it wasn't necessarily enough, as I was bound to admit.

'We're going to have to start considering an unpalatable possibility,' Daphne ventured when we were most of the way back to the car.

'I know.'

'Maybe she really isn't here. Maybe she never was.'

I nodded grimly. 'Maybe not.'

'How long do we go on looking?'

'A few days more.'

'All right. But then?'

'You tell me, Daphne.' I looked round at her. 'You tell me.'

But she couldn't. We were out of options. Unless Eris chose to give us another, of course. All along, she'd opened the doors I'd walked through. Vienna. Tollard Rising. Guernsey. They'd served her purpose, for whatever reason. Perhaps this time it was different. Perhaps this time no doors were going to open. Nor ever again.

The thought festered in the silence that fell between us. We started back towards St Peter Port as the warm afternoon petered into dusk, stopping halfway at the Fermain Tavern to try Eris's picture and the usual questions on whoever was in the bar. But the place was empty and the barman couldn't help. It was just another waste of time and effort. We sat at a corner table to finish our drinks. Daphne picked up a discarded copy of the *Guernsey Evening Press* and leafed through it. I stared into space and waited for some inspired notion to hit me. None did. Several minutes slipped by. I drained my glass and looked at Daphne, and saw she was frowning intently at the newspaper in her hand.

'What is it?'

'Something . . . odd.'

'What?'

'Nyman told you he met Eris in Greenwich Park, didn't he? Near the Royal Observatory. Where she'd been to see the camera obscura.'

'Yes.'

'Did you know there was one on Guernsey?'

'No. Let me see.'

She turned the page round towards me and pointed at a boxed advertisement. THE HARBOUR VIEW YOU WON'T HAVE SEEN BEFORE, ran the blurb. LA FAUCON-NERIE CAMERA OBSCURA – AN EYE-OPENER RESTORED. 'Another coincidence, do you think?' asked Daphne as I glanced up at her.

'Too much of one. Wouldn't you say?'

She hesitated, then nodded. 'This time, I would.'

La Fauconnerie was a fine old Georgian house set in sub-tropical gardens on a lofty perch near the summit of the hill overlooking St Peter Port. From the street I could

255

see a dovecote on a knoll off to one side behind the house, where it enjoyed an uninterrupted panorama of the town and shoreline. The shape and metallic texture of its cupola were distinctive, and confirmed the location of the camera obscura. I was all for calling on the owner that evening, but Daphne insisted we wait till the advertised hours of opening next day, which was undoubtedly wise, even if it was frustrating.

Promptly, at ten o'clock on Thursday morning, we were back. The gates of the house stood open and signs pointed the way to the Fauconnerie Camera, as they called it. At closer quarters the house itself seemed less imposing than it had from the other side of the wall. Dilapidation was setting in. The gardens were likewise in need of care and attention, with overgrown borders and a tumbledown orangery. The converted dovecote was a different story, however. It looked to be in immaculate condition, the redundant perches gleaming white in contrast to the glimmering black cowl of the cupola that clearly held the mirror and lens of the camera.

We'd reached a paved area round the door at the front of the dovecote before catching the attention of a powerfully built middle-aged man engaged in hammering new struts into a cucumber frame away to our right. He waved and strode over to greet us.

'Sorry,' he said, grinning through a ginger beard as thick as a hedge. 'We don't normally get any customers this early. Though it's more or less perfect visibility.' He gazed away to the east, where Castle Cornet at the mouth of the harbour, and the whale-backed silhouettes of Herm and Jethou beyond, stood out clearly in the sunshine. 'No question about that.'

'I had no idea there was a camera obscura on

Guernsey,' I remarked. 'Until I spotted your advert in the paper.'

'Only recently restored. Brand-new optics. But it was originally set up in the eighteen twenties, we think. It's hard to be sure. We're hoping to make quite a thing of it. If we can turn it into a tourist attraction we might be able to do up the house properly. Talking of which, it's two pounds fifty per adult.'

I handed over the money and he showed us in. The interior was a standard arrangement: a screen set on a circular table in the centre of the room, with blackout curtains all around and pulleys to adjust the lens. Our host fiddled with the angle and focus for a while, until we had a view of the yachts moored in the harbour pin-sharp on the screen, then he panned the camera to either side with a motorized unit and let us admire the strange and powerful trick of the device. Most of St Peter Port, the roofs and the roads, the cars and the people, the bobbing boats and the wheeling gulls, slid slowly past in the foreshortened eye of the lens above us.

'If there's anything you're particularly interested in,' he said, 'you only have to—'

'Who installed the original camera?'

'Fellow called Byfield.' I felt Daphne grasp my elbow in the darkness. 'An Englishman. Don't know much about him. Amateur astronomer, I suppose.'

'He lived here?'

'Yes. Not sure how long. But long enough to see the potential of this site. Amazing coverage of the coast, isn't it?'

'Breathtaking,' murmured Daphne.

'Did he do anything else?' I persisted.

'How do you mean?'

'I'm not sure. Anything . . . historically significant, perhaps?'

'Not that I've heard of. Good view of Sark coming up, actually.'

'Would anyone else know about him?'

'Byfield? Don't think so. Why should they? Like I told a chap yesterday—'

'Someone else was asking about him?'

'Yes.'

'About Byfield?'

'Look.' Our host abruptly switched off the motor, pulled back the curtains and pushed the door open, admitting a flood of sunlight in which he blinked reproachfully at us. 'It's quite obvious the camera doesn't interest you. It was the same with your friend.'

'Not a friend.'

'Well, whatever. The fact is I know next to nothing about Lawrence Byfield.'

'Tell us about the other visitor who asked after him, then,' suggested Daphne. 'Did he give you his name?'

'Yes. Well, that was the point really. He seemed to think his brother might have been sniffing around here a few months back. Late brother, apparently, though I never quite—'

'Quisden-Neve?'

'You obviously do know him. Yes, that's the name. It meant nothing to me.'

'Quisden-Neve's brother is here?'

'Well, he was yesterday.'

'Maybe he saw your advert,' said Daphne.

'No. He already seemed to know more about La Fauconnerie than I do myself. He was surprised I'd never met his brother. Asked me over and over again in case I'd forgotten, though I'm not likely to have, am I, with a name like that?'

'Do you happen to know where we can find him?'

'Oh yes. He told me the hotel he was staying at. Just in case I remembered something about his brother. But I think he said he was leaving today, so—'

The St Pierre Park was a modern multi-star hotel backing on to its own golf course just beyond the western outskirts of St Peter Port. We were there far sooner than the niggardly island speed limit allowed, hoping against hope that the sibling Quisden-Neve hadn't checked out early. We were in luck – but only just. A man whose voice, bearing and washed-out blue eyes I recognized immediately was clearing reception as we entered. He looked like Montagu with the benefit of more exercise, less Pomerol and a plainer taste in clothes. But, then, he was in mourning. Day-Glo bow ties weren't exactly appropriate. As I steered Daphne on to an interception course, I reminded her in an undertone to say nothing that implied I was the errant witness to his brother's murder. We were going to have to tread carefully as well as swiftly.

'Mr Quisden-Neve?'

'Yes.' He stopped and frowned at us, every crease of his expression calling up the spirit of the dead Montagu. 'What can I do for you?'

'I knew your brother.'

'You did?'

'My name's Ian Jarrett.'

'I don't recall Monty mentioning you.'

'I knew him only slightly. And recently. This is a friend of mine, by the way. Daphne Sanger.'

'Charmed, I'm sure.' Even in bereavement, he

259

summoned a flirtatious smile, and seemed to dally with the notion of kissing Daphne's hand rather than merely shaking it. 'Valentine Quisden-Neve.'

'My condolences,' said Daphne. 'I never met your brother myself, but . . . you were close?'

'Twins.'

'Then I'm doubly sorry. Losing a twin . . .'

'Is akin to losing a limb.' He shook his head dolefully and sighed. 'I'm sorry, but I have a plane to catch. When you say you knew Monty . . .'

'I met him not long ago . . . in connection with a mutual acquaintance.'

'How very enigmatic. Monty would have approved. But I'm confused. You met him here, on Guernsey?'

'No. Bath.'

'Then why . . .'

'We've just come from La Fauconnerie,' said Daphne. 'We know a little, a very little, about Lawrence Byfield.'

'As it seems do you,' I continued.

'On the contrary. I know nothing.' He looked at each of us in turn, then moved towards the exit. 'May we talk on the hoof, as it were? I really must catch that plane. The funeral's tomorrow. And there's a great deal yet to be arranged. Tell me about the acquaintance you had in common with Monty, Mr Jarrett.'

'A young woman called Eris Moberly,' I explained, as we reached the open air and headed for the car park. 'She's gone missing. We're trying to find her. She and Monty shared an interest in this man Byfield.'

'Hence your visit to Guernsey?'

'You could say that, though there are other—' I broke off, aware I couldn't afford to get in too deep. 'Look, I was shocked to read of your brother's death. The

260

circumstances sounded quite awful. I'm just wondering—'

'The circumstances weren't half as awful as the theory the police have come up with. They think Monty may have been killed by some kind of homicidal rent boy. Rough trade, as I believe it's called. The fact that his predilections went quite the other way is lost on them. A bachelor, found strangled in an InterCity toilet. Q.E.D., apparently. God help us all.'

'What brought you to Guernsey, Mr Quisden-Neve?' asked Daphne.

'The conviction that Monty was murdered for some altogether more sinister reason. He'd been uncharacteristically secretive in recent months, even with me. "Got something a little hush-hush on, Val," he'd say whenever I asked. "Could be my entrée to the big time." Well, so much for that. He was obviously out of his league. But which league had he strayed into? That's what I'd like to know. Since the police don't seem to want to find out, I've decided to do their job for them, as best I can. I was at his flat on Saturday morning, sorting things out, when the post came. It included a reminder for an unpaid bill from a genealogical researcher here on Guernsey. Fellow called Lefebvre. Unlike the police, I'd wondered where Monty was going on the train. They assumed London, but his bag, along with whatever tickets he was carrying, was missing. And I was sure he meant to be away several days. His toothbrush and shaving tackle weren't in the bathroom. Could it have been Guernsey? I phoned round the airlines and, bingo, there he was, booked on a flight from Heathrow to Guernsey last Thursday afternoon. I couldn't contact Lefebvre until Tuesday, because of the damned holiday. He wouldn't reveal what his bill was for over the phone, but in person it was a different story, especially when I paid him what he was owed. Settling debts never was Monty's strong point, I'm afraid.'

'What was Lefebvre working on?' I asked. 'Lawrence Byfield?'

'The very man. Tenant of La Fauconnerie, back in the eighteen twenties.' We'd reached Quisden-Neve's hire car. He opened the boot, dumped his bag inside and looked round at us. 'Bit of a dead end, wouldn't you say?'

'Not necessarily.'

'Nothing worth murdering Monty for. That seems clear.'

'Does it? What had Lefebvre found out?'

'I really don't have the time to go into it all. Why not ask him yourself?' He fumbled with his wallet. 'Here's his card. Look, if you do turn anything up . . .' He scribbled something on the back before passing it to me. 'There's my phone number.'

'Thanks. But look—'

'I have to go. Sorry.' He moved round to the driver's door, but pulled up smartly when Daphne laid a restraining hand on his shoulder.

'One last thing, Mr Quisden-Neve.'

'What is it?'

'Show him Eris's picture, Ian. Just in case.'

'All right.' I took it from my pocket and held it out for him to see. 'Ever met her?'

He grabbed it from me and peered closely at the likeness. 'As a matter of fact, I think I have. Here, in St Peter Port. Yesterday.'

'*What?*'

'A strange business, actually. But there's been so much—'

262

'Tell us.' Daphne interrupted. 'Please.'

'I didn't think at the time . . .' He shrugged. 'Lefebvre's office is in a tiny alley near the market. I'd parked down at the harbour, on one of the piers. I'd just got back to the car and was about to get in when another car leaving the pier, some kind of Lotus, bright yellow and brand new – eye-catching number, no question – squealed to a halt right by me. The driver's window was down. It was her. This woman. She was at the wheel.'

'You're sure?'

'Can one ever be absolutely sure of such things? I think it was her. I *feel* sure, looking at this picture.'

'What happened?'

'She stared at me. Almost through me. As if she'd seen a ghost.'

'She mistook you for your brother,' murmured Daphne.

'That's possible, if, as you tell me, she knew Monty.'

'Did you speak to her?'

'No. She just stared at me for . . . what? . . . half a minute. Then she raised the window and drove away. I thought no more about it.'

'She's here,' I said, half dazed by such a bland, unlooked-for delivery of proof. 'Alive and well. On the island.'

'This is important, isn't it?' asked Quisden-Neve, handing the picture back to me. 'This is what it's all about.'

'Almost certainly not,' said Daphne with a calm perversity that somewhere, at the back of my mind, I saw the sense of. 'Eris has a lot of problems. But they're unlikely to have anything to do with your brother's murder.'

'Let me be the judge of that, Miss Sanger.'

263

'Of course. Look, here's *my* card.' Seeing Quisden-Neve's brow furrow at the sight of her professional title, Daphne added, 'I was treating her. You'll understand I can't go into details. But if you want to talk further when we get back . . .'

'I'm sure I shall.'

'Then please phone me.'

'Or we'll phone you,' I said, smiling in an attempt to assure him of our good faith. It was just as well he had a plane to catch. He had too many questions. And those I was able to answer I couldn't afford to – yet.

'I'm not going to let this rest, you know,' he declared, as if to the world in general, as he climbed into the car.

'Don't worry,' said Daphne.

'Neither are we,' I concluded, before she could say it herself.

The Lefebvre Family History and Lost Heirs Service was housed in attic rooms over a hairdressing salon in the centre of St Peter Port. The receptionist-cum-secretary told us, through a headful of cold, that Mr Lefebvre wouldn't be back till three o'clock. We made the nearest we could to an appointment and left.

The next few hours hung heavily. I had no appetite for lunch and little inclination to describe my reaction to Valentine Quisden-Neve's sighting of Eris. Daphne took a good guess at what it was anyway, as we walked the pier car parks in an aimless reconstruction of the scene, and wondered if at any moment the yellow Lotus might reappear.

'What would she have done if it had been you rather than Quisden-Neve? That's what you're asking yourself, isn't it, Ian? Are we falling over backwards to give her the benefit of the doubt? Is she ill and in need of help

264

– or just having a good laugh at our expense?'

'You think that if you want. I'll go on believing in her, thank you very much.'

'Because you have to.'

'Because I *choose* to. I love her – unconditionally. It's as simple as that.'

'As a psychotherapist, I have to tell you love is neither simple nor unconditional. You love the woman you met in Vienna. She's not necessarily the woman hiding here on Guernsey.'

'We'll see about that.'

'Yes. We will. I'm merely trying to prepare you for the possibility that—'

'Save it, Daphne. I'm not going to argue with you about this.'

'Just with yourself.'

'For God's sake.' I pulled up and rounded on her. 'This is getting us nowhere. Why don't we go our separate ways until four o'clock and meet up then at Lefebvre's?'

'All right.' She eyed me thoughtfully. 'You're going to spend all that time here, aren't you? Just watching and waiting.'

'Maybe.'

'And, if you do see her, you'd prefer me to be elsewhere.'

'I suppose I would.'

'You seem to have forgotten something.'

'What's that?'

'We're supposed to be on the same side.' She sighed. 'But have it your own way.' Without another word she turned and walked away. I watched her go with a squirming sense of relief. Everything she'd said was true. But now at least I didn't have to hear it said.

Nothing happened. Lightning didn't strike twice. Or maybe Eris knew better than to return to the same place so soon. I spent so long pacing round the piers and marinas that I began to wonder if Quisden-Neve could have been mistaken. But I knew that was only frustration doing my thinking for me. He'd seen her. But I wasn't going to. Not yet, anyway.

Daphne was waiting for me by the market arcade, opposite the entrance to the alley that led to Lefebvre's office. It was just gone ten to three by the town church clock.

'You're early,' she said, with a softness in her voice that hinted at regret for the harsh words we'd exchanged at the pier.

'You, too.'

'That's because we're suddenly short of time. I've had an urgent message from a psychiatrist I work with. A patient he referred to me has tried to commit suicide. Quite a serious attempt, apparently. I'll have to go back right away.'

'Of course. Eris is only one case to you. I do see that.'

'Ian—'

'You have to go. It's all right. I understand.' Part of me was pleased. When I found Eris, I wanted to be alone with her. 'I didn't see her, by the way. You didn't expect me to, did you?'

'No. I didn't.'

'Because you think it's me she's hiding from.'

'Let's talk about it later. I'm booked on a flight to Heathrow at five o'clock. I can still come with you to see Lefebvre if you'll drive me to the airport afterwards.'

'All right. Let's go.'

Lefebvre was alone in his office, having sent his ailing secretary home. 'She was no use to me, sneezing and snuffling all over the place.' Not that he looked a fastidious man. The greasy hair, dirty fingernails and frayed shirt suggested he dealt with most of his clients by post. But he was nothing if not adaptable. 'I conducted the Byfield research for the late Montagu Quisden-Neve. It was a confidential transaction. The information itself, though, is still for sale, so to speak, at my usual terms.'

'What are they?' asked Daphne.

'They're, ah, set out in this leaflet.' He began to rummage in his desk. 'Now, where—?'

'Just tell us,' I interrupted.

'Very well.' He stopped rummaging. 'Fifty pounds.' He smiled. 'For this kind of thing.'

'For work you've already been paid for,' Daphne pointed out.

'I charge what the market will bear.' His smile broadened. 'And there is of course no VAT to worry about.'

'Here.' I handed him the money. 'Let's get on with it.'

'Do you want a receipt?'

'All we want is everything you told Quisden-Neve about Lawrence Byfield.'

'Of course. And we're all busy people. I quite understand.' He pocketed the cash and composed himself. 'Well, now, this was an unusual assignment, I can't deny. Famous ancestors and unclaimed bequests are my normal province. Mr Quisden-Neve had more abstruse requirements. They amounted essentially to everything I could learn about Lawrence Byfield, whom he believed to have lived here during the eighteen twenties. The most difficult task was confirming that the man had indeed been a resident on the island. I eventually traced him through the poor rate registers. He held the lease of La Fauconnerie, a rather handsome property up on—'

'We've seen it.'

'Ah. Right. Along with the camera obscura?'

'Yes.'

'Bernard Cresswell's done an excellent restoration job, don't you think?' He paused, expecting, I suppose, a chorus of enthusiasm. When none came, he merely raised his eyebrows and continued. 'Good. Well, Byfield leased the house from March 1819 until his death in October 1824, during which time he installed a camera obscura in the dovecote and won something of a reputation in the community as an amateur scientist.'

'He was trying to follow in her footsteps,' Daphne whispered. The same thought had come to me. Rogue or not, Byfield had appreciated the potential importance of heliogenesis. A camera obscura was a good starting point. As to how much further he'd gone . . .

'What sort of reputation?'

'I can't really be more specific. He was a founding member of La Société Scientifique de Guernesey. There was a brief obituary in their archives. I had to have it translated from the original French. I incur many such expenses in this line of work, let me tell you.'

'How did he meet his death?' asked Daphne. 'He'd still have been a relatively young man in 1824.'

'Thirty-nine, according to evidence given at the inquest.'

'Not natural causes, then?'

'By no means. Byfield was killed in a duel – or as a consequence of one, perhaps I should say. He fought a Frenchman by the name of Paulmier on the sands at Vazon Bay. Sabres were the chosen weapons. Byfield suffered a minor injury from which he was expected to recover, but for some reason the bleeding couldn't be staunched.'

'He bled to death.'

'Yes.'

I looked at Daphne. The illness from which Byfield had supposedly been convalescing when he came to Tollard Rising; the limp; the minor injury; the unexpected death. Byfield was a haemophiliac – the one Quisden-Neve had been looking for.

'Why was the duel fought?' asked Daphne.

'Not recorded, I'm afraid. Paulmier fled the island, fearing prosecution. The Procureur was known to be down on all that kind of Gallic excess. The seconds claimed not to have been told. Mr Quisden-Neve asked me to look for a woman in the case and I did turn up a coincidental death which struck him as significant. The suicide of an unidentified Englishwoman a week before the duel. She threw herself off the harbour wall into a stormy sea and drowned.'

'Oh God,' murmured Daphne.

'It was suggested at the inquest that the events were connected, but an old friend of Byfield's who'd travelled from England to attend his funeral and stayed on for the inquest—'

'Joslyn Esguard,' I put in with fatalistic certainty.

'Yes. Esguard *was* the name.'

'He did his best to *dis*connect them, did he?'

'As a matter of fact he did. He said, in evidence, that his friend had fought several duels back in England over gambling debts, and suggested that was almost certainly the cause on this occasion.'

'Are you sure the woman was never identified?'

'We're talking about 1824. It's pure luck I turned up this much. Without the duel it wouldn't have been

269

sensational enough to warrant such a detailed press report. The drowning was small beer.'

'What else did you find out?'

'Nothing to speak of. Byfield died without issue and—'

'Without legitimate issue, you mean?'

'Er, yes, quite. As you say. At all events, no widow or grieving relatives cropped up at the inquest. And La Fauconnerie was re-let. Byfield was buried in an unmarked grave at the town cemetery. I can give you the plot reference if you require it.'

'That won't be necessary.'

'What about the unidentified woman?' asked Daphne.

'How do you mean?'

'Where was she buried?'

'Oh, I couldn't say.' Lefebvre shrugged. 'Does it really matter?'

We reached the airport in time for a cup of tea in the cafeteria before Daphne went through to board her flight. We hadn't said much since leaving Lefebvre's office. The doleful implications of what he'd told us didn't seem to need spelling out. Marian had traced Byfield to Guernsey after seven years of searching, and found a man of straw not worth the hunting down. Perhaps she'd hoped all along that he really had been more than Jos's puppet. But perhaps he'd had enough decency to disabuse her on the point, to be honest with her for the first and last time. Hence her despairing dive from the harbour wall. And hence his quarrel with a short-tempered French swordsman. A second suicide, dressed up as a *mort d'honneur*. Leaving his old friend from England to sift through the wreckage – and to

270

squirrel away certain facts for future use. Quisden-Neve had died with the last piece in the jigsaw close at hand. But for us it was only the first piece. And the picture it formed part of remained a mystery.

'Do you think Eris knows what happened to Marian?' I asked as the minutes ticked by.

'Knows – or senses?' Daphne looked across at me, her voice barely audible above a toddler's temper tantrum at the table behind her. 'It would at least explain what brought her here. In part.'

'And the other part?'

'Something to do with Niall. It must be.'

'I thought you were unconvinced he was on the island.'

'I'm unconvinced by everything. Except the need for caution. I'll be back as soon as I can. By Sunday, hopefully. Until then—'

'I'm to walk on eggshells?'

'Just tread carefully. Quisden-Neve got himself murdered, remember.'

'I'm not about to forget.'

'What is there worth killing for in this, Ian? I understand that least of all.'

'It has to be Marian's photographs. They'd fetch a fortune. And people never like sharing fortunes. Especially not people like Niall Esguard.'

'Stay out of his way, then.'

'I will if I can. I'm not interested in finding the photographs. Only in finding Eris.'

'That's what worries me. In the end, they could turn out to be the same thing.'

It was a valid warning. But I was convinced, maybe because I needed to be, that Eris was in some kind of danger, and was only hiding from me to ensure I didn't get dragged into it as well. But, if there was any sacrificing to be done, I meant to be the one to do it. And staying out of Niall Esguard's way wasn't how to start.

For the time being, though, he was no easier to track down than Eris. They were both on the island. I didn't doubt that. But where? My only clue was a bright-yellow Lotus, driven in St Peter Port just the day before. It should be possible to trace it, I reasoned. It really should.

After I'd seen Daphne off, I did the rounds of the airport car-hire desks. Lotuses weren't exactly their speciality, but I was told which dealer to go to in search of one, and their showroom was, like just about everything else on Guernsey, only a few miles away. It was still open when I arrived, and a salesman with the last half-hour of a Friday afternoon to while away gave me the benefit of his wisdom.

'Sounds like a mainland model. I certainly can't recall anything as exotic as that going through our books. It's not as conspicuous as you might think, actually. The millionaires like to be seen around in customized sports jobs, even though the speed limit here means you get a ticket for just changing into third. Most of the cars sit in air-conditioned garages up at Fort George conserving their second-hand value. What a waste, eh?'

Fort George was an estate of luxury residences laid out within the walls of the old British garrison on the headland south of St Peter Port. I drove round it that evening, gazing at the hacienda-style rooflines and the manicured lawns, at the locked gates and the closed doors. It was no place to ask questions, let alone expect answers. Apart from anything else, there was no-one *to* ask. A pedestrian would have been more noticeable than a whole motorcade of Lotuses.

It should have occurred to me sooner, but the thought actually came to me there, prowling round the culs-de-sac and corniches of Fort George. I was missing the point. If Eris had come to Guernsey to retrace Marian's footsteps, she had to have visited La Fauconnerie. But Daphne and I had left the house that morning in such a hurry we'd not even tried out Eris's picture on the owner.

I drove straight there. The camera obscura was closed, of course. The evening was drawing in. But the gate was unlocked. I went through and pulled the bell at the front door of the house.

A tall woman in an outsize cardigan and a long, paint-spattered dress answered. She had a mass of greying curled hair and a harassed expression. The sound of scales being played on a violin drifted out from the hallway, along with the tang of a spicy dinner.

'Mrs Cresswell?' I ventured, using the name Lefebvre had dropped earlier and hoping I'd judged the relationship correctly.

'Yes?'

'I'm sorry to trouble you. I visited the camera obscura this morning. I wonder, could I—?'

'Someone about the camera, Bernard,' she shouted behind her. 'Can you have a word, please?'

'It's not actually—'

But I was too late. Already the bearded figure of her husband was bearing down on me. 'You again. Not more about bloody Byfield.'

'Not exactly. Could I . . . step in for a moment?'

'Why not? Two pounds fifty isn't just for a camera obscura display. You get unfettered access to the house at any hour of the day or night thrown in.'

'I'm sorry if we got off on the wrong foot this morning.

The fact is I'm very worried about a friend of mine who's gone missing. She was last seen in St Peter Port. Now, she happens to be very interested in photographic history, so she might have visited your camera obscura. I have a picture of her if you'd care to take a look.'

'Working on the basis that we get so few visitors I'd be bound to remember her?'

'Bernard!' snapped his wife, who'd lingered behind him in the hallway, listening. 'What's got into you? The poor man's only asking you to *look*. He needs our help.'

'Yeh, sorry.' Bernard grimaced apologetically. 'A lot of bills come in at this time of year. It's the end-of-fiscal-year blues. Let's start again, shall we? Show me the picture.'

I handed it to him and watched as he gave it a long, shamefaced stare of scrutiny. Mrs Cresswell looked over his shoulder at the same time. Eventually, they both shook their heads.

'Are you sure?' I pressed. 'Just hanging around the street outside, perhaps? Or driving by – maybe in a yellow Lotus?'

'I don't think so,' said Bernard.

'Nor me,' added his wife.

'What about the violinist?' I signalled with my eyes.

'Might as well ask, I suppose,' agreed Bernard. 'Jamie!' he bellowed up the stairs. The scales died at once. 'Come down a sec.'

Jamie, a solemn little boy of twelve or so, appeared at the top of the stairs and pattered down to join us.

'Recognize this lady?' prompted his father.

Jamie frowned at the picture in fierce concentration, then gave his verdict. 'No.'

'Never mind,' I said, hardly sounding as if I meant it.

'Perhaps Niall knows her,' Jamie remarked.

'Niall?'

'Our occasional lodger,' Mrs Cresswell explained, apparently oblivious to the shock that must have been written all over my face.

'Niall . . . Esguard?'

'No. Hudson, actually.'

'Ah. I see. Sorry. I thought . . . but it's obviously not the same man.' Except that it was. Obviously and undoubtedly.

'He comes over from England on business every few weeks. When he does, he lodges with us.'

'Helps with those bills I was complaining about,' said Bernard.

'Is he . . . here now?'

'As it happens,' Mrs Cresswell replied. 'Well, staying, I mean. But he's out at the minute.'

'He'll probably be back soon,' said Bernard. 'If you want to leave the picture.'

'Better not,' I responded, retrieving it from his grasp. 'Only copy.' I grinned. 'And if Mr . . . Hudson . . . doesn't live here permanently, well, there's no real point in bothering him.'

I turned towards the door, trying not to break into a run. 'Thanks for your help.'

I sat in the car, several doors down from La Fauconnerie, as the dusk deepened and the street lamps came on, waiting and watching. Sooner or later Niall was bound to show up. And I was willing to wait and watch for as long as I had to. What I'd do when he did appear I wasn't sure. For the moment, all I wanted was to be certain it really was him.

What was he up to? I turned the question over in my mind as time slipped by and night slowly fell. The answer had to involve Marian's photographs. Did he believe there was a cache of them at La Fauconnerie? Or did he believe Byfield had mastered photography himself and produced some pictures of his own? Either way, lodging with the Cresswells gave him the chance to find out. He'd stolen the negatives Quisden-Neve had extorted out of Eris, but still he was greedy for more. Well, that was no surprise. He struck me as the greedy type.

Did he know Eris was on the island? Did *she* know *he* was, come to that? Had she heard about Quisden-Neve's murder and deduced who was responsible? If she had, it would explain why she was so shocked to see his twin brother on the pier. If only I could communicate with her in some way. If only I could make her understand help was at hand.

The passenger door was suddenly wrenched open and, before I could react, Niall Esguard had slid into the seat beside me. He was dressed in his trademark black and was grinning wolfishly.

'Jarrett,' he said with caricatured amiability. 'Thought it must be you. Piece of advice. Always check the back way. It's generally how I come and go.'

'Esguard, I—'

'Hudson, if you don't mind. You could do worse than throw a few aliases around yourself. Might make you less predictable. But that wouldn't be difficult.'

'What are you doing on Guernsey, *Mr* Hudson?'

'I could ask you the same question.'

'I'm looking for Eris Moberly.'

'Still no luck there? Sorry to hear it. You don't think she's on the island, do you? That'd be a weird coincidence. Me being over here on business and all.'

'What business is that?'

'None of yours.'

'That bookseller you referred me to – Montagu Quisden-Neve. I hear he came to grief.'

'I heard the same thing. Can't help wondering if he didn't have the same problem as you.'

'What's that?'

'An inability to keep his nose out of other people's affairs.' Niall leaned closer. I could smell the tobacco on his breath, as stale and pungent as the menace in his voice. 'Another piece of advice for you. Sincerely meant. Leave Guernsey.'

'Why should I?'

'It's a dangerous place.'

'That's not what I've heard.'

'You've been listening to the wrong people. For *you*, it's dangerous.'

'Are you threatening me?'

'Take it how you like.' He leaned back and eased open the door. 'Can't stop, I'm afraid. Much as I'd like to.'

'Before you go—'

'Yes?'

'Take this how you like. If I find Eris has come to any harm because of you, then you'll be the one in danger.'

'Thanks for the tip.'

'I'm serious.'

'I know.' He pushed the door wide open, climbed out and threw back a parting remark to me. 'So am I.' Then he slammed the door and walked away. I watched him in the rear-view mirror until he vanished at the next corner, then slapped the steering wheel in frustration. The encounter had achieved nothing, except to put Niall on his guard. There was no such thing as a free threat.

I drove down to the harbour, parked on Castle Pier and stared out to sea through the curtain of darkness, while the clink of halyards against masts in the marina behind me kept up a mournful rhythm. I was tired. I was weary of the chase. If she was here, why couldn't she show herself? If she knew I was looking for her, as she must do, how could she bear to keep her distance?

I whirled round, hope and instinct meeting in the fleeting certainty that she was just behind me. But there was nobody there. The pier was empty. I was alone, as I'd been too often since the madness of Vienna. Passion had curdled into bloody-minded obsession. There was an answer and I meant to have it. There was a meaning and I would know it. There was nothing else I could do but go on.

I drove back to the hotel – a ten-minute journey across St Peter Port. As I walked across the car park towards the entrance, I barely registered the sound of a car pulling out of a parking space behind me and accelerating throatily towards the road. Then the note of the engine caught my attention. I looked round. It was a pale Lotus, its colour bleached by the street lamps. I started running towards it as its brake lights blinked at me like the red eyes of a creature hiding in the forest. Then it swung out into the road and sped away in a burst of sound.

Cursing the sour mood that had made me so unobservant, I raced back to my car and drove off in pursuit. But there was never a chance I'd catch up. I drove by guesswork, round the western periphery of the town to Fort George, then out along the main road to the airport. It was a shadow chase, scarcely better than standing in the hotel car park and doing nothing.

That's where it ended, an hour or so later. I'd asked the receptionist, the porter and the barman if they knew the driver of a yellow Lotus and their answer had been no. Eris hadn't gone into the hotel, of course. She'd stayed outside, lying in wait for me. She'd wanted to see me. But not to *be* seen. Not to speak or touch or utter a single word of explanation. I shouted her name into the night and heard only my anger in the silence that followed.

Daphne phoned next morning. I was glad to speak to her, but reluctant to tell her anything. There was secrecy bedded in my soul now, a furtiveness about my every word and thought.

'Things are more complicated here than I'd anticipated, Ian. It may be several days before I can get away.'

'Don't worry. It can't be helped.'

'Are you all right?'

'Yes.'

'Have you turned anything up?'

'Not a thing.'

'What will you do?'

'Carry on looking.'

'Are you sure that's wise? You sound tired.'

'I feel fine.'

'I don't believe you.'

'I'm not one of your clients, Daphne. You don't need to concern yourself with my state of mind.'

'Be careful.'

'Of course.'

'And phone me at once if anything happens.'

'Naturally.'

'I'm sorry, you know.'

'What about?'

'Having to leave.'

'Don't be. You had no choice.' And to myself I added silently, *It's better this way. I prefer to face it alone. Whatever it is.*

It was Saturday morning. I walked the crowded streets of St Peter Port, searching the jumble of faces for one I knew I wouldn't see. I traversed the piers, scanning the ranks of parked cars in vain. I sat in a quayside pub and tried to stop thinking. But I couldn't. I had nothing else to think *about*. My existence had been reduced to the narrowing circle of my search.

I went back to the hotel, intending to drive out to Fort George again and look for a gardener to interrogate. But there was no need. An answer of a kind was waiting for me at reception.

'Package for you, Mr Jarrett,' the girl said brightly. 'By special courier.'

She slid a small Jiffy bag across the desk to me, and I guessed at once by the size and shape who it was from and what it contained. I picked it up and stared at the courier's label. It showed the name of the sender and the time and place of despatch: E. Moberly, Guernsey Airport, nine o'clock that morning.

'Do you want your key, Mr Jarrett?'

'What?'

'Your key.'

'Oh yes. Sorry. Thanks.'

I took it from her and ripped open the Jiffy bag as I turned away towards the stairs. A tape slid out into my hand. There was no note. But obviously there *was* a message. I turned back to reception.

'Do you know today's flight times?'

'They're in the paper. Here you are.'

She produced a copy of the *Guernsey Evening Press*

and opened it for me at the travel information page. The first flight to London on a Saturday was at nine thirty-five. That was it, then. Eris was no longer on the island. She was gone. But not without saying goodbye. There was another tape now. And this one was meant for me.

'Not leaving us, are you, Mr Jarrett?'

'No. But, actually, I won't need this.' I dropped my key back on the desk. 'I have to go out for a while.'

I pocketed the Jiffy bag and strode out through the door. The only cassette player I had with me was in the car. I propped the tape in its jaws as I drove out of the hotel and headed for the coast road. As soon as I was clear of St Peter Port, trundling north around Belle Grève Bay, I pushed the tape home.

Chapter Ten

What was the last thing I said to you, Ian? You remember, when I phoned you at Lacock. 'Don't try to find me.' That was it, wasn't it? *'Don't try to find me.'* It was good advice. It was the only thing I've ever said to you that you should have acted on. But you couldn't let go, could you? You just couldn't do it.

My name isn't Eris Moberly. I'm thirty-two years old, yes, but I'm not married and I don't live in Mayfair. I've never been to a psychotherapist. I don't suffer from fugues or flashbacks to another life. I didn't come to Guernsey to figure out how Marian Esguard died. And I won't be on the island when you hear this. Which is just as well. It wouldn't be sensible for me to be anywhere near when you learn the truth. It's time for you to find out the name of the game we've been playing. You won't like it. Trust me on this. You're going to feel bad about it. Very bad.

I'm sorry, Ian. Really, I am. This doesn't give me half the pleasure I thought it might. That's why I won't prolong the agony. I'll lay it on the line. I'll tell you as much as you need to know and no more. I'll make it clear to you where we stand, you and me.

We didn't meet by chance in Vienna. It was planned and staged. It was a set-up from the word go. I was told to get close to you, to tangle myself up in your life any way I could. Well, sex was the obvious draw. I've always been good at it. Better than I've been at a lot of things. I was told you'd be . . . susceptible. And you were. So was I, come to that. You know what I mean. It was good. Bloody fantastic. If it makes you feel any better to hear me say it. Which it won't. Not when you realize that, all along, I was getting an extra kick out of knowing what it was leading up to.

You couldn't have escaped. If you'd turned me down that first time, I'd have found some other way to get to you. There always is another way. I learned that lesson from a good teacher. But I didn't have to try too hard anyway. You were there for the taking. I'm sorry about the photographs, by the way. I didn't destroy them just to protect my anonymity. I was told to do it. You had to be prised away from your profession as well as from your family. I had to become the centre of your world. First by being there. Then by not being there.

I've been on Guernsey ever since, waiting for you to turn up. I set things up last year with those stints as Dawn Esguard's lodger. Plus the slice of wedding cake, of course. You couldn't miss, once you'd been pointed in the right direction. That's where the tapes came in. Daphne's in on it, too, you see. In fact, she knows more than I do. Like why you were targeted in the first place. That's the part of this I don't understand. I don't want to, either. There's a reason. Of course there is. Maybe you already know what it is. If not, I reckon you'll find out soon enough.

Is it tied up with Marian Esguard? I mean, I don't

know where all that stuff came from. I just read my lines. But it sounded genuine. And not just because it was supposed to. You *are* a photographer, after all. Or were. Before you dedicated your life to finding Eris Moberly.

I never met Milo Esguard, despite pumping Dawn about him. Niall, yes, of course. He's one of us. I can't say I like him, but I guess he has his uses. He never threatened me. Neither did Quisden-Neve. I went into his bookshop once, to size him up, just so I could describe him on the tape. But that was it. I've never been sure how much he knows about what's going on. His twin brother's been on Guernsey this week. I was told to let him see me. He was bound to mention it to you with Daphne on hand to jog his memory. That was the signal for the final phase to begin. First Daphne got out. Now me. Niall, too, I imagine. You're on your own.

Eris Moberly doesn't exist. That's what it comes down to. She's a fantasy. I didn't experience any of the things described on the tapes. Do you understand, Ian? It's all been a lie. The fugues, the ancient negatives, the whole bag of tricks. None of it happened to me. To somebody else, maybe. But not to me. And not to Eris Moberly.

You'll want to know why I did it. How I could bring myself to. First and foremost, of course, there's the money. This is the best-paid job I've ever had, by a long way. My employer's very generous. Even when I had to hang around Guernsey for weeks on end he gave me the use of a flash car and a luxury pad with heated swimming pool to compensate. And I didn't exactly slum it in Vienna. I can't complain about the pay and conditions.

One thing you ought to know. I've had to get by in the past by making men believe I cared for them, by convincing them I liked the things they liked. But, in your case, I didn't have to pretend. It really was as good for me as it was for you. Just a pity it couldn't last. I'm sorry, Ian. It wasn't quite good enough to make me forget who's paying the bills.

And who *is* that? Your tormentor-in-chief, I mean. The man who set all this in motion. I first met him a couple of years ago. I was at a pretty low ebb then, but he recognized my potential. He's good at spotting people's strengths – and their weaknesses. Yours included by the look of it. He's asked me to do some strange things since I started working for him, but I guess this counts as about the strangest of the lot. I know he'll have his reasons, though. He always does. Just like I always know better than to ask what they are. A man who treats me as well as he has doesn't have to justify himself to me.

It's different in your case. He's put you through hell, one way or another. I reckon you're entitled to an explanation. Well, he's the only one who *can* explain. So, why don't you ask him? Apparently you'll know how to find him. His name is Conrad Nyman.

PART THREE

DEVELOPMENT

Chapter Eleven

Shock hit me like a wave a few minutes after I had the sense to pull off the road at the northern end of Belle Grève Bay. I stared out at the brilliant blue sea and the cloudless sky, my mind and heartbeat racing. I played the tape through one more time, listening to her voice and the mockery coiled within it. Then shock gave way to sudden frenzy. I screamed abuse at her, drowning out the words that pieced together the lies she'd told me. I wrenched the cassette out of the player so quickly the tape snagged on the heads. It tore as I yanked at it, but I no longer cared. I jumped out of the car, threw the cassette to the ground and stamped on it hard, several times, then watched the wind catch the unravelled tape and blow it away like a strand of seaweed.

I was angry with myself for being so easily fooled, but angrier by far with those who'd done the fooling. What gave them the right to tear my life apart? What had I done to deserve it? Nothing that I could even remotely imagine. They'd all been strangers to me, until they'd decided to become my enemies. But why? In God's name, *why*?

Conrad Nyman could tell me. He was *going* to tell me, whether he wanted to or not. Even Eris had agreed I was owed an answer, and I meant to have it. My dismay was less than my determination to force the truth out of Nyman. Why me? Why now? Why the whole damn thing? What the hell was it *for*?

'I'm going to find out,' I said aloud. Then I climbed into the car and started back towards St Peter Port.

I couldn't get a berth on any of the catamarans, so I had to opt for the traditional ferry, a slow overnight run to Weymouth. That left me with a frustrating afternoon and evening to kill, when all I wanted to do was go after the man who'd been pulling the strings in the puppet show my life had become. The delivery of the tape had been well timed, like all his other ploys. A Saturday at the end of Easter week was just about the worst possible day to try to leave Guernsey at short notice.

I called at La Fauconnerie to check what Eris had said. Sure enough, Niall Hudson had flown back to England on sudden and urgent business. I could have tried to book a flight myself, of course, but I reckoned I'd need the car when I arrived. There was nothing for it but to sit it out. I rang Daphne, but got only her answering machine. There was no point in leaving a message. I meant to deliver one in person sooner or later.

It all came back to Nyman. Where he lived I had no idea, but Nicole might know. She wasn't answering either, though. I left a message, but she hadn't rung back by the time I booked out of the hotel and headed for the ferry terminal. I just had to hope she wasn't away for the whole weekend. It was better to confront Nyman at home, where he might feel vulnerable, than amidst the security of Nymanex's Docklands HQ. Besides, I didn't want to wait one minute longer than I had to. Everything he'd told me had been part of the lie. The meeting with Eris in Greenwich Park and her pursuit of him, the letters and the phone calls – none of it was true. He'd been enjoying himself at my expense. And now I meant to call him to account.

The ferry docked at Weymouth early on a grey morning. The roads were empty and I made it to London in not much more than two hours. If Nicole was spending the weekend at home, I was sure to find her in, quite possibly in bed. The guy she'd been entertaining when I'd called before Easter was a worry, though. New boyfriend meets old wasn't a scene I needed.

As it turned out, there was no answer to my repeated rings at the bell. It looked as if she hadn't left the answer-phone on just for cover. I sat and fretted in the car a while, then doorstepped the neighbour on his way out for a paper. I recognized him, but it was probably just as well he didn't seem to remember me. He might not have been so responsive to my plea of urgency.

'Away for the weekend, I'm afraid. I think the wife said she'd gone to see her parents.'

That was good news and bad perfectly balanced. At least I knew where she was. But I wouldn't be a welcome caller in the midst of their cosy Sunday. They rattled around a big old mock-Tudor house on the outskirts of Bedford. I'd been summoned there when it still seemed possible I might be charged with causing death by dangerous driving following the accident on Barnet Hill. Old man Heywood had wanted to impress on me how important it was that Nicole's name shouldn't be mentioned in court. None of us was likely to remember the encounter with pleasure or desire a repetition, but, since I didn't have their phone number, and directory enquiries refused point-blank to tell me what it was, there was no way round it.

It was late morning when I arrived, and about as untimely as it could be. The drive was full of cars, the garden aswarm with children and their doting parents: Nicole's numerous siblings and their still more numerous offspring. One of the mothers recognized me by some weird kind of laser-sharp facility for recalling trouble spots in her sister's past. Nicole was fetched from indoors and I was left to wait for her on the farthest patch of lawn from the house. It was as if Mr and Mrs Heywood's health wasn't reckoned to be equal even to a glimpse of me. And Nicole's equanimity didn't seem to be any more durable.

'I thought Fran was joking,' she said by way of barbed greeting, her thunderous expression clashing with the sunny riot of poppies on her dress. 'What can have possessed you to come here, Ian?'

'I had to speak to you.'

'Couldn't it have waited? It's my parents' ruby wedding anniversary. You're not the surprise I had in mind.'

'Give them my congratulations.'

'I won't give them the slightest hint you've even turned up if I can avoid it. What the hell do you want?'

'Information.'

'The police would like some as well, I gather. From the witness who fled the scene of Montagu Quisden-Neve's murder, for a start. What exactly have you got yourself into?'

'I don't *exactly* know. But Conrad Nyman knows. I have to speak to him.'

'So speak to him.'

'Today.'

'The best of luck. He's not coming to our party. I can't help you.'

'Where does he live, Nicole?'

'How should I know?'

'You profiled him. Remember?'

'I profiled his business. *Chez* Nyman didn't come into it.'

'You must have some idea.'

'Oh, all right.' She tossed her head in exasperation. 'Will this get rid of you?'

'It will.'

'It better had. I only know because the architectural press wrote it up. He's restored an old Lutyens house in Sussex. Derringfold Place, near Cuckfield.'

'Address?'

'You'll have to ask around. That's as much as I can tell you. But it'll be well known in the area, I expect. You'll find it. Though what kind of a reception you'll get from Nyman I couldn't say. *If* he's there. He doesn't like to have his privacy invaded, that I do know. I'd think twice about cold-calling him if I were you.'

'There's nothing to think about. This won't exactly be an unexpected visit.'

'Then why did you have to come to me to find out where he lives?'

'Because he likes to play games. But, as you know better than most, *I* don't.'

A hard, fast drive south got me to Cuckfield as the pubs were thinning out after the lunchtime rush. The landlord of the first one I tried enlisted the help of three regulars keen to show off their local knowledge, and I was soon heading down the lanes towards Derringfold Place.

Its massive chimneys and galleried windows showed themselves beyond the hedges for half a mile or so before I pulled in through an open gateway and sped up a curving drive. The mature grounds, splashed with spring blossom, made the house look even more elegantly manorial than it must have done when Lutyens finished it a hundred years or so ago. No wonder the architectural press was interested. Painstaking restoration had made it glowingly photogenic. If Nyman had wanted to buy an aesthetic reputation along with a chunk of mid-Sussex squiredom, he couldn't have chosen better. There was nothing cheapskate about Derringfold Place. It was the real thing, even if its owner wasn't.

Not that I had a clue what sort of man Nyman truly was. He'd been slick and amiable enough when we'd met, but that had clearly been an act. I meant to find out what the act was designed to conceal. I stopped as close to the house as I could get without actually driving up the front steps, bounded up to the porch and yanked at the bell pull. There was a bull's-eye window set in the door, with a sinuous N worked into the glass.

I'd given the bell three tugs before there was an answer. A Hispanic maid opened the door and greeted my demand to see Nyman with a placid smile. 'Oh, Mr Nyman, he plays tennis right now.'

'Where?'

'Out back. Shall I tell him you're here?'

'Don't bother. I'll tell him myself.'

A gravel path led off behind a privet hedge towards the rear. I left the maid in mid-remonstrance and started along it. It followed the line of the house, round the broad circular foot of the principal chimneystack and through an arched gateway into the garden. Lawns fell away ahead of me towards clumps of azalea and rhododendron, with mature trees beyond. Away to the right was a swimming pool and a screen of fir trees, through which I could glimpse a wire-mesh fence and the tramlines of a tennis court. Then I heard the plop-plop-plop of a rally, and a male voice raised in encouragement. 'Bad luck.' It was Nyman. I moved at a jog across the lawn and along the path linking pool and court.

He had his back to me as I rounded the last in the row of firs and pushed through the gate onto the court. He was standing casually, racket in hand, waiting to receive service, dressed in the white trousers, shirt and sweater of a bygone era. His opponent, a girl in shorts, sweatshirt and baseball cap, was gathering a ball from the back of the court. Somebody else, a woman, was sitting in a chair by the sidelines near the net. But they hardly registered in my mind. I was only thinking about Nyman and his responsibility for everything I'd endured since that fateful morning in Vienna.

'Nyman, you bastard!' I shouted. As he turned, I hit him, somewhere around the left cheekbone. I heard the breath grunt out of him as he fell, the racket clattering away across the court. He lay on his back for a second, then rolled onto his side, propped himself up on one elbow and raised his other hand to his cheek.

'Oh my God,' the woman near the net cried. 'What . . . what are you doing?' She jumped up, and the flash of her colourful sweater caught my eye just as the familiarity of her voice froze my thoughts. I looked across at her, unable to believe whose face I saw looking back at me. Then I shifted my gaze to the girl at the other end of the court.

'Dad?' Amy called nervously. 'What's happening?'

'Are you out of your mind?' said Faith as she rushed to Nyman's side, her eyes blazing at me. 'You must be. This is . . . this is insane.'

'Don't worry,' said Nyman, smiling gamely as she crouched beside him. 'I'll live.'

'What are you doing here?' I barked out at Faith. 'What have you brought Amy here for?'

'A relaxing weekend. What the hell do you think we're here for?'

'With *Nyman*?'

'Do you two know each other?' called Amy, advancing cautiously to the net.

'I'm afraid we do,' said Nyman, rising to his feet with Faith's superfluous assistance and letting me see, with a flicker of a glance, that I couldn't have suited his purposes better than by hitting him in full view of my wife and daughter. He was the new man in Faith's life. He hadn't set out merely to destroy my life. He'd positioned himself to take it over. 'I should have mentioned it, Faith. I'm sorry. I didn't want to worry you. He came to see me at work just before Easter, throwing all kinds of threats around. I never thought anything like this would happen.'

'Threats?' Faith stared at me incredulously. 'Ian, for God's sake . . .'

'He's lying. I didn't threaten anyone.' But what I'd just done implied the exact reverse. I could almost see the conclusion forming in Faith's horrified gaze. 'This isn't how it looks. He's set me up. And you. Both of you.'

'Oh, Dad.' There was sorrow in Amy's voice as she rounded the net and moved closer, sorrow and the beginnings of pity. 'What's happening to you?'

'Ian,' said Faith. 'Is this about . . . *jealousy*?'

'Of course not. I didn't even know you were seeing each other.'

'Then why did you go to Conrad's office?'

'He tried to warn me off,' said Nyman, wincing as he fingered his reddening cheekbone. 'Said if I didn't leave you alone . . . Well, it seems he meant it.'

'You walked out on our marriage, Ian.' Faith's eyes were still fixed on me. 'You left me for another woman. How did you expect me to deal with that – by going into a bloody nunnery? You don't have the right to *comment* on my choice of male company, let alone—' She broke off, tearfulness suddenly overcoming her. 'This is . . . You make me so ashamed, you know that?'

'Hey, don't get upset,' said Nyman, slipping his arm round her, and looking straight at me as she turned towards him for comfort. 'I'm not going to sue for assault. Ian's just . . . overwrought. Right, Ian?'

'No. Wrong, *Conrad*. You think you're very clever, but let me tell you, you're not going to get away with it.'

'Away with what?'

'Wrecking my life. Stealing my wife and daughter.'

'Stealing? You talk as if they belong to you. As if they're your property.'

'You're twisting my words. Faith, I didn't mean—'

'*What* didn't you mean?' She glared at me. 'That you'd fallen in love with someone else? That we had no future together? Wasn't I supposed to believe you?'

'I didn't know what was going on. I was being manipulated. By the man you seem to think is some kind of white knight in shining armour.'

'My feelings for Conrad have nothing to do with you. You made it obvious you couldn't care less about me. Amy, too. She was expecting to hear from you over

297

Easter, you know that? She trusted you to call. But did you? Did you hell.'

'He made sure I couldn't.' I pointed accusingly at Nyman, who looked as uncomprehending as I knew he wasn't. 'He got me out of the way. Had that tame psychotherapist of his lure me off to Guernsey.'

'I'd heard you were seeking help.' Nyman sounded almost compassionate. 'I have to say, I think you need it.'

'Why? Planning to try to convince them I'm mad, are you?'

'For God's sake, Ian,' said Faith. 'You're doing a fine job of that yourself.'

'I'm telling you the truth.'

'You're accusing your psychotherapist of working for Conrad?'

'She is.'

'That's crazy, Dad,' said Amy gently. 'Seriously crazy.'

'If you have her number, we could phone her now,' said Faith. 'We could try to sort this out.'

'Oh, I have her number. And your boyfriend's.' I nodded at Nyman. 'It's the same.'

'You're not making any sense.'

'I'm not meant to be. But I am. Daphne's on the payroll. So's Eris. She was working for him when I met her in Vienna.'

'Eris? I thought her name was Marian.'

'Just another lie. Told at his bidding.'

'You can't believe that.'

'I'm afraid he does,' said Nyman with syrupy reason-ableness. 'I'm very much afraid he believes every word.'

'Listen to me, Faith. You, too, Amy. Leave here now. Get away from this man. He's dangerous. Don't trust him. He plans to harm all of us.'

Nyman shook his head. 'Why would I want to do that?'

'You tell me. It's why I came here. To force you to tell me.'

'But I can't. Because it isn't true. I don't know this . . . Eris. Or Daphne. They aren't working for me. I met Faith by chance, not as part of some grand scheme to hurt you.'

'How did you meet her?'

'I'm really not sure I—'

'In the National Gallery,' Faith put in. 'Admiring the *Bathers at Asnières*.'

'Your favourite picture,' I said, eager to claim a fragment of our lost intimacy.

'Mine, too,' stated Nyman placidly.

'Here's a test for you, Faith,' I went on, refusing to take my eyes off her. 'Try to find some shred of evidence that he had the slightest interest in Seurat – *before* it suited his purpose to claim one.'

'Stop this, Ian,' she insisted. 'It's grotesque.'

'I'm not sure he *can* stop,' said Nyman. 'It's a self-fulfilling prophecy. He left you; I must have tricked him into it. I like the same kind of art as you; I must be faking. I deny persecuting him; I must be lying. I advise him to go to his psychotherapist for help; she must be working for me. I don't think you're too far gone to realize, Ian, that what this amounts to is classic paranoia.'

'I realize that's what you want it to amount to.'

'Why don't we phone Daphne?'

'Because she'd only say what you've told her to say.'

'See what I mean?' He looked at Faith, then slowly round at Amy. They saw. And they believed. Him, not me. 'I'm sorry about this, Amy, honestly I am, but I think your father's very sick.'

She nodded. 'You need help, Dad.'

'And we'll give you help,' said Faith. 'If you'll let us.'

'Oh, I'll let you. If you'll help me find the truth.'

Nyman smiled softly. 'I think you just heard the truth, Ian. You didn't like the sound of it. But it *was* the truth.'

'Bullshit. I'm not mad. Even though you've done your best to drive me mad. You're not going to get at me that way.'

'I'm not trying to get at you in any way.'

'I'll find out why you're doing this. Daphne knows, doesn't she? Eris let that much slip. And Eris doesn't seem to realize Quisden-Neve's dead.'

'Who?'

'Weak links, Conrad. Someone else in the know. And a murder you'd better hope I can't pin on Niall. Because, if I can, I reckon he'll happily implicate you. He doesn't strike me as the loyal type.'

'I'm afraid I haven't the first idea who or what you're talking about.'

'I'll prove you're behind it all.'

'You won't. *It* doesn't exist. Except in your mind.'

'I *will* prove it. And when I do . . .'

'Yes? What then?'

'I'll make you pay for what you've done.'

'Conrad would be within his rights to call the police, Ian,' said Faith. 'The way you're behaving, I wouldn't blame him if he did.'

'Let him. I've nothing to hide.'

'Neither have I, Ian,' said Nyman, sounding as sincere as ever. 'But I've no wish to see you arrested in front of your daughter. Have you any idea what you're doing to Amy? You're not well. She's doing her best to understand that. Don't make it any harder for her. Please. For her sake.'

'*Her* sake? Practising the role of stepfather already, Nyman? Well, let me tell you—' I stopped and looked at Amy. She was crying. She was staring straight at me, with tears coursing down her cheeks.

Faith turned towards her, then glanced over her shoulder at me. 'Get out of here, Ian.' Her voice was low and husky. 'Leave us alone.' She let go of Nyman, walked over to Amy and led her slowly away to the court-side chair.

'Easy,' whispered Nyman. 'You're making it too easy.'

'What?' I rounded on him. He gazed blithely back at me. 'What did you say?'

'Nothing. I never said a word.'

'You bastard. I'll get you for this.'

'You need help. You really do.'

I looked across at Faith and Amy. They'd turned away from me, hugging and consoling each other as best they could. Nyman was their friend now, while I was . . . some kind of shared tragedy in the making. And there wasn't a single thing I could do that wouldn't make it worse.

'Well, Ian?' Nyman murmured, knowing Faith and Amy were too far away to hear him, let alone detect the sarcastic edge to his words. 'What are you going to do next?'

'Go to hell,' I muttered. Then I turned and walked off the court, heading for the path round to the front of the house. I needed to be alone, to make sense of what had happened and find a way to deal with it. Nyman was right. I was adding self-destruction to his brick-by-brick demolition of my life. For the moment, all I could do was stop.

I went back to London, driving more slowly now, my mind circling sluggishly round the invidiousness of my position. A defeatist weariness had swept over me. I couldn't seem to think clearly. Nyman had been too clever for me. Why shouldn't he go on being? Why should the downward spiral ever stop if I couldn't even reason out why it had begun?

I parked the car somewhere off Ladbroke Grove and walked down to Notting Hill Gate through the mild spring sunshine, aware of the indifference of the city pressing in on me. Nobody cared about me. I hardly cared myself. Perhaps I was mad after all. Or perhaps this was how madness began.

Yet I still had one friend left. I might have forgotten him, but he hadn't forgotten me. Tim Sadler was waiting on the doorstep when I reached the flat.

'Faith called me from Sussex,' he explained with a smile that somehow managed to convey sympathy for both of us. 'She told me what happened.'

'But not why, I'll bet. Want to hear that part of the story?'

'It's why I came.'

'Is it? Or did Faith ask you to assess my condition?'

'Well, that too, since you mention it.'

'And how would you describe my condition, Tim – in a word?'

He hesitated, pondering the point, then said, 'Not good.'

'That's two words.'

'Great.' He summoned a cautious grin. 'At least you can still count.'

Tim took a brief look inside the flat before insisting he drive me to his house for a rustled-together meal, over which I recounted the events that had engulfed me since our last meeting. I couldn't tell whether he believed me, but he seemed to want to. And that was a start.

'It's a pity you destroyed Eris's last tape,' he mildly observed when I'd finished.

'I was angry.'

'No wonder. But the other tapes – where would they be?'

'At Daphne's practice. But she's probably already wiped them.'

'Which is why she's gone to ground. Yes, I see. Give me her phone numbers and I'll try them again now.'

'It won't do you any good.'

It didn't. He could only raise an answering machine, at Daphne's home *and* her office. 'You don't know where she lives?'

'I've only ever had the phone number. The first time I met her was in Hampstead and the area code certainly puts her out that way. But she's ex-directory, of course. As you'd expect.'

'You think the Harley Street practice is a sham?'

'No. I checked up on her. That side of things is kosher.'

'So it is.' He nodded. 'I checked up on her myself.'

I blinked at him in surprise. '*You* checked?'

'To make sure you were going to be in good hands. Faith wanted to be . . . reassured.'

Suspicion didn't need much to take hold of me. 'You're not still reassuring her, are you, Tim? Will you be reporting back to her about what you've been able to learn by pretending to take my claims seriously?'

303

'I'm not pretending. Faith thinks you're mentally ill. There's no point fudging it. That's what she believes. But I don't.'

'Why not?'

'Because your psychotherapist should be more actively concerned about you than she seems to be if you really are so very far gone. Because I don't think you're capable of murder, yet Quisden-Neve *was* murdered, presumably for some compelling reason. And, oh yes, because I don't trust Conrad Nyman.'

'You talk as if you know him.'

'No. But I have met him. I took Amy to the cinema on Easter Monday. Least I could do considering how her father had let her down. Nyman was at the house when we got back, oozing charm from every pore. I wasn't impressed. Of course, it wasn't me he was trying to impress, but even so . . .'

'Yes?'

'There's something about him. He's too smooth, too good to be true. And Faith isn't his type. So the question is, why's he trying to convince her she is?'

'To get at me.'

'Maybe so. But *why*?'

'I don't know.'

'There has to be a reason, Ian.'

'Of course. But I'd never even heard of him until Nicole mentioned his name.'

'Is that the connection, then – Nicole?'

'Why should it be? It was all over between us years ago. And we were the only people it hurt.'

'Not quite.'

'Well, Faith, of course, but—'

'I didn't mean Faith.'

'Who, then?'

'Who suffered the most in all that?'

'The most? Well, I suppose it has to be—' I broke off and stared at him, confused but already half-convinced. 'You don't mean . . .?'

'The woman you killed.'

'Yes, but for Christ's sake—'

'You killed her. That's undeniable. Whether accidentally or not might make little difference to someone who loved her.'

'Nyman?'

'It's possible.'

'I saw her friends and relatives at the inquest. I don't remember anyone like him. But then . . .'

'What?'

'I was doing my best to avoid eye contact with them.'

'So Nyman could have been there.'

'I suppose so. But . . . why wait five years? And why give me some long-dead proto-photographer to chase after? Why not just . . . run me down in his car . . . if revenge is what he wants?'

'Who can say? But there's a real similarity between what's happened to you and what happened to Marian Esguard. As Byfield was to her, so Eris has been to you: a treacherous lover. And Marian was a photographer, remember. Just like you.'

'Was she? I can't help wondering if Nyman didn't just make her up to torment me.'

'No doubt you can't help wondering. But you don't believe it.'

I looked long and hard at him. 'No. I don't.'

'It all means something.' Tim stood up and walked to the window. 'Of course, we should really be worried about what he may have planned for Faith and Amy.'

'I already am. But all I've done so far is drive them into his waiting arms.'

'If you could prove he knew the woman you killed . . .'

'Her name was Isobel Courtney. She was thirty-six years old. Blond hair, cut short. I remember noticing, when they lifted her up on the stretcher to take her away, how very blond her hair was, once most of the blood had been washed out of it by the rain. The rain was one of the reasons I hit her. The windscreen was smeary. I should have stopped and cleaned it properly. I was thinking about Nicole and how good it had been with her. I was so bloody pleased with myself, accelerating down the road towards the railway bridge, not concentrating, not caring. And then . . .' I shrugged. 'Bang.'

'I've never heard you say so much about it before.' Tim was gazing at me from the window. 'I suppose . . . Isobel Courtney . . . got overlooked amidst all the strife between you and Faith.'

'Well, Faith was more interested in why I'd been to Barnet in the first place than whether I could have avoided the accident if I'd been quicker to react, that's for sure.'

'And could you have avoided it?'

'Maybe. If I'd been just a bit more careful. Who knows?'

'But it was still an accident.'

'I certainly didn't mean to kill her. I was under the limit, the drink limit anyway. As for speed, there were no witnesses to contradict what I said.'

'Was it true?'

'No. I deliberately underestimated my speed. Who wouldn't in the circumstances? The police couldn't make out a case against me. You could hardly expect me to make it out for them.'

'But Isobel Courtney's nearest and dearest?'

'I don't know. None of them spoke to me at the inquest. I didn't go to the funeral. I've no idea what they thought. At the time, I was grateful they didn't get in touch. I had a lot on my mind.'

'So did they.'

'Yes. But five years on? They must be over it by now.'

'One of them may not be.'

'You mean Nyman?'

'If you can link him to Isobel Courtney, I don't think Faith will be able to go on believing he met her by chance.'

'But how can I do that?'

'I think you're going to have to do what you couldn't face doing five years ago. Contact Isobel Courtney's friends and relatives. Get to know the person whose life you unintentionally ended. And somewhere in her past . . .'

'I'll find him.' I took Eris's photograph from my pocket and looked at it. 'And maybe I'll find somebody else, too.'

Isobel Courtney. I thought about her that night almost for the first time. Five years before, she'd merely been the name-tag on a problem that imploded the lies and evasions I'd used to keep marriage to Faith and my affair with Nicole running together on parallel tracks. They might never have overlapped but for two simultaneous lapses of concentration: Isobel Courtney's and mine. I knew only too well what had been on my mind. But I'd never so much as wondered what had been on hers. I hadn't wanted to find out the kind of person I'd killed. So long as she remained just a name-tag, I could cope with what I'd done. I'd photographed dead people

307

before. I'd looked through a camera lens at incinerated Iraqi troops outside Kuwait and learned how to disregard the memories and the hopes that had ended for every one of them. It hadn't been so very difficult to apply the same technique to Isobel Courtney. It had been an accident, after all. It hadn't been my fault. There was nothing I could have done.

But there was. I knew that. Maybe Conrad Nyman did, too. And maybe he'd decided to remind me. In his own particular way.

The inquest hadn't excited much press interest. But there'd been at least one reporter in attendance. I'd noticed him jotting away in his notebook during the proceedings. I'd never seen his report. I'd never wanted to – till now.

A local weekly seemed the best bet. I drove out to Barnet next morning and tried the public library. And there it was. Not difficult to find, since I knew the date I was looking for only too well. BARNET ROAD DEATH A TRAGIC ACCIDENT. It hadn't even made the front page.

I scanned the meagre paragraphs, recognizing my own name and a more or less accurate snatch of the measured words I'd used to describe what had happened. '*I was driving south down Barnet Hill at about thirty miles an hour when a figure dressed in dark clothes ran straight out into the road in front of me. I braked, but she was too close for me to avoid a collision.*' The coroner had gone along with that and the police had been obliged to. The jury hadn't quibbled either. '*Miss Courtney was probably hurrying because of the heavy rain falling at the time,*' the coroner was quoted as saying in his summing-up. '*Tragically, her haste cost her her life. There is no evidence to suggest that Mr Jarrett was driving recklessly or carelessly.*

No blame can be attached to him.' No blame. No blame at all. Officially.

And the victim? My gaze tracked back to the opening paragraph. '*A verdict of accidental death was recorded at an inquest held this week into the death, following a road accident on Barnet Hill on 23 March, of Isobel Courtney (36), a Sotheby's valuations expert, of Smollett Avenue, Clapham.*' That was all there was by way of an obituary for the woman I'd killed. Now that I saw it in print, I vaguely recalled the police officer who'd interviewed me saying that she'd had 'a promising career in the arts world'. He'd said it reproachfully. It was as close as he'd allowed himself to get to accusing me of responsibility for her death. The absence of witnesses had prevented him getting any closer. And I'd stonewalled him at every turn.

I walked from the library through the shopping centre as far as the Underground station, and looked down Barnet Hill towards the railway bridge. The morning was still and bright, unhaunted and unechoing. But, if I closed my eyes, I could still remember the sound of the impact and, what was worse, the pitch of the car and the thud beneath it as I drove over her.

Why was she in Barnet? Who did she know there? Where was she born? Who were her friends? The questions milled in my head, questions I'd been determined five years before not even to ask, let alone answer. Then one question focused the rest. What kind of material had she valued for Sotheby's? What could it have been?

It was a guess, but somehow not a wild one. I went back to the car, rang Sotheby's and asked to speak to their photographic expert. I was put through to his assistant, a courteous but reticent woman who identified herself as Mary Whiting.

'I'm afraid Duncan Noakes is in New York this week,' she informed me. 'Can I help you in any way?'

'Perhaps. It's a long shot, and you'll think it an odd question. But was Mr Noakes's predecessor a Miss Isobel Courtney?'

'Yes. She was. But . . .'

'Miss Courtney's dead. I know. Did you . . . work with her?'

'Well, yes.' She hesitated. 'I did.'

'Closely?'

'As her assistant.'

'So you knew her reasonably well?'

'Yes. Very well. I had an extremely high regard for her.'

'Would you be willing to meet and tell me a little about Isobel, Ms Whiting? I'd be enormously grateful for any information you can give me.'

'Why should you want information about somebody who's been dead for, what must it be, five years now? You'll forgive me, but the request seems positively macabre, Mr . . .'

'Jarrett. Remember the name?'

'I can't say I do.'

'I was the driver of the car that hit her.'

'You were . . . I beg your pardon?'

'The driver. The man responsible. I . . . feel I've never properly . . . faced up to what I did. It might help me to do so if I could . . . find out what sort of person Isobel was.'

'A very fine person, Mr Jarrett. That I *can* tell you.'

'Would a brief meeting be asking too much, Ms Whiting?'

'Well, I . . . I suppose not.'

'Today?'

'I'm afraid I'm extremely busy.'

'Too busy for lunch?'

'I'm really not sure I can—'

'Please, Ms Whiting. You have to have lunch. Why not have it with me?'

She was a middle-aged woman who combined stylish dress sense with a seemingly deliberate plainness of hair and face. My first impression, when I met her outside Sotheby's Bond Street entrance, was of somebody set complacently in dullish ways, but I soon realized that was merely a pose. She had quick wits and a sharp mind. As well as a disquieting gift for implying she knew she was being told less than the truth.

'Were you really the driver of the car that hit Isobel?' she asked over a modest risotto and a glass of house red in the nearby trattoria she'd chosen for our lunch.

'Yes. I was.'

'And five years later you've been visited by the compelling desire to get to know her.'

'You sound as if you don't believe me.'

'It's just that it seems rather late in the day for your conscience to be pricked.' She eyed me deliberatively before adding, 'But what exactly do you want to know about her?'

'Anything you can tell me.'

'Well, as I told you on the phone, she was somebody I had a great deal of respect for, both personally and professionally. That makes her very rare in my experience, believe me. My knowledge of her was confined to work, of course. We didn't meet socially. But, being her assistant, I observed her at close quarters for several years. One gets to know someone pretty well in such circumstances.'

'How would you describe her?'

'Honourable. Devoid of malice. Even to the extent of pretending she hadn't heard office gossip, let alone participating in it. She was capable of extreme kindness. Her solicitude while I was easing myself back into work after a serious illness was quite touching. At other times, with other people, she could seem aloof, even insensitive. But that was only because of her dedication to the job in hand. She had remarkable powers of concentration.'

'What exactly was the job in hand?'

'Valuing and acquiring collectable photographs for auction. Mostly the rare and/or antique variety. Her knowledge of photographic history was second to none. Mr Noakes is a journeyman by comparison, though competent enough in his way. But Isobel had, well, let's call it an eye. A sense for photographic *art*, if you understand me.'

'Yes. I think I do.'

'She was a considerable connoisseur in her own right, actually.'

'Really? Whose work did she like?'

'Early Victorian female photographers. The earlier the better. Julia Margaret Cameron, obviously. But others less well known: Lucy Bridgeman, Augusta Crofton, Fanny Jocelyn . . .'

'Marian Esguard?'

'I beg your pardon?' But she'd heard. I knew that by the startled look on her face.

'Wasn't there a famous pioneer photographer called Marian Esguard?'

'No. I don't believe there was.' She frowned. 'I've certainly never heard of her. When was she active?'

'I'm not sure. Very early on, I think. But, forgive me,

your reaction . . . I could have sworn the name meant something to you.'

'It did, yes.' She softened. 'I'd never thought it might have a photographic context, though, considering I'd be bound to have come across at least a reference to her by now if she'd produced any significant work. But I never have. Not once, that I can recall. And I'm not the forgetful type, I can assure you.'

'So you'd remember where you heard of her before?'

'Oh yes. She was mentioned to me at, well, at Isobel's funeral.'

'Who by?'

'One of the other mourners. A friend of Isobel's. Not a colleague, I mean. Nor a relative, so far as I could gather. She didn't actually specify how they knew each other. Perhaps from school or university. I'd have said she was a little older than Isobel, though, so—'

'What did she say?'

'Well, it was the strangest thing. We went back to Isobel's house in Clapham after the funeral. It wasn't a large party. A dozen or so, all told. It was a rather stilted affair, standing in Isobel's drawing room, which I'd never been in before, with her mother and father pressing cakes and sandwiches on us that I for one had no stomach for, surrounded by Isobel's collection of early Victorian photographs on the walls. There was a particularly fine blown-up print of a Cameron portrait over the fireplace. *Mrs Duckworth, 1867*. It's quite famous, actually. I was admiring it when this friend of Isobel's, as I took her to be, approached me, puffing a slim cigar, of all things, and—' She broke off, noticing my reaction to the description. 'You know her?'

'I shouldn't think so. Go on. You were going to tell me what she said.'

'Yes. So I was. Well, she asked me how I knew Isobel and I explained. I must have asked her the same question, but something else cropped up before she could answer. Or she avoided the issue. I can't remember which. At all events, she got me chatting about what a wonderful person Isobel was to work for, then suddenly asked, "Did she ever talk to you about Marian Esguard?" Just like that. When I said no, she asked if I was sure. When I said I was, she changed the subject, then pretty niftily moved away to talk to someone else. All in all, rather odd behaviour. That's why it's stuck in my mind. But as for Marian Esguard being a notable early photographer, well, I'm afraid you're wrong there.'

'Am I?'

'Why, yes. If she had been, Isobel would most certainly have been interested in her, and I'd have heard of her as a result.'

'I suppose so. Tell me, who else was at the funeral?'

'Oh, two or three other people from Sotheby's. Several neighbours. Various relatives: an aunt and uncle, a cousin. Assorted friends.'

'Any . . . male friends?'

'Not that I recall.'

'She lived alone?'

'As far as I ever knew. That was my . . . impression. Not that there mightn't have been . . . occasional admirers . . . but Isobel wasn't in the habit of volunteering details of her private life.'

'Ever heard of Conrad Nyman?'

She thought about it for a moment, then shook her head. 'No.'

'Debonair business type. Robert Redford looks. Cartloads of charm.'

'I've never met him.'

'If he wasn't at the funeral, maybe he phoned Isobel from time to time.'

'No. Definitely not. What makes you think otherwise?' She was growing suspicious now and I could hardly blame her. 'Am I to assume, Mr Jarrett, that there really is more at stake here than your unquiet conscience?'

'I think you've assumed that all along, haven't you?'

'Yes.' She cocked her eyebrows frankly at me. 'I have. I've also assumed you aren't going to tell me what it is.'

'Who else could I ask about Isobel?'

'Members of her family, I suppose.'

'And where would I find them?'

'Her parents were shopkeepers in Chichester. They kept a tobacconist's business. Five years ago, at any rate. They could have retired since, of course. Or died. Like Isobel.'

'Yes. So they could. Any idea of the name and address of the shop?'

'None. But there's something I can tell you. Something I *ought* to tell you. Mr and Mrs Courtney were good people, good, gentle people who loved their daughter very much. That was my abiding impression of them. They weren't bitter about what had happened to her, just very, very sad. I asked Mr Courtney how he felt about the driver of the car. About *you*, that is. He said he didn't blame you – accidents happen. But he also said you should have attended the funeral. Or written to them at the very least. He thought he had a right to expect that much of you. I thought so, too.'

'Yes.' I tried not to flinch as I looked at her. 'And you were both right.'

I was in Chichester by four o'clock. All the way down, the accusation in Mary Whiting's voice had lingered in my thoughts. I should have attended the funeral. Or at least written to Isobel Courtney's parents. It was true. So I should. But my solicitor had advised me to say as little as possible to her family for fear of implying I was in any way at fault. I'd told myself that hearing from me would only upset them further. Besides, I'd still had the police breathing down my neck at the time, as well as a hurt and angry wife. I hadn't been short of excuses. Some of them had even been genuine. But they were all played out now.

Chichester itself, bustling with shoppers in the afternoon sunshine, seemed edged with mystery, strung with invisible threads that I brushed through at every step. Isobel Courtney had grown up in the city. Just like Marian Esguard. Whose past was whose? I wondered. Whose story came first?

I parked where Eris had claimed to, at the Festival Theatre, and walked down North Street towards the centre. At the first newsagent I came to, I asked if they knew of a specialist tobacconist in the city and was recommended to try the Pipe Rack in South Street.

'I think I've heard of it,' I said. 'Is it run by the Courtneys?'

'Well, just Sam Courtney now. Doris died a couple of years ago. Sam's been on his own since. I think he only keeps the place going for the company. Sad, really.'

And sad it surely was. The window display was more like a faded museum exhibit, sun-bleached posters recalling long-forgotten tobacco advertising mottoes – 'Trust Gold Leaf to taste good' and the like. The shop itself looked as though it had been closed down months ago and was awaiting a refit, pending which the vestigial stock of pipes, tobacco and smoking

316

accessories had been left to gather dust.

But the sign on the door insisted it was open for business and, a minute or so after the bell had tinkled into silence behind me, a small, round, white-haired old man in a threadbare cardigan, frayed shirt and rumpled trousers wheezed out from the rear, cleared his throat with evident difficulty, peered at me through jam-jar-bottom glasses and asked if he could help.

'Mr Courtney?'

'Yes. Do I know you?' He squinted at me. 'I do, don't I? I'm afraid my memory's not what it was.'

'I'm Ian Jarrett.' I offered him my hand. 'The driver of the car that killed Isobel.'

He looked at me blankly for several seconds, then my words seemed to register. 'Of course. Yes, I remember you from the inquest. The driver of the car. Jarrett, did you say?'

'Yes. I should have contacted you at the time to say how extremely sorry I was. I know it's late in the day, but will you . . . accept my condolences?'

I was still holding my hand out. Abstractedly, he shook it, then pulled out a stool from beneath the counter and sank down onto it. He was breathing rapidly and shallowly, the wheeze threatening at any moment to turn into a convulsing cough. 'Your condolences. Yes, of course. You've, er, come a long way?'

'From London.'

'And after such a long time, too. Ian Jarrett. Yes, that was the name. Kind of you to call.'

'Not really.'

'It's a pity you didn't come before. While Doris was alive. She might have appreciated it.'

'I am sorry. About all of it. Especially the accident, of course. I wish to God it hadn't happened.'

317

'I wish that, too.' He looked down. 'Still, good of you to make the effort. Thank you.'

'Mind if I . . . ask you a few questions about your daughter?'

'Mind? No. Got nothing else but memories to live on. You may as well jog a few. If you want to. Can't see what you'll gain by it, though.'

'Was Isobel born in Chichester?'

'Oh yes. Right upstairs.' He nodded towards the ceiling. 'We thought she'd be the first of two or three, Doris and me. But . . .' He shook his head. 'Isobel turned out to be our only child. It's a grievous thing to outlive your own child, Mr Jarrett. Not natural. Not in the order of things.'

'And she grew up in the city?'

'Yes. Till she went away to university. She was a bright girl, our Isobel. Clever as they come. That's how she did so well for herself. Had a good job with Sotheby's. A *very* good job.'

'As a photographic expert, I believe.'

'That's right. She loved photography, even as a little girl. She took over my old Brownie box camera when she was about ten and built up whole albums of pictures. We bought her a smart new camera one Christmas, but she went on using the Brownie. Then she got into developing the pictures herself. Set up a club at her school and used their darkroom. It's a funny thing, really. Hundreds of pictures there must be upstairs, taken by her. But hardly any *of* her.'

'Occupational hazard.'

'Come again?'

'Never mind. Tell me, do you know East Pallant?'

'It's just round the corner.'

'What about number eight? It's a legal practice.'

318

'Not with you.'

'What I mean is did Isobel . . . take an unusual interest in a particular house in East Pallant?'

'No. Why should she have? She took lots of pictures round Chichester. Liked Georgian architecture. East Pallant's the place for that if anywhere is. But . . . number eight? I don't know what you're getting at.'

'She never married, did she?'

'So?'

'I just wondered if she was . . . planning to.'

'Not that Doris and I knew of. We didn't see as much of her as we'd have liked, though. She was always . . . busy. Well, that's London for you. If there was a man . . .' He shrugged. 'We didn't hear from him afterwards. That's all I can tell you.'

'Did she ever mention the name Conrad Nyman?'

'Who?'

'*Conrad Nyman.*'

'Never heard of him.'

'What about Daphne Sanger?'

'Her neither.'

'I gather she attended the funeral. A friend of Isobel's presumably. A cigar-smoker. Slim. Ash blonde. Glasses.'

'I don't remember her.'

'Really? A colleague of Isobel's at Sotheby's said she met her there.'

'Maybe she did. But I don't remember. It was an upsetting time.'

'Of course. I'm sorry. I didn't mean to . . .' I sighed and glanced round at the shabby remnants of the Courtney family business, aware how little right I had to badger this sad old man with his hoarded memories of the camera-crazy girl that had grown into the photograph-haunted woman. 'Isobel's colleague said she had a fine collection of early Victorian photographs. What happened to them?'

'Her solicitor dealt with all that. Cleared the house before it was sold. We couldn't bear to have any of it here.'

'No mementoes?'

'We had mementoes enough.'

'Yes. I suppose so. Did they include . . . I mean, I know you said there were hardly any, but . . . do you have a photograph of Isobel, Mr Courtney? I've never . . . actually seen her . . . If you know what I mean.'

'There *are* photographs, yes. Doris had one framed . . . afterwards. You can see it . . . if you want.'

'I'd like to. If I may.'

'Go through to the back.' He reached out and raised the flap to let me through the counter.

A small sitting room lay beyond the doorway, crowded with oversized Fifties-style furniture. The air was frowsty, heavy with dust and cigarette smoke. The remains of a meal stood on a table near the window, adding stale soup to the mix of odours. But the past was stronger than all of them.

I crossed to the mantelpiece above the gas fire. Framed photographs stood on either side of the clock in the centre. One was a wedding shot of Sam and Doris Courtney long ago, the other of a slim blond-haired woman in her mid to late twenties, standing in a walled pathway near the cathedral. A transept and part of its spire could be seen in the background. She was dressed casually and was smiling warmly at the camera, posing for her mother, perhaps, during a weekend down from London. Her hair was longer than I recalled. There was nothing as such for me to recognize. It was an unstudied insignificant snapshot. But it was how the Courtneys had chosen to remember their daughter. Young, cheerful and free of foreboding. Except that, to my eye, there *was* something, in the stiff edge to her smile and the faint wariness of her gaze, that implied she wasn't the untroubled or uncomplicated girl her parents would have wished to believe. Even then.

'You had a lovely daughter, Mr Courtney,' I said, walking back into the shop. 'I'm truly sorry. I wish . . . Well, you must know what I wish.'

'But wishes aren't wands, Mr Jarrett. You can't wave them over your sorrows and make them go away.'

'Why was Isobel in Barnet that night, by the way?'

'Visiting a friend.'

'Which friend was that?'

He looked at me sharply, aware, it seemed, that he'd spoken without thinking. He was holding something back. That was clear. I'd suspected it all along. But he had a crucial advantage that meant I couldn't press him to reveal what it was. He was the aged father of the woman I'd killed. He owed me nothing. Not even honesty. 'I can't remember,' he mumbled at last.

'Were they at the funeral?'

'I . . . I'm not sure. I suppose so. My memory's not as sharp as it used to be. I forget. Except the things I want to forget. They don't go away.' He stuck out his lower lip pugnaciously. 'I try to think of Isobel as she is in that photograph, but my mind won't always let me. Sometimes, too often, it puts a different picture in its place. The picture of what I saw on that slab in the mortuary when I went in to identify her. How she was after you'd . . .'

He flapped his hand, at me or the memory, I couldn't tell which, and caught a small tower of tobacco tins with one of his fingers. The tins toppled across the counter, several skidding off onto the floor, where they rolled and rattled slowly to rest.

'I'd like to close up now,' he said, breaking the silence that followed. 'Would you mind leaving? I'm rather tired.'

Sam Courtney was tired. Maybe I was, too. Or maybe my confidence was ebbing. It was no more than a five-minute walk to East Pallant. Number eight stood at the end of an elegant parabola of Georgian houses. Like most of the others, it had been converted into offices, whose occupants were beginning to leave for home, strolling away in the mellow late afternoon sunlight, briefcases in hand, coats over arms. Everything was ordinary and orderly. Nothing was out of place.

But if I raised my gaze to the rooftops and the sky and let my mind discard the sights and sounds of the present I could almost imagine that, with enough thought and concentration, enough desire to make it so, I could look down again and see Marian Esguard emerging from the door of her father's house into the world she'd known. The same bricks and mortar, the same railings and paving stones. It wasn't so very different, nor so very far away. She'd been here. Maybe, in some sense, she still was here.

But when I did eventually look down, all I saw was a schoolgirl walking slowly past me and on along the street. I hadn't heard her approaching and I watched her receding figure with a fixity of mind I couldn't quite fathom. She was wearing school uniform – boater, blazer and pleated skirt – and was carrying a satchel over her shoulder. Her long blond hair bounced on the collar of her blazer as she walked. She was probably about Amy's age, and I could easily imagine what Amy would say about having to wear a boater, though this girl didn't seem to mind. She glanced back at me, or at something behind me, as she crossed to the other side of the street, then vanished from sight round the curve of the buildings.

I didn't think any more about her until I was driving north out of the city, back towards London. Then it came to me. It was still the Easter holiday. There shouldn't have been any schoolgirls in uniform on the streets of Chichester. Not now. Not at this point in time.

Chapter Twelve

Nyman had so far eluded me, but Daphne surely couldn't hope to deny her friendship with Isobel Courtney. Mary Whiting had met her at the funeral, and I'd have taken a bet she was living in Barnet at the time. Isobel had gone there to see her, perhaps to seek help in dealing with whatever affinity she felt with the lost and long-ago soul of Marian Esguard.

I couldn't see my way much further into the mystery than that and I wasn't sure I wanted to. There was another possible explanation for everything that had happened to me. It was the most horrifying one of all and the backward glance of the schoolgirl who'd passed me in East Pallant lingered in my mind as a glimpse of just what that explanation would mean: that nobody was to be trusted, least of all me.

But I wasn't going to believe that until I was forced to. Next morning I went straight to Harley Street and tried the bell at Daphne's practice. There was, as I expected, no answer, so I tried the next bell on the panel, for an osteopath called Ramirez, and talked his receptionist into letting me in.

'Miss Sanger will be away for at least another week,' she informed me. 'It was my understanding that she'd been in touch with all her clients to explain the situation.'

'She must have missed me. I need to write to her, actually. Do you have her home address?'

'I can't give that out, I'm afraid. But, if you write to her here, we'll forward it on.' With a tell-tale downward glance, she slid one envelope over another in her out-tray.

'It's an urgent matter. I'm not sure I can—' I snatched up the envelope she'd just covered and looked at the name and address on it.

'Give that back to me at once,' she demanded, flushing angrily, though partly perhaps at her own stupidity.

'Certainly.' I handed it over smartly. 'Don't worry. I won't tell if you won't.'

It was a small house in a select reach of West Hampstead. The empty drive, the firmly latched gate, the closed windows and the milk dial set on zero told me what the answerphone had already implied: she wasn't there. She couldn't stay in hiding for ever, but maybe she thought she could stay there long enough to seal my fate in whatever way Nyman had planned. I could chase them, but it seemed I could never catch them.

A neighbour was eyeing me suspiciously over the hedge and I decided to capitalize on her watchfulness. Predictably, she had no idea where Daphne had gone, nor when she'd be back. But she saw no harm in satisfying my curiosity on one point. Daphne had moved into the area four years before – from Barnet. They could stay ahead, but it seemed they were never quite out of sight.

Clapham proved the point. I worked my way along
Smollett Avenue, drawing blanks at every door. Five
years was a long time. The name meant nothing. And
why should it, when people kept themselves to themselves, and Isobel Courtney might well have done so
more assiduously than most? But somebody knew something. They always do. And the elderly Asian woman at
number forty-seven was that somebody.

'Miss Courtney lived right next door, at forty-five. Oh
yes, I remember her well. She was very pleasant. I liked
her. Not like the couple who live there now, with their
noses in the air and their big car. He drives like the man
must have done who killed Miss Courtney. Hurry,
hurry, hurry and hang the consequences. Miss Courtney
was a very nice lady. She never said a bad word about
anybody.'

'Did she get many visitors – friends coming and
going?'

'No, no. She lived very quietly. No noise, no parties,
no people. I used to say to her, "You should find yourself a good man before it's too late." But she never did.'
She grinned at me. 'The men only come now it *is* too
late.'

'Men?'

'You're not the first to ask about Miss Courtney.
You're not even the best-looking. But don't worry.
You're not the worst-looking. There was a gentleman in
a pink bow tie I didn't at all—'

'Quisden-Neve?'

'That could be his name. He gave me his card, but I
don't . . .' She frowned thoughtfully. 'Quisden-Neve.
Yes, it was something like that.'

'When was this?'

'I forget. Two years. Three. Who knows?'

'What did he want?'

'Same as you. Same as the first one.'

'The good-looking one?'

'Yes. He came about a year after Miss Courtney's death. Very smart. Very handsome. Very . . . well spoken. Who were her friends? What happened to her possessions? What did I remember about her? Always it's the same. She's dead. Why don't you let her rest in peace? There's nothing I can tell you. She was here. Then I heard she was killed. I went to her funeral. I met her parents. Good people, very sad. A van came and the house was emptied. Then it was sold. What more can I say?'

'The first man. Was his name Nyman?'

'I don't remember if he said.'

'But handsome? Blue eyes? Grey-blond hair? Maybe just blond then? Tanned and well dressed? Touch of the film star about him?'

'That would be him to a likeness.'

'Then it *was* Nyman.'

At last I had something to show for my efforts. Isobel Courtney was a common denominator between Nyman, Daphne and me. She'd played a part in all our pasts. Now I knew so for a fact, I was determined to force the knowledge on Faith and oblige her to take my allegations seriously.

I could think of only one way to be absolutely sure of speaking to her alone. I phoned her office in Hounslow, checked she was at work that afternoon, then drove out there and parked just far enough down the road to be able to monitor arrivals and departures without drawing attention to myself. I had a clear view of her car in the car park. It was only a matter of time.

She left early, which I'd half expected with Amy home from school. She was clearly in a hurry as well, though not enough of one to slip past me. I was at her side while she was still stowing her bag and an armful of files in the boot. And I was waiting to surprise her when she closed the boot and turned round.

'Oh my God!' she said, starting backwards. 'What are you doing here?'

'We need to talk, Faith,' I replied, reminding myself to sound calm and reasonable.

'I disagree.' She made to move past me to the door, but I blocked her path. 'Please, Ian,' she said, pulling up and treating me to the tight-lipped frown I knew so well. 'You're being impossible.'

'I just want to talk. It won't take long.'

'But *I* don't want to.'

'A few minutes of your time. That's all I'm asking for.'

'No, it's not. You're asking me to listen to more of the kind of paranoid nonsense you served up on Sunday.'

'A few minutes, Faith.' Despite what she'd said, I could see she was softening. She still felt something for me, even if it was mostly pity. 'Come on.'

'All right.' She shook her head in irritation. 'But if you start accusing Conrad of conspiring against you again—'

'I won't accuse him of anything. I just want to draw a few facts to your attention. It's up to you what you make of them.'

'A few facts? Somehow I doubt it. But get in the car anyway. If we stand here arguing any longer we'll have an audience.' She nodded towards the office windows behind me, then brushed past.

She'd already started the engine by the time I lowered myself into the passenger seat. With a crunch of gears, she started off, sweeping out of the car park and round two corners to a quieter road bordering a school playing field. There she pulled in and stopped.

'Well? What are these facts, Ian? As far as I'm concerned, the clock's started ticking on your few minutes.'

'I'd better come straight to the point, then. You remember Isobel Courtney?'

'Of course I remember her. What's she got to do with this?'

'Daphne Sanger, my psychotherapist, the one who contacted you, she knew Isobel Courtney. She even went to her funeral. What's more, five years ago she was living in Barnet. Isobel must have gone there to see her.'

'"Must have" doesn't sound like a fact to me.'

'I think I can prove it if I have to.'

'You don't have to for my benefit. I don't care why she was there. I know all too well why you were.'

'You spoke to Daphne. You know she exists.'

'So?'

'She's gone missing. From home as well as from her practice. Phone her yourself and see.'

'Why should I want to?'

'Because Conrad also knew Isobel Courtney. Her old next-door neighbour in Clapham will happily describe the man who called round asking questions about her within a year of her death. And you'll recognize the description. I promise you that.'

'No, I won't. If you think I have the slightest intention of—'

'It was *him*, Faith. Don't you see? Isobel. Daphne. Conrad. Me. You. We're all connected.'

'Rubbish.'

'How much do you know about him?'

'Enough.'

'Precious little, I suspect, when you analyse it. I'll bet he's a biographical blank. A man of mystery. Maybe that's part of his appeal. But ask yourself this: what's he hiding?'

'Nothing. He's a sane and sensitive man. You just don't recognize the type.'

'Where was he born?'

'I don't know. I haven't asked him.'

'Are his parents still alive?'

'I . . . He hasn't mentioned them.'

'Any brothers or sisters?'

'Not as far as I know.'

'What did he do before Nymanex? I mean, what career path has he followed?'

'*Stop it.*' She turned round in her seat and glared at me. 'I'm not going to let you interrogate me. Certainly not about Conrad.'

'You haven't been able to answer a single question about him, Faith.'

'Where are the facts you promised me?'

'In front of you. The ones I've turned up. And the ones you *haven't.*'

'I haven't been trying to. I dare say Conrad couldn't quote my life history back at you if you challenged him to. Are you suggesting *I'm* hiding something?'

'Just think it through. You met at the National Gallery, right? Who made the first move? Who spoke to who?'

'Mind your own business.'

'It was Conrad, wasn't it?'

'What if it was?'

'You've been set up. Just like I have.'

'Oh, for God's sake.' She sighed and ran her fingers

330

through her hair in a typical gesture of exasperation. 'This is getting us nowhere. I'd like to drive home now, Ian. *Alone.*'

'Promise you'll be more inquisitive about his past.'

'I'll promise nothing.'

'He'll be evasive. And, if you persist, he'll lie. I guarantee it. He's not what you think.'

'You don't know what I think. I'm not sure you ever have.'

'At least keep Amy away from him.'

'Get out of the car. Please.'

'All right. I'm going. But for all our sakes, Faith, don't trust him.'

'I'll tell him what you've said. All of it. Just because I do trust him.'

'There'll come a day when you won't.' I eased the door open and searched for some parting words that would linger in her mind after I'd gone. 'I don't expect you to admit to any misgivings about him. But I'll bet you have some. I'll bet, deep down, there's something about him that worries you. Believe that feeling even if you don't believe me.'

'Goodbye, Ian,' she said firmly, though no more firmly than she would have done even if my warning had struck home.

I knew better than to say any more. I could only hope I'd said enough. I climbed out onto the pavement and watched as she drove away. It could go either way now. She might see through him. Or not. And I wasn't sure which was the more dangerous outcome.

I had no wish to return to the all but empty flat that was the closest I had to a home, so I stopped off at Tim's lab. He was just packing up and needed little persuading to step down to the White Horse for a drink. I told him more or less everything that had happened since Sunday, everything that I could swear to anyway. He seemed less impressed by my discoveries than I'd hoped and unconvinced by my tactics where Faith was concerned.

'You should have waited till you had some hard evidence. I don't think Nyman will have much difficulty talking his way out of what you've come up with so far.'

'I can't afford to wait. He may spring some new surprise on me at any moment. I don't like him being close to Faith. And I especially don't like him being close to Amy.'

'She'll be back at school and out of harm's way next week.'

'Yes. So she will. But next week seems an eternity away. I have to pin something decisive on him. And I have to do it quickly.'

'How?'

'I don't know. There's no-one else I can question about Isobel Courtney.'

'You'll have to go after Nyman himself, then.'

'Yes. Which means talking to Nicole. She may be able to give me some clues about his past. But she isn't going to like being asked, I can tell you. I virtually had to promise she wouldn't hear from me again just to get his address out of her.'

'Do you want me to ask her?'

'*You?*'

'Why not? At least I'll be able to reassure her you're not in the grip of a personal fantasy.'

'Are you sure I'm not?' I looked him in the eye, offering him the chance to say whatever he truly felt.

'As sure as I can be.' But he hadn't quite met my gaze as he'd replied. Even for Tim, there remained an element of doubt. Just as there did for me.

'You know,' I began, 'while I was in Chichester . . .' Then my voice trailed into silence as my desire to confide in him faded. Some secrets were better not shared. 'Forget it. It doesn't matter.'

'What about Nicole – *do* you want me to speak to her?'

'Yes, please, Tim. It's a good idea.'

'Well . . .' He beamed at me. 'Somebody has to have them.'

Tim's good idea left me nothing to do. And nowhere to go. I should have gone back to the flat after we'd parted. Instead, I drove across Putney Bridge and round to Castelnau. I parked some way from the house and approached on foot. There were lights in the downstairs windows and one on in Amy's bedroom as well. If she twitched back the curtain, she'd see me standing beneath the streetlamp, looking up at her. But the curtain didn't move and I went no closer. It was too soon to try again. If Nyman was there, it would end badly. And, if he wasn't, it might end no better. Tim was right. I needed more than second-hand coincidences. I needed proof. Until I had some, I could only turn and walk away. Like a wandering loner who sees the lights of someone else's home and feels a stab of envy as he passes by, I couldn't afford to stop.

Back at the flat, I stared round at the bare walls and sparse furnishings. The place looked and felt unoccupied. I'd been living in it for nearly three months without even unpacking. It held nothing of me. Maybe, I thought, as I ran my finger through the layer of dust on a tabletop, there was nothing of me to hold.

I walked across to the bed and lay down, letting my

eyes rest without focusing on the blank grey ceiling. Fear was creeping up on me. I could sense its approach. It wasn't some sudden panic. It was a gradually mounting terror of what I'd be if this went on for another three months. Everything was slipping away from me: job, family, lover; security, self-confidence, sanity. I'd walked into quicksand and all my struggles had only sucked me in deeper.

I started with surprise at the first bleep of the phone, jumped from the bed and hurried across to where I'd left it on the table.

'Hello?'

'You've been busy, Jarrett.' It was Nyman's voice, cool and dark as the night beyond the uncurtained windows. 'Hope I'm not interrupting anything important.'

'What do you want?'

'I'd like to arrange a meeting. Just you and me. For a confidential word about matters of mutual interest.'

'I'm on to you, Nyman. I know what this is about.'

'Clearly you think you do. Faith was quite upset by your allegations. I really can't have you harassing her in this way. Since you believe me to be orchestrating a conspiracy against you, I suggest we discuss it man to man and put an end to the whole sorry saga.'

'Suits me.'

'Good. Now, as you know, I'm a very busy man. Accommodating you in my schedule at short notice is far from easy, but it can be done. I have a breakfast meeting tomorrow morning at the Savoy. The company launch will be collecting me from Charing Cross Pier at ten o'clock to take me back to Canary Wharf. Why don't you join me aboard and we can talk on the way?'

'Makes no difference to me where we meet, Nyman. I just want the truth.'

'Excellent. I'll see what I can do for you. Tomorrow at ten.'

It was another ludicrously perfect spring morning when I walked down through the parks next day to Whitehall, along the Embankment and under Hungerford Bridge. The cherries were in blossom, the tourists were out, and nothing – absolutely nothing – in the riverside vista echoed my sense of imminent crisis.

The launch was moored at Charing Cross Pier as promised, a sleek rapier-flanged craft with the vainglorious name *Nyman Aqua* recorded in ultramarine copperplate on the bow. I was welcomed aboard by the pilot. He was polite but unsmiling. And clearly expecting me.

'Mr Nyman's not here yet,' he announced. 'Make yourself comfortable while we wait.'

There was a large and airy cabin beneath the wheelhouse, but I preferred the bow, where I could scan the Embankment for Nyman. As it was, I didn't have to wait long for him to appear. No sooner had I looked up than I spotted him, halfway between Cleopatra's Needle and the pierhead, strolling casually along, the breeze ruffling his hair. He was speaking into a mobile phone as he walked, but, seeing me, paused by the parapet to conclude the call. As soon as it was finished, he nodded down to me and walked on.

A minute or so later, he was on the pontoon, exchanging a cheery word with the pilot. Then he was aboard, the engines were throbbing into life and we were casting off. Nyman tossed his briefcase into the cabin and joined me in the bow. He was wearing an immaculately cut lightweight suit and was smiling as broadly and warmly as if I were an old friend he hadn't seen for far too long.

'Grand day,' he remarked as we nosed out into the river and the Embankment slowly sheered away from us.

'I wouldn't know,' I replied, keeping my eyes fixed on his.

'Not getting to you, is it? Surely any photographer worth his salt should have a feel for the weather. Light. Temperature. Visibility. Don't they all play a part?'

'I'm not here to take photographs.'

'No. Of course not. Just as well, probably.' He spun round and stretched an arm towards the receding flank of the Houses of Parliament. 'Correct me if I'm wrong, Jarrett, but didn't your hero, Roger Fenton, take a famous photograph of that when it was still under construction, with sailing barges in the foreground and Big Ben shrouded in scaffolding?'

'You're not wrong.'

'When would that have been? 1857 or so?'

'About then.'

'And Fenton was born . . . when?'

'1819.'

'Before photography was invented.'

'Supposedly.'

'Yes. Quite.' He turned back to me, still grinning from ear to ear. 'Quite so.'

'Forget Fenton, Nyman. You and I both know this has nothing to do with photography.'

'Does it not?'

'You're out to take some twisted kind of revenge for what happened to Isobel Courtney.'

'"What happened to her." Don't you mean "What you did to her"?'

'You admit it, then?'

'I suppose I do. In a sense. But as for it having nothing to do with photography, well, you couldn't be further from the truth.'

'It was an accident, you know.'

'What was?'

'Isobel's death.'

'Really?' He followed some spot on the South Bank with his eyes as we passed under Waterloo Bridge, glanced at his watch, Rolex gold flashing in the sun as he twitched back his cuff, then slowly returned his gaze to meet mine. He was no longer smiling. 'Even if that were true, the question arises: does it make a difference? I mean, do intentions mitigate consequences? What do you think, Jarrett? If, just for the sake of argument, somebody ran over Amy in their car and killed her, would it make you feel better or worse if you thought they'd done it deliberately?'

'There's obviously a difference. To any sane person.'

'As to sanity, I believe the doubt hovers over yours, not mine. But bear with me. Would it make you feel better or worse if you thought they'd done it deliberately?'

'Worse. Naturally.'

'You reckon so?'

'I've just said so.'

'Yes. So you have. Still, it's pure conjecture on your part, isn't it? I mean, you've never actually experienced such a thing. You don't really know. Do you?'

'Not from—'

'Then let me tell you.' His voice was suddenly harsh, his expression intense. 'Based on my personal experience. You're wrong. Murder presumes a motive. And a motive gives you something to hang on to. It confers meaning on tragedy. Whereas stupidity and carelessness reduce death to a farce. And enable the killer to evade responsibility. "It was only an accident. It wasn't my fault. I'm not to blame." Does that accurately paraphrase your moral position in this particular debate, Jarrett?'

'It accurately paraphrases the coroner's summing-up at the inquest. If you'd been there, you'd know that.'

'I was unavoidably detained elsewhere. But I read a transcript of the proceedings later. I know exactly what was said. And what was concluded. I just don't happen to accept the conclusion.'

'You blame me for Isobel's death.'

'That's right. You're catching on awfully fast.'

'Were you in love with her?'

We were past the Oxo Tower now, homing in on the centre span of Blackfriars Bridge. Nyman glanced at his watch again. He took a slim gold case from his pocket – monogrammed N like the bull's-eye window in the front door at Derringfold Place – and opened it, offering me a cigarette. I shook my head. He went ahead and lit one for himself, savouring the first draw as we passed beneath the bridge.

'Well?' I persisted. 'Did you love her?'

'All other things being equal, I'd be happy to satisfy your curiosity on every single point. But they aren't equal. I'm constrained by . . . tactical considerations.'

'What the hell does that mean?'

'It means your lucky guess that Isobel and I were . . . connected . . . has obliged me to step up a gear in our little . . . *jeu de mort*.'

'Our *what*?'

'I underestimated Quisden-Neve and had no choice but to take drastic action against him. It was of necessity clumsily done. But, apropos of my earlier comments, it

338

didn't insult him by being accidental. The point is that I don't propose to make the same mistake twice. I have to limit your freedom of movement before you succeed in turning Faith against me.' His smile returned. 'The game still has rules, though, even if they're harsh ones. I'll give you a chance. Not a good one, but a chance nonetheless. We're going to drop you at Swan Lane Pier, just before London Bridge. You can make it to Bank Tube station from there in five minutes, if you put a spurt on, then you can travel straight through to Notting Hill Gate on the Central line. Ten stops. What do you reckon? Twenty minutes from Swan Lane to your flat if you go like a bat out of hell and get lucky with the Tube schedule? Half an hour's a more plausible minimum, I suppose. Let's say that. You could take a cab, of course, but the traffic's diabolical today. Well, every day, really. I'd opt for the Tube myself. But it's your choice.'

'What the hell are you talking about?'

'Eris is at your flat. Has been since ten o'clock. That's who I was speaking to on the phone. I should have a word with your landlord about the locks on that place if I were you. Not exactly top security. But you'll soon have more pressing matters on your mind, so let's not dwell on it.'

We were approaching Southwark Bridge now. Nyman took another draw on his cigarette and checked his watch yet again. 'At ten forty-five Niall will join her. Eris is expecting *you*, actually. Niall will be a surprise for her. And not a pleasant one. They don't exactly get on. I'm none too fond of Niall myself. He has some deeply unappetizing characteristics. It's one of those characteristics he'll be giving expression to this morning.'

Nyman paused while we went under the bridge, the engine noise bouncing back at us from the stonework above and around us. Then we were back in the sunlight again. 'He's going to kill her, Jarrett. In your flat. He's going to make it look like your handiwork, of course. And, needless to say, I'm not going to supply you with an alibi.'

I looked at him, disbelief somehow confounded by the mildness of his expression. He meant it. Every word. There was absolutely no doubt. It was going to be as he'd said.

'I don't think you'll get there in time to intervene, let alone prevent it happening. Consequently, you'll be in prison when Faith marries me and Amy becomes my stepdaughter. I'll have taken your life away from you. Just like you took Isobel's. Only you won't be dead. And you'll have the privilege of knowing it wasn't in any sense accidental.'

We passed under Cannon Street railway bridge. London Bridge lay dead ahead. The launch slowed fractionally and veered in towards the pier on the north bank. My thoughts couldn't seem to keep pace with what was happening. He was mad. He had to be. But he was also clever. And in Niall Esguard he had a confederate who was willing if not eager to put his plans into effect.

'You could phone the police, of course. But you have to weigh your chances of persuading them to take the call seriously against the time you'd lose. And then there's Niall to consider. He may jump the gun and turn up earlier than instructed. He does so love his work. In that event, all you'd be doing is strengthening the case against you. The call would look like a ham-fisted attempt to cover your tracks. You could walk away from it, of course. Abandon Eris to her fate and try to prove you were somewhere else when she died. But you care about her, don't you, even though she tricked you? And there's just a chance you can save her. Maybe you'll get there quicker than I've allowed for. Maybe she'll stall Niall long enough to make a difference. Maybe you'll have a slice of luck. Who knows? That's part of the game.'

I looked at his smiling face, then round at the approaching pier, then back at him again. 'You've done all this because, five years ago, I killed Isobel Courtney in a road accident that was as much her fault as mine?'

'It's made you remember her, hasn't it?'

'I hadn't forgotten.'

'I'll have to take your word for that. One thing's certain, though.' He leaned closer. 'You won't ever forget her now.'

'I'll find some way to stop you.'

'I doubt it. You're welcome to try, of course. Indeed, you *should* try, because the futures I have planned for Faith and Amy aren't ones you'd approve of, especially Amy's. By the time you get out of prison, she's going to be a seriously troubled young woman if I have anything to do with it. And I *will* have something to do with it. Rather a lot, actually. The middle teens are such a vulnerable period in a girl's life, don't you think?'

'You bastard.'

'Sticks and stones, Jarrett. And even the words are over now. Time for you to jump ship.'

A river tour boat was already moored at the pier. The launch approached at some speed, slowing suddenly and slewing round as it came alongside the vacant end of the pontoon. A man mopping down the deck of the tour boat stopped to gape at us in bemusement as white water churned and the engines roared.

'There's not a moment to lose,' said Nyman. 'I should start moving if I were you.'

I wasted another precious few seconds grappling mentally with a situation I still couldn't quite believe, even though I knew it really was happening. There was only one thing for me to do. He'd made sure of that. I'd spent three months searching for Eris. Now I was certain to find her. But there was only the slimmest of chances I'd find her alive.

'What's it to be, Jarrett?'

All I could deny him was an explicit reply. My dash to the opening in the port rail must nevertheless have been exactly what he wanted to see. I jumped onto the pontoon, raced along it and started up the ramp to the street. From there I carried straight on up Swan Lane without looking back, running hard and fast, as if the Devil were behind me – as, in a sense, he was.

The traffic round the Monument and approaching London Bridge looked as heavy and slow-moving as Nyman had predicted. The Tube really was likely to be the quickest route, even though it could hardly be quick enough. I ran on up King William Street, dodging other pedestrians as I went, dashing headlong across side streets, ignoring the squeal of brakes and the blare of horns. A subway to Bank station appeared ahead. I plunged gratefully into it, sprinted through the concourse to buy a ticket, then took the escalator down to the Central line two steps at a time.

And at the bottom I found myself reduced at once to the slow and steady pace of London Underground. 'NEXT TRAIN: 6 MINS,' declared the overhead display on the westbound platform. It wasn't open to negotiation. That was how long it was going to be. I thumped the nearest pillar in frustration. I was going to be too late. There was hardly a doubt in my mind, far less a hope in my heart. I wasn't going to make it.

But still I had to try, as Nyman had calculated I would have to. The six minutes grudgingly passed while I prowled the slowly filling platform. All the anger at Eris that had boiled up in me as I'd listened to her last tape drained away into despairing forgiveness. She'd duped me. She'd made a fool of me. But I didn't want her to die. Some small part of what had happened in Vienna remained precious in my memory. I saw that now as the crowning irony of Nyman's campaign against me. It had only worked as well as it had because Eris and I had unwittingly stepped outside it and found a place where deception didn't matter any more. Perhaps Nyman realized that. Perhaps that was why he'd decided she had to die. Not merely because it suited his purposes, but because she was the weak link in the chain he'd bound around me.

I held on to the thought as I boarded the train. It made everything better and worse at the same time. It meant Nyman's plans could sometimes misfire. But it also meant that, if Eris died, it really would be my fault.

The journey was a void. I refused to let myself look at my watch. I stared at the tunnel walls beyond the window opposite my seat and tried to fill my mind with their blankness. St Paul's; Chancery Lane; Holborn: people got on, people got off. Tottenham Court Road; Oxford Circus; Bond Street: one day, I knew, it would all be different. Marble Arch; Lancaster Gate; Queensway: one day, I'd know what had already happened.

Notting Hill Gate. I was running again now, along the platform and up the escalators, through the barriers and up the steps to the street. I fumbled with my keys in my pocket as I dodged and weaved along the crowded pavements. Everyone else seemed to be moving with exaggerated slowness. I was like the blur of a mobile figure in a Fenton photograph: the man who'd been there but couldn't be seen. My mind flashed forward to what might be waiting at the flat. Niall was capable of anything. Killing her wouldn't be enough for him. The worse it looked, the worse it would turn out for me. That would be all the encouragement he needed. '*I can't say I like him*,' she'd told me on the tape, '*but I guess he has his uses*.' And so he did – more than her guesses could ever have encompassed.

But now guesswork was at an end. I was past the front door and bounding up the stairs. The door to the flat lay ahead. I rammed the key into the lock, turned it and flung myself through.

The first thing I saw was Niall's face. And he was smiling.

But the smile was a rictus of death.

He was lying in the centre of the room, his back propped against the armchair, his head lolling sideways. His shirt and trousers were wet with blood, and a slick of it lay black-red on the carpet beneath him. There was blood on his chin, too, and on the cushion of the sofa, as if it had poured from his mouth. His eyes were wide and staring, his mouth fixed in a grin.

I stood with my back against the door as the details of the scene slowly lodged themselves in my mind: the grey pallor of his face, the apron of blood, the frozen clench of his fists. Then I noticed a narrow coil of dark material trailing from between the fingers of his right hand. I stepped closer. It was a black leather tie. *His* tie, presumably, though I'd never seen him wear one. The rest of his outfit was standard: black jeans, black leather jacket, white shirt, the breast pocket stretched round a blood-soaked pack of Camel cigarettes. I remembered the manner of Quisden-Neve's death and wondered if Niall had tried to strangle Eris with the tie. Maybe that's how he'd done for Quisden-Neve. No doubt it had struck him that by using the same *modus operandi* he could saddle me with both murders and so kill three birds with one stone.

But somehow Eris had got the better of him. She'd shot him or stabbed him – I couldn't tell which – and then . . . I turned slowly in a circle. Was she still here? Half of me wanted her to be. The other half was very frightened. There wasn't a sound, except the drip of the kitchen tap. It was too rapid for me to have overlooked when leaving earlier. I walked into the kitchen and immediately noticed droplets of blood and bloody water on the floor and draining board. There were some in the sink as well, along with spatters of vomit. The roller towel was stained pink in patches. The physical debris of violent death was waiting everywhere.

I checked the bathroom. It was empty. That left me back in the bed-sitting room with Niall Esguard's corpse and a limited ration of time in which to decide what to do. He was a tall man and his splayed legs seemed to fill the space between the armchair and the door. I edged round him to the window, flung it open and leaned out to breathe the clear spring air. I ran a hand across my sweat-bathed face and was almost surprised, when I looked at it, that it wasn't covered in blood. Out of the corner of my eye, I could still see the dark and jagged shape slumped against the armchair. It wasn't going to go away. I hadn't dreamed it. Niall Esguard really was dead, there, in the room behind me.

In some strange way, it was actually a relief. The things I'd imagined on that torturous Tube ride from the City were infinitely worse than this. Eris dead, raped, mutilated – anything. And all of it wildly off the mark. Had she been ready for him? Or just lucky? It didn't matter which. The result was the same. She'd killed him, thrown up in the kitchen sink, washed the worst of the blood off and gone. But there would still have been a lot of blood on her clothes. She'd surely have attracted attention. Or perhaps . . .

I left the window open and, giving Niall another wide berth, crossed to the wardrobe. The door was ajar. I swung it wide open and saw at once that my raincoat was missing. She'd taken it to cover the bloodstains.

How long had she been gone? I wondered. I looked at my watch and did some mental arithmetic. It came down to ten minutes at the outside, possibly less. She might have been hurrying out onto the street even as I was racing up the steps from the Underground. I fervently wished then that she'd stayed. It didn't matter about Niall. We could have sorted something out. We could have helped each other. Not that she could have known I was about to arrive. Maybe she would have stayed if she had. Maybe . . .

And, anyway, it did matter about Niall. Of course it did. He was dead, in my flat. Someone had killed him. Murdered him, the police might well conclude. Who would they suspect? There was only one candidate. Me. And what would they find when they checked Niall's background? Me again, asking about him in his local pub, and mentioning Quisden-Neve into the bargain. I'd soon be nailed as the witness who'd done a runner at Chippenham railway station. After that I'd be lucky not to end up charged with double murder. Nyman's plans had misfired again – Niall hadn't turned out to be as efficient a killer as he'd supposed. But maybe that didn't make a lot of difference. Maybe Nyman always had a fall-back position, and this was it. If by some fluke Eris killed Niall, or I killed him trying to rescue her, I still carried the can. Heads he won, tails I lost.

I sat down stiffly on a chair by the table and tried to think. What would Nyman like me to do? What would suit him most of all? For me to incriminate myself, of course. For me to make it worse. What had he said? '*You could walk away from it. You could try to prove you were somewhere else.*' Fat chance. All I'd achieve by making a run for it would be to set myself up more clinchingly than Nyman had done. No. That wasn't the answer.

What was, then? I stared at the blood-bibbed figure in front of me and he stared vacantly back. Death had already drained him of menace. He was just a macabrely broken dummy, a carapace of the crude and vicious schemer he'd been, not really Niall Esguard at all any more.

That was it. I almost smiled at the simplicity of the idea. How would the police know who he was if I didn't tell them? Nyman could hardly volunteer the information. And Eris was running for her life. It was only my links with Niall that put me in the frame. If he was an anonymous stranger I'd found murdered in my flat, I was in the clear. Not completely, of course. I'd still be a suspect, even if the police didn't say so. But none of my clothes were bloodstained. There was no murder weapon, certainly not one with my fingerprints on it. Forensically, I was clean. And there was no shadow of a motive that made sense.

It was a risk. But everything else was even riskier. This way I had a good chance of talking my way out of trouble rather than into it. But it depended on Niall's anonymity. I'd have to remove and destroy any identification he was carrying. It wasn't likely to be much. A man with his fondness for aliases would surely carry as little as possible that proved who he really was. But there'd be something, even if it was only a credit card. Whatever it was, it had to go. And it had to go without leaving a trace – in the flat or on me.

I rose, fetched a fork and spoon from the kitchen drawer, returned to where Niall was sprawled and crouched down in front of him. I lifted the sides of the jacket away from him with the spoon and checked for pockets. There was one inside. A probe with the fork revealed nothing. The outer pockets were visibly empty. The shirt pocket, of course, contained his cigarettes. So far so good. As for his jeans, the bulge in the right-hand pocket was unmistakably that of a wallet. I pushed the wallet slowly out with the spoon and plucked it clear. The left-hand pocket held only a handkerchief. The hip pockets, as far as I could see – and feel with the fork – were empty. A bunch of keys hung from one of his belt loops – a couple of Yales, a mortice and another sporting a Porsche shield on its fob. I unclipped the ring, taking great care not to touch the belt loop as I did so, and took the keys and wallet over to the table.

The wallet held several hundred pounds in cash, plus three credit cards, each bearing a different name – Esguard, Hudson, Sherwood. That was it. He'd died as he travelled: light.

I washed the fork and spoon in the bathroom and replaced them in the kitchen drawer. Then I wrapped a length of toilet tissue round the keys and stuffed them, with the wallet, into an old envelope, Sellotaping the flap and seams. I wrote a note to Tim to accompany the package.

Tim,
Whatever happens, hold on to this until you
hear from me. Tell nobody and *please* don't
open it.
I'm relying on you.
Ian

My story was going to be that, with no phone in the flat, and having left my mobile in the car – which happened to be true – I'd decided to make my way to the police station in Ladbroke Grove to report my gruesome discovery. It was only a few minutes away, so it wouldn't sound so very odd, not when I laid it on about not wanting to spend a moment more than I had to alone with a dead man – which also happened to be true.

Far more importantly, however, there was a post office on the corner of Ladbroke Grove, where I could buy a padded envelope and dispatch the package to Tim. Once I'd convinced the police I was on the level, I could reclaim Niall's wallet and keys from him. The contents of the wallet had revealed nothing. But the keys would get me into 6 Bentinck Place, where I reckoned there'd be some kind of evidence to convince Faith that Nyman had known Niall. That would surely be enough to make her doubt him.

But doubt cut several ways. Were the police really going to believe the dead man was a stranger to me? Given the turnover of tenants in a flat like mine, and the dubious character of a lot of them, it wasn't so very improbable that one or more had kept a duplicate set of keys – removed by the killer, presumably. Why they'd gone there would be a mystery, but that suited me well enough. It could be months before the police made a connection with a man reported missing in Bath, *if* anyone ever did report Niall missing. Anxious friends and relatives weren't exactly a feature of his life.

I looked back at him before closing the door, and realized, with sudden dismay, that as far as I knew the Esguard line ended here, unworthily and anonymously. For Niall and the rest of them it was over. But not for me. And not for Conrad Nyman. We'd both make sure of that.

Chapter Thirteen

'You must be mad,' said Tim. It was the morning of the following day in Parsons Green. He was eyeing me across the breakfast table in his kitchen with apparently genuine concern for my sanity. The police had released me the night before, after a solid afternoon and evening of questioning, without charge and without, so far as I could judge, any active suspicion that I'd murdered the nameless intruder I'd found dead in my flat. The flat itself was sealed as a crime scene, so I'd had little choice but to impose on Tim's hospitality. Clearly worried by my revelation late the previous night that the dead man was none other than Niall Esguard, he was now positively horrified by my announcement that Niall's wallet and keys were likely to be landing on his doormat any minute. 'Have you any idea the risks you're running? I mean, for God's sake . . .' He threw up his hands in despair at my conduct.

'You think I should have told the police everything?'

'For innocent people, it's normally the wisest course of action.'

'But I wouldn't have been believed. You know I

wouldn't. What could I do to help Faith and Amy from inside a police cell?'

'That's all very well. But if the police learn you've lied to them they'll think you murdered Niall Esguard *and* Quisden-Neve.'

'Nobody murdered Niall Esguard. It was self-defence.'

'Maybe so. But it doesn't look like self-defence, does it? Did they tell you how it was done?'

'He was stabbed once, in the neck, severing the carotid artery. I think Eris must have smelled a rat and taken a knife with her for protection. When Niall tried to strangle her, she lashed out to save herself. It was probably just a lucky blow.'

'Not for Niall. Has it occurred to you she was expecting to meet you there? If she was carrying a knife . . .'

'It was to protect herself from me? I don't think so. Remember, she didn't seem to know Quisden-Neve was dead when she recorded the last tape. Maybe she'd found out since getting back from Guernsey. Maybe that's what put her on her guard. She knows Nyman. Therefore she knows there's plenty to be frightened of.'

'She does now. And I take it Nyman will realize what this means . . .' Tim flapped the newspaper at me. It was folded open at an inside page carrying a brief report of the discovery of a man's body at a flat in Notting Hill Gate, closing with the words, '*The police are treating the death as suspicious.*'

'I imagine he already knows. He'll have made discreet enquiries when Niall failed to make contact.'

'So both you and Eris are in considerable danger.'

'Potentially. But Eris will have gone to ground now. We know how good she is at that.'

'Which leaves just you.'

'I've been in danger ever since Nyman decided to punish me for Isobel Courtney's death. It's no worse now than it ever was. But that's not the point. He made it crystal clear to me that he planned to get at me through Faith and Amy. Especially Amy.'

'How can you stop him?'

'By staying out of police custody and proving to Faith that he isn't—' There was a rattle from the letter box and the plop of mail on the doormat. I got up at once and rushed out into the hall. 'It's arrived,' I shouted back to Tim, snatching up the package and tearing it open. 'So that's a load off your mind.' He was watching me from the kitchen doorway as I dropped the keys and wallet into my pocket. 'Burn the envelope, just to be on the safe side. We don't want you branded as an accessory, do we?'

'Technically, I already am one. Strangely enough, though, that's the least of my worries. You're going to Bath, I assume.'

'Right now. I had to promise the police I wouldn't leave London without informing them, so, if they phone, could you be as vague as possible? Like I said in the note you haven't read, I'm relying on you.'

'In that case, I shouldn't neglect my duties as your adviser. If there's anything to incriminate him at Bentinck Place, Nyman will try to remove it.'

'I aim to beat him to it. Besides, he won't necessarily know it's there. I'm banking on Niall's double-dealing nature.'

'Also, there's no telling how Nyman may react to Niall's death. It's his first serious setback. It could tip him over the edge.'

'Into what?'

'I don't know.'

'Neither do I, Tim.' I shrugged on my coat and made for the door. 'Let's hope we don't find out.'

I'd surrendered my car to the police for forensic examination. 'For the purposes of elimination,' they'd said, meaning just in case they found a bundle of bloodstained clothes in the boot. 'You can reclaim it in the morning.' But, now it had come to it, I couldn't afford the time. It seemed quicker and easier to make for Paddington and catch the next train to Bath: the nine fifteen, getting in at ten forty.

I took a taxi from Bath Spa to the corner of Bentinck Place and gave number six one slow, watchful walk-by before concluding that the coast was clear. I marched smartly up to the front door, got lucky with my choice of Yale key and let myself in.

The hall was as Eris had described it: shabby and silent. I walked straight across to the door of Niall's flat, unlocked it and stepped inside.

I was in a high-ceilinged drawing room, the thick curtains tightly closed. There was a hollow sound to the closing of the door behind me, suggesting the contents didn't amount to much beyond the three-piece suite I could make out in the gloom-filled centre of the room. Wooden sliding doors were set in the wall to my right, with a gleam of bright light around the frame. I slid them open and looked through, only to be momentarily dazzled by sunlight flooding through the uncurtained rear windows of the house.

Once my eyes had adjusted, I could see the little there was to see: a sitting room wallpapered and carpeted in faded Sixties style, and almost devoid of furniture. A table stood against one wall, with a single chair drawn

354

beneath it. In the centre of the table was a telephone, beside a well-filled ashtray and a half-empty bottle of lager. There was nothing else. It was as if Niall had stripped the flat of his family's possessions and replaced them with none of his own. I turned back towards the drawing room.

And stopped in my tracks at the sight of Daphne Sanger, lying full length on the sofa, her head propped on the arm, her brow furrowed, as if in mild academic curiosity about my next move. The gold frames of her spectacles glistened in the shaft of sunlight that stretched past me. 'Hello, Ian,' she said, sitting up with a nervous lick of the lips. 'I've been waiting for you.'

'*You've* been waiting for *me?*'

'Yes.' She glanced at her watch. 'An hour or more.'

'What the hell are you talking about?'

'Nyman sent me to check the place over. He was too busy to come himself.'

'Busy with what?'

'I don't know.' She rose and walked slowly towards me, stopping when she reached the nearer of the two armchairs. She rested against it and I noticed her fingers trembling as she trailed them along the back. 'I never know.'

'What are you checking for?'

'Incriminating material. Anything mentioning Nyman. Or me, of course. There's nothing. I can save you the bother of looking. Niall seems to have distrusted records of all kinds. Apart from some clothes, you'd be hard pushed to find any real evidence that he ever lived here. Not much of an epitaph.'

'How did you learn he was dead?'

'Nyman has contacts everywhere. He learns what he wants. Did you kill Niall?'

355

'No. Eris killed him. In self-defence. I'm sure you know what was planned.'

'Actually, I don't. Nyman said he couldn't account for what had happened.'

'He set it up, for God's sake. Niall was to murder Eris at my flat and frame me for the crime. She somehow got the jump on him. I found him there, dead from a stab wound. Eris had already left.'

'Clever girl. I'm glad she's safe. I never thought it would come to this, you know. You have to believe me.'

'Why should I? You've lied to me all along.'

'The lies are over, Ian. We've got to stop Nyman. That's why I waited for you. We have to end it.'

'*We?*'

'I'm offering to do whatever I can to prevent any more damage being done.'

'You can start by telling my wife just what sort of a man she's mixed up with.'

'All right.'

'You'll come back with me right now to London and tell her?'

'Yes.'

'Just like that?'

'It's what you want, isn't it?'

'Of course it is. But I want the truth as well. I want to know what made you think you had the right to throw my entire life into turmoil.'

'Isobel gave me the right.' She didn't blush or flinch. Her expression gave me clearly to understand that she recoiled from whatever Nyman might do next, but didn't regret a single thing she'd already done to help him. 'Nyman said you'd guessed. So there it is. We loved her, he and I, in our different ways. And we hated you for taking her from us. You deserved to suffer for

356

that. I'm damned if I'll say otherwise. But you've suffered enough. We all have. This can't be allowed to continue.'

'Too right it can't. But there's a problem. I don't trust you. Your change of heart could be just another of Nyman's set-ups.'

'So it could. And I can't prove it isn't. But we don't have time to debate the point. I'll answer all your questions. And I'll tell Faith the whole truth. What more can I do?'

'It's not enough.'

'It'll have to be. Right now, I'm all you've got.'

I stared at her, my anger and distrust slowly weakening before the overriding imperative to act.

'My car's outside,' she said softly. 'Shall we go?'

'Who *is* Nyman?' I demanded, as soon as we were clear of the city, heading north towards the M4.

'He's Isobel's brother.'

'That can't be. Her father told me she was an only child.'

'Not true. Isobel had a younger brother, Robert, christened Robert Conrad. He was the black sheep of the family, clever but uncontrollable. A promising university career was cut short by a prison sentence for drug trafficking. Not just dealing, but recruiting other students, mostly female, to smuggle the merchandise in from abroad. His parents disowned him. "You're no son of ours" stuff. Meant literally, as you've discovered. Only Isobel kept in touch with him. Visited him in prison and stayed in contact afterwards, without her parents' knowledge or approval. From her brother's viewpoint, only her love was unconditional and therefore only she was worth caring about.'

357

'Is that why he wasn't at the inquest – because he was in gaol?'

'Yes. But not for the same offence. He went abroad after his release and got mixed up in bigger-league crime. He was in a Swedish prison serving a sentence for organizing microchip thefts when Isobel died. He acquired a fresh identity and a dry-cleaned business reputation when he got out. You only have to look at the financial press to see what a good job he's done. He hasn't gone straight, of course. He's more crooked than ever. What he's gone is respectable. Dirty money, clean hands.'

'How do you know all this?'

'I know the family history because Isobel told me. We were lovers. I think you should understand that. It's the bond between Nyman and me. Isobel is the only person either of us has ever really loved.'

'I thought she was your client.'

'She was. At first. But then it went further. Falling in love with your psychotherapist is pretty common, actually. It's just not supposed to be reciprocated. Abuse of a position of privilege. Unprofessional. Irresponsible. It's the big no-no. But with Isobel . . . none of that mattered. I took precautions. I knew it was wrong. But I went on. *We* went on. Until one of those precautions killed her. She used to park at the station when she came to Barnet rather than outside my house, in case the neighbours noticed the car was still there in the morning. Which is why she was crossing Barnet Hill that night on foot.'

'It *was* an accident, you know.'

'No doubt. But that doesn't make her loss any easier to bear. Nyman came back to this country after his release looking for her. His parents hadn't even told him

358

she was dead and he couldn't understand why she'd stopped visiting or writing. Eventually he tracked me down and persuaded me to tell him what she'd been consulting me about.'

'Flashbacks to the life of Marian Esguard?'

'Correct. She'd been troubled by them since childhood, although at first she didn't understand what they were. They grew much worse and more intense after she'd passed thirty, the age at which Marian disappeared. She came to me for a cure, but there was no cure. I convinced myself – and her for a while – that the Marian persona was a psychopathological delusion. But it wasn't. We both realized that in the end. Somewhere, somehow, by some strange intersection of consciousnesses, Isobel and Marian were one. You can call it reincarnation if you want. I'd call it shared identity. Isobel couldn't help remembering being Marian. Maybe Marian couldn't help foreseeing being Isobel. I don't know. At some point outside time, they meet; they *are*. I can't explain it. I couldn't then and I can't now. But it *was* true. And it was way beyond my power to cure in any sense. It was also fascinating, of course. I don't deny that. I urged her to keep coming. I waived my fee. At first out of curiosity to see what we could uncover about Marian. Then . . . out of love.'

'Did Nyman know you were lovers?'

'Oh yes. Isobel told him about the relationship during her last visit to him in Sweden. He hadn't realized I was her psychotherapist, however. He hadn't realized she even had one. She'd kept the Marian problem from him. Hadn't wanted to worry him with it. Investigating that part of her life became a key element in the grieving process for him. By encouraging it, I thought I was helping him come to terms with his loss.'

'But not so.'

'No. Not so at all. I lost touch with him after a while and assumed that was the end of it. I noticed his meteoric rise in the business world with wry amusement. It was the exact opposite of my own career. I somehow lost my confidence after Isobel's death. I couldn't seem to trust myself as a therapist. I grew cautious and aloof. My client list shrank. I started to suffer from depression. Then, this time last year, Nyman made contact again. He was ready for what he'd evidently been planning all along: to move against you. Well, you must know by now what it was he proposed. Trick you into leaving your wife, abandoning your career and wasting months in a search for somebody who didn't really exist, while Nyman took over your family much as he would some corporate minnow.'

'And you went along with it.'

'Yes. He set me up in Harley Street and gave me a renewed sense of purpose. The tapes Eris recorded were doctored versions of taped sessions I'd had with Isobel, grafted onto Nyman's elaborations on what he'd subsequently learned about the Esguards, past and present. He'd met Niall and Milo during his investigation of Marian's life. Niall's weakness was money, of course. There wasn't much he wouldn't do if the pay was good. One of the few things I *did* find at the flat was a file of statements from a Guernsey bank account in the name of Niall Hudson, showing a very healthy balance.'

'So you were both on Nyman's payroll.'

'I never accepted a penny beyond the Harley Street rent. Nyman made it easy for me. In return for just a little play-acting, I got a ringside seat at your humiliation.'

'And that's what you wanted?'

'Since you ask, yes. I thought you deserved what you

got. Deceiving you also gave me my confidence back. My practice is on the up and up. I'm suddenly in fashion. And there was a stick as well as a carrot. Nyman could make out a good case of unprofessional conduct against me any time he chose.'

'You're saying he blackmailed you?'

'I'm saying he might have done if I hadn't co-operated. But I did co-operate. Gladly. You didn't give a damn about Isobel. I could see that at the inquest. She was just a stupid woman who'd been inconsiderate enough to walk into the path of your car. I bet you don't feel that any more. I bet she matters to you now.'

'Yes. She does.'

'That was all we were supposed to be doing, according to Nyman. Reminding you, painfully but justly, of the consequences of taking a life.'

'And what are the consequences, Daphne? You can tell me, now you've had some experience of it yourself.'

'I had no part in Quisden-Neve's murder. A private disagreement between him and Niall. That's what Nyman told me. It was never supposed to happen.'

'You believe that?'

'I *did*. I let myself believe it. But now . . . I wonder if even old Milo's fatal heart attack was entirely natural. Niall was with him at the time. Maybe he . . . gave him a helping hand. I don't know. As for Quisden-Neve, I think he worked out what was going on. Isobel had visited Milo, much as Eris described, only years ago, when Milo was still living at Bentinck Place. Milo later told Quisden-Neve about her strange familiarity with the life of Marian Esguard. Quisden-Neve tried to trace her, only to learn she was dead. He must have found out as much as he could about the circumstances of her death. When you went to see him, he'd have recognized your name from the inquest. He knew Nyman was paying Niall to set you up and he suddenly knew why. Maybe he had doubts about Milo's death himself. What he certainly had was a saleable story about Nyman. The press would have gone for it in a big way, don't you think? Remember, it was worse than Quisden-Neve knew, with Nyman's criminal past likely to emerge if they dug deep enough.'

'So Quisden-Neve had to go.'

'That's my reading of it. As for Eris, I never had the slightest inkling Nyman was planning to have her killed and you framed for her murder. But he must have been, right from the start. I see that now. It was to be the *coup de grâce*.'

'I'm not so sure. I think he took against her because she wasn't as indifferent to me as she was supposed to be.'

'Maybe. It doesn't really matter, though, does it? We're all running now.'

'Where will Eris have run?'

'I don't know. Nyman made sure we knew as little about each other as possible. We've only met once. I have the impression Nyman rescued her from bad times. But it's only an impression. I don't even know her real name. We're virtually strangers. Maybe Nyman thought that would mean I wouldn't care what happened to her. But I'm not willing to be a party to her murder – or anyone else's. I'm going to call a halt to what he's doing once and for all.'

'How can you?'

'To begin with, I can open your wife's eyes to his true nature.'

'That won't stop him.'

'No. But the threat of exposure will. I could ruin him

overnight. Who'd trust Nymanex with their money once they'd learned what its founder had done on his way to the top?'

'Not many.'

'Exactly. I think he'll see reason. I think he'll realize he's gone far enough.'

'Are you sure?'

'No. But it's worth a try. There has to be a way out of this. For all of us.'

'Does there?' I stared at the road ahead. 'I wonder.'

Neither of us spoke for quite a while after that. We drove on, absorbed in our own thoughts. I hadn't a shred of a hope that Daphne could talk Nyman into giving up. He was going on to the end, whatever the end was, and I was going with him. But, before we got there, Faith and Amy had to be made to understand what was happening, and only Daphne could accomplish that. Until then, I couldn't afford to question her strategy.

Anger wouldn't have helped much either. Strangely enough, though, there was none to suppress. Close to the heart of everything Nyman had done to me was a truth I was slowly bringing myself to acknowledge. I hadn't cared about Isobel Courtney. I hadn't wanted to know. But now I did care. Now, for the first time, I genuinely wanted to know.

'Tell me, Daphne,' I said as we neared Reading, 'have you ever seen Isobel . . . since her death?'

'Since her death? What do you mean – a ghost?'

'Kind of.'

'No. Nothing. I wish I had. Why?'

'It's something that happened while I was in Chichester. I'm not sure what it was, exactly. But the only thing separating us from the past, or the past from us, is time, right? I mean, when I walk along East Pallant, so does Isobel, so does Marian, in a sense.'

'But *only* in a sense.'

'A photograph lifts the barrier, though. It's a snapshot of time as well as people and places. To take a photograph, as Marian did, before anyone else even understood what a photograph was, must have been . . . incredible. Did Isobel really find those negatives?'

'No. That part was one of Nyman's inventions. Though it seemed to me, when I heard how he'd told Eris to describe them, well, it seemed almost as if . . .'

'What?'

'As if he'd seen them.'

'How could he have?'

'I don't know. But when he wasn't building up Nymanex I reckon he was devoting himself to the mystery of Marian Esguard. How did he know Byfield settled on Guernsey, for instance? It must have taken a lot of painstaking research. Either that or he discovered some source of information Isobel had never come across.'

'Of which the negatives could be part.'

'It's possible. They always sounded real to me. He grew up with Isobel, remember. He saw and heard more about her strange obsession than anyone else. I suppose that gave him a crucial advantage. Quisden-Neve spent years ferreting after the truth, but Nyman gave him a head start and still got there first. He told me the negatives didn't exist, that they were just imaginary devices to lure you further into the thicket. But he only ever told me what he judged I needed to know. He could easily have been lying. He does it for a pastime. He's not going to find it easy to go on lying, though.'

'He won't like that, will he?'

'No. Not at all.'

'How will he react?'

'You want my professional opinion?'

'Yes.'

She pondered the point as we sped through another grey motorway mile. 'Badly.'

We drove straight to Faith's workplace in Hounslow. I sat outside in the car while Daphne went in ahead of me. No good was going to come of my being present when Faith learned what game Nyman was playing. I didn't want her to think I was revelling in her disillusionment. What I wanted above all was for her to have no room for doubt in the matter. She had to be shown what he really was. And she had to believe it. Beyond question.

Looking in from the car park, I spotted them in a ground-floor room. Faith was at the window, staring out expressionlessly, just too far away for me to be able to tell if she was looking at me or not. Daphne was behind her, in shadow, walking a few paces to and fro as she spoke. They could have been discussing any workaday problem. The gestures would have been much the same. Daphne was trying to sound calm and reasonable. Faith was pretending to be unmoved. But the dumbshow didn't fool me. This was the shattering of a dream. I let it go on for ten minutes or so. Then some marginal loss of intensity in their tight-lipped exchanges told me it was time to join them. Faith knew now. She understood – if she was ever going to. Whether she railed at me or not was irrelevant. We had to plan ahead.

They were waiting for me in silence, standing apart in the room, avoiding each other's gaze. Faith seemed determined to avoid my gaze, too. She didn't turn round as I entered.

'Faith?'

'It's all right,' said Daphne. 'She believes me.'

'How couldn't I?' said Faith dully. 'She's not a wayward husband with doubtful motives, is she?'

'I'm sorry.'

'Really?'

'Yes, really. I'm not enjoying this.'

'Neither am I.'

'We need to decide what to do.'

'I *have* decided.' Now she did look at me. 'I'm going to take Amy to stay with my parents until the new term begins.'

'And then?'

'That's none of your business. I have Daphne's promise that Conrad Nyman will be off our backs by then.'

'Faith's supposed to be meeting him at the Waldorf this evening at six thirty for drinks before going on to the theatre,' Daphne explained. 'I've suggested you and I meet him instead and propose a pact. A clean break on both sides. No police, no enquiries, no questions.'

'Which has the handy advantage of leaving her professional reputation miraculously intact.' Faith's tone was flat, her meaning plain. 'Nevertheless, I'm willing to go along with it.'

'He's a dangerous man, Faith.' I held her gaze, urging her to remember what was far more important than all our petty resentments. 'We have to give him a way out.'

'Then you'd better make sure he takes it.'

'He will,' said Daphne. 'It's an offer he can't refuse.'

'I'm relying on you, Ian.' Faith looked straight at me. 'Don't let me down.' The unspoken word *again* hovered in the air. 'Don't let Amy down.'

'I won't.'

'Are we agreed?' asked Daphne.

Faith and I nodded. Then, realizing I was about to speak, she cut me short. 'I don't think anything more needs to be said.' I shrugged, trying to communicate some of the sympathy and the regret she clearly didn't want to hear put into words. 'Only I do have work to do. And so, it seems, do you.'

'She took it well,' said Daphne as we walked away down the corridor.

'You think so?'

'Nobody likes to be made a fool of. And nobody likes to analyse the experience. It was a shock, naturally. Nyman's been the perfect suitor. Too perfect, in a way. For what it's worth, I think she was half expecting something to go wrong. It was all too good to be true.'

'What about Nyman? Will he be expecting something to go wrong?'

'I don't know. It doesn't really matter, so long as he accepts our offer.'

'And will he?'

'He has to.'

'Simple as that?'

'Yes.' She paused before adding, 'If it works.'

The appointment Nyman didn't know he had with us left me time to call in on Tim to check if the police had been looking for me. They hadn't. But someone else had.

'Nicole? What did she want?'

'Information about Nyman. It seems he was supposed to be at a press conference this morning to unveil Nymanex's annual report, but he didn't show. She seemed to think you might know why.'

'Well, I don't.'

'I told her you wouldn't. It gave me the chance to quiz her about Nyman, though, like I said I would. His past really is a total blank, apparently.'

'Not any longer, Tim. I know as much about him as I need to know. And far more than I like.'

Daphne was already sitting in the bar, nursing a gin and tonic and a half-smoked cigar, when I reached the Waldorf shortly after six o'clock.

'You look worried,' I said as I joined her.

'I am.'

'I thought it was all going to be very simple.'

'I thought that, too. But I was wrong.'

'Aren't you being rather defeatist?'

'No. Accurate. There was a message waiting for me when I arrived.' She passed me a crumpled sheet of Waldorf-crested notepaper. 'From Nyman.'

'But . . . he couldn't have . . .' I flattened the sheet on the table and read the message aloud. ' "Miss Sanger, Mr Nyman presents his apologies and regrets he will be unable to join you and Mr Jarrett as planned." ' I looked up at Daphne. ' "*As planned.*" He knew. How? Surely Faith wouldn't have told him.'

'I hardly think so. He must have guessed.'

'*Guessed?*'

'There was a car, a few places behind us, all the way along the motorway, just too far back for me to see the driver. I noticed it a couple of times, but I didn't like to mention it. I . . . thought I was just being . . . paranoid.'

'You think he followed us from Bath?'

She nodded. 'Yes. I do.'

'That's why he wasn't at the press conference.' I

waved away her frown of puzzlement. 'And he'll have known what it meant when we left the motorway at Hounslow.'

'I'm afraid so.'

'Where's Faith now?'

'*En route* to her parents' with Amy, I hope.'

'You *hope*? Christ almighty.' It was all going wrong. I could sense it falling apart around me. I pulled out my mobile and punched in my old home number. Faith answered at the first ring. Her words and the tone of them told me at once what was wrong.

'Amy – is that you?'

'It's not Amy, Faith. It's me.'

'Ian? Do you know where she is?'

'Amy? Of course not. Why isn't she with you?'

'She wasn't here when I got home. I've been phoning round her friends, but none of them have seen her. She must have gone shopping or something. I don't know. A walk, maybe. It's a fine evening. She'll probably be back any minute.' But she didn't believe that. Any more than I did. 'Are you at the Waldorf, Ian?'

'Yes. Nyman isn't coming here, Faith. He left a message. He knew what we were planning.'

'How?'

'I don't know. What matters is Amy. Would she go with him, if he spun a plausible enough yarn?'

'Probably.' Her voice was flat, more despairing than grudging.

'Then that's what must have happened.'

'Not necessarily. She may still—'

'He's taken her, Faith. You know it; I know it. Nyman's taken our daughter. And we have to get her back before—' I broke off, unable to frame the thought in words.

'Before what?'

'Never mind. Just stay where you are.'

Faith didn't know the kind of man we were dealing with.
The charmer had been revealed to her as a liar and a
manipulator. But he was worse than that. I just wasn't
sure I had the heart to tell her how much worse.

It took us nearly an hour to reach Castelnau through
the early evening traffic. By then Faith had phoned every
last friend of Amy's with the same result, several of them
for a second time. She'd also phoned Derringfold Place,
as well as Nyman's Barbican flat *and* his Docklands
office. But he wasn't at any of them. And nor was Amy.

'Why didn't you warn me he might do something like
this?' she demanded.

'It wouldn't have made any difference,' reasoned
Daphne. 'He was probably already on his way here while
we were talking about him at your office.'

'But what does he hope to accomplish? Amy will soon
realize he isn't taking her to meet me. He can't keep her
against her will.' She looked from one to the other of us,
hoping, I suppose, that we'd agree. 'Can he?'

'There's nothing to suggest he's personally capable of
physical violence,' said Daphne.

'Is that supposed to reassure me?'

'Listen, Faith,' I began. 'We need to stay calm.'

'This is all your fault.' She rounded on me, sounding
anything *but* calm. 'If you hadn't leapt into bed with that
tart in Vienna—'

'He'd have found some other way to get at me. At *us*.
You still don't seem to understand.'

'Don't tell me what I do or don't understand. I want
Amy back.'

'So do I. But shouting at each other isn't going to get us anywhere.'

'All right, all right.' She waved her hand at me, then walked to the window and back, twice, breathing deeply, searching for some kind of mental balance. 'Should we phone the police?'

'I wouldn't,' said Daphne. 'There's no proof Amy's with Nyman. She's fourteen years old. The police won't take her absence seriously until tomorrow. By then Nyman may have made contact.'

'So we just *wait*?'

'I think that might be best.'

'But she's not your daughter, is she?'

'No, I realize—'

'I don't think you do. I don't think you have any idea. Come to that, how can I be sure you're really trying to help? For all I know you could still be working for Nyman.'

'You have to trust me, Faith. Nyman promised me no-one would get hurt. I had no reason to expect he'd do anything like this.'

'Where's he taken her?'

'I don't know. I'm not his confidante. He's deceived me as well as you.'

'Derringfold Place, perhaps. The maid said he hadn't been there all day, but maybe she'd been instructed to say that.'

'I doubt it. It would be too obvious.'

'Somewhere else, then.'

'Yes. Somewhere only he knows about. Somewhere he's prepared for just this contingency.'

'*Prepared?* You think he's been planning this for some time?'

371

'Maybe. Like I told you, *I don't know.*'

'You don't know,' Faith repeated dully. 'He doesn't know,' she added, her voice cracking as she pointed at me. She was on the verge of tears now, but anger, with me, with Daphne, with herself, was holding them back. 'None of us—'

The telephone was ringing. It was as if it had been ringing for several minutes without anyone noticing. But now it was loud and clear in our ears. For a second, we stood stock still, staring at each other. Then Faith ran past me into the hall and grabbed the receiver.

'Amy?' It was more a hope than a question. And the hope died in the dull silence that followed. When Faith spoke again, she sounded sullen, almost resentful. 'Yes. All right. Hold on.'

'Who is it?' I asked as she walked back into the room.

'Tim.'

'*Tim?*'

'Yes. He wants to speak to you.'

'How did he know I was here?'

'Don't ask me. Just get rid of him. And *don't tell him anything*. OK?'

'OK.' I went out into the hall and picked up the telephone. 'Tim?'

'I have to see you right away, Ian.'

'I really don't think I can—'

'Get over here, will you? There's something you have to . . . *Just get over here*.' And with that he put the phone down.

I stared at the dead receiver, wondering if I should call him back. But Tim was the most phlegmatic of people. He never made a fuss. He never exaggerated. He always meant what he said. And what he'd said I couldn't ignore.

Already, I was certain it had something to do with Amy.

'I have to go over to Parsons Green,' I said, returning to the lounge. 'Can I, er, borrow the car, Faith?'

'You . . . *what*?'

'It's urgent.'

'Amy's missing. Possibly kidnapped. Isn't that urgent?'

'Of course it is. But Tim will think it odd if I don't go. We don't want him to realize there's something wrong.'

'What can possibly be so urgent? Tim's life runs like clockwork. *He* has nothing to worry about.'

'Look, it won't take long. I'll be back within the hour.'

I caught a suspicious glance from Daphne. But Faith was too distracted to be suspicious. 'Oh, for God's sake,' she snapped, marching out to fetch the car key.

'What's going on?' asked Daphne in an undertone.

'I'm not sure.'

'It's Nyman, isn't it?'

'Maybe. If so, it's best I go alone, don't you think?'

But the only answer Daphne could give me was an assenting nod as Faith rejoined us.

'Here,' she said icily, handing me the key. 'Help yourself.'

'I'm sorry about this.'

'Really?' She stared at me. 'I don't understand you any more, Ian, you know that? I don't understand a single thing about you. Amy needs you, not Tim. If you had a shred of decency . . .' She shook her head in weary condemnation.

'I have no choice.'

'There's always a choice.' She paused, weighing her words. 'It's just that you always choose wrong.'

Tim must have been looking out for me. He opened the front door as I ran up the path and slammed it shut behind me.

'Amy's missing, isn't she?' he asked in the flat tone of one who already knew the answer.

'Yes. We think Nyman has her.'

'You're right.'

'How do you know?'

'He told me. Over the telephone, about half an hour ago.'

'He rang *you*?'

'Yes. Because he had a message for you and you alone and reckoned I could get it to you.'

'What did he say?'

'You can hear for yourself. He told me to ring off and switch on the answerphone, so he could call again and record a message.' Tim led the way into the lounge and over to the telephone as he spoke. 'Ready?'

I nodded and he switched the machine on. There was an electronic bleep, then Nyman's voice, echoing faintly on the tape so that it sounded almost disembodied.

I hope you're listening to this, Jarrett, because it represents your only chance of seeing Amy alive again. She's here with me now, safe and secure. But she can't move and she can't speak. And she'll never speak again if you don't find us before dawn tomorrow. It's not long, I know, but it's long enough for someone as sharp-witted as you. Oh, I nearly forgot. You don't know where we are, do you? You'll need a clue. Well, here it is. I first came here with Isobel, a long time ago. In fact, it was the very last time we were all

374

together. Be seeing you, Jarrett. Or not. As the case may be.

Tim switched the tape off and looked at me questioningly. 'Do you think he means it?'

'Yes.'

'So do I. When I spoke to him I had the impression, the very distinct impression, that he meant every word.'

'It's been leading up to this all along. An eye for an eye. I don't have a sister. But I do have a daughter.'

'A *sister*?'

'Nyman is Isobel Courtney's brother.'

'Flesh and blood.'

'Exactly.'

'What are you going to do?'

'Find them. By dawn tomorrow.'

'How? Did that . . . "clue" . . . mean something to you?'

'I'm not sure. Maybe. Play it again.'

Tim rewound the tape and stood watching me as I listened to Nyman's sneering voice, in which there was also some bubbling undercurrent of desperation. '*I first came here with Isobel, a long time ago.*' But where? Where had they gone? '*In fact, it was the very last time we were all together.*' He wanted me to work it out. He needed me to solve the puzzle. And he reckoned I could.

'Again, Tim. Once more.'

'*I hope you're listening to this, Jarrett . . .*' Oh, I was listening. I was listening so hard I could almost see the pictures in his head, the pictures of what had been and what was yet to come. '*Be seeing you, Jarrett. Or not. As the case may be.*'

'That's it.' I snapped my fingers. 'Photographs.' I looked across at Tim. 'Will you do me a favour?'

'Name it.'

'I've got to go now. Give me an hour's start, then take this tape to Faith. Tell her to do as she thinks best. Contact the police, whatever. I doubt it'll make any difference, but . . . she has to know.'

'Know what, exactly?'

'That I'm doing the only thing I can to save Amy.'

'And that is?'

'Just what Nyman wants me to do.'

Chapter Fourteen

It was gone ten o'clock when I reached Chichester. The night was mild and windless and Chichester itself seemed eerily empty. There were no lights showing at the Pipe Rack. If Sam Courtney was still up, I reckoned he'd be in the small sitting room behind the shop, with Isobel's photographically preserved smile waiting for him whenever he happened to glance up at the mantelpiece. Not that I much cared. I was sure he'd be at home and that was all that mattered. I'd break the door down if I had to.

But I didn't have to. I added a few thumps on the woodwork to my slams at the knocker and soon saw a wedge of lamplight towards the rear of the shop, then made out a stooped figure slowly rounding the counter.

'Who's there?' the old man ventured when he was closer.

'Ian Jarrett,' I shouted. 'I have to speak to you.'

'Who?'

'Jarrett. You remember, Mr Courtney. I was here Monday afternoon.'

He hesitated so long you'd have thought Monday was

a distant memory. Then he said, 'What do you want?'

'It's urgent, Mr Courtney. A matter of life and death. Please open the door.'

'I've got nothing to say to you.'

'I think you have.'

'Well, I don't.'

'It concerns your son.'

'What?'

'You heard, Mr Courtney. Your son. Robert. Middle name—'

He reached up and slipped the top bolt. It snapped back explosively, silencing me. I waited as he released the bottom bolt, turned the key in the lock and edged open the door. Amber light from the nearest street lamp shimmered on the thick lenses of his glasses. His eyes, blurred and magnified behind them, gaped at me in alarm. 'I've got no son,' he muttered, as if repeating a mantra. 'Isobel was our only child.'

'Why don't we talk about it inside?'

'There's nothing to talk about.'

'Then why did you open the door?' I stepped in slowly and he moved back, letting me enter with a shrug that was two parts submission to one of stubbornness. 'The "friend" Isobel was visiting in Barnet the night she died was her psychotherapist, Daphne Sanger.' I pushed the door gently shut behind me. 'Her psychotherapist and . . . something more.'

'I don't know what you mean.'

'Yes, you do. It's why you denied all knowledge of her when I mentioned her name on Monday. You're pretty good at closing your mind to things you don't want to think about, aren't you?'

'Fat lot you know about it.'

'Come on, Mr Courtney. I know *all* about it. Isobel and Daphne were lovers.'

'Rubbish.'

'And Conrad Nyman is your son.'

'No. He isn't.'

'Yes, he is. Much as I wish he weren't. He's Isobel's brother and he holds me to blame for her death.'

'You *are* to blame.'

'Yes. I am. But my daughter isn't.'

'Your daughter? What's she got to do with it?'

'Amy. Fourteen years old. Nine when Isobel died. Entirely blameless, wouldn't you agree?'

He frowned at me in confusion. 'I never said she wasn't.'

'He's kidnapped her.'

'Who?'

'Your son.'

'*I have no son.*'

'He's kidnapped her and he's threatening to kill her.'

'I don't believe you.'

'Got a cassette player?'

'What?'

'*A cassette player.*'

'Well . . . Yes, I've got one.'

'I have a tape I'd like you to listen to.' I slid the extra copy of the tape Tim had made for me out of my pocket and showed it to him. 'Then I think you *will* believe me.'

He stared at me for half a minute or so before leading the way, at a shuffling pace, back across the shop. It was hard to tell if he was trying to stall me or just short of breath. But eventually we reached the sitting room. *News at Ten* was playing with the sound turned down. The old man stooped to switch it off completely, then pointed to a bureau in the corner. A radio cassette player was stationed there, flanked by a bowl of wrinkled apples and an empty vase. 'Isobel gave it to us a couple of Christmases before she died,' he said. 'Doris used to listen to her Val Doonican tapes on it, but I only bother with the radio. You'll have to work it.'

'All right.' I moved to the bureau, switched on the machine and set the tape running. Sam Courtney listened in silence, his shoulders hunched, his jaws clenched so tightly the muscles created their own shadows on his sunken cheeks. Nyman's voice filled the void between us, his words echoing in the loudspeaker – and in the room that had once been his home. Then he was done. I stopped the tape and rewound it. 'Do you want to hear it again?'

'No.'

'It *is* your son's voice, isn't it?'

Sam looked at me and nodded dolefully in confirmation. Then, defeated by his own admission, he sat down slowly in the armchair.

'We did our best for that boy,' he murmured, as if to himself. 'He wanted for nothing. He had a good upbringing. We taught him the difference between right and wrong. We were firm but fair. We treated him the same as Isobel. But he didn't turn out the same. There was always something . . . evil in him.'

'But he loved his sister.'

'Oh yes. He loved her well enough. And she loved him. So much that she went on seeing him and writing to him after we'd . . .' He shook his head despairingly.

'After you'd disowned him.'

'Well? I couldn't stop him defying us. But I could stop him disgracing us.'

'Have you seen him since he got out of prison?'

'No. He knew better than to come here.'

'But you were aware he'd turned himself into Conrad Nyman?'

'Only when I saw his face in the county magazine, showing off that house of his over at Cuckfield.'

'Too close for comfort?'

'He never did concern himself with my comfort. I heard nothing from him when Doris died. Not a word.'

'Nor did he from you when Isobel died.'

Sam flushed slightly. His voice thickened. 'I shouldn't be in any hurry to side with him . . . now you know what he's capable of.'

'How far do you think he might go?'

'As far as he wants. He's never accepted any limit on what he does. The only person beside himself he's ever cared about . . . is Isobel. If he's got your daughter like he says . . .' Sam swallowed. 'She's in danger of her life.'

'Will you help me find them?'

'How can I?'

'"*The very last time we were all together.*" What does that mean?'

The old man shrugged. 'I don't know.'

'Think, for God's sake. "We" could be him and Isobel, but "we all" must be the family. You, your wife and your two children. Together. For the very last time.'

'Maybe.'

'When would that have been?'

'Well . . . I'm not sure. Before he . . . went to prison, I suppose, the first time. But he'd been keeping his distance from us for years. I mean, he lived under this roof, at least until he went away to university, but . . . you wouldn't call that . . . being together.'

'What would you, then?'

'When we still did things together. Properly. As a family.'

'What things?'

'Holidays and such.'

'What was the last holiday you took, then – all four of you?'

'Oh, that would have been . . .' He paused to think, his brow furrowing with the effort. 'The Norfolk coast. Summer of Seventy-three. Isobel was seventeen that year and Robbie was . . . fifteen.'

'Where did you go – precisely?'

'A caravan site. At a place called Wells-next-the-Sea. It was Isobel's idea. She said she'd always wanted to photograph the area.'

'Why?'

Sam gave another of his vast and helpless shrugs. 'I don't know. You couldn't question her about her photographs. She had her reasons and we went along with them. Made a change from Weston-super-Mare, I'll say that, though the wind off the North Sea was as cold as charity. That caravan was all draughts. But Isobel didn't care. She was out every day round the country-side with Robbie. They hired a couple of bikes to explore on.'

'And what did they explore?'

'No idea. Doris and me were just grateful Robbie was being kept out of mischief. It meant we could relax on the beach – when it wasn't blowing a gale. There was some big estate a few miles inland – a house and park open to the public. They hung round that quite a bit, I think.'

'Taking photographs?'

'Isobel always took photographs.'

'But Robbie was with her this time.'

'Pretty much.'

'You said on Monday there are hundreds of Isobel's photographs upstairs.'

'So there are.'

'Including the ones she took in Norfolk?'

'I suppose. I mean . . . I'm not sure. We couldn't bear to throw any of them away. But I've never . . . sorted through them to check . . . what's there and what isn't.'

'It's time we did, then. Don't you think?'

The photographs were stored in a wardrobe in the bedroom that had once been Isobel's and was now a dusty jumble of her youthful possessions, hoarded by her grieving parents: school books, fluffy toys, the Brownie box camera she'd taken her first pictures with, pop records she'd bought as a teenager – and albums and shoeboxes piled one upon the other, filled with the photographs that had been her passion.

I dragged them out onto the floor and began sifting through the unmounted prints and negatives while Sam wearily turned the leaves of the old-fashioned black-card albums. Almost at once I began to recognize the subjects of her photographs – Chichester, Bath, Dorset: the triangulations of Marian Esguard's life. There was East Pallant, in seemingly infinite variations of light and angle. Here was Bentinck Place, pictured again and again on a sunny day long ago. And this, surely, was the empty patch of downland near Tollard Rising where Gaunt's Chase had once stood. She'd followed the trail, long before she knew where it led – or even why it led there.

'Here's the caravan,' Sam interrupted, lowering himself onto the bed and holding the album open for me to see. 'This is the Norfolk holiday.'

It was a black-and-white shot, like most of the others. Isobel seemed to have had no taste for colour. The caravan was viewed from one end, with a plumper, younger Sam and a woman who was obviously Doris sitting beside it at a picnic table, teapot and cups and saucers before them, plus two bottles of Coca-Cola, one with a straw in it. Ten yards or so behind them, a youth dressed in denim jeans and jacket sat astride a bicycle, one arm propped on the handlebars, his hand supporting his chin. He had a mass of blond hair and a blank, unsmiling gaze. He was Robert Courtney, alias Conrad Nyman, at fifteen years of age.

There was another shot of him on the facing page, striding along a bank and viewed from below, silhouetted against a mackerel sky. 'That was the path into the village,' said Sam. 'The caravan site was half a mile out, at the mouth of the harbour.'

I turned the pages. There were long shots of a grand house set in parkland; of formal gardens, an obelisk, a monument of some kind, cottages and lodge gates bowered in summer-heavy trees. 'The country estate?' I queried. Sam nodded. I turned on. Most of the remaining pages in the album were devoted to one particular building: a medium-sized stone-and-slate Georgian country house of no obvious architectural interest, viewed from the end of a curving drive, from further along a road running past it, from a field to the rear, from another field to one side, from a hill half a mile away, then much closer to, right outside the pillared and pedimented front door, on the lawn, on the terrace, even on the threshold of the wisteria-draped French windows, in which a reflection of Isobel could just be discerned in one of the panes, her face obscured by the fringe of her hair as she looked down into the camera.

'She wore her hair long then,' I murmured as the memory of another glimpse of it tugged at me.

'Oh yes,' said Sam. 'Lovely it was.'

'Do you remember this house?'

'No. She and Robbie must have found it.'

'But where?'

'Somewhere in the area, I suppose.'

'Hold on. There's a name.' I peered more closely at the photograph taken from the end of the drive, in which a nameplate could be seen on one of the gate pillars. 'Brant's Carr Lodge. Mean anything to you?' Sam shook his head. 'Nothing at all?'

He shrugged. 'She liked Georgian architecture.'

'But it's run of the mill. You could see a dozen houses like this in the average country parish.'

'I don't know, then.'

I turned over the last page and found myself looking at Isobel's teenage brother, pictured in profile, leaning, hands in pockets, against a finger-post at some rural crossroads, with a telephone box in the background, against which two bicycles were propped. All four direction markers on the post were legible: BURNHAMS 3½; WELLS 3; CREAKES 2½; WALSINGHAM 4½. 'Where was this taken?' Once more, Sam could only shrug. 'Haven't you any idea?'

'Not really.'

'But within easy cycling distance of Wells. That's obvious, isn't it?'

'Well . . . Yes.'

'Have you got an atlas?'

'What sort of atlas?'

'Any kind.'

'Well . . . There's an old AA handbook downstairs. There are motoring maps at the back of that. But it's years out of date.'

'More than twenty years out of date?'

'Easily.'

'All the better. Come on.'

He was seriously short of breath by the time we'd reached the sitting room and ferreted out his well-thumbed and nearly thirty-years-old AA members' handbook from the bureau. I held it under a lamp and leafed through the map section to the north Norfolk coast. There was Wells-next-the-Sea, about halfway between Hunstanton and Cromer. It had a caravanning and camping symbol against it. My eye followed a circle inland. Great and Little Walsingham lay to the south, North and South Creake further to the west, Burnham Market and a clutch of other Burnhams further west still. In the middle of the circle was a historic-house symbol and the name Holkham Hall.

'Holkham,' panted Sam. 'That was the estate. I remember now.'

'The crossroads must be about here,' I mused, tapping the map just below the hall, where several minor roads intersected. Then I looked back at the photograph I'd removed from the album. Nyman's younger self wasn't looking in any of the waymarked directions, but out across the fields, somewhere to the east, towards . . . Brant's Carr Lodge. It had to be. He'd promised me a clue. And this was it.

Chichester to Wells-next-the-Sea had to be 200 miles. More with the diversion round London. I wasn't likely to get there in much under four hours, and first light in mid-April was going to be in the region of half-past four to five o'clock. The cloudless sky would show the very first streaks of dawn out on the east-facing flatlands of Norfolk. I was already short of time and I might need a lot of it to track down Brant's Carr Lodge. Nyman had judged it to a nicety once more. It wasn't impossible, but it wasn't exactly probable either.

Yet I had the feeling he wanted me to make it. There was a challenge implicit in his threat. I could offer to take Amy's place. Maybe his contempt for me made him doubt I would, but there, at least, I could prove him wrong. I couldn't stop thinking of Amy as I drove north along the night-tunnelled roads towards Norfolk. Of the things I'd done for her. Of the times I'd spent with her. Of the love I'd given her. They'd never been enough, any of them. A crumbling marriage and nomadic career had made me a poor kind of father. But Nyman had given me the chance to change all that.

If he really had given me the chance, that is. The long dark miles of night driving revived fears I'd not examined till then. The worst of them was that Amy was already dead and that Nyman was merely tormenting me with the delusion that I could save her. If so, Faith would blame me for throwing away the only frail hope we'd had by setting off alone and in secret on a fool's errand. Though no more than I'd blame myself, of course.

I stopped for petrol at the last services before leaving the motorway system and seriously considered phoning Faith to tell her where I was going and why. What stopped me was the mad logic of Nyman's ultimatum. The scant understanding I had of him suggested that Amy's only chance lay in trusting my instinct that this was between him and me and no-one else. I filled the tank and drove on.

The A10 ran out at King's Lynn. From there I headed north-east across a dark, flat, empty landscape towards the coast. I knew I was close when I reached Burnham Market. The road signs gave the distance to Wells-next-the-Sea in single figures now. And the dashboard clock confirmed I was still on schedule – but only just.

Suddenly the headlamps caught a cluster of tourist signs for Holkham Hall – the gardens, pottery, house and some sort of agricultural museum. I turned round in the entrance to the hall, drove back the way I'd come and took a succession of lefts, reckoning they were bound to lead me south of the park. But the narrow, high-banked lanes were a maze of potential wrong turnings. I ended up on the Fakenham bypass, way off course, and had no choice but to follow the signs back to Burnham Market.

Nothing had been moving in the village when I first drove through. This time I spotted a milkman starting his round and stopped to ask him if he knew Brant's Carr Lodge. No joy.

I had another stab at circumnavigating Holkham Park then, forcing myself to drive more slowly and study every finger-post I passed. It was painstaking, but it paid off when the headlamps picked out a blob of telephone-box red at a crossroads ahead. I pulled up with the lamps trained on the finger-post and studied the waymarkers. BURNHAMS 3½; WELLS 3; CREAKES 2½; WALSINGHAM 4½. There couldn't be any mistake. I turned off the lights, stopped the engine and climbed out to get my bearings. I was at a corner of the park, a boundary wall and a belt of trees behind me, open fields in front. In the deep rural darkness, it was hard to be sure of anything else. Except that the darkness wasn't as deep as it had been. There was a barely perceptible lightening of the sky. And then I realized that it wasn't as silent as it had been either. A few birds were already singing in the park. Night was nearly done.

I jumped back into the car and took off along the Walsingham road, which was the closest route to the direction Nyman had been facing in the photograph. Left at the next crossroads was just a guess and not a lucky one. There were no roadside houses and the first turning off, bar a few muddy tracks, led me back along the boundary of the park to the telephone box. I set off again towards Walsingham and chose a different turning at the next crossroads more or less at random.

I slowed to inspect the first building I came to, but it was only a barn. A little way ahead was the concreted entrance to a drive of some kind. My hopes soared when I saw the name on the roadside board: Brant's Pit Farm. It couldn't be far now. I decided to give myself a couple of miles, then, if necessary, backtrack to the farm and ask there.

But it wasn't necessary. Soon a straggling garden hedge appeared on my left, then the white pillars of a gateway. I slowed as I drove past and caught a glimpse of a gravel drive and the roof-tree and chimney stacks of a house, outlined against the ever paler sky. I coasted on for twenty yards or so, then pulled off the road and stopped.

The dawn chorus was louder now. It seemed to fill the twilit air as I climbed from the car and hurried back along the soft grass verge towards the gate. The sky was an opaque and sickly yellow, weirdly shot with something that would soon be blue. There were no lights showing in the house. I couldn't see a car on the drive. But the nameplate was where it had been in Isobel's

389

photograph. I rubbed some grime clear of the letters and saw what they spelled. Brant's Carr Lodge.

I stepped gingerly across the gravel and took to the long weed-pocked grass of the lawn as soon as I could, though stealth made little practical sense in the circumstances. Nyman would be watching out for me. He'd see me coming, whatever precautions I took.

The overgrown garden, the unlit windows and the carless drive all hinted at desertion, as perhaps they were meant to. I surveyed the front of the house from the shelter of a vast rhododendron bordering the lawn, watching and listening closely. But there was nothing to see or hear: no shadow across the window, no flicker of a curtain, no creak of a board. The house seemed not merely empty, but vacant. It couldn't be, though. Nyman had brought me here for a reason. And he wanted me to know what that reason was.

My patience snapped. Caution wasn't going to do me any good. I strode out across the lawn, the moist grass squelching beneath my shoes. As I reached the driveway in front of the house there was a sudden loud switch to crunching gravel. Then I was at the door.

It was open. As I touched the handle it swung slowly away from me. I stepped into a broad, bare-boarded hall that ran the depth of the house. The French windows Isobel had photographed from outside more than twenty years ago were ahead of me, viewed now from inside. A staircase curved away to one side. Doors stood open to left and right, leading to empty reception rooms. None of the floors was carpeted, none of the windows curtained, none of the rooms furnished. There were bulbs in the overhead light sockets, though, and when I flicked one of the switches the bulb lit. There was no dust on my finger either. Somebody had been there.

'Nyman?' I shouted his name angrily, certain he was somewhere in the house, waiting for me. There was no answer. I moved to the stairwell and shouted again. Still no answer.

Then I heard something. A rustle, carrying with it some slight papery echo. It seemed to come from above. I bounded up the stairs to the first-floor landing and caught sight of the edge of a rug in one of the rear bedrooms.

The rug covered the floorboards round a narrow bed, on which somebody had recently lain. There was an uncased pillow at the head, dented in the centre, and a jumble of blankets across the mattress. A pair of hand-cuffs hung from the bed-rail, steel clinking faintly against brass in time to my footfalls. What had Nyman done? Where was he? Where was Amy? I was here by dawn. I'd met his terms. He had no right to cheat me again.

A drift of smoke came to me as I stood looking at the bed. I swung round and saw the faltering glow of embers in the tiny fireplace. A fire had burned there for some time to judge by the accumulation of ash in the grate. It must have been fed till the last few hours.

Then I saw the large square sheet of paper Sellotaped by its corners to the chimney breast. One of the corners had lifted the tape off the wall. It was its sudden curl of release I'd heard from the hall. I pressed it down again, then stepped back to switch on the light. The sheet of paper was a large-scale map of the area, showing every field and building, including Brant's Carr Lodge by name. A circle had been roughly drawn in red round a spot a few miles to the east of the house. Its centre was a point where the old runways of a disused airfield inter-sected with a lane. It was a message from Nyman.

And its meaning couldn't be doubted. For there, lying

on the narrow mantelpiece in front of me, was Amy's wristwatch. I recognized the pink leather strap. It had been a present from Faith and me for her eleventh birthday. The face was decorated with a yellow sun and a blue quarter-moon, given grinning human features. But I couldn't see the sun *or* the moon. Because the watch had been smashed – as if by a hammer blow.

The airfield was a Second World War relic spread across an empty windswept plateau, beyond which the sun rose as a swollen fireball in the clean chill air. I pulled off the road onto a grass-seamed expanse of fifty-year-old concrete at the centre of the X formed by the runways. There were a few patches of stunted woodland nearby, planted as windbreaks presumably, and a row of old hangars that looked to have been converted into grain-stores by a local farmer, but nothing else, except the wind tugging at my hair as I climbed from the car. Man-made desolation stretched in every direction.

Then I saw it – a dark shape on the south-western horizon, moving fast along one of the runways towards me, maybe a quarter of a mile away across the plateau. I walked clear of the car, deliberately making myself visible, as the shape coalesced into a black Range Rover, pitching and jolting as it sped through the potholes. It was Nyman. It had to be. And all I could do now was stand where I was.

I'd expected the Range Rover to slow as it approached. Instead, it accelerated still further, engine roaring, suspension lurching. I willed myself to stand still, at least until I could be certain Nyman was at the wheel. But, as the car burst across the tarmac of the road, I realized the windscreen was smoked almost as black as the bodywork. He wasn't going to stop and he was heading straight for me. I started to run to my left, then hurled myself clear as the Range Rover surged past, the tyres thwacking over the patch of concrete I'd just been standing on, dust and grit spraying round me.

Only then did he slow. I saw the brake lights glare as he skidded to a halt thirty yards away. By the time I'd scrambled to my feet, he'd completed a U-turn and was facing me once more, engine revving. 'Nyman,' I shouted. 'Get out of the car.'

His answer took me by surprise. The engine cut out and silence suddenly engulfed us, so intense that I could hear the sleeve of my jacket flapping in the wind and a second later catch the distant cry of a skylark. Nothing moved. Nobody got out of the car. I started walking towards it.

I'd covered about ten yards when the gun went off. It was an explosion of sound within the car. The suspension rocked slightly with the impact. But none of the windows shattered. Whatever the bullet had hit, it had hit home.

One thought filled my mind as I sprinted towards the driver's door. He'd killed her. Nyman had killed Amy; had shot her there, with me as a helpless witness. What he meant to do next I didn't care. He could shoot *me* for all he liked, provided I could lay a hand on him first.

But what he'd actually done was the last thing I'd expected. As I wrenched open the door, he fell out to meet me. For a second, he was in my arms, his face close to mine, his blue eyes blankly staring. The left side of his head was a bloody mess of smashed bone and exposed brain. A tiny rivulet of blood was seeping from his mouth, down over his chin. The gun slipped from his trailing hand and hit the concrete. I watched the first bright-red drop of blood reach the pearly cream collar of his shirt. Then, as his legs slid off the seat, I was pushed back by the weight of him. I let go. He fell heavily, the last breath he'd drawn shooting out of him as he struck the ground.

I scrambled past him into the cab, my mind already bracing itself for what I might see. But there was nothing. Amy wasn't there. I craned over the backs of the seats to be sure. But it was true. She simply wasn't there.

Then, as I turned round, I saw it, propped between the dashboard and the windscreen, where Nyman knew I couldn't miss it.

A tape.

Chapter Fifteen

This is in case I don't kill you, Jarrett. I haven't made my mind up yet. Should it be you or Amy? Or both? Or maybe even neither? Let's think it through, shall we? Let's weigh the pros and cons.

One thing's certain. There might be a way out of this for you and Amy. *Might*. But not for me. I'm going down. Nymanex has the skids under it. Ask your very good friend, Ms Heywood. She knows all about it. A Colombian banker of my acquaintance, Orlando Vecerra, was arrested six weeks ago in Frankfurt on money-laundering charges. Apparently he hasn't stopped talking since. And Nymanex is a subject he keeps coming back to. I didn't miss yesterday's press conference simply in order to check up on Daphne. I also wanted to dodge some awkward questions. But you can only dodge for so long. Sooner or later, the men in ill-fitting suits will be coming for me. I just don't intend to be there when they do.

I can't go back to prison. Not for a third time. It's unthinkable. Only I *do* have to think about it. And what I think is that I won't let it happen. That's what I swore when I got out last time. Never again. I was going to go straight. Can you believe it? You ought to. Because Isobel was the one who talked me into it. And the one who could have helped me make it work. Instead, what did I find when I came home? That she was dead. That *you'd* killed her. And that nobody had even bothered to tell me.

Isobel was the only person who ever stood by me. She was my big sister all her life. She *mattered*. That's what this has been about. Making her matter all over again. Forcing you to remember what you did to her – and to regret it. I reckon I've succeeded. You'll never forget her now. You'll never be free of her. Even if I let you live. Especially then, perhaps. Because I don't think you'll be able to put your life back together again. Not as it was.

My mother had a pair of china rabbits that stood on her dressing table. Mr and Mrs Rabbit, we called them. Mr Rabbit had a pipe, Mrs Rabbit a shopping basket. Classic sexist stuff. One day, when I was playing hide-and-seek with Isobel – I'd have been coming up to ten, I suppose – I knocked Mr Rabbit off the dressing table. He broke into dozens of pieces. My father thrashed me for that. Anyway, Isobel stuck the pieces back together again. It took her hours to work out which piece went where, but she wouldn't give up. Mr Rabbit was more glue than china by the time she'd finished. You could see what he'd been, but you could also see how much of what he'd been wasn't there any more. I thought it would have been more merciful to wrap the fragments in newspaper and bury them in the bin. But thirty years later I don't feel very merciful. So maybe I'll just let you go on, like Mr Rabbit, glue and all.

I've burned the negatives – the physical proof of

Marian Esguard's achievement. I found them here, where I'm recording this, in Brant's Carr Lodge, in a compartment hidden under the lower steps of the staircase, just like I had Eris tell you *she* found them at Bentinck Place. I only altered the location. I had to destroy them. I can't take the risk of you turning yourself into some kind of celebrity by using them to rewrite the official history of photography. You do see that, don't you? I can't allow you to gain anything from this beyond an awareness of just how much you took out of the world when you killed my sister.

You'll be wondering how the negatives ended up here. It's an instructive lesson in the dangers of jumping to conclusions. I bought the house three years ago when it came onto the market. I was still investigating the parts of Isobel's life she hadn't told me about then. I knew Brant's Carr was significant because of the interest she'd taken in it during our holiday at Wells. She kept coming back here to take photographs. Even crept into the garden to take close-up shots when the people who lived here were out. She couldn't seem to stay away. I didn't understand why, so I researched the history of the house. It used to be part of the Holkham estate. The archivist there let me look through the records. Maybe you've heard of Thomas Coke, the agricultural reformer. He inherited Holkham in 1776 and ran it until his death in 1842. In 1817 he let Brant's Carr Lodge to a Francis Drew. The documents in the archives describe Drew as a veterinarian. Coke was keen on good veterinary practice, and Drew was one of the best. He went on to become a founder member of the Royal College of Veterinary Surgeons. Back in 1817, he must have been just the sort of bright young man Coke liked. He came to Norfolk from Sussex with his wife, Ann, maiden name

Freeman. With me yet, Jarrett? I'll be disappointed if you're not.

I'm not going to spell it out for you. I don't need to, anyway. The answer's in a letter Barrington Esguard received in September 1851, some thirteen years after his brother Joslyn's death in the fire at Gaunt's Chase. It was one of the items Quisden-Neve was carrying in his bag when Niall . . . bumped into him on the train. He must have got it from Milo. It didn't quite tell him enough, though. Still, it would only have been a matter of time before . . . But see for yourself. I've sent all the documents Niall stole from Quisden-Neve to his brother. As next of kin, he's entitled to them. And whatever good they may do him. I'm sure he'll be happy to let you take a look.

I was sorry about having to take such drastic action against old Q-N. It was a poor reward for his persistence. And it's only bought me a couple of weeks. The trouble was that Niall was just itching to do it. In case you're wondering, it was Nicole who warned me what he was up to. I've been making it worth her while for some time to run with the hare *and* hunt with the hounds. It's been money well spent. A financial journalist is a useful person for someone like me to have on his side. I'd planned a more relishable enlightenment for you on the point, of course, but events have got the better of me. Nicole thought Quisden-Neve only had commercial dirt to dish. The realization that something far more sinister was going on, and that her old boyfriend was involved in it, would have overridden her understanding with me for sure. So, you see, I had no choice but to let Niall off the leash.

His was a brutal nature. Maybe he was some sort of

throwback to Joslyn. He told me Milo died of natural causes fair and square, but I later learned he'd taken the old boy out for a day at the races when it happened. It was convenient for me, so I never asked any questions. And I was grateful for his ruthlessness where Quisden-Neve was concerned. Setting him on Eris was too much, though. I was hurrying by then, trying to finish you off before Vecerra finished *me* off. But it's no excuse. Eris didn't deserve that. I'm glad it didn't work. Not for your sake, but for hers.

I met Eris in prison. I'm not joking. Her father was the only other English con in the prison the Swedes put me in. He died there. She'd been to see him once to my knowledge, then came over again to arrange for the body to be sent home, and visited me to ask how his last few months had been. I could tell, there and then, that she had real potential. After I got out, I found her holding down some dead-end job, eager to take any opportunity I offered her. When it comes to finding things out, or playing a part, well, she's the best. As you've discovered.

Her real name . . . But I'm not going to tell you that. Knowing her as well as I do, I think you've seen the last of her. All those months of searching are going to leave you . . . nowhere. No Eris, no Nicole, no Faith. None of them will have you, Jarrett. You're on your own.

Except for Amy, of course. She'll stand by her father. But will I let her? That's the question I keep coming back to. Can I do it? Should I do it? I don't have long to decide. You'll be here soon, I reckon. But not soon enough to forestall me. I can promise you that.

I'd better go upstairs now and see how she is. She won't have had a comfortable night, what with the gag and the handcuffs. Not to mention the fear. She is *very* frightened. And with good reason. She doesn't know what's going to happen. She doesn't know what I'm going to do. Neither do I. Let's find out, shall we?

Chapter Sixteen

I live with this now. I will always live with it. It ravels and unravels in my mind, as if governed by some mechanism of perpetual motion. Nyman's body, sprawled on the runway, his blood seeping into the cracks and crevices of the concrete. His taped voice, playing to its questioning end. Emptiness all round. And Amy, her absence part of the blank horizon, her voice half heard in the wind.

'Where is she?' I shouted at Nyman, stooping over him in the absurd hope that he could somehow hear me. 'What have you done with her?' But he'd said all he was ever going to say. And he'd already done whatever it was he'd decided to do.

I ran to my car and started driving, back the way I'd come, clinging to the notion that he meant me to find her and had therefore given me as much of a clue as I needed. The photographs still held the answer. He wouldn't have broken his own crazy rules. The photographs would tell me where to go.

Wells-next-the-Sea. It had to be. The cosy seaside resort where the Courtney family had holidayed all those years ago. I'd seen the pictures, as I'd been meant to. I'd already been shown the place he'd taken her to.

It was only a few miles to the coast, and only a few more along it to Wells. I covered the distance in a matter of minutes, navigating by the map I'd torn from the wall at Brant's Carr Lodge. I was aiming for the caravan site marked at the far end of the road running out along the western side of the harbour to the lifeboat station.

The town was quiet, the beach road a straight, flat run. There was a miniature railway to my left and a high bank to my right, blocking the view of the salt marshes. I glanced up at the bank, somehow expecting to see a figure silhouetted against the sky, as in Isobel's photograph of her brother – dark, solitary, determined. But there was nobody there.

As I looked back at the road, I saw what was waiting for me at the far end. And I knew what it meant at once, even though I didn't want to believe it. The map showed a car park in the lee of the pine-topped dunes above the beach. And there, ahead of me, flashing like blue tinsel against the green smudge of the trees, were the lights of police cars.

At least half a dozen of them were drawn up in a group. I heard the crackle of the static on their radios as I pulled in behind. Uniformed figures were milling round either side of a blue-and-white tape strung across a path that led into the trees. Raised and urgent voices were carrying on the wind blowing in from the sea. The tape was stretching and snapping taut like a whip.

I was intercepted before I made it from the car to the trees. I had Nyman's blood on me and a wild look in my eyes. What the policeman who grabbed my arm must have thought I can only imagine.

'There's a girl's body on the beach, isn't there?' I shouted at him. 'You may as well tell me. It's Amy. My *daughter*, for Christ's sake. Nyman shot her, didn't he? Just like that. The bastard. He really did it.'

A plain-clothes officer heard me and hurried over. 'What exactly are you saying, sir?' he asked, his eyes narrowing as he led me to one side.

'My daughter. Amy. Nyman killed her.'

'Who's Nyman?'

'The murderer. Don't you understand?'

'Not really, sir. How do you know there's been a murder? Were you here earlier?'

'No. Of course not. Otherwise I'd have—'

His glance over my shoulder was fleeting but anxious. I whirled round and saw the tape being lifted clear as two men in overalls carried a stretcher out past it to a van. The rear doors of the van stood open in readiness. There was a figure on the stretcher, covered in a plastic shroud.

I started running across the car park. There was a shout from behind me, but I ignored it. The stretcher was half in and half out of the van now. The men carrying it looked up at me in alarm. I pushed past a policeman who hadn't seen me coming. The shroud was some kind of body bag, zipped at the centre. I lunged forward, stretching into the van to reach the fastener. Somebody grabbed my shoulders and pulled me back. But the zip came too.

I see her face now, as it was then. I see it in my dreams. There was a time when I saw it if I merely closed my eyes for a second, branded on my retina as if I'd stared into the sun. Amy. Her face pale and strangely tranquil, her eyes closed as if sleeping, her cheeks flecked with tiny spots of blood. And there, in the shadow of the shroud, where her hair should have fallen clear of her temple, was a deeper shadow still. Then nothing. A blank. White noise. A siren. Or a scream. I can't tell.

PART FOUR

EXHIBITION

Chapter Seventeen

Fearing the worst is a kind of talisman. Subconsciously we hope it will act as a self-averting prophecy. Once I'd realized Amy was in Nyman's hands and at his mercy, the fear of what he might do to her gave me the confidence to believe he wouldn't harm her at all. He knew her. Maybe he even liked her. She'd done nothing to hurt him. Not a thing. I was the guilty party if anyone was. Amy was innocent of blame. She didn't deserve to die.

That was why he killed her, of course. Because she was blameless, like Isobel. And because she was my daughter, a part of me just as Isobel had been a part of him. In destroying her, he broke me, beyond restoration if not repair. Like his mother's china rabbit, I'd go on, glued together, a thing of fragments and fears fulfilled.

'*It's a grievous thing to outlive your own child*,' Sam Courtney had said. '*Not natural*,' was how he'd put it. '*Not in the order of things*.' And this was Nyman's gift to me. This was the price he'd put on his sister's life. Now, at a time and place of his choosing, the price had been paid.

*　　*　　*

I don't remember the next few hours with any real clarity or grasp of sequence. My mind doesn't seem ready yet to let me relive the events as they unfolded. Maybe it never will be.

I was taken to the small police station in Wells, which had become the crowded and noisy centre of a murder inquiry, and held there for questioning, presumably as a suspect, though I don't recall being aware of such a status. How the truth and meaning of what had happened were going to emerge seemed unimportant to me. My thoughts and actions were paralysed by the enormity, the unalterability, of Nyman's revenge.

His body had already been found, by a farm manager doing his rounds of the converted hangars up at the airfield. The pathologist probably told the police it looked like suicide there and then. Apparently the Range Rover matched the description of a vehicle seen speeding out of the beach car park at Wells by a caravanner shortly before he stumbled across Amy's body in the dunes. At some point I gave them Faith's phone number. They didn't seem to want me to contact her direct. Not that it made any difference, since the Met were monitoring Faith's calls by then in the hope of hearing from Nyman. Faith had called them in as soon as she'd listened to the tape. Her estimate of my chances of success had turned out to be exactly right.

By the time she arrived in Wells a few hours later, the local police had pieced together most of the story and satisfied themselves as to where I figured in it. Faith and I met in the stark privacy of the station's one and only interview room. I can't remember what we said. But I can remember her eyes, bloodshot and brimming with tears. And the silences between whatever words we stumbled over, silences heavy with grief and anger and condemnation.

An inspector called Forrester, who'd accompanied Faith from London, badly wanted to talk to me. There was the small matter of Niall Esguard's murder to be thrown into the pot. He knew I'd lied about that from his questioning of Daphne. He was treading carefully, but he was suspicious all the same. Whether the second tape made him less suspicious or more I neither knew nor cared. It was over. Everything now was *post mortem*.

By early evening he'd finished with me and I was, in that chilling masterpiece of police-speak, free to go – at least for the time being. Tim was waiting to collect me. Faith had asked him to make sure I came to no harm. She'd gone to Norwich, where Amy's body had been taken. Her parents were driving over from Cheltenham to meet her. There were arrangements to be made in the wake of what had happened, but no-one supposed for a moment that I was capable of making them.

I have a memory of walking with Tim along the harbourside at Wells, fishing boats bobbing at anchor, the setting sun gilding the salt marshes, neither of us speaking because there were no words equal to the horror that had overtaken us. The world proceeded on its placid way while we stumbled in a void.

It was dark when we started back for London. Nightfall seemed to cut me off from Amy more profoundly than ever. She was in the past now. With every nightfall to come she'd slip further and further away. Her death had been instantaneous, the work of a moment. But I was going to lose her, bit by bit, memory by memory, for the rest of my life.

*   *   *

I stayed with Tim overnight. Early next morning Faith's father phoned from Norwich to say they'd be taking her back to Cheltenham with them. There was a clear implication that I should stay away. I wanted to share my grief with her. Maybe she wanted to share hers with me. But too much had gone wrong between us for that to be possible. Each of us instinctively recoiled from the only person who could truly understand how we felt.

The press were on the scent by then. Nyman's suicide started as a shock to the business world, and turned with bewildering speed into a features-page sensation. Money and murder made an irresistible combination. Luckily for me, none of the papers got wind of the revenge element. Nymanex's shady dealings and its founder's violent end, spiced by Nyman's murder of his lover's daughter as a brutal prelude to the taking of his own life, were more than enough to be going on with.

Not for the police, however, who called me in for further questioning about the deaths of Niall Esguard and Montagu Quisden-Neve. I didn't object to being given such a going over. The events they wanted me to recount would have filled my thoughts wherever I went and whoever I talked to. Nothing could be changed and nothing gained by their recital. But it had to be done. And it had to be better than being left to my own devices.

Daphne had already made a clean breast of her part in Nyman's machinations. The fact that her account matched mine no doubt made it easier to believe us both. The links with the long-ago life of Marian Esguard confused them, though. They seemed reluctant to dwell on the point. Vengeance, conspiracy, persecution and violent death formed a coherent pattern beyond which they were reluctant to stray.

The one loose end they *were* interested in was Eris. I

don't think they swallowed my contention that she'd killed Niall in self-defence, even with Nyman's posthumous testimony to back me up. They wanted to find her. But neither Daphne nor I could tell them how to. Nyman had given them a clue, though not much of one. That apart, she was as elusive as ever.

At some mid-point of that long day of questions and answers, I realized I for one had opted out of the search. Eris could hide or show herself as she pleased. My obsession with her was over. Nyman had killed that, too, when he'd held the gun to Amy's head and pulled the trigger. He'd made an end of everything.

Daphne was waiting for me when I left the police station. The condolences she proffered were doubtless genuine. Her desire to punish me for Isobel's death hadn't run to any of this. What Nyman had done he'd done alone. Nevertheless, her words struck a false note. Her regrets merely added to the waste and hopelessness Nyman had left behind for me to sift through.

She offered to drive me back to Parsons Green and I couldn't seem to find the energy to refuse. It was a Saturday afternoon. The traffic moved sluggishly in fume-hazed sunshine. A football crowd was making its way home from Stamford Bridge. I stared out of the car at their faces as they passed, unable to connect with the world they inhabited. I'd never felt so lonely in my life.

'I can only imagine how you're feeling, Ian,' said Daphne as we crept forward. 'I never thought Nyman would do such a thing. He must have been insane.'

'Aiding and abetting a madman. Quite an achievement for a psychotherapist.'

'I won't be a psychotherapist much longer. The police have made it obvious they'll see to it that I'm not allowed to continue practising, whether or not they press charges against me.'

'Are you expecting sympathy?'

'No. Of course not. I—'

'Anyway, Nyman wasn't insane. You know that as well as I do.'

'Yes,' she murmured in response. 'You're right. He knew *exactly* what he was doing.'

'And we never stood a chance of stopping him.'

'Probably not.'

'*Definitely* not.'

We crawled on in silence to the next red light. Then she said, 'If there's anything I can do to—'

'Help? I don't think so, do you? Some things can't be helped.'

'No. They can't.'

'I'll get out here and walk.'

'There's no need for that.'

'Yes, there is.' I opened the door. 'The truth is, Daphne, I can't bear my own company, let alone yours.'

'I'm sorry.' She looked round at me. 'Really.'

'I believe you. You're sorry. I'm sorry. Everyone's sorry. But Amy's dead.'

I climbed out and slammed the door and walked away down the nearest side street. I couldn't have said what direction I was heading in. It didn't matter anyway. No direction led me where I wanted to go. Back to all the days before yesterday.

'Ian.'

Nicole's voice reached me through the amber-leached darkness as I walked along the road towards Tim's house several empty hours later. She was standing by her car a few yards further on, her face tight and drawn and pale.

'I guessed I'd find you here.'

'You were always good at guessing.'

'The police told me about Amy. And Nyman. And Isobel Courtney, too. Is it really true?'

'Depends what they told you.'

'The whole thing, Ian. For God's sake. Amy was killed . . . for revenge?'

'Yes. Effective, wouldn't you say?'

'I just can't believe it. He never . . . I mean, there was nothing to—'

'Give the game away? There wouldn't have been. That's what he called it, by the way. A game. And he was quite a player, wasn't he?'

'How's Faith . . . taking this?'

'Without me. That's how she's taking it.'

'I had absolutely no way of knowing what he was up to. He never even hinted—'

'That the money he was paying you wasn't just a straightforward bribe? I don't suppose he did. But straightforwardness wasn't in his nature. As Nymanex's shareholders are going to discover.'

'If it comes out that I was on his payroll, I'll be finished. You realize that?'

'Finished? I don't think you know the meaning of the word, Nicole. I say that as someone who's just beginning to.'

'I'm sorry, Ian. God, I'm sorry.'

'Join the club.'

'It seemed such easy money. If I'd ever once thought—'

'How well did you know him?'

'I didn't know him at all. It was just a . . . financial arrangement.'

'Really? What about that night when I called round to

413

warn you of the danger I *thought* you might be in? You said you had an important guest. It was Nyman, wasn't it? A bit late for a financial arrangement, wouldn't you agree?'

She said nothing. But her answer was clear enough. Nyman had been thorough in his inventory of my past and present – and in its demolition.

I sat up most of that night with Tim, drinking whisky and remembering Amy. Tim was the only one left I could talk to freely, the only piece of me Nyman hadn't touched. He was also Amy's godfather. We'd both wondered what sort of a woman she'd grow into. Only we hadn't acknowledged as much until this second night of so many without her. When we knew we'd never find out.

At dawn, we walked down to Putney Bridge and watched the sun rise slowly over the river, swollen and benign and cruelly beautiful.

'It's going to be a lovely day,' I said. 'Nyman even fixed the weather.'

'This is as bad as it gets,' Tim said after a pause. 'Remember that. It has to get better. Eventually.'

'You're probably right. But eventually's a long time. And I don't seem able to look far enough ahead to see it. I'm not even sure I want to.'

'Amy would have wanted you to.'

'Yes. She would. But she's not here to tell me that, is she? It's too late now. For everything.'

'It can't be.'

'Why not?'

'Because you're here to say it, Ian. Why else?'

I gave him a weary smile and squeezed his shoulder. We stood watching the sunrise for another minute or so.

Time doled out a few grudging increments. Then we turned and headed back across the bridge.

The press didn't trouble me over the next few days. I suppose they had plenty to keep them busy without delving into Nyman's reasons for targeting my family. Murder and suicide committed in the face of commercial ruin and probable imprisonment summed up the public explanation of his actions. I was left out of it. The reckoning between Nyman and me remained a personal affair. As perhaps he would have wished.

I stayed with Tim until the funeral. It was held in Cheltenham. The choice of venue was Faith's. There was no dispute about it. I was willing to go along with whatever she preferred. On some unwritten scale of sentimental values, the mother always outranks the father. And in this case there was another factor. Behind Nyman's primary responsibility for what he'd done lay my own secondary responsibility for making him do it. It was something I couldn't dodge. It was going to be with me as long as I lived. And I was going to think of it every time I thought of Amy.

Doubtless it was in her grandparents' minds, too, when we met at the church near their home – the very church in which Faith and I had been married sixteen years before. The funeral became a ceremonial confirmation of what it still took a gigantic effort of will to believe: Amy was gone. Sixteen years reduced themselves to the bleak realization that we'd come full circle – and found the circle empty.

Faith travelled in the undertaker's limousine with her parents and her sister, Jean, who'd flown from Australia to attend the funeral. I rode in Tim's car. The result was that Faith and I had exchanged no more than a few

415

stilted words and an awkward hug by the time I saw her slip away from the gathering of friends and relatives in her parents' drawing room. She caught my eye as she left and, after asking Tim to cover for me, I followed.

We went upstairs, to the bedroom she'd slept in as a child and was clearly now sleeping in again. The photograph I'd taken of her and Amy that had hung in the hall at Castelnau was standing propped up on the narrow mantelpiece, facing the bed.

'I drove down and fetched it a few days ago,' Faith said, noticing the direction of my gaze as she closed the door behind us. 'I just wanted to see us together again. To look at her face. To be sure she existed.'

'I know what you mean.'

'Do you? Sometimes I wonder if you've ever known what I meant.'

'If I haven't, it's too late to start now.'

'Far too late.'

'I mourn her, too, Faith. You can't doubt that.'

'I don't. But I can't seem to stop blaming you for her death.'

'I *am* to blame.'

'No, you're not. At least not exclusively. Nyman played on my weaknesses as well as yours. It took both of us to let him get close to Amy.'

'But if I'd gone straight to the police when I guessed what the clue he left on the tape meant . . .'

'He'd still have killed her. I'm certain of that.'

'So am I. But it doesn't help, does it – being certain?'

'Not one little bit.'

I walked to the window and gazed out for a minute or so at the vapid Cheltenham skyline, then looked back at Faith and said, 'What are we going to do now?'

'Sell the house. If you agree. Split the proceeds and . . .'

'Go our separate ways?'

'When Jean flies home next week, I'm going with her. I'll stay a month at least. Then . . . I don't know. Maybe I'll stay for good. A fresh start. A new life. Something like that. It's too soon to say.'

'Is that why you've had Amy buried here? Because you think your parents will take better care of the grave than me?'

She shook her head. But she also looked away.

'I'll go along with whatever you want to do about the house.' I shrugged. 'And about us.'

'It's all over, Ian.'

'It certainly feels like it is.'

'Are you still looking for her?'

'Eris? No. Not any more.'

'You should look for *something*.'

'Why? Where's it ever got me?'

'That's not the point. You're a photographer. If you stop looking, you stop living.'

'Good advice.' I stepped across to the mantelpiece and traced Amy's photographed smile with my finger. 'But I may not take it, even so.'

A few days later, I moved back into the home I'd walked out of three months before. But it was a home no longer. I'd volunteered to house-sit until a buyer could be found, and to pack up the contents for storage or shipment to Australia or whatever Faith ultimately decided to do with them. If you stripped away the memories, it was just so much clutter. But the memories couldn't be stripped away. I found myself slowly but surely packing up my own past. With no future to go to.

417

*   *   *

I might have stopped looking for Eris. But others hadn't. Inspector Forrester of the Metropolitan Police for one. A prospective buyer was due the morning he chose to call round. I made no effort to disguise the inconvenience of his visit. I wanted an end to questions that had no answers. But how can a question end *except* in an answer?

'I'm hoping you might have heard from Miss Moberly, sir – or whatever her real name is.'

'No, Inspector. I haven't.'

'Pity. You're about our only chance of finding her now.'

'Weren't the Swedish authorities able to help you?'

''Fraid not. Turns out there *was* another Brit in prison with Nyman. George Latham. A Londoner. Murdered a prostitute in Malmö. Died of hepatitis a year before Nyman's release, aged fifty-three. But he had no recorded next of kin. And, as far as we can tell, no visitors from this country. We think Nyman may have been having us on.'

'Having *me* on, more like. He probably hoped I'd follow the trail.'

'A trail that leads nowhere.'

'Exactly.'

'Like the rest of this inquiry when you come down to it. With Nyman dead and Miss Moberly missing, there's not much of a case against Miss Sanger. The SFO will pick over the bones of Nymanex. Otherwise . . . it'll run into the sand.' He sighed. 'Well, while I'm here, there is one other thing. On the tape you found in his car, Nyman referred to an old letter Niall Esguard stole from Montagu Quisden-Neve.'

'I remember.' It would have been truer to say I'd

forgotten – until that moment. 'He sent it to Quisden-Neve's brother.'

'Who was happy to show it to me.'

'And?'

'And nothing. What you might call the historical side of this has had me fuddled all along anyway. I wondered what you'd made of it.'

'I haven't seen it.'

'You haven't?'

'No.'

'I felt sure you must have.'

'Why?'

'Curiosity, I suppose.'

'I'm right out of that.'

'And conscience.'

'That, too.'

'*And conscience*,' he repeated.

'What do you mean?'

'Montagu Quisden-Neve's murder isn't strictly my pigeon. With Niall Esguard dead, there's never going to be a trial anyway. But, once all the reports are in, there *will* be an inquest. And you'll be the principal witness. It just seems hard to make the poor bugger's twin wait till then to hear how it happened. From *your* lips. If you know what I mean.'

I knew what he meant. And he was right. I wasn't out of curiosity. Not quite. Maybe it's an ineradicable component of the human condition – whatever the circumstances. I still had the card in my wallet that Valentine Quisden-Neve had given me in Guernsey, with his phone number written on it. I rang the number as soon as Forrester had left. An answering machine took my message. And Quisden-Neve phoned back six hours later.

*　　*　　*

He lived at Northiam, on the Kent–Sussex border, in a tile-hung cottage – a pair of cottages, more accurately, knocked together to form a spacious residence overlooking a lush stretch of water meadows. And he looked so like his brother that I couldn't really have said for sure which of them I'd found dead on that train. Or which of them I was now telling the truth to, for the first time, over whisky and water, in a sun-dappled country garden.

'I'm sorry I couldn't tell you this in Guernsey. I reckoned it was safer for you not to know about Niall. He was a dangerous man. It was safer for me as well, of course. I'm not trying to dress it up as a white lie. I was chasing too many shadows to trust anyone.'

'Rather like Monty, it seems. As the police have done their best to explain.'

'I should have explained myself. Before now.'

'But you've been visited by a loss surpassing that of a brother, Mr Jarrett. I have no complaint. What I may have, however, is a surprise for you.'

'A letter written to Barrington Esguard in September 1851?'

'Yes. It was one of a number of documents I received through the post, bundled together in an envelope, and without any note of explanation, on Friday the eleventh of April. The Norfolk postmark meant nothing to me. It was only when I read of Nyman's suicide and your daughter's dreadful murder, also in Norfolk, on the very same day, that I realized there had to be a connection. When the police played me the tape Nyman left behind, the connection became clear.'

'And what's the surprise?'

'The identity of the writer of the letter.'

'Who was it?'

'Somebody you were led to believe had died by her own hand twenty-seven years before the letter was written.'

'Marian Esguard?'

He smiled and nodded in answer.

'That can't be.'

'Oh, but it can. The envelope also contained a letter she'd written to her father in April 1817. Aside from the changes in penmanship you'd expect with age, the hands are unquestionably the same.'

'I don't understand.'

'No. But you will. When you read the letter.'

He took me into his study, where the letter was lying ready and waiting on the desk, with the earlier letter lying alongside it to confirm they were written by the same person. They undoubtedly were. I sat down, aware of Quisden-Neve slipping out of the room behind me and closing the door. The desk was solid mahogany, old enough to pass for the one Barrington Esguard had no doubt sat at in his house in Bath to read the very same unexpected communication. Not much separated us in this instant of discovery, except the opaque but invisible curtain of time. And even that seemed to be twitched back as I read.

Euston Hotel, London
Sunday 7th September 1851

My dear Barrington,

I am as surprised to find myself writing this letter as you may well be to receive it. To break a silence after such a long interval is a strange thing, is it not? Nearly thirty-four years have

421

elapsed since we parted in the ball-room at Midford Grange. I do not suppose you expected to see me again during those years any more than I expected to see you again. But I dare say there have been many unlooked-for reunions amid the milling throngs at the Crystal Palace this summer. The Great Exhibition has worked many a human wonder among its mechanical marvels.

Perhaps, had we not both been so startled by the sight of each other, we would have found a few fitting words of greeting. But the explanations we should then have been obliged to offer to our respective companions would undeniably have been as embarrassing to them as to us. Perhaps, therefore, upon reflection, it is as well that we passed by without exchanging more than a glance of recognition.

It was gratifying to see how well you are carrying your years, and I do sincerely hope that Susannah's absence from your side had no doleful significance. The middle-aged gentleman to whom you were talking was surely dear Nelson. He did not notice me or catch your glance in my direction, and might not have recognized me even had he done so. But the face of the child is there in the man and in the face also of the child who was tugging impertinently at your coat-tail, who I would surmise must be your grandson.

Was it you, I wonder, who led your party to the photographic exhibits? I have not forgotten our last conversation, and nor, I suspect, have you. It was a poignant experience, I cannot deny, to see what others have accomplished in the years since I was forced to abandon my research in the field of heliogenesis, as photography might now be called but for your brother's – how shall I phrase it? – rigidity of mind.

I do not wish to traduce the dead, nor lodge claims of scientific primacy which others would regard as preposterous. What was done was done, what was lost lost. There is an end of it. We are both too old to squander our remaining years on futile regrets. My purpose in writing to you is entirely sentimental and I pray you will respond in kind.

It has occurred to me that your evident shock at catching sight of me yesterday may have been occasioned by your harbouring till then the belief that I was dead. It is a belief Jos would have been pleased to entertain himself and to encourage in those of his friends and relatives who knew me. Perhaps he hoped that I had died of a broken heart. He had, after all, done his very best to foster conditions in which I might easily have done so. I feel sure you are familiar with the sordid details of his conspiracy with Mr Byfield to break my spirit and imperil my sanity. What you may not be familiar with are the exact circumstances of our final parting. I can hardly suppose that he gave you an accurate report of them. If, however, his distortion of the facts persuaded you that I had embarked upon a fore-doomed quest after the errant Mr Byfield, you will not have been misled. I wasted seven years of my life – seven years of my precious freedom from your brother – in such a quest. At its end I tracked Mr Byfield to his hiding place on the island of Guernsey. I succeeded. But what a success!

I will tell you the truth of it in the hope that my candour will find an echo in your own soul. On the crossing to Guernsey I made the acquaintance of a woman who had believed herself to be Mr Byfield's wife until his desertion of her and their child some years previously and her subsequent discovery that she was not his first such victim. It was a bigamous union, quite possibly not the only one Mr Byfield contracted in his amorous career. The child had died. The woman was close to despair. She had, like me, traced his whereabouts in the face of many difficulties. She proposed to throw herself upon his mercy. For she loved him still, with a shameful passion. He was ever one to command such emotions. I speak, of course, from personal experience.

What was I to do? Confronted by this ample proof of Mr Byfield's duplicity and my folly, I did not disembark with the woman when we reached Guernsey. I remained on the ship and returned to England, sadder and wiser and quite possibly harder hearted than I had been before. To have found him out was in the end more important than to seek him out.

I shall not weary you with an account of my doings in the years since. Suffice it to say that, if I have not always been happy, I am now at least content. Where I live and how I live are matters you need not concern yourself with. Indeed, my experiences at your brother's hands have left me reluctant to disclose too much of myself to any member of his family, including, alas, you, dear

Barrington. Forgive me if I am too harsh. Forgive me and confer blame on the one who should bear it.

Jos is dead and I will say no more about him. It is the manner of his death that concerns me. I had fondly imagined that there would eventually be an opportunity for me to revisit Gaunt's Chase and to retrieve my heliogenic records and equipment, all of which I was obliged to leave behind. But the fire destroyed everything. I saw that for myself when I paid the house a surreptitious visit some weeks after reading of the disaster. All was gone.

Or was it? I remember your interest in my heliogenic researches. I remember your proposal to take them forward under your stewardship. And I remember your curiosity about the heliogenic picture I made of you and Susannah. It occurs to me – as no more than the frailest of hopes, I grant – that you may have rescued something of my work from Gaunt's Chase, either with Jos's consent or, more probably, without it. It occurs to me, as rather more of a guess than a hope, that you must at least have tried, if I read your character right.

You can tell me whether I do or not. You can, with the munificence of the venerable, reassure me that I did not dream my former accomplishments. Our chance meeting of yesterday prompts me to beg this favour of you. I hope the same chance will prompt you to grant it, if not for old times' sake, then for family's sake.

A letter or a package, or whatever you are able to send, will reach me if sent care of Miss

Arabella Humphreys, Arnwick House, Burnham Market, Norfolk. She is a good friend of mine and her discretion is absolute.

I wish you well, and close this letter wondering if I will hear from you as you have now heard from me, in a spirit of reconciliation.

Yours most sincerely,
Marian

After I'd read the letter, I went back out to the garden, where Quisden-Neve was waiting. He cocked his eyebrow questioningly at me as I sat down opposite him. Then he leaned forward to pour me some more whisky.

'I did say it was a surprise, didn't I, Mr Jarrett?'

'You did.'

'I take it you assumed Marian Esguard was the woman whose suicide apparently prompted Lawrence Byfield's fatal duel on Guernsey. Monty would have known better, of course, already being in possession of the letter. He was very close to the answer, wasn't he? Too close, as it turned out.'

'I'm afraid so.'

'I further take it Barrington Esguard had indeed helped himself to some of the negatives Marian left at Gaunt's Chase and was sufficiently moved by her letter to return them to her via her friend in Burnham Market.'

'It looks like it. Marian's sister and her husband lived at Brant's Carr Lodge. I think Marian lived with them. But perhaps she didn't confide in them about her photographic work. Maybe they didn't approve of women dabbling in science. That would have been another reason for using Miss Humphreys as a go-between. And for hiding the negatives under the stairs. Where they remained until Nyman discovered them.'

'And subsequently destroyed them?'

'Yes. He probably burned them on the fire in the bedroom. The ashes were still warm when I arrived.'

'What would such items be worth – if he hadn't burned them?'

'A lot.'

'How much is a lot?'

'Enough to have made your brother a wealthy man. Enough to have run quite a few risks for.'

'But not enough to get killed for.'

'Nothing ever is.' I glanced away and sipped some whisky, eager suddenly to talk of anything but death. 'What will you do with the letters?'

'I don't know. Donate them to the Royal Photographic Society, perhaps. What are they worth, without the negatives?'

'Financially, very little, I imagine. They could be mid-Victorian forgeries. Or Marian could be lying. No-one but Nyman ever saw the negatives. He could have been lying, too.'

'But you don't think so?'

'No. I'm sure they existed. And I'm equally sure they don't exist now.' I sighed. 'Nyman was good at destroying things.'

I was planning to drive straight back to London when I left Quisden-Neve's house. Just a few miles outside Northiam, however, I spotted a sign for Bodiam Castle. Instantly and completely, sharper than any photograph, the memory came back to me of going there one summer Sunday with Amy. The castle was a picture-book medieval relic that could have been made for children, with its battlements and portcullises and crumbling spiral staircases. Amy had adored it.

A school party was swarming over the place when I arrived. They looked to be about the age Amy had been then. I walked round the lilied moat, listening to their voices filling the air. Somewhere, I knew, if I looked hard enough, I'd be able to find the film I'd had in my camera that day. But Amy wasn't on it. I hadn't taken any pictures of her or the castle. I'd let the visit go unrecorded. And now, just like Marian Esguard's secret experiments with light and paper in the spring and summer of 1817, there was no proof it had ever happened. What I was remembering I could just as easily be imagining. Nyman had erased the past as well as the future.

Chapter Eighteen

The only thing left in an empty life is time. I could almost touch it as it passed that spring and summer. Amy's existence slipped away behind me like a single turning on a long straight road. I looked back at it fixedly, fearing that if I once glanced away it would vanish for ever. The world I was in wasn't her world any more. And it didn't feel like mine either.

The house sold easily, for a good price. I banked my share of the money and moved into a rented flat in the centre of Barnes. Faith wrote to say she'd taken a book-keeping job with a wine shipper in Adelaide and was staying on in Australia, for six months or so at least. She hoped I was getting back into photography. I didn't reply. It seemed fairer to let her think I was too busy.

The reality was that a kind of wilful inertia had settled over me. Hours and days seemed to flash by while I did nothing but walk the streets and stare at the sky. Sometimes I simply lay on my bed and watched the light change as the sun moved slowly round me. I took no photographs. In a sense, my life had *become* a photograph: a Fenton landscape in which I was the silhouetted figure in the middle ground, back turned to the camera, face unseen, purpose unknown. Every moment was frozen. And every moment was the same. I was slowly losing sight of everything that should have mattered but no longer did. I was spiralling down into a dark place where I could neither see nor be seen, but felt, in some strange way, safe from every kind of harm.

Tim was just about my only human contact. He'd look at me during his periodic visits with such a despairing expression that I'd momentarily want to break out of the cycle I was trapped in. Then the desire would fade and I'd tell him not to worry.

Tim had most of his advice and encouragement thrown back at him. But he didn't give up. And, despite his denials, I detected his hand in the unexpected offer that came my way at the beginning of September. My agent broke the silence he'd maintained since the Vienna-in-winter fiasco with a weird and grudging proposition. The Icelandic Geodetic Survey wanted a set of up-to-date photographs of the island's volcanoes to combine with their maps of the areas and the descriptive writings of some eminent vulcanologist in a definitive study of the subject. The vulcanologist was the problem. She was an eruptive character in her own right, and so notoriously reckless that no local photographer could be found who was willing to work with her. They'd all had their fingers burned one way or another. And so, like the runner who finishes last in the race, only to be handed the winner's medal because everyone else has been disqualified, I was chosen for the job.

I'm not sure why I took it. I think the finality of the opportunity shocked me into acceptance. Last chances are difficult to turn down. Besides, I knew nothing about volcanoes and I'd never been to Iceland. The whole project was alien to me. Which was the essence of its appeal. It was more of an escape than a challenge.

Or so I thought until I stepped off the plane at Keflavík and met Dr Asgerthur Sigurthsdottír. She drove me into Reykjavík at what seemed foolhardy speed through a rainstorm that lifted only occasionally to reveal glimpses of an arid black landscape, treating me as we went to her contemptuous views of men in general and male photographers in particular.

She was a large, flame-haired, gruff-voiced woman of forthright opinions and no discernible reserves of either patience or tact. 'They told me your daughter was murdered a few months ago,' she bluntly announced as we approached Reykjavík. 'They think that will make me gentle on you. Maybe you think that also. Think again. You are here to work. I will work you. We start tomorrow.'

Over the next six weeks we travelled the island, by Jeep and plane, and sometimes on foot, in all weathers, more of it foul than fair, trying to pin down, in her words and my pictures, the mood of the strange places she took me to. Asga – the diminutive she came to accept from me in preference to my mangled pronunciation of her full name – had been obsessed by the volcanoes of her native land since the explosive offshore birth of Surtsey in 1963, when she'd watched its column of ash rising into the sky from her school classroom 100 kilometres away. Since then, she'd been approximately 100 kilometres closer to every big bang the geodynamics of Iceland could supply – which was quite a few. Witnessing an eruption was, she said, 'like sex with a man who knows what to do – rare, violent and unforgettable'.

431

I let that and all her other provocative remarks pass me by. I was content to concentrate on photography. Iceland was a place like no other I'd ever been. Its vast, black, smoking wildernesses soaked into my mind, along with the wind and the rain and the cold dazzling sunlight. I felt removed into a realm of heightened vision, where some kind of photographic perfection was within my grasp. I filled film after film with hallucinatory images of glacial white and sulphurous yellow and deep drowning blue. I returned to the only thing I did well with an eagerness I could neither control nor deny. The pictures imposed themselves upon me.

Early autumn was hazardously late to be visiting some of the sites, but that didn't seem to bother Asga. And the volatility of the weather gave my photographs a menacing hue I could almost taste. There was an edge to them I couldn't help relishing. I already knew they were going to be some of the best work I'd ever done.

The nearest we came to disaster wasn't, as I'd anticipated, in the grey deserts of the interior, where Asga's giant-wheeled Jeep took swollen streams and sandstorms in its stride, but on Snaefellsjökull, the dormant volcano near the far western end of the Snaefellsnes peninsula, Jules Verne's famous starting point for his *Journey to the Centre of the Earth*. We approached from the south-east, climbed as high as possible in the Jeep, then took a chance on the weather allowing us to make it to the summit and back on foot before nightfall. In the event, a blizzard blew up from nowhere, we lost our way, went down the wrong side of the mountain and reached the coast road in a state of near-collapse, with the light all but gone.

Asga had just about enough breath to blame me for

the position we found ourselves in. 'You're supposed to be the cautious one, lens brain.' But she also had the sense to realize we weren't going to make it back to the Jeep and the local knowledge that led us to an old fish-drying shed, fitted out as an emergency shelter, where we holed up for the night.

It was there, 1,000 miles and more from all my previous experiences, that I finally explained to somebody who'd never met Amy how she'd died and why. 'It's too cold to sleep,' Asga said. 'You'd better tell me your story.' It was her prickly way of admitting she wanted to hear it. And to my surprise I wanted to tell it. The time had come to do more than picture the horror and the waste of it in my mind. The time had come to speak. And in some inchoate way to accept. It was done and couldn't be undone. I was going to live through it. Something in my nature was going to force me to survive. Whether I wanted to or not.

Asga gave every impression of having forgotten all about our heart-to-heart by morning, when we trudged back round the coast road to the Jeep. She never so much as mentioned Amy's name. Or Nyman's or Eris's or Isobel's or Marian Esguard's, or any of the others I'd felt at the time she was taking such clear and cogent note of. She said nothing about any of them. Until the night before I flew back to England, that is, when she stood me a farewell dinner at a seafood restaurant near the harbour in Reykjavík. Then, at last, when I'd come to think she never would, she broke her silence.

'I've been thinking about your story, Jarrett. Best brain-food I've had from one of you click-clickers.'

'Glad it entertained you,' I said, way past taking

433

offence at any remark she made, however insensitive.

'I don't know the people in it. Not one. I reckon that's why I see it clearer than you.'

'Do you?'

'Sure thing. So I wanted to tell you, before you left, where you've got it wrong. You missed something, Jarrett. You didn't get the picture. It must have caught you without your camera.'

'What must?'

'Nyman lied. On the tape. He *didn't* destroy the negatives.'

I smiled at her across the table. 'What makes you think that?'

'Obvious. Because he lied about the reason for destroying them. He could have cut you out of the deal easy as slicing by sending them to Quisden-Neve's brother along with the letters. Or just by leaving them where they were. They didn't belong to you, did they?'

'But he didn't leave them where they were. The police searched the house from top to bottom and found nothing. And he didn't send them to Valentine.'

'Because he didn't have them.' She grinned triumphantly. 'The other lie proves that.'

'Which other lie?'

'The one about Eris. About how he first met her. He didn't want you to find her. Don't you get it? *She* has the negatives.'

'Rubbish.'

'Don't you ever *think*, Jarrett? I mean, just for a few minutes at a time? If not, listen to somebody who does. He sent Eris to your flat, didn't he, planning for Niall to kill her there and make it look like you did the crime?'

'So?'

'What was your motive going to be?'

434

'What do you mean?'

'The negatives, stupid. She was carrying them. They were what the police were supposed to think you'd murdered her *for*.'

'That can't be.'

'And she's still got them.'

'No. Nyman burned them.'

'He made you *think* he'd burned them. That's not the same thing. Trust Dr Sigurthsdottír on this. She has them. And that's how you'll find her. Because they're worth big bucks, right? So, when she thinks it's safe, when she thinks she's left it long enough, she'll try to sell them. And she'll have to show herself to do that, won't she? That's when you'll have her. If you want her. But do you want her, Jarrett? Do you *really*?' She puffed at her cigarette and frowned at me. 'That's a question only you can answer.' Then she added after a pause, 'And maybe not even you.'

I tried not to think about Asga's theory when I returned to London. There was plenty to keep my mind off it, given how spectacular the prints were that Tim made from the films I'd brought back. He agreed with me that the pictures really were quite something. So did my agent, who reckoned he could interest other people besides the Icelandic Geodetic Survey in them. He even gave my 'career' an optimistic mention.

But none of it was quite enough. As I emerged from the shock of Amy's death, old attractions and stubborn curiosities reasserted themselves. Could Asga be right? Where was Eris? And what was the answer to that other nagging question?

I phoned Mary Whiting at Sotheby's in a spasm of impatience with my own inability to draw a line under the past and the people in it. There weren't many ways Eris could sell the negatives for what they were worth without attracting the attention of Sotheby's photographic expert, Duncan Noakes, and hence his keen-eyed assistant, Mary Whiting. If she could assure me that her boss had seen and heard nothing relating to such items, Asga's theory, while not disproved, would at least go unsupported. That would have satisfied me. And it was what I confidently expected to happen. But something else happened instead.

'Did you hear I'd been trying to contact you, Mr Jarrett?' she asked, before I'd had a chance to explain what I wanted. 'I'd quite given up hope of tracking you down.'

'I've been out of the country.'

'Well, no matter. The situation resolved itself anyway.'

'What situation?'

'Oh, it was that name you mentioned to me in connection with poor Isobel. Esguard. It cropped up a few weeks ago. As soon as it did, I thought of you. I couldn't help wondering if you knew the identity of our mysterious client. She was offering us some antique negatives, you see. One of them bearing the name of Esguard.'

I met Mary Whiting that evening after work in a pub near Berkeley Square. She was sipping an orange juice when I arrived and clutching her briefcase in her lap like a nerve-racked spy about to pass on state secrets.

'I read of your dreadful loss in the newspapers, Mr Jarrett. Please accept my condolences. Am I correct in supposing that this matter and Isobel's death are connected with what happened to your daughter?'

'Conrad Nyman was Isobel's brother, Miss Whiting.'

'I had surmised something of the kind, I can't deny. It seems quite . . . dreadful.'

'It was. It is. But tell me about your client. She's what brought me here.'

'She wrote to Mr Noakes a few weeks ago. It was the strangest kind of letter. Delivered by hand, so there was no postmark. No address either. And no phone number. No way of replying at all, in fact.'

'Anonymous?'

'Not exactly. There was a name. She signed herself Kay Bradshaw. But I couldn't help doubting if that was genuine.'

'What did the letter say?'

'It asked Mr Noakes if he was interested in handling the valuation and subsequent sale of what the writer described as "very early photographic negatives". She claimed to have seven in all and enclosed a photocopy of a print of one as a sample. I've brought it with me.' She snapped open her briefcase. 'Would you like to see it?'

'Oh yes.'

Suddenly, there it was in front of me, wavering slightly in Mary Whiting's hand. It was only a photocopy, of course. But I knew the Regency couple standing at the foot of those broad stone country-house steps. I knew them as if I'd seen them before. As in a sense I had. Often enough to know what the caption said without reading it. *Barrington and Susannah Esguard, Gaunt's Chase, 13 July 1817*.

'This was the only reference to the name?' I asked. 'There was no mention of *Marian* Esguard?'

'None.' She slipped the piece of paper back into her briefcase and closed it. 'But it set me thinking, even so.'

'Did it set Mr Noakes thinking?'

'Naturally. It could easily have been a forgery. A

photocopy proves less than nothing. But such tantalizing possibilities cannot be ignored. The date alone, with the clothing of the subjects as partial confirmation, sufficed to arouse his curiosity. Miss Bradshaw said she would phone in a day or so to see if he wished to examine the originals. If he did, a meeting could be arranged.'

'And did she phone?'

'Yes. And an appointment was made for her to call. Mr Noakes was very excited. I think he envisaged a professional as well as a financial coup.'

'But you didn't?'

'I was simply cautious. Miss Bradshaw's extreme secrecy and the appearance of that name Esguard on the caption worried me. Hence my unsuccessful attempts to contact you. As it turned out, though, I needn't have worried.'

'Why not?'

'Because Miss Bradshaw didn't turn up. She failed to keep the appointment. And she hasn't been in touch since.'

She'd lost her nerve. That had to be the explanation. Getting a valuation from Noakes, let alone selling the negatives, ran the risk of alerting the police, who, for all she knew, were convinced she'd murdered Niall. And then there was the risk of alerting me. My feelings were probably as unclear to her as hers were to me. I wasn't even sure myself how I'd react to meeting her again. But for her, Nyman's conspiracy might never have got off the ground. Then Amy would still be alive. She didn't have Daphne's excuse of avenging a lost love. Yet in some irrational part of my mind I knew I might still be prepared to excuse her.

Mary Whiting promised to alert me to any renewed approach from Kay Bradshaw. Eventually, she'd try to cash in on what she had. That seemed obvious. But when? How much longer would she wait? Just how cautious would she be?

Tim advised me to forget her, which was only what I'd already told myself to do. To some extent, I'd actually succeeded. I wasn't looking for her now as I had nine months before, in longing and despair. My mood was different, tempered by the blows I'd been dealt. Yet still I yearned for a resolution of some kind. Without an ending, how could I begin again?

By having to, came back the bleak but oddly consoling answer. I had some money behind me. I'd rediscovered my self-confidence as a photographer. I even had an idea: to tour the former Soviet Bloc countries of Eastern Europe, photographing changed people in a changing world, the failures as well as the successes. There was a story there for the telling – in pictures. I was sure of it.

While I was still planning the trip, one of the Sunday supplements bought three of my Icelandic photographs. The features editor liked them so much he commissioned me to take some pictures of an eccentric Welsh sculptor and the massive rock-form creations he'd scattered across an Anglesey hillside. Then Latent Image, a gallery in Pimlico so new I hadn't even heard of it, offered me a quarter-share in an exhibition of landscape studies. My stock was suddenly rising. There's nothing like being forgotten for making you potentially fashionable. As if to prove the point, *Time Out* gave me a write-up that almost qualified as a rave, even if it was confined to a single paragraph.

*   *   *

The *Land and Lens* show ran for the first two weeks of November. It was halfway through the second week that I heard from Mary Whiting.

'I thought you ought to know, Mr Jarrett. Miss Bradshaw's been in touch.'

'And?'

'She has an appointment with Mr Noakes. Tomorrow. At three o'clock.'

I pretended to myself that I might stay away. I went through the motions of regarding the matter as fifty-fifty – a chance I might or mightn't take. But at a quarter to three the following afternoon I was there.

The sky was grey. There was a cold drizzle in the air, a foretaste of dusk. Lamps burned brightly in the glittering shopfronts of Bond Street. Cars, vans, taxis and courier bikes wound their way south towards Piccadilly. Logo-laden shoppers streamed along the pavements. Outside the blue-canopied entrance to Sotheby's a pair of pinstripe-suited punters clutching catalogues debated lot prices over fat cigars. They'd have made a good subject for a photograph. But I didn't have my camera. '*I don't like having my picture taken*' was virtually the first thing she'd said to me. So this time there'd be no pictures.

I stood in the lee of one of the pillars flanking the entrance to Rennor House, five doors north and across the street from Sotheby's. I had as clear a view as the traffic allowed. Whether she arrived on foot or was dropped off by cab, there seemed no way I could miss her. Once she was inside, she couldn't escape me. And then . . . I didn't know. I had no idea what I'd say to her, let alone what reply she might give. I was nervous. My hands, holding open the newspaper I wasn't reading, were damp with sweat. It would have been easier, after all this time and all this searching, to walk away. But I kept on watching. And waiting. And wondering.

Three o'clock approached. It would be soon, I told myself. Any minute now I'd see her. People drifted by Sotheby's. Some went in. Others came out. The cigar-smokers vanished. Taxis pulled up. Figures flitted past, crossing the road, hurrying by, window-shopping, gossiping. I scrunched my shoulders, forcing them to relax. I looked up and down, then back across the street. Nothing. She still wasn't here.

Three o'clock came. And went. She was late now. Not too late. Not yet. Five past. Ten past. The odds were lengthening. I glanced round. So many people. So many faces. But not hers. Not now. Not—

I pulled out my mobile and phoned Mary Whiting. I almost wanted her to say she'd slipped in past me. That would have been better than believing she wasn't coming at all.

'I'm sorry, Mr Jarrett, but she hasn't turned up. And there's been no message. It looks as if she's going to stand us up again. There's time yet, of course. She might still be on her way.'

So she might. But time only stretches so far. I stayed there, as the damp grey twilight strengthened, till the point where it snapped, finally and absolutely. That's when I knew: I was waiting for something that wasn't going to happen.

Then I turned and walked away. I was alone. And almost glad of it.

I met Tim for a drink at the White Horse that evening and told him about Kay Bradshaw's no-show. He was more worried by my conduct than he was mystified by hers. I think he'd hoped I'd given up the search altogether. Now he was afraid I might throw myself back into it all over again.

'That isn't going to happen,' I told him.

'Sure about that?'

'I think so.'

'Only *think*?'

'Well, sooner or later, if she really does have the negatives, she'll sell them. It stands to reason. Overseas, maybe. Or through an intermediary. When she does, it'll be big news. I'll hear of it whether I want to or not. It's inevitable. This year, next year, eventually, she'll show herself.'

'And then?'

'Then we'll find out if it's over. Or if I'm kidding myself by thinking it is. There's no other way to be sure.'

'And *until* then?'

'I live with the uncertainty.' I glanced away, thinking of the woman I'd known in Vienna and the stranger I'd been looking for ever since. 'And so does she.'

I drove to Cheltenham next day. It was my first visit to Amy's grave since returning from Iceland. I bought some flowers on the way, only to find them redundant amidst the spray of carnations and chrysanthemums left by my mother-in-law. The rain that had kept them fresh was still falling, dank and pattering, on the soft green grass. The sky was grey, the light thin.

'AMY JARRETT, BELOVED DAUGHTER AND GRANDDAUGHTER,' read the inscription Faith had chosen. 'FOREVER YOUNG IN OUR HEARTS.' And so she was. In our memories, too. Young and precious and more vulnerable than we'd ever realized. I could picture her smile in my mind, could almost hear her laughing voice. But reality was a headstone in a municipal cemetery. It was the mud and leaf-mush beneath my feet. It was bonfire smoke drifting across a line of trees. Amy wasn't part of it any more. Except for the part of her that remained in me. I swung a long, slow punch towards her nose. And hit the empty air.

I began to cry. The tears suddenly filled my eyes, distorting the image of my fist held out in front of me. Even that, it seemed, was only a picture. But the tears were real. And different from those I'd shed before. They were for Amy now, not for me. They were for the tomorrows she'd been denied, not the yesterdays I couldn't alter. They were for letting go. And moving on.

Land and Lens closed that weekend. I drove round to Latent Image on Sunday afternoon to collect my unsold pictures. The manager of the gallery, Roz, had said she'd be there all day, setting up a new exhibition. Her notorious mood swings were currently near the top of their sine curve, so she was all smiles and good cheer, keen to use my arrival as an excuse to stop for a cup of tea.

'The show was great,' she enthused. 'Only one or two for you to take away. Oh, and there's this. Somebody put it through the door. It was here when I arrived this morning.' She handed me a board-backed buff envelope – the kind that carries the request PLEASE DO NOT BEND printed on it in red. My name was written on the front. In a hand I recognized. 'I suppose you really know you've cracked it when fans send you their work for an opinion.'

I tore the flap open and slid out the contents: a single black-and-white photograph in ten by eight enlargement. It looked to have been taken with a zoom lens from the far side of Maddox Street, across the angle of its junction with Bond Street. There was a lot of blurring from intervening vehicles and pedestrians. But the man leaning against the pillar on the left-hand side of the entrance to Rennor House was in sharp focus. He was holding a newspaper open in front of him, but the jut of his chin and the bunching of his brow made it clear he was looking over the top of the page at something on the other side of the road.

'No note?' asked Roz.

'No need for one,' I murmured. 'The message is in the picture.' I stared down at my face in the photograph. Looking, without seeing. Seen, without knowing. Whether red against the snow, or grey against the drizzle, she eluded me. But I couldn't elude her. Unless I stopped looking. That was the only escape. For either of us.

'What's your next project?' Roz tossed the question back over her shoulder as she walked across to switch off the kettle. 'Something exciting?'

'Something different,' I replied, slipping the photograph back into the envelope and letting it drop into the large metal waste-paper bin beside me as I spoke. 'That's all I know.'

I stopped in Putney on my way home from Latent Image and walked out onto the bridge, to the exact spot where I'd stood with Tim seven months before, watching the sunrise. I remembered how inconceivable any kind of future had seemed that day. Yet here I was, in that unimaginable place: the rest of my life. The sun was obscured by thick, drizzling cloud. The light was spare, raw and granular. It held no more secrets.

Photographs don't discriminate between the living

and the dead. I understand that now. In the fragments of time and shards of light that compose them, everyone is equal. Marian, Isobel, Amy, Eris, Conrad, even me – we're all the same. Now you see us; now you don't. It doesn't matter whether you look through a camera lens and press the shutter. It doesn't even matter whether you open your eyes or close them. The pictures are always there. And so are the people in them.

THE END

BEYOND RECALL
by Robert Goddard

At a wedding party in Cornwall in the summer of 1981, Chris Napier is shocked to recognise a dishevelled intruder as his childhood friend Nicky Lanyon, whom he has not seen since his father, Michael Lanyon, was hanged for the murder of Chris's great-uncle, Joshua Carnoweth, in 1947.

It was the inheritence of old Joshua's fortune that led the then humble Napier family to their present state of affluence. When Nicky subsequently hangs himself, Chris sets out on a journey into his own and others' memories of the tragic events of 34 years before. Driven on by Nicky's firm belief in his father's innocence, he begins to doubt the official version of those events and to question the conduct of several members of his own family.

Then other present-day mysteries begin to dog his footsteps into the past and soon his search for the truth becomes a desperate struggle for his own survival.

'Satisfyingly complex . . . finishes in a rollercoaster of twists'
Michael Hartland, *Daily Telegraph*

'The narrative has a compelling seductiveness. There are no flashy literary devices, just good old-fashioned story-telling'
Peter Millar, *The Times*

0 552 14225 5

OUT OF THE SUN
by Robert Goddard

Harry Barnett is shocked to learn that he has a son –
David Venning, a brilliant mathematician, now
languishing in hospital in a diabetic coma. And this is
only the first and smallest of the mysteries he is about to
encounter.

David's condition is attributed to an accident or suicide
attempt. But Harry discovers that his mathematical
notebooks are missing from the hotel room where he was
found and two other scientists employed by the same
American forecasting institute have died in suspicious
circumstances. Driven on by the slim hope of saving the
son he never knew he had, Harry goes in search of
the truth and finds himself entangled in several different
kinds of conspiracy – none of which he ought to stand
the slightest chance of defeating.

Harry Barnett was the flawed hero of Robert Goddard's
earlier novel, the award-winning *Into The Blue*. But
nothing in that experience prepared him – or the reader
– for the baffling conundrums and heart-stopping
suspense of *Out Of The Sun*.

0 552 14224 7

A LIST OF OTHER
ROBERT GODDARD TITLES
AVAILABLE FROM CORGI BOOKS
AND BANTAM PRESS

14223 9	BORROWED TIME	£5.99
13840 1	CLOSED CIRCLE	£5.99
13839 8	HAND IN GLOVE	£5.99
13281 0	IN PALE BATTALIONS	£5.99
13282 9	PAINTING THE DARKNESS	£5.99
13144 X	PAST CARING	£5.99
13562 3	TAKE NO FAREWELL	£5.99
14224 7	OUT OF THE SUN	£5.99
54593 7	INTO THE BLUE	£5.99
14225 5	BEYOND RECALL	£5.99
04266 2	CAUGHT IN THE LIGHT (Hardback)	£16.99